Praise for R.J. Ellory

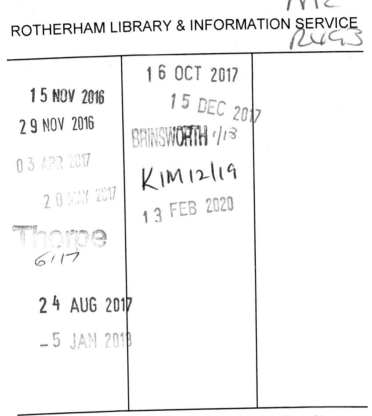

R.J. Ellory is the author of thirteen novels including the bestselling *A Quiet Belief in Angels*, which was a Richard & Judy Book Club selection and won the Nouvel Observateur Crime Fiction Prize in 2008, and *A Simple Act of Violence*, which was the 2010 winner of the Theakstons Old Peculier Crime Novel of the Year. Both *A Dark and Broken Heart* and *A Quiet Belief in Angels* have been optioned for film.

R.J. Ellory's other novels have been translated into twenty-five languages, and he has won the USA Excellence Award for Best Mystery, the *Strand* Magazine Best Thriller 2009, the Quebec Laureat, the Livre de Poche Award, and the Readers' Prize for the Festivals of St Maur and Avignon. He has been shortlisted for a further twelve awards in numerous countries and four Daggers from the UK Crime Writers' Association.

Despite the American settings of his novels, Ellory is British and currently lives in England with his wife and son. To find out more visit www.rjellory.com or follow him on Twitter @rjellory

By R.J. Ellory

Novels
Candlemoth
Ghostheart
A Quiet Vendetta
City Of Lies
A Quiet Belief in Angels
A Simple Act of Violence
The Anniversary Man
Saints of New York
Bad Signs
A Dark and Broken Heart
The Devil and the River
Carnival of Shadows
Mockingbird Songs

Novellas
Three Days in Chicagoland:
1. The Sister
2. The Cop
3. The Killer

Mockingbird Songs

R.J. ELLORY

An Orion paperback

First published in Great Britain in 2015
by Orion Books
This paperback edition published in 2016
by Orion Books,
an imprint of The Orion Publishing Group Ltd,
Carmelite House, 50 Victoria Embankment,
London EC4Y 0DZ

An Hachette UK Company

1 3 5 7 9 10 8 6 4 2

ISBN 978 1 4091 2135 0

Typeset at The Spartan Press Ltd,
Lymington, Hants

Printed and bound in Great Britain by
Clays Ltd, St Ives plc

To my brilliant editors, Jemima Forrester and Jon Wood;
to my tireless agent, Euan Thorneycroft; to my fellow
Whiskey Poet, Martin Smith, and his wife, Sue,
in appreciation of her limitless patience and hospitality
as we recorded the first album.

A man could not be blessed with better friends.

As always, to my wonderful wife, Vicky, and my son, Ryan,
for everything that's been, and everything yet to come.

ONE

"A clear conscience is nothing more than a bad memory."

For what it was worth, this was the last flawed pearl of wisdom offered by Evan Riggs on the day that Henry Quinn was released from Reeves County Farm Prison.

It was July of 1972, and Henry Quinn had served precisely three years, three weeks, and four days—a handful of hours, too, but up against the time he'd already done, such a detail didn't count for much. Not until the final night. That final night the mattress seemed more unforgiving, the cell more claustrophobic, the sound of caged men more terrifying than anything he'd experienced since the day he'd arrived. Evan Riggs, there on the bunk above him, just slept through it all. Riggs had done more than two decades. If something disturbed his sleep, it was unknown to Henry Quinn.

Quinn knew that the teenager he'd once been—shuffling ankle-bound along the gantry to his new home, wearing nothing but shorts and shorn hair and a fierce, burning shame—was now so removed from the man he'd become that . . . well, it was as if his soul had been stolen and replaced by another.

He had served his time, had listened, perhaps learned. He'd been beaten, battered, bruised, close to broken, but had somehow survived. Much of the latter had been down to Evan Riggs, and for this he owed a debt that could never truly be repaid. Should he ever forget that debt, he merely had to look in the mirror at the scar that traversed his midriff from beneath his right shoulder to his ribs on the left. That had been a bad night, and it was a night he would not have survived alone.

And when—at last—Henry's final hours in Reeves approached, Evan Riggs sat with him and they talked of everything but goodbyes.

"Success does not vanquish demons," Riggs told him. "Remember that, kid. I tried to drown my demons in liquor, but they swam real good. That's the trick right there. That passion for something, that burning desire to be somebody bigger than you are . . . well, that's the thing that drives you to do whatever you gotta do, but it never sleeps, you see? The hunger that drives most creative people is the thing that ultimately kills them."

"Why so many of them do drugs, I guess."

"Maybe . . . Couldn't say. Never took that route. Hell, in my own way I guess I did, but I just looked for some kind of peace in the bottom of a bottle. Looked real hard, never found it. Liquor doesn't make people do bad things. It just makes them believe there are no consequences. Truth is, you get drunk enough, then everything and nothing makes sense. You'll cry about it all; you'll laugh about it all. Solutions to life's problems are as clear as day after two-fifths, but when daylight actually comes, you realize you're still as dumb as a box of rocks. Every sunrise I believed things would get better. Every sunrise I was wrong."

Evan Riggs, onetime guitar picker, onetime singer, onetime West Texas radio star, onetime murderer, looked intently at the young man sitting on the edge of the facing bunk and then he smiled.

"And now the talking's all done, Henry Quinn," he said, perhaps as some kind of in-joke, for Riggs was laconic at the best of times. In the main he was quiet, watchful, an expression on his face like he knew that what he wanted to hear would never be said. "Talkin' is all used up, and you gotta go do whatever you're gonna do with this life of yours."

Riggs was a hard man with a hard history, not yet fifty years old and already twenty-plus years of jail behind him. A few more years and he'd have seen half his life through bars. Henry Quinn would leave, someone else would take his place, and they in turn would see freedom before Evan Riggs. How many cellmates Riggs had seen, he'd never said. Of his own thoughts and feelings, he ventured little at all. Maybe that was West Texas; maybe that was just Riggs's way. Many was the time Henry Quinn had wondered why Riggs tolerated his chatter. There were a million ways to die; perhaps loneliness was the worst. Maybe that was all there was to it: someone's voice—anyone's—was better than silence. For Quinn himself, the silence had grown exhausting within a week of his arrival, for in the spaces between sounds, his mind nagged and tugged at everything for some kind of explanation for his situation. There was none. That was—at last—the conclusion. Sometimes life, fate, God—whoever or whatever—just dealt you a hand that left you wondering if you should scratch your watch or wind your balls.

"Can hear the man comin' to get you," Riggs said.

Quinn heard footsteps then, out along the gantry, down the

steps, and onto the landing, that all-too-familiar ring of heels on metal, the first night like some surreal death knell, the last like some liberty bell beckoning one and all from deep beneath the ground. The battle was done. The war was over.

"Evan—" Henry started, but Evan raised his hand and silenced him.

"We ain't doin' none of that goodbye shit, Henry. I've listened to you for the better part of three years, and I don't have a mind to hear much else. Have to say I'm lookin' forward to a little peace and quiet."

"I just wanted to say thank you—"

"Just need you to find my daughter and give her that letter, kid. You do that for me, and I'll still owe you beyond anything I might have done for you."

"I gave you my word, Evan. I'll find her and give her the letter."

"I know you will, kid. I know you will."

Henry turned as a warder appeared on the other side of the cell bars.

"You lover boys done finished your kissin' and whatever?"

Evan winked at the screw, gave him a wry smile. "Oh, there's plenty more left for you, Mr. Delaney, sir. Don't you worry your pretty little head about that."

"You are such an asshole, Riggs. Of a mind to come on in there and—"

Henry Quinn stood in such a way as to block Delaney's view of Riggs.

"Ready, boss," Quinn said.

"Hell, you done wastin' your time in here talkin' to this crazy old fuck, I'll never know," Delaney said. "Anyways, you's all done and dusted now. Reckon we'll be seein' you again real soon, though. I guess Riggs'll have found himself another pretty little bird by then."

"Oh, hell no," Riggs said. "Savin' myself all up for you, Mr. Delaney, sir."

Delaney disregarded the comment, turned left, and barked, "Open up seventeen! Man goin' out!"

There was a wave of catcalls, whistles, and hollers from the block. Toilet rolls came sailing over the gantries and landings like inauguration-day ticker tape. Men hammered dents into coffee cups against cell bars.

Henry Quinn felt a firm hand grip his shoulder, and without

turning around, he placed his hand over Riggs's and held it for just a second.

"Remember how I told you, kid. Eyes and ears open, mouth shut. Pretty much no one out there who ain't lookin' for some way to fuck you. And when you get to hell, you keep an eye out for me. I'll be waitin' there someplace with a bottle."

Quinn merely nodded. He could not turn and face the man. He did not want Riggs to see the tears welling in his eyes.

Some people—a rare handful—left their fingerprints on your soul.

Processing took four hours. There was a lot of waiting and clock-watching, but Henry Quinn was used to it. Seated on a hard plastic chair in an antiseptically clean corridor that still somehow managed to smell of regret, Henry looked at his hands for a while. Where once there were calluses from playing guitar, there were now calluses from hefting pick and shovel and hammer, from breaking rocks and throwing rocks and piling rocks together. It would be a good while before he could play like he had before.

He had to go see his ma in San Angelo. He was torn six ways to Sunday. Last time she visited, he'd asked her not to come again. That had been more than a year ago. She was crazy-talking, like, *We are the same, aren't we? Sometimes I feel like my mind is so small I'm nothing more than a prisoner inside . . . Other times my mind is so big I could walk for years and never see the boundaries*. Not what she said, but how she said it. As if she were talking to more than one person when there was no one but Henry in front of her. One of the wardens asked Henry if she was okay. Henry said she was fine, just tired from the journey, a little stressed maybe. Henry knew she was drinking. Not for thirst but for medicine, and that kind of medicine caused its own panoply of ailments, the cure for which was just more liquor.

So Henry thought about his mother and pretty soon reckoned he didn't know what to think, and thus he tried to think of something else.

And then he splayed his fingers and looked through the spaces at the black-and-white tiled floor beneath his feet, a checkerboard he had cleaned so many times he knew it intimately.

Had to collect his guitar, his gear, his pickup truck, and then head southwest toward the Mexican border, find a town called Calvary. Evan Riggs's estranged brother, Carson, was sheriff down there, and from what Evan had told him, Carson had been—to all intents and purposes—the legal guardian of Evan's daughter after Evan had been

4

jailed. Once Quinn found her, once he'd fulfilled his promise and delivered the letter, then he was on his own. That promise to Riggs meant a great deal, as much as any word he'd ever given, and Henry Quinn knew he'd be damned if he didn't fulfill it.

Evan Riggs—a man to whom Henry had spoken endlessly, a man who'd patiently listened to everything that Henry had uttered, a man who'd somehow become a seemingly limitless well for all that Henry Quinn had to say—remained an enigma to Henry still.

Evan Riggs would die right there in Reeves County Prison. The only other possibility was a prison transfer, and that meant dying somewhere else that looked just the same.

Life. No hope of parole. Life that meant *life*. And all for nothing.

I told them I didn't remember what happened, and I didn't. They don't wanna hear that, however. A man who doesn't remember must be a man with something to hide. Like I always say, a clear conscience is nothing more than a bad memory. Doesn't stop me knowing in my bones that I killed that man. And for what?

Some said that Evan Riggs didn't get the chair because he was a country singer with a long-playing record to his name. Others said that it was because he'd done two years in the military, '43 to '45, just like Governor Robert Allan Shivers, Angelina County-born, Austin alma mater, a man who liked that old-timey a-pickin' and a-singin' as much as the next conservative Democrat. Army men respected army men, and that had been enough to keep him alive.

Some said that Evan Riggs didn't see death row because there was a ghost of doubt in the back of everyone's mind that he was, in fact, the one who beat that man to death in a cheap motel in Austin in July of 1950.

Whys and wherefores aside, Governor Shivers signed the paper; Riggs went to Reeves County Farm Prison for life without parole. The dead guy, some slick Charlie who went by the name of Forrest Wetherby, was simply consigned to history.

Riggs was hauled semiconscious from his own motel room, still reeking of rotgut. Said he remembered nothing at all—not the man he'd supposedly killed, not the hollering, not the fistfight. Had no explanation for the blood on his knuckles or the rips in his clothes. He did know one thing, however. He knew he was a drunk, and not a good one, that he possessed the capability and capacity to kill a man. He'd done army time. He'd seen conflict in Europe. Train a man to kill and it's only a matter of time before he ups and does it.

Riggs pled no contest, accepted the first lawyer the Public

Defender's Office afforded him, reconciled himself to the three Moirai, those fateful Greek characters who spun the threads that connected every event of one's life from start to finish. The Moirai did not treat him well, but they could have treated him worse. Governor Shivers intervened, and Riggs didn't tap-dance on linoleum while the state boiled his brains.

Those who knew Evan Riggs wondered why he didn't fight a better fight. Some said he must be a Bible-reading man, that whatever avoidance he may have engineered on earth would only catch him later. Better to take the punishment now, be done and dusted within his own lifetime than look forward to an eternity of damnation in the hereafter. Some said a man may be guilty of something else entirely, that God finds a way to bring justice to a sinner, and there was no lack of evidence of Riggs's drinking and womanizing and wanton lifestyle. After all, weren't the very songs on that long-playing record of his about one and the same thing? Hell, even the name of the record—*The Whiskey Poet*—said all that needed to be said about Riggs's source of inspiration. "Lord, I Done So Wrong." "This Cheating Heart." "I'll Try and Be a Better Man." Take those pretty tunes away and you may as well have called it a confession.

People were always of a mind to think what they wanted, and there was often no relationship between that and the truth.

Such were Evan Riggs's circumstances, and however many times he might have tried to rewind his life, it would not be rewound. Hindsight was as close as anyone could ever get to living things differently, but hindsight was nothing more than a ghost of what might have been with a promise of nothing new.

Henry Quinn and Evan Riggs had been drawn together, it seemed—by design, by default, by destiny, who knew? They crossed paths, like stray dogs looking for a home that never was and never would be. The dynamics and circumstances that brought them together were similar, if only that there had been liquor and a long night and a jail term at the end.

As for Henry, he saw the capacity in Riggs to kill, certainly the capacity to fight like a cornered hound. Had he been pressed for an opinion, he would have said that Riggs did kill that man in Austin, and even though he claimed his memory was blank to the event, he'd seen it writ large on his heart. The internal truths are the ones that can never be truly buried.

If Evan Riggs's life had been changed by a fistfight, then Henry's had been changed by a bullet. The bullet that had changed Henry's

6

life was the very same one that near-fatally wounded Sally O'Brien. Irony being what it was, that .38-caliber slug had not been intended for her. In fact, it hadn't been intended for anyone at all.

It was just one of those things. An accident, a coincidence, once more the spinning of those fateful threads. Beyond that, it was God's will, and there was no fathoming that.

How Henry Quinn wound up at Reeves went like so:

Sally O'Brien's husband, Danny, was already at work. The two eldest kids, Laura and Max, had run out to the school bus no more than twenty minutes earlier, and Sally was alone with the baby, Carly. Sally was dressed in one of her husband's T-shirts and a robe. It seemed to be a regular day, a day just like yesterday, just like the day before, save it wasn't. Sally's life would dramatically change for the worse before that minute was out, and she had never even suspected it.

The bullet that came through the window at 9:18, morning of Monday the third of February 1969, made a sound like a blown lightbulb as it punctured the pane. Sally barely heard the sound, had no time at all to register its source. It traversed the last six or seven feet to where Sally stood stirring eggs on the stove, and it entered her neck at a near-perfect angle to cause the maximum amount of damage without actually severing her trachea or spinal column.

The radio was playing some song by the Light Crust Doughboys, not the original lineup, but the later crew that Smokey Montgomery put together. Sally could listen to that kind of thing all day and all night and all day once again, folks like Tommy Duncan and Bob Wills and Knocky Parker. Her husband said it was too old-timey, but then her husband said a great many things to which she didn't pay no mind.

Involuntary response caused Sally to grip the spoon she was using to stir the eggs, and for a moment she stood there—stock-still, her eyes wide—and then she keeled over sideways and hit the linoleum. The spoon caught the edge of the pan, and hot scrambled eggs scattered across the floor around her.

Carly—all of one year and four months old—started giggling. She didn't understand the game Mommy was playing, but it was funny. She went on giggling for a mere twenty or thirty seconds more, and then she figured that this wasn't such a fun game anymore.

Another thirty seconds and Carly was crying, and would go on crying for a further twenty minutes before the mailman, a sometime drinking buddy of Danny O'Brien's called Ronnie Vaughan, appeared at the door with a package requiring a signature.

Vaughan knocked on the screen, on the inner door. Then he rang the bell. He could hear the baby crying, and yet there was no response. The inner door was locked, and so he walked around the side of the house and approached the building from the rear. From the rear porch he could see sideways into the kitchen. He did not notice the neat hole in the other window; nor did he see Sally O'Brien lying on the linoleum in a pool of blood and scrambled egg. He could see the baby, however, and the fact that no one seemed to be attending to her raised sufficient alarm for Ronnie Vaughan to call the police.

A black-and-white arrived at 9:43 a.m. The attending officers, James Kincade and a recent academy graduate named Steve French, surveyed the scene. Kincade rang the bell, rapped repeatedly on the front door, and then obtained the telephone number for the O'Brien property. He had Dispatch call that number three times, allowing the phone within to ring for a considerable time. By 9:51, Ronnie Vaughan, James Kincade, and Steve French came to the collective conclusion that something was awry. Kincade and French went in through the rear kitchen door, and before Kincade had even taken three steps, he was aware that he was traipsing not only through Sally O'Brien's breakfast, but also her blood. Kincade, later acknowledged as having taken action that ensured Sally's survival, stuck a finger in the bullet hole and prevented any further blood loss. He kept his finger in that hole even as she was lifted onto a gurney, even as she was driven the eight and a half miles to San Angelo County Hospital triage.

Had James Kincade not done his Little Dutch Boy routine, then Sally O'Brien would have bled out. But she didn't bleed out; she made it. There was a darn good chance she would never speak again, but she was alive.

Then came the investigation. Why would anyone want to shoot a woman like Sally O'Brien in the throat while she was making eggs? Why would anyone want to shoot her at all?

Took Officer James Kincade all of twenty-five minutes to find the hole in the fence that ran adjacent to the O'Brien property. Running a line of cord to ascertain trajectory from the other side, he found a ricochet mark on the side of a water barrel. He surveyed the area extensively, and with his not-insignificant knowledge of firearms, he concluded that there was only one place from which that bullet could have originated and yet still be possessed of sufficient power to pass through a fence, ricochet off the water barrel, and puncture a woman's throat. The yard that backed onto the O'Brien property became the focus of his attention. The property—a rental—was occupied by a woman called Nancy Quinn and her son, Henry. Finding no one home, Kincade went over the back fence of the property and discovered empty beer cans and shell casings. He didn't touch a thing.

Two and a half hours later, he and French returned with a warrant, a detective by the name of Oscar Gibson in tow, an Oklahoman by birth, a West Texan by default. He'd been San Angelo PD for eight years, was a good man, an honest cop, and he waited patiently while Kincade and French hammered on the door, rang the bell, came to the inevitable conclusion that there was no one home.

Vaulting the O'Brien fence and surveying the scene with a clear and unbiased eye, Gibson came to the same conclusion as Kincade, albeit unsupported and hypothetical. Someone or some persons had drunk beers and fired a handgun in the Quinn yard. One of those bullets had passed through the fence, ricocheted off the water barrel, punctured the window, and penetrated the throat of the O'Brien woman. The bullet had done its worst around nine a.m., presumably the sound of gunshots unnoticed and unreported because it was a weekday and a working neighborhood. Whether the beers had been drunk at the same time as the firing of the gun and whether those who had drunk beers had been the same as those who had pulled the trigger was unknown. Henry Quinn was the name they had, unless his mother, Nancy, was some kind of errant modern-day Annie Oakley with a taste for Buckhorn.

The kid was rounded up within two hours. They had him dead to rights. First questions asked and answered in the affirmative—*Were you at home this morning, drinking beers in the yard? Did you fire a handgun?*—saw him arrested on the spot. Nancy Quinn was fetched from work, and by the end of the day, she saw her son charged with unlawful possession of a weapon and assault. They let him slide on the underage liquor beef. Gibson proclaimed he had a forgiving and lenient side. The kid had dug himself a deep hole; no one, least of all Henry, needed it deeper.

Henry Quinn, two days shy of his eighteenth, was charged as an adult, arraigned, remanded to San Angelo City Jail. Preliminary hearing would be a formality. The kid had no defense. He was drunk, he fired the handgun, and Sally O'Brien got a slug in her neck. The slug was confirmed as having been fired from that very same hand-gun and no other. Had Sally died, it would have been manslaughter. Counsel from the PD's Office told Nancy O'Brien that if her son got a sympathetic jury, he'd do three-to-five, more than likely in Reeves County Farm Prison. He made a point of telling her that Sally O'Brien wouldn't be so lucky. Prognosis for vocal recovery was not looking so good. Said that Henry Quinn should keep a weather eye out for Danny O'Brien after his release.

The trial went as expected. Henry got a sympathetic jury. Defense counsel, PD Office or otherwise, was a great deal more astute and purposeful than that provided for Evan Riggs back in August of 1950. Henry Quinn got the three-to-five, was shipped out to Reeves after sentencing on Monday, June 16, 1969. Hendrix had just been busted for heroin possession. Apollo 10 had been launched and was short of the moon surface by nine miles. The toll of Americans dead in Vietnam had just exceeded those lost in Korea. "Get Back" by the Beatles topped the Billboard.

That was the way it happened.

To say that prison life came as a shock to Henry Quinn would have been an understatement. More than an understatement. Everything that had taken place between the day of his arrest and his arrival at Reeves possessed a spectral and transparent quality. None of it was real, and none of it mattered. He would wake soon, of course, secure in the knowledge that it had been nothing but the fun-house mirror of imagination distorting his worst fears into a far worse reality. But it was not reality. It was dreamland. He didn't need to worry.

There was no Sally O'Brien. There had been no drunken gunplay in the yard. There had been no bullet, no ricochet, no Carly O'Brien left crying as her mother nearly bled out on the linoleum. No public defender, no preliminary hearing, no charge, no arraignment, no trial, no conviction. And the day of sentencing? That had merely been the precursor to his moment of waking.

A moment of waking that never actually arrived.

The reality of who he was, where he was, the surreal diversion his life had suddenly taken, came home to him with the sound of a heavy door, a door that slammed shut behind him that first night in June of 1969.

There is nothing comparable to that sound, almost as if the very nature of that sound is somehow ingrained into the spiritual woof and warp of human existence. We have all heard it. We all know what it means. It never loses its potency or power. Such an old sound for such young ears.

You are no longer a free man, Henry Quinn.

You will eat when we say. You will piss when we say. You will smoke and walk and talk and work and shit when we say. You will not see girls or guitars or a good breakfast for a long time to come, sonny. That's the way it is. Deal with it or hang yourself in the latrines with six feet of twisted bedsheet and a prayer that no one finds you until your eyes glaze over and you soil yourself.

This is a done deal.

Henry Quinn lay in prison that first night. He did not sleep. He was on suicide watch, as were all greenhorns. First seven nights alone, first seven nights in a cell with nothing but bars. Guard on duty changed every four hours so there was no chance of sleeping on the job. Men cried. Men sobbed. Men prayed. The guard said nothing; it was the others who hollered for the noisy ones to keep their goddamned mouths shut.

Quit your fucking whining, you asshole, or I'll come in there and cut you good.

Henry did not cry, nor sob, nor pray. He lay in silence and wished the night away. Somehow it worked, for each night seemed briefer than the last, and after three days, he slept, sheer exhaustion snatching him away into a fitful but thankfully dreamless slumber.

On the morning of the eighth day, he was integrated. He was showered, deloused, issued a second set of denims, a pair of rubber-soled shoes, no socks. Socks had been withdrawn from standard uniform at Reeves after the 1959 riot. Men had brought fist-sized rocks back from the fields, dropped them into socks, felled some guards, killed one, brought the place to a standstill for two days straight. The National Guard came down, and eight dozen wannabe soldiers restored order with fire hoses, batons, and sheer force of numbers. Closest any of them would get to war, but the inmates gave them a good run for their money.

Warden at the time was "retired," and the new man, a seasoned veteran by the name of Frank Colby, was brought in to kick Reeves in to shape. And he did. Convict leasing was reestablished—external work parties, chain gangs—and the pent-up frustration and inherent anger within Reeves County Farm's populace was channeled into constructive and socially contributive endeavors. A NATURAL FORCE FOR GOOD. COLBY SWEEPS THE CORRIDORS CLEAN. REEVES: A ROUTE TO REHABILITATION. It was all so much whitewashed horseshit. Colby was on the make, had always had an eye for a bribe and wasn't scared to take it. He was a generous man, however, and officials the length and breadth of Reeves County and beyond took advantage of that generosity. The farm prison became a proverbial horn of plenty, and thus the beatings, the unduly harsh solitary terms, the inmate injuries and accidental fatalities were overlooked.

It was into this new and improved correctional facility that Henry Quinn found himself integrated, and he had known—within a matter of days—that here was a place that would make him or break him.

TWO

Whichever way you told the tale, Henry Quinn was an accident.

To be raised with such a knowledge does something to a kid, no doubt.

Nancy Quinn, all of twenty-two years old, had never intended to get pregnant, and Jack Alford had never intended to be the man who'd done it to her.

But he did, all hot and sweaty and half undressed in the back of a Buick Super four-door sedan, the drunken moment most memorable for the fact that Nancy Quinn whacked her elbow on the white Tenite steering wheel and couldn't stop laughing for three minutes straight. The sex itself had not been memorable. Waking alone and clothed in her own bed the following morning, Nancy was aware of two things: her elbow still hurt and her underwear was missing. She prayed that she hadn't gotten knocked up. Her prayer, like so many others, went unanswered, and within a week she knew. She just *knew*. The mental and psychological hurricane through which she survived over the subsequent weeks was biblical, but she never said a word to her parents. She confided in her sister, and her sister said that the only thing to do was cross the border into Ciudad Acuña or Piedras Negras and get an abortion. As far as she understood, all of Nancy's worldly problems could be solved with a length of hose, a liter of lye, and about seventy-five bucks.

Whether it was the horror stories she'd heard about backstreet abortions, whether it was guilt, innate compassion, or a sense that something like this happened for reasons she could never begin to understand, she made a decision. That decision occurred to her while she sat in a movie theater in San Angelo. The film—*Edge of Doom* with Dana Andrews and Farley Granger—did not engage her attention. However, it was during that film that she was overcome by an emotion she could describe only as *peaceful*. Accompanying that emotion was the certainty that she would see the pregnancy through; not only that, but she would tell her parents the truth.

It didn't go well. Her mother said little of anything. Her father

13

called her a *hussy*, gave her two hundred dollars, and told her that this was the limit of his financial and parental responsibility. She was twenty-two years old, she had a job (she worked as a secretary for the San Angelo County Library Department), and she rented her own apartment. Whether she kept the child or not would be her own decision. He knew what he would decide, but he was *not* her and this was *not* his problem.

Not unsurprised by her father's reaction, Nancy left the house somewhat reconciled to the fact that this was a one-way ticket. Even her mother, trying to console her at the threshold with a *Don't worry, dear . . . he'll come around in time* didn't allay her fears. It was a fearful thing, after all, and whatever the whys and wherefores, Nancy didn't believe it was right for her family to abandon her. The sense of abandonment became a sense of injustice became a sense of self-righteous indignation, and by the time she reached the second trimester, she knew that if her father came crawling on his knees for forgiveness—not that he ever would, mind—she would turn him away unsympathetically just so he'd understand how he'd made her feel.

Her father never came, the self-righteous indignation tempered and softened, and by the time Nancy Quinn gave birth on February 5, 1951, she was a different woman. She called the boy Henry. Just Henry. No middle name, no ancestral relevance, nothing but the simple certainty of a two-syllable sound that felt right for the little one who returned her gaze unerringly and melted her heart. Had there ever been a ghost of doubt in her mind about the rightness of her decision to see the pregnancy through, that doubt was exorcised and vanquished in a single beat of that selfsame melted heart.

If anything, time alone served to vindicate that decision, for Henry Quinn—by any standards—was no normal kid.

To say he was bright would have been an understatement. The child was incandescent. It was not that he asked questions, for out of the mouths of babes the questions are endless and routine. It was the questions asked that puzzled Nancy, and those questions often left her lost for words. And sometimes Henry would make a statement as if that statement were nothing less than fact, and from a child so young it just baffled the hell out of her.

Why is it that some days go really fast and some go really slow, even when they have the same amount of hours in them, Ma?

Turn the music up, Ma. It makes me feel like nothing bad could ever happen to anyone.

14

This from a child merely a year past his first words.

And then, one night, lying in her arms, he looked up at her and said, *My heart goes twice as fast as yours. Is that because I love you twice as much as anyone else?*

These were the things that told Nancy Quinn her boy was different. These were the joys and wonders that her father would never discover. Henry's maternal grandfather died before Henry was three, and Nancy never once regretted harboring the resentment she felt toward him. Even if she couldn't hold on to a man, she sure as hell could hold on to a grudge.

Nancy took Henry to the funeral, told him that he was going to meet his grandmother for the first time. Henry seemed to take the whole thing in his stride. He charmed everyone, men and women alike, and when Grandma Quinn picked him up and hugged him, she cried more than she'd ever done for the loss of her husband.

That day saw the resolution of any conflict or disharmony that may have existed between mother and daughter. Marion Quinn paid for Nancy and Henry to move out of the cramped apartment where they'd lived since forever and into the rental house where she and Henry would remain until that fateful morning when beer was drunk, a gun was fired, and a water barrel deflected a bullet into the throat of an unfortunate and unsuspecting Sally O'Brien.

The years between the funeral of Walter Quinn and the arrest of the grandson he never met were quietly eventful in their own way. Henry Quinn attended a local school, jumped grades twice, graduated, attended college, and though his academic prowess was never questioned, his motivations were. Henry Quinn did not care. That was the way it seemed. He read books by the handful, sometimes two or three simultaneously; he wore out his library card and his shoes with the sheer number of trips he made to the library. Nancy, still employed by the San Angelo County Library Department, herself a remarkably well-read woman, made lists of recommended volumes. Henry not only read the books on those lists, but he strayed wildly down odd literary avenues into obscure genres and rare subjects. Everything from English classics to contemporary American poetry passed through Henry's hands, through Henry's mind, and thus into Henry's psyche. Equally at ease quoting *Twelfth Night*, H. P. Lovecraft, or a stanza from Helen Adam's *Margaretta's Rime*, Henry Quinn confounded people. The person folks expected Henry Quinn to be and the person Henry Quinn actually was were never the same thing. In fact, Henry seemed to take an inordinate degree of pleasure in defying people's expectations of him. Perhaps they anticipated someone with such an intellect to be superior, even condescending, but Henry could not have been more humble had he tried. He was neither self-deprecating nor riddled with internal doubt, but he exuded an air of carefree nonchalance that somehow eased the air around him. However quick his mind might have been, his manner was slow, his speech measured, as if everything he uttered had the flavor of something planned and practiced and yet could never have been.

The truth, if there were such a thing, was that Henry Quinn thought in terms of music. He lived his life as if everything he heard were merely a soundtrack. From his first discovery of T-Bone Walker and Freddie King, he did as he had done with books. He wandered wildly through myriad genres and subgenres, listening to Red Garland, Charlie Christian, Harry Choates; then suddenly it was Shostakovich and Rachmaninoff, once more veering wildly back to Ernest Tubb and the Texas Nightingale, Sippie Wallace.

When Henry Quinn was nine, Nancy bought him a Teisco EP-7 electric guitar from a secondhand store. The guitar was already four or five years old, looked like it had maybe been used to row a boat out of a muddy swamp, but it cleaned up well and looked close enough to the one Freddie King used that she knew it would make Henry happy.

When Henry saw it, he cried.

Subsequently, and almost without variation, Henry returned from school, completed his homework, did his chores, and then headed for his room. Rare was the night when Nancy did not find him asleep in his clothes, the guitar still clutched in one hand, pieces of paper scattered around the floor covered in hieroglyphics, lyrics, musical annotations of one variety or another. Sometimes she would stand in the hallway and listen to Henry as he played a phrase from some scratched Bakelite disc on his Symphonic 556 record player over and over and then tried to replicate it himself. She marveled at the boy's patience and determination, and when she started dating a music teacher by the name of Larry Troutman from San Angelo High, she watched as Henry literally bled the poor man dry for knowledge and a better scope of understanding.

"Boy's as hungry as a Cuban boxer," Larry told her. "Never seen anything like it. Darn kid has a sponge for a brain . . . Don't matter how much I tell him; he wants to know more."

The relationship between Nancy Quinn and Larry Troutman did not last. Henry's passion, however, went from strength to strength.

The songs he started writing were old songs. At least that's the way they sounded to Nancy. Lines like *Every time I die, someone steals my shoes* from the lips of a fifteen-year-old seemed both terribly wrong and terribly right. *He understands whiskey, women, and God, and everything in between.* That was another one she heard as she crossed the hallway to the bathroom, and she stood there a moment and wondered if Henry was actually hers. Maybe they had switched babies on her in the hospital. Maybe this kid was some kind of gypsy. She knew as well as she knew her own name that it wasn't so, but still she wondered at the source of this angled perspective and the strange wisdom it seemed to precipitate. Maybe Jack Alford was responsible, the errant and irresponsible one-night-stand father of Henry Quinn. She could not know, and never would, for she hadn't known Jack then, and she doubted she'd ever see him again for long enough to find out.

A few months after Henry turned sixteen, there was a talent show at the Tom Green County Fair. Henry got up on a makeshift stage in front of a tough crowd, and with his beat-to-hell Teisco EP-7 guitar and a Lafayette LA-75 amplifier, he played a song of his own composition called "Easier than Breathing to Love You." Where he got the words from, Nancy did not know. She wasn't privy to everything her son did, but she was pretty sure he hadn't yet found a girl and lost his virginity. However, that song had been written by a man whose heart had been broken more times than he cared to recall. That's how it sounded. It must have sounded that way to Herman Russell, a scout from a small record company in Abilene. Herman Russell was as wide as he was tall, kind of rolled enthusiastically forward, a crooked smile on his face like he knew everyone was a trickster, nevertheless certain he was trickier than most. Had a habit of wearing suits with a vest, a watch and chain, a pocket handkerchief that matched his tie. A Southern dandy with a penchant for two-toned shoes and pomade.

"Seen a hundred thousand of these talent shows in my time," he told Nancy Quinn.

Henry stood by, guitar in hand, aware of nothing but the fact that he'd dropped a bar on the middle eight, hit a half dozen bum notes, and on the final refrain pitched a semitone flat. As far as he was concerned "Easier than Breathing to Love You" had sounded like a pet store burning down.

"Kid's got a voice, a good playing style as well," Herman Russell said, and then turned to Henry and asked, "Who writ the song, boy?"

"I did, sir," Henry replied.

"Straight up? You don't say," Herman said, and knocked his hat back an inch from his brow. He squinted against the light and looked at Henry as if for the first time. "You don't say," he repeated, as if somewhere deep inside him was a cave that served up echoes. "You got some more tunes like that?"

"He's got a ton of them," Nancy said. "All he ever does, aside from school and chores, is play guitar and write songs, Mr. Russell."

"Oh, you go on and call me Herman. No one calls me Mr. Russell, save the cops and the IRS!"

Herman looked at Henry's boots, his raggedy jeans, his rolled cuffs and youthful face. Youthful he was, no doubt about it, but if this scrawny kid had writ a song such as that, then there was something going on that didn't make sense.

Herman, however, was the kind of man who attended church more often than Easter and Christmas and believed that it was right to trust a man until he gave a reason to do otherwise. Hence he had no motivation to consider that Henry Quinn had not writ that song, and a good song it was, the kind of song that could be pressed into a 45 and sold to a hundred or more West Texas music stores under the Crooked Cow label. For that's who Herman Russell worked for—the Crooked Cow record label—and he was Abilene born and bred, had different boots and suits for every day of the week, ties and kerchiefs that matched, and he prided himself on a square deal for a square service. Henry, if all was as appeared, was not only a square deal but the real deal, and there weren't so many of those that came along in a straight month of county fairs.

Herman Russell suggested a visit on up to Crooked Cow in Abilene, and Nancy—seeing such a thing could do no harm in either the short or the long term—went with her son on the bus, tickets paid for by Herman Russell with a Crooked Cow business check at the Greyhound depot that same county fair afternoon. They took the bus ride just a week or so later, on Thursday, same day the Beatles released *Sgt. Pepper's Lonely Hearts Club Band*, and in a small anteroom outside a large recording booth, Henry Quinn stared at a picture of a country singer called Evan Riggs. He knew the man and his album, *The Whiskey Poet*, but he did not know of Riggs's current whereabouts, that he had already served seventeen years of

18

a life sentence at Reeves for the murder of Forrest Wetherby in an Austin hotel corridor in July of 1950, and had Henry known then that he himself would share a cell with the man he now looked at, he would have smiled his Henry Quinn smile and said, "You know what? You're just plumb crazy..."

Henry cut a tape demo of "Easier than Breathing to Love You" that afternoon. He felt more relaxed, and there was no one watching him, at least no one he could see, and the man who spoke to him through the headphones seemed unhurried, as if all the time in the world were at their disposal. He had Henry sing the song a couple of times, "Just to check the levels, son..." and then told Henry that they were finished.

When the man appeared, he was all elbows and knees, sapling-thin, had a smile as contagious as a summer cold.

"Folks just settle down when they think they ain't on tape," he explained. "Great trick, but works only one time. You done good, son. Got a good song there, nice voice. Few years more you gonna sound as fine as anyone I've recorded."

Henry took the compliment. He expected nothing. He'd just bused it to Abilene for the adventure.

Herman Russell took the recording away, told Henry and his ma to talk a walk around the corner to a soda shop, have a root-beer float or some such, come back in a while.

They took a walk, they had a float, came back in a while, and Herman was awaiting them.

"Spoke to the big boss with the hot sauce, played him your song. He was very impressed, but he ain't gonna tape you now. Wants to wait a coupla years, let your voice mature a touch. Wants to know if you'd be interested to sign a holding contract."

"A holding contract?" Nancy asked. "What on earth is that?"

"Nothing really binding," Herman explained. "Just means that you're gonna give us first refusal on your songs should anyone else express an interest in Henry, professionally speaking. We give you five hundred bucks, we get first refusal on your material if someone else wants to record and distribute you, and when Henry here turns eighteen, he comes on up here again and we cut some more demos and see what's cooking."

"And the five hundred bucks? If we want to go with some other record company?" Nancy asked.

"They buy Henry out for the same amount. Like I said, it's kind of informal, to be honest. More a gentleman's agreement than a legally binding contract. No one's gonna go see a lawyer for the sake of five hundred bucks, Mrs. Quinn."

Henry signed the paper. Nancy signed it as his legal guardian, even though she thought five hundred bucks was little short of a money mountain. Herman signed it, too, but with a flourish, like it was the redrafting of the Constitution. He gave Henry the money right there and then, and in a music store two blocks east, Henry bought a 1968 Gibson Les Paul Custom guitar for two hundred and sixty-five bucks.

Henry knew he wanted it the moment he saw it. It was like meeting an old friend.

"Guitars is like guns, son," the salesman told him. The salesman's name was Norman. He had it woven above the pocket on his chambray shirt. "There's a gun for every man. Soon as he picks it up, he knows. Feels like he's shaking hands with someone he can trust. Guitars is the same. You got yourself a bargain there. Good as new, should be about three twenty-five, but we sold it six months ago only for this lightweight feller to come back and tell us it was too heavy. Not a mark on it, not a scratch. Coulda sold it as new, but that'd be dishonest, and we ain't dishonest."

Nancy stood aside. She said nothing. It was like listening to a different language. A conversation between aliens. Alabama rednecks, maybe.

"You got yourself an amplifier, son?"

"Got a Lafayette."

Norman smiled, said, "That'd be like putting cookin' oil in a Cadillac. Need yourself a Fender. Should git yourself one of these here Princeton Reverbs."

Norman took Henry into the back. Nancy stood a while and felt like Henry now loved something just as much as he'd once loved her. She knew the music thing was inside of him like a blood-borne virus. There was no cure, only a medicine with which the symptoms could be managed and allayed. That medicine was playing and singing and being the center of attention and all else that went with the life her son had evidently chosen. Or maybe the life had chosen him—she wasn't so sure which it was.

Henry walked out of Abilene's Finest Music Store with his new gear and enough change for a good dinner. He and his ma went to a diner a couple of blocks from Arthur Sears Park, and here they talked a little of the past, a great deal about the future, and Nancy

Quinn understood in her heart that soon her son would be leaving this life for something unknown, untried, untested.

As it turned out, less than four months shy of that scheduled return to Abilene, a trip that might very well have seen Henry Quinn cutting records for Herman Russell and Crooked Cow, Henry would get drunk and play fool with a loaded .38.

By the time he was released from Reeves in July of 1972, a great deal of life would have happened. The United States had apparently put a man on the moon, though Henry Quinn would have been among the first to question that; Mary Jo Kopechne drowned at Chappaquiddick; the hippies found free love and peace, and Manson lost his mind; even the demise of the Beatles could not keep Vietnam from the headlines; trigger-happy National Guards, much the same as those who had quelled the Reeves riot in 1959, shot four students dead at Kent State; Arthur Bremer tried to assassinate George Wallace, and J. Edgar Hoover's ghosts and paranoid delusions finally provoked a heart attack big enough to kill him.

The young man who bought a ticket for Calvary at the Greyhound depot in San Angelo was a changed man in a changed world.

He carried with him a backpack, that selfsame Gibson guitar he'd bought in Abilene all of five years earlier, and a letter to a girl called Sarah from a father she'd never seen.

Henry Quinn believed that Evan Riggs's friendship had helped him maintain his sanity in Reeves. He'd said he would go down to Calvary and speak to Evan's brother. He'd said he would find Evan's daughter and deliver the letter.

As far as Henry Quinn was concerned, there was no real difference between a promise given and a promise kept. That was just the way he was made.

21

THREE

Rumor had it that Calvary was once called Calgary. Just as in the Bible, the place of the skull. The place they nailed up the king of the Jews.

"They sure as hell done that 'fore any Texians done got here," someone once said. "Texians here too darn drunk and too darn lazy to do anything so fancy. Woulda just shot the dumb sucker 'stead of buildin' all that fancy riggin' and whatnot. Shot the boy and then thrown him in a ravine or some such. Let the coyotes git 'im."

Way back before all the border wars and suchlike started, Texas didn't rank so well in the popularity stakes. It was too far from the other colonies, there were too many Indian raids, and something about the endless panorama of dust and nothing debilitated the soul.

Calgary, if it was even called that back then, came about by accident.

Lincoln's election in 1860 saw South Carolina set on secession, and five other lower South states followed suit, Texas among them. The Civil War played out, the army of Northern Virginia finally surrendered, and Reconstruction began. Congress welcomed Texas back into the Union in 1870, but it seemed once more that Texas was like a distant and unruly cousin, bad-tempered, prone to drunken outbursts, volatile at the best of times. Invitation was little more than a resentful obligation, the loutish and unsophisticated uncle at a genteel Southern party. While everyone was drinking watermelon juleps and talking politics, Uncle Tex had cleared half a bottle of bourbon and was trying to fuck the help. Texas seemed to offer nothing but agricultural depression, unrealistic demands, and a landscape sculpted by wind and an endless caravan of hard wheels and hooves.

Until the oil. Until black gold burst from the ground south of Beaumont in January 1901, and Spindletop defined the new Texas. Seemed there was no looking back. Texas possessed a currency that everyone wanted and everyone could spend. But that did not make the state any more hospitable; nor did it prevent the Dust Bowl and the Great Depression. It was only the Second World War, the vast influx of federal money that built army bases, munitions factories, and hospitals that really changed the state's fundamental nature. Three-quarters of a million men left Texas to fight, and those who returned did not return to stare at featureless horizons and work an inhospitable land.

One of the Texans who did return from the war was Evan Riggs, twenty-one years old, and the homestead he returned to perhaps defied the seeming inclination toward progress that characterized so many other towns and cities statewide.

"One of those places Jesus forgot, or just plain gave up on," was the way Evan's father, William, described it, but he'd already set himself to farming all of three hundred and fifty acres of cereal, was stubborn enough to set his spurs as deep as they'd go into the haunch of West Texas.

Born in Marathon, just on the other side of the Stockton Plateau, in the late summer of 1896, William Riggs was West Texas in blood and bone and everything else that made a man. William bought a plot of land that he would, in time, expand and establish in his own methodical way. He was twenty years old when he went out there, but West Texas had a way of accelerating the years on even the most unsuspecting and naive young man, and by his second decade, William was as able and confident as would ever be required for survival.

On a clear-skied day in October 1918, William Riggs married a seventeen-year-old girl called Grace Margaret Buckner. Though he had known her less than six months, William loved that girl with a missionary zeal equaled only by those first Spanish colonists of the late 1600s.

Perhaps Grace agreed to the marriage as an escape route. Her own father possessed a skittish eye, as if always watchful of things others could not see. Stray dogs, lost kids seeking forgetful parents. Even ghosts. Folks called him crazy, but they meant something a good deal harsher. Rumor had it he *messed* with his own kids, and not just the girls. William Riggs saw the man had no manners. Never ate nothing but it wasn't with his fingers and straight from the pan, and when it came to the marriage day, Lester Buckner's face was nothing more than a twisted knot of grievance and displeasure.

However, Buckner had good sense enough to let his daughter go. The deal was done, and Grace was now a Riggs. Just seventeen years old, she went out to Calvary with her new husband, and though she may not have felt true love in her heart, she certainly did feel that the life ahead could only be better than the one she'd left behind. Thankfully, it was. Better, but no less tough. William Riggs was a good man, no doubt about it. He was honest and straight, a worker, a churchgoer, a good friend, and a decent husband. He did not want children, not yet, not until they had settled and stabilized, and this was something she could understand and appreciate. If you were going to bring a child into the world, then best make that world as good as it could be.

And so it was with trepidation and anxiety that Grace informed her husband that she was pregnant in April of 1919.

William stood stock-still and silent for some time. His expression was unreadable, but it was an expression Grace had not seen before.

He opened his mouth to speak, seemed to reconsider his chosen words, and then simply said, "No one to blame but myself."

William Riggs left the house and did not return until dusk.

Grace asked him if he was okay. He replied, "I was all set on gettin' myself angry about this, but now I don't feel so much like it."

Something had changed in the man. As if something inside of him was broke down and irreparable.

"It's going to be okay," Grace assured him, but she did not believe that, and it was obvious in her voice.

The pregnancy was endured. It was not easy, not at all. William spent all the hours God gave him in the fields. He hired extra hands, coloreds and Mexicans, worked them hard, paid them a decent wage in comparison to his neighbors. Riggs earned a reputation as a fair-minded and pragmatic man, even somewhat empathetic. To his wife he became a distant memory of something that might have been. He was never abusive or violent, far from it, but there seemed to emerge a cruel streak in him, a coldness perhaps. Whatever tenderness may have once been there seemed hardened and resolute, as if blame was being apportioned and he'd assigned her the lion's share. Perhaps he believed that his authority had been undermined. He'd said no to children, at least for a while, and yet here was a child on the way, like a letter in the mail that could not be delayed. Perhaps, as some men do, he took this as a sign that he was not master of all he surveyed, that there were other forces at work that could defy and derail his intentions. Whichever way it came, he had decided it was a bad thing.

The child came in January of 1920. Same day the federal government saw fit to prohibit alcohol.

William Riggs held his firstborn in his arms, a son, and when the child opened its eyes and looked at its father, the father felt little of anything at all. Riggs had sense and humanity enough to understand that this absence of feeling was wrong, but he could not force himself to feel something he did not. That the mother loved the child was evident in all she said and did around him, but Riggs did not connect with the boy. They called him Carson, and he was a strong boy, a fighter. He never sickened, he slept soundly, he ate enough for two, and he grew like a tree. But Riggs watched that boy as if he were the fruit of some other man's loins, and though he knew that such a thing was impossible, it still sat like a shadow among his thoughts. It repeated on him again and again, like sour milk on the palate. He desperately wanted to love the boy, but he could not. Grace saw this turmoil, this inner conflict, and she grieved in her own quiet way. The atmosphere was one of melancholy, akin to a wake, but she could not fathom what William believed he had lost.

When Grace told him she was again pregnant in the latter part of June, 1923, William stood in the kitchen and looked at her, a glass in his hand, a mustache of milk on his upper lip, and he said, "Seems like we're destined to have a family," which wasn't what he wanted to say, but some type of distant cousin.

The second child, once again a boy, arrived with a good deal less fanfare and drama in March of 1924.

Whatever internal knots were tied with Carson's birth seemed untied once more in the moment that William held Evan in his arms. The newborn gurgled and blinked, his tiny hands reaching toward his father, and the obdurate stone that had temporarily replaced William Riggs's heart gave up its tenancy without a fight. The man cried. Never would have admitted such a thing, but he cried. He carried that babe out to the veranda and stood silently while his exhausted wife slept. Carson, now four years old, was elsewhere, perhaps taking this opportunity to secrete further comestibles about his person as if continually allaying the risk of starvation. His dungaree pockets were a mess of crumbs and crusts, his fingers forever finding ways into Weck and Mason jars, his face a smear of chocolate or preserve. There was something simple, even base about the boy, William believed, as if his intent in life would never be anything greater than taking as much of everything as he could and yet giving as little as possible.

To him, even in those first moments, Evan was different. Never a man for poetic and elegant words, William was inspired to find terms such as *lightness* and *presence*. The child, even in those first few days of its life, brought something to the party. Carson, it seemed, was a taker. Evan was a giver. That was the only way William saw fit to define it. And though his temperament and love for Carson would never match that which he felt for Evan, nevertheless he believed that Evan had rehabilitated something he had lost. Evan showed his father what there was to love about his eldest son, for within those first few weeks of life, the newborn expressed an affection and affinity for his sibling that prompted comment from both parents.

Grace could not have been happier, for she recognized in her husband the man she had married, not the man she feared he had become.

William and Grace Riggs attended the small church in Calvary; she made preserves and cookies for the school bake sale; William brewed a potent fortified wine from blueberries and the like, and once a month he and a half dozen local farmers gathered for cards and cigars and ribald anecdotes. The Riggs were a well-liked and much-respected family, and within that environ the boys grew side by side, the slower Carson ever vigilant for the swifter-witted Evan, their similarities few, their mutual affection unquestioned.

And so it seemed that life would progress ever forward from good days to better days, and in the handful of years before the Great Depression, there was little for which William or Grace could have asked.

But then it seemed the devil came to Calvary. Wearing a hat and a coat and a crooked smile, blown in by some ill wind from beyond the Stockton Plateau and the Pecos River, a dark kind of trouble walked its way into the lives of William and Grace Riggs.

For so many inexplicable reasons, life would never be the same again, and it all began on Evan's fifth birthday in March of 1929.

FOUR

On the sidewalk outside an Eldorado gas station, a three-legged dog sat statue-still and watched as Henry Quinn rolled a cigarette and lit it with a match. Henry wondered about the leg, how it was lost, where it wound up, and how a dog like that would think about such a thing. Whether a dog like that would think at all.

A bus had stopped to refuel, disgorging its passengers, giving them time to use the restroom, stretch their legs, buy chilled bottles of root beer and sacks of potato chips before their own journey resumed. He had driven fifty-odd miles south on 277, would head east out of Eldorado, would perhaps make another brief stop in Ozona, and then cover the last handful of miles to Calvary.

The passengers gathered on the forecourt as they waited for the driver to fill the bus and fetch coffee, and Henry listened to the vignettes of conversation that snuck their way between the sound of the wheels against the highway and the passage of cars.

How am I doing? Spending money I don't have, drinking myself into an early grave. The usual, you know?

. . . three gross of Nibco 633 copper pipe unions . . .

. . . tell you now, ideas is like assholes. Everyone's got one, and they're usually full of shit . . .

To Henry they seemed like people of another race. In his mind he was still cell-bound. Would take a while to come out of it. Evan had spoken of such a thing.

Man's as likely to get someplace and ask for the smallest room he can get. Can't take too much space, you see? We don't care much for the un-familiar, and when you've been buckled up in an eight by ten for years on end, you don't feel so good unless you've got four walls arm's breadth apart and a door you can shut tight. People get over it, but it takes a while. Some of them never get over it, and they do something to get 'emselves brought right on back. You can feel their sigh of relief when someone locks 'em up again.

Henry knew whereof Evan spoke. There was a comfort in claustro-phobia. There was a comfort in routine. There was a comfort in never having to think about anything save the book you were reading or the conversation you were having. In jail you did not need to find the rent. In jail you did not miss a meal. There were a great deal of things you *did* miss, but even they seemed to fade from reality after a time. In a way it reminded you of being a child. You ate when you were told; you slept when you were told. Step out of line and there was always someone mighty keen to show you right where that line was and put you behind it once more.

But now it was all done. Now he was out and free, and though he could not leave the state for another year without telling someone, he was his own man.

Except for his promise to Evan and whatever was happening with his ma, he could do pretty much as he pleased.

The reunion had not gone well. She was still right there in the house where it all happened. The O'Briens, Henry was relieved to discover, were gone. Sally O'Brien had not lost the faculty of speech. A blessing, no doubt about it. Should Henry keep a weather eye out for Danny O'Brien? Maybe. Maybe not. Henry didn't know the man from Adam, thus could not determine his temper or taste for retribution. Seemed to Henry that when it came down to basics, there were two kinds of people: those who blamed everyone else for their situation and those who blamed themselves. Would take a broad perspective to accept that accidents and coincidences were of your own making, but given a choice between *yay* and *nay*, Henry would fall on the *yay* side. Even if such things weren't of your own design and decision, the mere fact of taking responsibility for them got you of a mind to do something about it, rather than just bitching like a cuckold.

Anyhow, all such philosophical ramblings aside, his mother was his mother, and she was slipping out through the gap between what was and what wasn't. The drinking didn't help none. Drinking, in Henry's experience, merely served to exaggerate what was already inside of you. Like money. Like power. Give those things to a man and he just becomes more of what he inherently is.

Reeves County Farm Prison transport drove Henry as far as Odessa. The driver said little, save that he wanted to stop at a roadside diner to get a cup of coffee and a bear claw. Henry waited on the bus. Driver never asked if he wanted anything and brought nothing back for him. Just sat and ate his bear claw, drank his coffee, lit a smoke, and then started out again.

By the time they arrived, it was nightfall. Henry slept at a shabby motel in a room that smelled of mold and bad feet. Didn't undress, for he doubted the sheets had been changed in a month. Even the water in the bathroom seemed uncertain of its own ability to clean anything. Wash your hands in it and they needed to be washed again elsewhere. It was not a good welcome back to the free world.

Henry took a walk around Odessa on the morning of the twelfth. Little things caught his attention. Colors seemed brighter, hair was longer, cars louder than he recalled. What had he expected, that time would wait for him unchanged and unmoved while he served his three years, three months, and four days? That it would be like dreamtime—a day in a second, a week in an hour—and yet upon waking the dreamer discovers that everything is the same? No, everything had changed. He could sense it. He could feel it. He did not like it, for it was a constant reminder that the time he'd spent in Reeves was as good as time lost forever. The only upside had been Evan Riggs, the fact that the man understood the need for music, that he'd shared some wisdoms and words that would count for something on the road to wherever Henry was ultimately headed. Where that was, well, Henry would find out in due course. Like Hemingway said, *It is good to have an end to journey toward; but it is the journey that matters, in the end.*

And so he walked, and he thought of how best to talk to his mother, to explain to her that he was not staying in San Angelo, that there was a road he was going to walk and its first wide part was somewhere called Calvary. Once that was done, the pledge honored, then where? He didn't know, and he didn't *need* to know. After a thousand or more days of regulations, he figured he could do without them for a while. Would she understand? There was no way of knowing until he got there and told her.

It was bad, but not as bad as it might have been.

A man had been staying in the house. That much Henry could determine from the shaving accoutrements in the bathroom, the shoes on the porch. Who he was and what his business was, his ma didn't say, and Henry didn't ask.

"You're leaving?" she asked. "I haven't seen you for a year and you're leaving?"

That first line he could have written before he left Reeves.

"I am," he told her.

"But why?" She stood in the kitchen doorway, her hand on her hip, something in her body language that said he was going nowhere

29

until she received some satisfactory answers. Her appearance was further confirmation that more than three years had passed. Her hair was close to silver, her eyes reconciled to the sight of an unappealing future. She did not look well.

"Have to deal with something, Ma," Henry said.

"But you need to spend some time here, spend some time with me, settle down, get a job. You need to get a job, Henry. A job should be your first order of business."

"It isn't, Ma. I don't expect you to understand, but there is something I have to do. I made a promise, and I gotta keep it."

"What about your promise to me?"

"What promise would that be, then?"

She changed the subject, went for the bourbon, took a slug that would have put Henry on his back after three years of no liquor. She started off on a detour concerning something or other that Henry did not understand, and in truth had no mind to. Seemed like she was working up enough courage for a fight, and that was the last thing Henry wanted.

"Look, Ma," he finally said, interrupting her midflow on some wild anecdote about a raccoon as big as a dog in the garbage, "I just have to do something. I'll be gone a little while. A few days, a week, a month maybe. As far as the rest of my life is concerned, I have to figure that out, sure, but that's not my priority right now."

"I am not happy, Henry," Nancy Quinn said.

"Is anyone?" Henry replied.

Nancy Quinn looked at her son like he was a stranger.

Henry smiled at her like she was the only mother in the world.

Compromising, Henry agreed to stay one night. His mother's gentleman friend arrived for supper. His name was Howard Ulysses Morgan.

"Hell of a story behind the Ulysses, if you're interested," which Henry was not, but Howard proceeded to tell the story anyway.

The story was no big deal, but politeness won over and Henry smiled at the end.

"And that, young man, is how I came to be Howard *Ulysses*," Howard concluded, pleased with himself perhaps, as if the oddity of his middle name somehow compensated for an absence of charm and personality.

Whichever way you painted the sign, Howard was a drunk. His was the bourbon, and he had no shame in keeping it to himself.

Only once did he offer some to Henry. Henry declined. Nancy took a second man-sized jolt, then switched to her own brand of poison, and the pair of them slid into semi-coherence, seemingly untroubled by the fact that Henry had just been released from prison and might have had an ache for company.

After an hour, he left them to their own devices. He went out back to check on his pickup, an Apache Red 1962 Studebaker Champ. Pride and joy, no question. Front driver's-side tire was down some and would need a breath of air; rust around the wheel arches was accelerated but not fatal. It had been tarpaulined, and the tarp had at least prevented animal or insect infestation and sun-bleaching. She kicked over on the first try.

"Y-you goin' s-someplace?" Howard slurred at him from the back door.

"No, sir," Henry said. "Not just yet. Just checkin' she's still runnin'."

Howard looked at Henry as if he'd forgotten the question he himself had asked, and then he raised his glass, smiled cheerily, and headed back indoors.

Henry heard Howard and his ma laughing about something, and then there was silence.

Maybe folks like Howard got through the day by convincing themselves it was still Christmas or New Year's or some such.

Half an hour later Henry was in his room. Evan Riggs's letter was there on the nightstand. It had one word clearly and carefully printed on the front. *Sarah*. Henry's guitar case sat on the floor at his feet. It had been underneath the bed all this time. The Princeton amp was still working. No reason for it not to have been, but when he switched it on and the transformer came to life, he was almost surprised.

Why there was a sense of trepidation as he leaned forward to open that case, he did not know. It was there, and he could not deny it.

Before Reeves, music had been his life, his being, his raison d'être. Glancing now toward the wall, seeing the stacks of vinyls that rested there—everything from Lead Belly and Sonny Terry to Gene Vincent and Johnny Burnette, British imported records like *Five Live Yardbirds* and *Piper at the Gates of Dawn*, the West Coast sounds of *Surrealistic Pillow* and *Easter Everywhere* from right here in Austin, Texas—Henry could see himself seated right where he was now more than three years earlier.

31

A moment. That's all it took. A moment of dumbass stupidity.

He was drunk. Four, five, six cans of beer, he couldn't even remember. He was in the funk. The black dog. He was pissed about something he couldn't learn, something that frustrated him. Nothing so simple as girl trouble; it had been soul trouble. Maybe something only musicians could understand, but there was a point where the body defied the mind. Maybe it was the same for athletes, as if you knew something could be achieved, but there was no clear way to achieve it. Regardless of reason or rationale, Henry had been down. He'd drunk most of a six-pack and then took the .38 into the yard and let off a few rounds. One degree up or down, one degree left or right, and that slug would never have ricocheted as it did, would never have made it across the yard and through the fence, would never have reached Sally O'Brien.

And he would not be here three years later with a void in his mind.

The weight of the guitar surprised him. Ten pounds, give or take, but it seemed so much heavier. The shape and feel was unmistakable, and the chords were still there, though changing was slow and clumsy. That would come back in no time at all. It was the riffs and lead lines that were gone, and where muscle memory had once put his fingers exactly where they needed to be, there was little of anything left.

Henry played the guitar for a handful of minutes, and then he laid it back in its case and just stared at it for a while. Finally, he kicked the lid closed with the toe of his boot.

He leaned forward, elbows on his knees, his head in his hands like a man taking delivery of heartbreaking news.

FIVE

"Ides of March," Grace Riggs told her husband on the morning of their youngest son's fifth birthday.

"What of it?"

"It's an important date."

"How so?"

"You don't know about Julius Caesar, sweetheart?"

"Can't say I do," William said. "He a stock farmer or grain?"

"You are teasing me," Grace replied. "You know exactly who Julius Caesar is."

William and Grace were in the kitchen, William sat tying his boots while she busied herself at the stove. Six in the morning, children still asleep, the early-morning routine as Grace fed and watered her husband before he went to work. This day was different, however. William would wake the children in a half hour or so, share breakfast, acknowledge Evan's birthday before he headed out.

"I do, indeed, my love," William told her. "He's that feller who done run into a steer with his tractor on—"

Grace swatted her husband with a dish towel. "Such an ignorant man, you are."

"Smarts is overrated," William replied. "Don't wanna git involved with none of that book-readin' business, now, do we?"

"I'm serious, Will," Grace said. "It's an important date. Historically significant. Lot of things have happened on the fifteenth of March. Columbus arrived back in Spain, the Red River Campaign, Tsar Nicholas abdicated—"

"I think you'll find, dear heart, that we human beings, for better or worse, have been around long enough to see a great many historical events on every day of the calendar. Besides, I don't think it's a good to idea to fill Evan's little head with such things. I know he's as bright as a star, but all this special attention is only going to make Carson feel left out. We spoke about this before, remember?"

Grace was silent for a moment, her expression as one readied for rebuttal, but nothing but silence was forthcoming. She knew her husband was right, said certainty not borne out of any requirement to bend to his will, for Grace Riggs was as righteously stubborn as any woman could be when she felt her self-determination was being subsumed, but out of simple agreement.

"Yes," she said. "You are right, my dear. Enough."

William reached out his hand toward her. She stepped closer, and he put his arm around her waist. He pulled her close and pressed the side of his face against her stomach.

"Different boys, different minds, but we cannot treat them differently," he said. "It will only be the cause of trouble they don't need."

Grace stood there beside her seated husband, one hand on his shoulder, the other touching the side of his face, and she looked out through the window as early-morning sun lit the fields like fire. She saw no purpose in reminding her husband of how distant he had been when Carson was first born. She was twenty-seven years old, and time with William Riggs had done nothing but strengthen her love and respect for the man. Never one for hearsay and rumormongering, she was nevertheless privy to words shared by wives in the postchurch gaggles that clucked and prattled beyond earshot of the minister. The husbands conspired to engage in late-night drinking and gambling, all the more ironic when the sermon had broached such things as temperance and abstinence, and the wives spoke ill of their husbands in such a way as Grace could never have countenanced.

An' I seen the way he looks at her ... what with her cheekbones tucked up tight and them bee-sting lips o' hers ...

Know when he's lyin' ... can see it painted all across his face like whitewash ...

Staggered home reekin' something devilish; told him to sleep in the barn, not to come near me with that disgusting thing o' his ...

For William, Grace had other words, words like *loyalty* and *dependability*, *trustworthiness* and *constancy*. He did not look at other women, save that they crossed his line of sight, and he kept on looking wherever he'd been looking and did not follow them as they passed. He did not drink to excess, and though there had been half a dozen times when he was a little worse for wear, he had always remained jovial, never angry, and certainly never violent. One time he danced a jig for her like some half-crazed Irish leprechaun, and she near lost her breath for laughing.

Other wives seemed to have found other kinds of husbands.

May-Elizabeth Crook once sported a shiner to rival those inflicted by Jack Dempsey upon the likes of Gene Tunney and Georges Carpentier.

"Crook by name, crook by nature, that's my husband," May-Elizabeth once told Grace, conveniently forgetting that she was a Crook herself.

Word was that Yale Killebrew was sharing his bed with Montie Jennings's new wife, and the womenfolk used words like *blowsy* and *sluttish*. Seemed to Grace that people should check for muddy footprints on their own porch before commenting on the state of others'.

And so Grace listened to her husband, not out of duty, but out of a mutual understanding and agreement that the life they shared was the life they created together. They stood back-to-back against the world, reliant upon no one but themselves for their own mental and emotional survival. Whatever bed they made, they would be lying in it, and that went for their children, too.

It was Evan's fifth birthday, and that was the only required significance for this, the Ides of March.

Until later, of course, but later had yet to arrive and thus was as unknown a territory as the rationale of Calvary's collective womenfolk.

Five years was old enough for a horse, and that's what Evan got. Set with saddle and stirrup and rein and bit, that narrow-haunched paint was a gentle beauty. Sire and dam were different, a bay and white for one, a sorrel and white for the other, and this one came up kind of hazel, except for a white hock-to-hoof splash on the forelimbs. Grady Fromme, two farms east, gave William Riggs a fair price for a good steed, ideal for a little 'un, and in the three days that William and Grace had kept that horse hidden in the barn, there had been nothing to indicate that the pony was anything but perfect in nature and temperament. He was a quiet one for sure, nudging up against William with an affectionate manner. William's experience was more bovine than equine, but he'd been around horses all his life and they were a good animal. Smarter than steer—that went without saying—and there was a devotion to be found in a horse that was equaled only by a hound. Good horse would carry you as fast as it could go until its own heart burst, and that was a fact. He'd seen it happen, heard of it more often, and that was something William could never fathom save were it for your own kin.

Breakfast done in a whirlwind of pancakes and spilled juice, Grace and William Riggs walked out to the porch with both of the boys. Carson was all of nine years old, had gotten his own pony at five but never really took to the thing. Two years on, William had sold it and bought the boy a bicycle. Didn't take to that, either. Each to his own, though what was Carson's own they had yet to learn.

Grace stayed up on the veranda with the boys, and William headed on down to the barn to fetch the paint. When he led him out across the yard and Evan saw him, there was a whoop of delight the like of which neither parent had seen nor heard before.

Grace sensed the envy. It seemed to swell around Carson. Like some sort of airborne virus, it infected the air as an unpleasant odor, an unsettling sound of indistinct origin.

"Go," Grace urged Evan, and Evan nearly tumbled appetite over tin cup as he barreled down the porch steps and hurtled across the yard toward his father.

The pony seemed untroubled by the whirlwind of arms and legs and laughter that gamboled toward it, and when William hoisted the boy up and settled his boots in the stirrups, when he started to lead that horse down the driveway and onto the grazing range, Grace couldn't believe how happy such a sight made her feel.

After ten minutes Carson wanted to go inside. He tugged at his mother's sleeve, but Grace wanted to stay and watch as her youngest bonded with the pony.

Carson went inside by himself, and when she heard a door slam upstairs, she knew there was a storm brewing.

It would not have been fair to say that Carson Riggs arrived into a world that did not love him. Despite his father's original reticence, the arrival of Evan had done wonders to smooth whatever edges and corners might have existed. Tradition seemed to dictate that the eldest was the favored, certainly when that eldest was a boy, but here it was different, tangibly so, and Grace was aware that Carson was aware, and that mutual awareness was something she wrestled with most every day. Those outside would perhaps have noticed nothing out of the ordinary but—as with all things—when you knew what you were looking for, you saw it all the time. Details, simple matters, the fact that William would pass the vegetables first to Evan, the fact that come an evening when William saw fit to listen to the wireless, he would have Evan on his knee while Carson sat cross-legged on

36

the floor below. The devil was in the detail, and Grace knew that if they were not cautious, then the devil might find its way into Carson as well. Having said that, Carson was not a bad boy. He was solid and reliable and conscientious in his own way. He was easy to love, for there was a simplicity in his outlook and manner that possessed its own immutable charm. Carson would never be fickle nor absentminded; nor would he be stricken with wild flights of fancy. Where Evan was akin to the newest and latest, Carson was the all-too-familiar sense of nostalgia that accompanied an old pair of boots that could never be discarded.

It being a school day, the boys were packed up with books and lunch pails by eight. Evan, predictably, didn't want to go, but he didn't put up a fight. Never one for tantrums and the like, Evan seemed philosophically resigned to the fact that though his elders were not necessarily always his betters, they still had the say-so in the general run of things. He hung back as William returned the pony to the barn, said goodbye to the thing, and headed for the road with Carson and his father.

"You gotta find that pony a name, son," William said.

"Will do, Pa."

"You any ideas yet?"

Evan shook his head. "Nope. He'll tell me when he's ready."

"Darn fool thing to say," Carson interjected. "Horses don't talk, you dumbass."

"Carson. Enough of that. Animals have a sense, and some folks have a sense for animals. Lot of things we don't understand—"

"Understand that horses don't talk," Carson jibed.

"Not another word out of you, young man," William Riggs replied, and there was a sharp edge in his tone.

Carson fell silent, knew better than to challenge his pa.

William drove them to school in the buggy, had some business over the other side of Calvary and school was en route. Little more than half a mile, they ordinarily walked and the walk was good for them. Got some air in their lungs, some limber in their muscles. And when school was done, Evan was all but falling over himself to get back to see his horse.

"That dumb pony done telephoned you and told you his name yet?" Carson needled.

"Don't be such a fool, Carson. Horses don't use telephones."

"And horses don't talk, you dumbass."

"You're the dumbass."

37

"You're the king of all the dumbasses in the world."

"I reckon you are so."

Thus it went on, back and forth, trading petty insults until the farm came into view and Evan started running.

Carson let him go. He didn't care to see the horse; nor did he much care that it was his younger brother's birthday. Birthdays were a whole heap of nothing disguised as something, and that you could take to the bank.

But it wasn't nothing. It was something. It was like a seed caught in a tooth that wouldn't give up. A hangnail that snags and catches. And Carson sat on it for three days before he did something cruel and foolish.

Perhaps it was nothing more nor less than jealousy, the innate knowledge that he was not as well loved, that the years before Evan's arrival were marked by some cool distance between himself and his father, but there was a ghost of something in the boy's mind. He loved Evan, no question there, but he envied him as well. Grace sensed it. William trusted Grace's female intuition about such things, and he was responsible enough to recognize that he was as much to blame for the situation as Carson himself.

Had the action been impulsive, it would have been seen as nothing more than childish and spiteful, albeit malicious, but it was the forethought that troubled both William and Grace Riggs.

Three o'clock in the morning, Monday the eighteenth of March, nine-year-old Carson Riggs, no slouch but never the brightest light in the harbor, crept out of bed, down the stairs, across the yard, and hurried out to the barn where his younger brother's pony was stabled. He then proceeded to let the thing loose. He raised a good ruckus, waving his arms and stamping his feet, and the little horse bolted. Had it been a bigger horse, with perhaps a sharper temper, Carson Riggs might have gotten his head kicked off, but no, the animal was just spooked some and took off like a whirlwind.

Took William a day to reunite heartbroken boy with skittish horse, and even then it came back of its own accord. William drove the perimeter of the farm, the farms adjacent, put word out that he was looking for a young hazel-colored paint, distinct for the white hock-to-hoof splash. Returned the first evening with no word of the thing, wondered whether it was gone for good. Evan had wept himself into a dreadful state, took no consolation from anything, and only when that pony made its cautious way up the drive toward the house did it look like the world was not actually at an end.

William and Grace Riggs knew who'd done it. It was obvious. Even the vain efforts to get involved in the search did not assuage their certainty that Carson had been responsible.

Once Evan was settled for the night, William took Carson aside and let him know.

"No use to lie, son," William said. "We know you let the pony go. No other way it could have happened. I am mad enough already, son. Don't get me madder by telling me it wasn't you."

Carson dropped his gaze to the floor, stayed silent.

"The last thing I wanna do is beat you, boy, but I ain't rulin' it out. You tell me now. You let that pony go, didn't you?"

Carson didn't raise his eyes or his head, but he nodded and said, "Yes, sir."

William sighed. "Now, what in the world inspired such a notion? Tell me that much at least. I got you a pony when you turned five. You never took to it. Even got you a bicycle and you didn't take to that neither. Evan's a little kid, son. What on earth did you hope to gain by breaking his heart like that?"

William knew that Carson was not sufficiently self-aware to answer such questions, but he had to ask them anyway. Had to get them out of his mouth; they tasted coppery and sour, and that taste would not dispel until the words were spoken.

"Don't know," was all Carson could manage.

"I know you don't, son, and I ain't really askin'. I'm groundin' you. You got extra chores, extra for you, and you'll be doin' Evan's chores for a month as well. In the morning you're gonna say sorry to your brother, and you're gonna mean it from your heart. You understand me?"

"Yes, sir."

"Now git, 'fore I change my mind and take your hide off with a horse whip."

Carson slunk away, shamed and disgraced.

Later, lying in bed, Grace said, "I think we got a live one, William. Scared he's not only troubled, but troublesome and a troublemaker to boot."

"Kids ain't dogs or horses. You can't train 'em the same way. They come with too much that's indelible."

"Where'd he get it from—that's the question," Grace said. "That streak I see in him worries me."

"I don't know, sweetheart, but punishin' him ain't gonna do nothin' but make it worse. You beat a child and you just provin' to him how he can rile you. Instinct gonna make him do it again just to get revenge."

"You're a good man, William Riggs."

"Was a champion asshole 'til I met you, though. Got the blue rosette and ribbon to prove it."

Grace laughed. She kissed him. They lay beside each other and settled into a restless sleep. William Riggs rarely dreamed, but that night he did. Come morning he would recall little of it save the vision of his eldest son saying something vicious through the bars of a jail cell.

SIX

Nancy Quinn had the radio on in the kitchen. Howard Ulysses was nowhere to be seen. George McGovern had won the Democratic presidential nomination.

Henry was in the doorway for a good thirty seconds before his ma realized.

"You leavin', then?" she asked. "Again?"

"I didn't leave you last time, Ma. I went to prison."

"Same thing, however you name it."

"I'm not gonna start a fight with you," Henry said. He could see she was hungover. Her actions were measured, as if trying to do everything without making a sound, as if to move suddenly would surprise even herself.

"Seems from my corner it's already started."

"Then you win," Henry said. "You are the undefeated title holder."

"You always had a sharp tongue."

"Had the best teacher, Ma."

Nancy Quinn turned from the sink. She looked her son up and down and then shook her head resignedly. "When did we get to this?"

"To what, Ma?"

"Sticking pins in each other to see who howls first?"

"Is that what we're doing?"

"You're still doing it, Henry. I didn't make you how you is, and I sure as hell am not to blame for you getting yourself in Reeves. You done that all by yourself."

Henry looked down at the floor. His feet were cramped into a pair of Luccheses that hadn't been worn for three years. They would stretch and give in a while.

"If you gotta go, then you gotta go," Nancy said.

"I gotta go."

"Do you know where you're going?"

"Some, yes."

"And why?"

41

"Gotta deliver a letter for someone."

"Someone you knew in Reeves?"

"Yeah."

"You ever gonna speak of it?"

"Nothin' to say."

Nancy frowned. "Three years in Reeves County and you have nothin' to say?"

"It's prison, Ma. You eat when they say; you sleep when they say; you shit when they say. Sometimes you get into a fight; sometimes you don't. Most people are lookin' to do whatever time they've got with as little heartache as possible. There's a few that are never comin' out."

"And the letter?"

"From a friend of mine to his daughter."

"This friend of yours ever gonna come out?"

"Nope."

"Daughter ever visit him?"

"I don't think she knows who he is, and I don't think anyone's ever gonna tell her."

" 'Cept you."

"Right."

"Mightn't be good for her."

"I know, Ma, but I made a promise, and a promise like that you don't break."

Nancy was quiet for a time, perhaps reflecting on promises made and never fulfilled. Maybe her life was full of them.

Then she smiled some internal smile and looked up at Henry. "Coffee's been on the stove a while. Probably not so good. Let me make some fresh. Have a bite to eat with me before you go, okay?"

"Sure, Ma."

By the time Henry hefted a knapsack and a guitar case into the back of the Champ, it was noon. Sun was high, sky was cloudless, air as crisp as crepe.

He started the engine, then climbed out and stood for a while as the engine ticked over. He smoked a cigarette and waited for his ma to come on out for the farewell.

She'd made him up a paper sack of sandwiches.

"Just some ham," she said. "Smoked kind you like."

"Thanks, Ma."

He held out his hand and she came to him. He was a head taller, and it felt like he was putting his arms around a child. She seemed frail.

"Where's Howard gotten himself to?" Henry asked.

"Work."

"He here often?"

"Often enough."

"He good for you?"

"He ain't bad for me."

"Drinks a lot, I noticed," Henry said.

"He's just thirsty."

Henry laughed dryly. "That the bill of goods he's selling, is it?"

"Same one we're all selling, Henry," Nancy replied. "Always got an explanation for what we do, what we done, what we're plannin' on doin'."

"He seems a little lost to me."

Nancy didn't reply. She didn't need to. Souls with similar afflictions gravitate toward one another. Usually it's not 'til they separate that they realize how similar they are.

"So, it's a goodbye, then."

"Au revoir, as the French say," Henry replied. "I'll be back soon enough."

"Well, I stood you gone for three years. Guess I can stand you gone for a while longer. You don't need to phone or nothin'. That'll just remind me that you could be here when you're not. I ain't gonna worry none, 'cause I know you can take care of things."

Henry hugged her close. "You always had more faith in me than I did in myself, Ma."

Henry stopped over at the garage on Pearsall.

"Where's Gus at?" he asked a stranger in rust-colored overalls.

"Gus Maynard?"

"Only Gus I know. He owns the place."

"Don't own it no more."

"How so?"

"He's dead."

Henry paused. Reminders of his absence were everywhere. Learning things like this just served to make him wonder what else he didn't know.

"You own the place now?"

"I do."

"What's your name?"

"Hoyt."

"I'm Henry. Been away for a while. Going on a trip now. Can you check her over, fill the tires, oil, gas her up, all that stuff?"

"Can do."

"I'm gonna go get a cup of coffee."

"At Stella's?"

"Sure."

"You come on back with a cup of coffee and a slice of angel food cake, I'll chip that off your bill."

"No problem, Hoyt."

Stella's had been there forever, and Henry was pleased to see that the end of forever wasn't arriving anytime soon.

In truth, Stella Roscoe wasn't even seventy, but the smoking and drinking had put at least a decade in her voice and on her face. When she spoke, her words were like chunks of coal floating up through a barrel of pitch.

"Henry Quinn," she announced as Henry appeared in the doorway of the diner.

"Stella Roscoe."

She came toward him, arms wide. "So, they let you out, then?"

"They did, Stella. They did."

She hugged him hard enough to crack ribs.

"You come sit yourself down and get some coffee and pie, son. Can't imagine you been eatin' anything but sowbelly and blackstrap."

"Some beans, too," Henry said. "Collard greens on Sunday."

"Oh, livin' the high life, eh?"

"Near as dammit."

Stella busied herself with coffeepots and pie dishes as Henry took a seat at the counter.

"Gonna take a drive out an' see some people," Henry said. "Hoyt there is fixin' up the Champ. He said Gus gone an' died."

"Yep. More 'an a year ago now. Liquor finally drained a hole through his liver, I guess."

"He liked a drink, that's for sure."

Stella laughed like a broken locomotive. "Think that there goes in the understatements ledger."

"His wife?"

"Hester. She upped sticks and went out to her sister's. Someplace near to Abilene. Baird, Cisco, Sweetwater. One o' them burgs."

"And Hoyt?"

"Hoyt is a good man. Don't know a great deal of anythin' but cars, but he owns Gus's garage now, so it kinda works out fine."

"He come from?"

"Somewheres oily," Stella said, cracking a smile in the leather satchel of her face.

She set a cup of coffee on the counter, followed it with a slice of buttermilk chess pie.

"So where's you headed now, boy?"

"Calvary."

"Man on a mission."

"Seems so."

"You gonna stay out of trouble?"

"Doubtful," Henry replied, cutting into the pie with the edge of his fork.

"Well, whatever trouble you get into, make sure you don't go back to Reeves, huh?"

"Do my best, Stella. Do my best."

"You know what they say."

"What'd that be?"

"Sometimes your best ain't good enough."

Henry smiled ruefully. "Thanks for the encouragement there, Stella Roscoe."

"You're more than welcome, Henry Quinn."

Henry finished up his pie and coffee, took another cup for Hoyt, the angel food cake, too.

Stella said there was no charge, but Henry left a couple of bucks anyway.

He bade her farewell, and she hugged him once more, told him to relay her best wishes to Calvary.

"They know you down there?" Henry asked.

She shook her head. "Nope, but that don't mean they shouldn't."

Over at the garage, Hoyt took delivery of the cake like it was Christmas.

Hands like that, Henry would have worn gloves to eat, but Hoyt didn't seem to mind. Maybe he had a hankering for greasy fingerprints. Maybe you got a taste for such things.

" 'S a good 'un you got there," Hoyt said. "Nothing wrong with her but a good run on the highway won't fix. Done your tires, oil, gassed her up, and she's itchin' to go."

" 'Preciated, Hoyt. How much I owe you?"

Hoyt told him and Henry paid up.

"Where you headed?" Hoyt asked, like the curiosity was con-spiratorial. What was the ex-con up to now? He off to find some other innocent woman needs a .38 in her throat?

"Calvary," Henry said it. "You know it?"

Hoyt shook his head. "Can't say I do."

"Fifty miles or so south, then west on 10 another seventy, eighty."

"West Texas," Hoyt said. "Folks pretty much live and die within a five-mile radius. Dirt they played in as kids is the same dirt they get buried in. Calvary may as well be France." He drank some coffee, maybe helped to wash them Valvoline fingerprints out of his mouth. "You have a good run. Hope you find whatever you're lookin' for."

"Thanks, Hoyt. See you when she needs a checkup."

"God willin'," Hoyt said, and disappeared into the shadowed cavern of the garage.

Radio worked fine. No reason it shouldn't have, but Henry was pleased all the same. He found an FM station out of San Antonio— KDXL 109.4—and they played a good mix of things he liked. Allmans, J. J. Cale, Barefoot Jerry, Bo Diddley, a bunch of soul stuff out of Muscle Shoals. Henry took 277 down through Eldorado to Sonora, headed west then to Ozona. On the other side of Ozona, almost to the Pecos River, he knew he'd gone too far. How he knew he wasn't sure, but he knew. He turned around, headed back the way he'd come, eyes peeled for signage.

After half a dozen miles, he saw pretty much the only indication that Calvary even existed. It was a right turn, said that his destina-tion was all of twenty miles, but the road he found was rutted and broken, like a dirt track aspiring to something more substantial. Calvary was a town, he'd guessed. Maybe it wasn't so much of a town as a backwater burg. For a place to have a sheriff, it surely had to be something more than a half dozen tar-paper shacks and a redundant water tower. Regardless, Evan's brother was down here, and if what Evan told him was true, then the sheriff knew of Sarah, perhaps had news of her current whereabouts. Hell, maybe she'd been here all along and this was going to be nothing more than a handshake, a postal delivery, and a hundred-and-eighty-degree about-face for home.

But there was a ghost of something. Maybe it was the fact that Calvary looked like it was hiding from the world down some beat-to-hell nothing of a road. Maybe it was the fact that whenever Evan had spoken of this brother, Carson, he'd worked up an expression like vinegar mouthwash. Henry sensed there was no love lost between the siblings, but that was all of an assumption, and history was wall-to-wall with examples of where assumption got you. No, there was no reason to feel anything other than the original sense of duty. He said he would do it, and do it he would. That was the start and finish of it.

He gunned the engine into life once more, put the radio back on to find T-Bone Walker had been waiting for him, and headed the Champ down that wheel-rutted road to Calvary.

SEVEN

The pony episode lost its strength of color in the natural tides of time.

The Riggs family survived through the Depression, William doing whatever he could to assist those who did not fare so well. He was an even-minded man, attended church and the like, held a personal philosophy that you got as good as you gave. That kind of thinking didn't come from the Bible; seemed to him it was common sense. Stock dwindled dramatically, simply because there was no place to feed and water them, but William had predicted this and sacrificed numbers accordingly. They wrestled themselves out of the twenties, and by the time things started to ease, it was 1936 and the boys were in their teens, Carson heading for manhood, Evan close on his heels.

And then Rebecca Wyatt showed up.

Rebecca's father, Ralph Wyatt, bought a farm to the west of the Riggses' land for a song in the fall of '37.

Ralph Wyatt had no wife. Where she was, no one seemed to know, and no one asked. The Calvary womenfolk chattered like sparrows about it, but none had an answer.

Wyatt hadn't been there more than a week when he came a-calling on the Riggs family. He was a big man, filled the doorway with his shoulders, forehead hard enough to hammer home fenceposts, hands sufficiently rangy and rough to spool five-strand barbwire and never catch a nick.

"Ralph Wyatt," he said, "and this here's my daughter, Rebecca."

Wyatt extended his hand, Rebecca curtsied politely, and William invited them in for lemonade.

Carson looked like he'd been trampled down by a longhorn, teenage hormones boiling under the surface as he sat across from Rebecca Wyatt at the long kitchen table.

Rebecca was fixing to be a heartbreaker, no doubt about it. Mid-teens, and already she had the grace of a swan. She did her best to hide it beneath dungarees and flat shoes and a mess of unruly bangs, but there was no denying the fact that she was destined to be a very beautiful young woman.

Grace busied herself with drinks and comestibles. Ralph Wyatt and William Riggs asked questions designed to plumb depths and ascertain toeholds. That they would grow to be fast friends as months became years was perhaps indicated by the warmth with which William spoke of Ralph Wyatt to Grace once the Wyatts had departed.

"Seems a good man."

"He does," Grace replied.

"Tough thing to raise a girl alone, but he sure seems to have done a fine job."

"Reckon Carson would agree with you on that one. Boy looked thunderstruck from the moment she walked into the house."

"Girl like that gonna break his heart."

"Everyone has to get their heart broken sometime, William. May's well get it done and over with."

William smiled wryly. "That's a hard line from such a soft woman."

"Who knows, eh? Maybe she'll take to Carson. He's a bright boy in his own way. Never was one for book learning, but you've done a good job, William. What he lacks in imagination, he makes up for in common sense and pragmatism. He's got a level enough head on his shoulders, and I think he's gonna do fine."

"*We*'ve done a good job, Grace. You have more patience than I've seen in anyone."

"That's very sweet of you to say so, William."

"Hell, Grace, you've been an absolute wonder with both of them. This music thing that Evan's so fired up about still leaves me speechless. Boy can sing just beautiful, and he's hankering for a guitar now and I don't see a reason not to get him one."

"He has a gift, that's for sure."

Grace, done with dishes and whatnot, came and sat beside her husband at the kitchen table. "So, we done congratulating ourselves on what fine parents we are, or you want to do some more?"

"We're done," William. "Only so much applause I can take."

"Has to be said that I don't worry about Carson like I used to."

"He was young, my sweet. He had a skewed idea about a few things, but I reckon he's pretty much straight now."

"I hope so."

"Sure loves Evan. No doubt about that. Takes care of him just fine at school."

"Way it should be. That's what big brothers are for."

"So let's see if the pretty girl breaks his heart, and we'll jump off that bridge when it happens."

The hammer of footsteps in the hallway, and Evan burst through into the kitchen, shouting loud enough for Ralph Wyatt to hear, "It's Carson! He done fell! Carson fell and there's blood everywhere!"

William leaped from his chair, Grace hard and fast behind him, running headlong after Evan across the yard and out to the barn where once Evan's pony had been stabled. A smaller barn now served that purpose, despite the fact that Rocket, as Evan had chosen to call him, was now full-grown. The barn where Carson lay bleeding had become a storehouse for machinery, a redundant tractor, an old flatbed that William had never found the time to fix or sell. Two-tiered, an upper hayloft that served no other purpose had become a play area for the boys when they were younger, and it was from this loft that Carson had fallen, dropping a good twenty feet and striking his head on the wheel arch of the flatbed as he landed.

The boy was out cold, and though Evan had declared that *there was blood everywhere*, there was very little blood at all, everything considered. Nevertheless, William knew enough of accidents and misadventures to understand that the external often did not reflect the internal. There was nothing to do but get the boy to the clinic in Sonora.

The entire family went, Carson and Grace in the back, Carson laid out, his head in his mother's lap. He was stirring within minutes of the journey's outset, and she merely held him close, a muslin wrap of ice close against the point of impact to inhibit the swelling. It was a bad collision, and when Carson's right eye flickered open, she could see it was crazed with blood. Hemorrhaging was her primary concern, that or some kind of fracture, and when they reached Sonora and the doctor told them that San Angelo was really the place for the boy, she fretted further.

"They have a radiography machine up there, Mrs. Riggs," the doctor explained. "That's why you need to get him there, see if there's some internal damage."

It was a fifty- or sixty-mile drive. The doctor offered an ambulance, but William said he and the family would take him.

"I'd send someone with you," he explained, "but I only got two people here—a nurse and a receptionist—and I need both of them."

"We'll be fine," William Riggs said. "We'll get him there, and everything will be fine." He said these words to allay his own fears as much as those of his wife. Carson was trying to speak, and it seemed like the muscles down the right side of his face weren't playing ball.

Evan said he'd come into the barn after Carson had fallen. He just found him there. Seemed intent on ensuring that no blame was being apportioned for the accident.

"Accidents happen," Grace told Evan, though there was hesitancy in her voice. Had she been pressed, she would have ventured the idea that everything happened for a reason, that *accident* was a label folks hung on things for which they weren't willing to be responsible.

It was late afternoon by the time they reached San Angelo. Things happened swiftly. The radiography machine was employed, and William and Grace and Evan sat quietly in the waiting room, hoping for the best, anticipating the worst. Not pessimism, just human nature.

When Dr. Gordon came to them, it was almost dark outside. They had been there for more than two hours, and there couldn't have been more than three dozen words shared.

"He's going to be fine," were Gordon's first words, and they produced a flood wave of relief. Grace shed tears. William held her. Evan just sat white-faced and wide-eyed.

"He has a hairline fracture here," Gordon said, indicating a point on his brow up and behind the right eye. "It really is very small, perhaps three-quarters of an inch, and it will heal quickly. There is no indication of internal bleeding, no hemorrhaging, no swelling of the brain. It was just a very bad concussion, and the external swelling is superficial. You get an impact, and blood rushes there as fast as possible to aid and speed healing. That's all you're seeing. Same principle as a bruise."

"That is wonderful news, Doctor," William said. "Thank you so much."

Gordon smiled. Three hours earlier he'd had to tell a father that he wasn't one, that his firstborn had died in childbirth. This was altogether better news to be delivering.

"He may have headaches for a while, and he certainly shouldn't be involved in anything strenuous or physically demanding for a month or so, but I don't see any reason why he shouldn't recover fully and with no adverse effects."

William stood and shook Dr. Gordon's hand. He clapped the man on the shoulder and gripped it firmly. "You have no idea how relieved we are," William said, but Dr. Gordon reckoned he did.

Carson stayed overnight. Grace stayed with him.

On the run home, Evan sat up front with his pa and once again explained that he hadn't been involved in the incident.

"I know that, Evan. We've been distracted. We were just worried about Carson. If we didn't pay you much attention, it was simply because of that."

Evan nodded. "Okay," he said, seemingly satisfied. "I just didn't want you and Ma thinking that maybe I pushed him for what he done to Rocket."

"Rocket?" William asked. "What did Carson do to Rocket?"

"When he let him loose, remember?"

Which William did, but that had been all of eight years earlier, and he couldn't have thought of it more than twice or thrice since.

It was an odd moment, somehow disquieting, and though they changed the subject and talked of many other things on the way home, William couldn't get it out of his mind that there must still be some shadow of resentment between his youngest and his eldest.

That did not sit right, and he made a mental note to speak of it with Grace.

EIGHT

Never one to judge by first impressions, Henry Quinn could not help but be a little surprised by Calvary. Expecting little more than a wide part in the road, Calvary seemed to him a fully-fledged town, long-established, boasting a main drag, a grain store, a couple of general mercantiles, a garage, two saloons, a pool hall, a brightly-lit supermarket, a boot maker, a saddler, and a host of other businesses and concerns that led away to a tall-spired church that had the look of fresh paint and generous accommodation.

He pulled the Champ up to the curb in front of a soda fountain, well-kept but outdated, a range of barstools and the long curved counter visible from the street. Even the soda jerk wore an outfit that wouldn't have gone amiss fifty years earlier.

If anyone were angling to haul Calvary, Texas, into the 1970s, they were slacking on the job.

Henry imagined there were a multitude of such places: quiet burgs minding their own affairs, unconcerned with whatever progress was being forged and hammered in San Antonio and Houston and Dallas. Rushing headlong toward the twenty-first century might be all the rage there, but this century was just fine for the likes of Calvary. Come to think of it, the last century might find even more favor.

Up at the counter, the place empty but for himself and the man serving, Henry asked after Sheriff Riggs.

The man smiled as if he knew something that was a secret to most others.

"Well, son," he said, "Sheriff Riggs is not only the law; he's pretty much a law unto hisself also, so where he'd be right now I have not the slightest notion."

"Is there a Sheriff's Office?"

"Oh, I'd say there'd be about a half dozen offices where Sheriff Riggs attends to his business, if you know what I mean."

Henry frowned. "I don't understand . . . I'm sorry—"

"Merl," the man said. "Name's Merl. As I say, Sheriff Riggs'll be

53

out and about, doin' something or other," he explained, which in truth was no explanation at all. "Time we have?" he asked himself, and looked back at the clock on the wall. "Somewheres around four. I guess he'll be back at the department office in an hour or so. You carry on the way you was headin'; maybe a quarter mile after the church, take a right—cain't miss it 'cause it is the only right you can take—and you'll see the building down there. Low-slung place, one story, painted blue. If there's a sheriff's car outside, then he's in. If there isn't, he ain't."

"Appreciated, Merl."

"No bother, son. What's your name, anyways?"

"Henry. Henry Quinn."

"Well, good luck on finding Sheriff Riggs there, Henry Quinn," Merl said, as if to imply that such a thing was some kind of Holy Grail escapade.

Henry, resisting any sense of obligation to get a soda, went back to the pickup and drove past the church. He pulled up facing the turn of which Merl had spoken. He could see the roof of the blue, one-story building and guessed he would stay there until Sheriff Riggs appeared.

For an hour he didn't see a single car, and then a tired-looking Oldsmobile Cutlass crawled past. The driver's eyes looked straight ahead, and the passenger—a girl of no more than five or six—stared at him blankly, as if seeing right through him, her expression unchanging even when he smiled. There was nothing to read into it, but it nevertheless provoked a sense of disquiet.

Merl's seeming air of dismissive nonchalance, the girl's vacant stare, and here was Henry Quinn in his pickup waiting for the brother of his cellmate. As if to remind himself of his reason, Henry reached back into the knapsack and took out Evan's letter. *Sarah*. That was it. Just the forename. Evan said that Sarah's mother was dead and he did not know the name of the family who'd adopted her. All he otherwise knew was her date of birth—November 12, 1949—and the fact that his brother, Sheriff Carson Riggs of Calvary, Texas, would be able to help.

As if to echo that thought in reality, a black-and-white appeared in Henry's rearview and headed on down the road toward him. As it slowed and turned, he was aware of being scrutinized by the driver, by assumption alone the one and only Carson Riggs. Beneath the hat and behind the sunglasses, Henry had no way of determining if this was indeed Evan's brother, but there was only one way to find out. He waited for the car to turn and head down to the Sheriff's Department building and then followed on after it.

Exiting his car, Henry felt sure that the driver of the sheriff's vehicle was undoubtedly Carson Riggs. His sunglasses removed, there was a distinct likeness, perhaps not in specific physical characteristics, but certainly in presence and posture. Where Evan was rangier, attributable perhaps to the Reeves diet, Carson was heavier-set in all aspects. A whisker shy of six feet tall, his hair full yet grayed, he leaned against the car, his thumbs tucked into the Sam Browne belt, his hat now tipped back and his hand raised against the last glares of the setting sun.

Henry got out of the pickup and paused before speaking.

That pause was sufficient for Sheriff Carson Riggs to get the first words in.

"Howdy there, son. Can we do for you?"

"I was looking for Sheriff Carson Riggs."

"I'd call your mission a success, then."

"You are he?"

"Am indeed, head to toe and all in between."

"My name is Henry Quinn."

"Is that so?"

"Yes, sir. It is. I came looking for you on an errand from your brother."

Carson Riggs stood up straight, took off his hat, and wiped his brow with the back of his hand. "Well, well, well. If I'd had to make a list of all the things you'd say, that there'd be pretty much the last."

"He said you might be surprised."

"Well, you can tell him I was," Riggs said, and put his hat back on.

"I came to ask you about his daughter."

Riggs seemed to take a step back then, not physically, but spiritually. That was the only way Henry could have described it.

"His daughter?"

"Yes, sir. His daughter."

"I take back what I said earlier. That would have definitely been the last thing on my list."

"You know where she's at?"

"Not the faintest clue, Mr. Quinn. You have any idea how long ago this was?"

"I know her name is Sarah, and she was born in November of 1949. Your brother said that you were her legal guardian after he was jailed."

55

"He said what?" Riggs looked positively baffled.

"That you became her legal guardian."

Riggs smiled wryly, and yet there was a sympathetic tone in his voice when he spoke. "I guess more than twenty years in Reeves has finally turned the poor son of a bitch's mind, Henry Quinn. He said that I became her legal guardian? His daughter? Hell, that is just the wildest notion I ever did hear. You do know she was adopted, right?"

"Yes, sir."

"And did my hapless, hopeless, half-crazy brother happen to tell you the name of the people who adopted her?"

"He said he didn't know that."

"And I guess you met him in Reeves."

"Yes, sir. I did."

"Bunked with him?"

"Uh-huh."

"And he set you on this foolhardy errand to find a girl he hasn't seen for more than two decades who is someplace with a family whose name he does not know?"

"That's right."

Riggs smiled sardonically. "And you agreed to this?"

"I did, yes."

"Might I ask why?"

"Because he is my friend. Because he helped me out at Reeves."

"Well, son, you are a better man than me. I mean, hell, I'm a sheriff. I have the entire Redbird County Sheriff's Department at my disposal, and I would be hard-pressed to find that girl. I think my brother has set you on a coon hunt where there ain't no coons."

"Perhaps you would be willing to help me find her, Sheriff Riggs."

Riggs frowned and once again removed his hat, but this time he tossed it through the open window of his car. He eyed Henry warily, as if the young man had said something that might be read one way or another, and both meant some fashion of trouble.

"And why would I do that?"

Now it was Henry's turn to be puzzled. "Because he's your brother... because the girl is your niece—"

"Well, son, you're assuming that such a thing gives Evan Riggs an entitlement to my time and efforts, and I can assure you that it does not. You are assuming that just because he is my brother, he is also my friend."

Henry understood, or at least believed he did. Sheriff Carson Riggs's brother was a convicted killer, not only that, but up in Reeves for life. To assume that there were issues between him and his sheriff brother would be pretty safe as assumptions went.

Henry wondered where that left him and his obligation to Evan. He wasn't no detective, and he sure as hell couldn't afford to hire one. Three years' prison salary amounted to three hundred and eighty-five dollars and change, and with the little he'd given his ma, the work on the car, just his expenditures since leaving Reeves, Henry Quinn had less than three hundred left.

"So, I don't know where that leaves you, son. Guess you could ask around. Some of the old-timers might be able to help you some. Not many of them go back that far, but if you check in the saloon, you'll see 'em. I'm sure a slug or two of the good stuff'll get 'em talking."

"That's much appreciated, Sheriff. Thank you for your time, and I am sorry if I stirred up something you aren't comfortable talking about."

"Oh, don't give it a thought," Riggs said. "I'm just a little saddened to know that poor old Evan has finally lost his senses." There should have been a smile in his voice, but Henry didn't hear it. "I do have one question for you, though."

Henry knew what it was before it was asked.

"What you do to get yourself in a place like Reeves?"

"Malicious wounding, unlawful possession."

"How long they give you for something like that?"

"Three years."

"Seems like a darned fool thing to have brought on yourself."

"It was."

"But you is all rehabilitated now, I guess."

"Yes, sir, I am."

"And you have a probation period?"

"No, sir. I do not. I am required to inform the authorities if I want to leave the state anytime in the next year, but no probation."

"Good 'nough. 'Cause I don't wanna be hearing about no trouble in town."

"You won't, sir."

Riggs stood a little taller. "I know that you can't generalize about these things, but I guess there are folks whose trust you gotta earn, and there are those who trust you from the get-go and will go on doing so until you betray that trust. I err toward the latter philosophy, despite the number of people who try to dissuade me from it." Riggs smiled coolly. "Don't be one of those people, Mr. Quinn."

"I won't, sir. I am not here to cause any trouble for anyone."

"Good to hear. Now, I guess you is plannin' on stayin' overnight."

"Yes, I am."

"Ask at the Calvary Mercantile. Man there name of Knox Honeycutt. He'll see you right."

"That's very kind of you," Henry replied.

"Don't mention it," Riggs replied, and headed into the office building.

Henry stood there for a moment, uncertain as to how he felt. Like he'd left the store only to realize he'd been short-changed. More than that, like Sheriff Carson Riggs had just told him to leave Calvary without saying any such thing at all.

NINE

For a long time everything stayed the same, and then suddenly everything changed.

Because of the girl.

Grace knew it, could see it as plain as day after night, and even though William wasn't blessed with female intuition, he could see it, too.

Neither believed it was anything so troublesome as jealousy or envy. It didn't possess that dark a shadow. Perhaps it was nothing but physics, the simple truth that the world appeared to work in binary ways. Two were company, as they say, but three was plain awkward.

Rebecca Wyatt was fifteen years old. It was the outset of 1938, and just two weeks after the New Year's celebrations, the Riggses were looking at Carson's eighteenth. No doubt about it, the boy had become a man, at least physically speaking.

"He doesn't catch fire like Evan," William said, and not for the first time.

"Longer fuse doesn't necessarily mean any less of a firework."

William smiled at her. "You ever anything but glass half full, Grace Riggs?"

"Saddens me that he's a disappointment to you," she said.

"I don't think—"

Grace touched her husband's sleeve as they sat there at the kitchen table. It was early morning, a few days before Carson's birthday, and neither boy was yet awake. "I see it, William. I reckon Carson sees it, too, though he doesn't know what he's seeing. Must be hard work being the less favored."

"I don't intend to be that way toward him."

"I don't think you ever intended a mean thing in your life. Sometimes the way we want to be and the way we are just don't work out. People can see it, and sometimes you are easier to read than the funny pages."

"Is it that obvious?" William asked.

"It is obvious how much you love Evan," Grace said, and would not be pressed for further comment.

And then they spoke of the girl.

"She is a beautiful girl," Grace said. "Will be an even more beautiful woman. But she's a gypsy."

William frowned.

"No mother, raised by her father, and she has an errant spirit," Grace explained.

"Meaning what?"

"Some people are content with whatever life brings to the doorstep. The rest go out and look for more. Carson is the first. Evan is the second. I think our Miss Rebecca Wyatt is far more like Evan than she is Carson."

"She's a child," William ventured.

"No, she isn't," Grace replied. "Girls get grown faster than boys in every way. And she's a bright flame, that one. She'll go one of two ways. She'll want someone to keep her grounded, remind her that life isn't all Ferris wheels and fireworks, or she'll do what Evan's going to do."

"What Evan will do?"

"You don't think he's going to run out of here the first moment he sees a way? That boy is going to take the road less traveled; of that I am sure. Music, you know? He's an artist. He'll never be a farmer. What Carson will do, I do not know, but those boys could not be less alike if we had planned it."

"I see how Carson looks when she is around," William said.

"And I see how she looks when Evan shows up," Grace replied.

"We shall see who wins, eh?"

"My concern, if you want to know the truth, is that everyone will lose."

"I would hate to see either of them hurt."

Grace smiled, her expression slightly distant, as if remembering something tinged with sadness. "Steel yourself, William Riggs. Life has a habit of disappointing most of us."

The birthday arrived. Carson Riggs, eighteen years old. Hard to fathom how such a number of years had passed, but they had. The boy was a man, and Grace had him in a suit and a bow tie, his hair slicked with pomade, his shoes shined Sunday best. He looked the part more than he acted it, but it was his birthday, so allowances were made.

The Wyatts came over. Ralph brought him a knife with a bone handle. Rebecca delivered up a pocket watch that had once belonged to Ralph's cousin Vernon Harvey. Vernon was born in Snowflake, Arizona, and died in France twenty-two years later. During something called the Meuse-Argonne Offensive, Vernon's legs were blown clean off. Whoever thought such a thing would be appreciated took the time and trouble to empty Vernon's pockets and get those personal effects back to his family. Vernon's sister couldn't bear to have anything in the house, and thus the effects were scattered far and wide. How the dead soldier's watch ended up in the possession of Rebecca Wyatt, even Rebecca was uncertain, but she believed that Carson would value it, and thus she wrapped it in tissue and presented it to him on the occasion of his eighteenth. Carson was polite, but he did not really get the point of someone else's dumb old pocket watch. Evan, however, was fascinated, and wanted to know everything there was to know about Vernon Harvey and the legs he'd left behind in the Argonne Forest. Rebecca embellished the story for him, detailing acts of selfless heroism performed by Corporal Vernon Harvey, the lives saved, the children rescued from burning French farmhouses, the German marksman he tracked for three days and nights, sleepless, without food or water, until finally cornering him and killing him stone dead with a single bullet to the heart.

Evan Riggs was fourteen years old, and he could feel the history in that watch. He could also feel something in his lower gut that told him he would think of Rebecca Wyatt last thing before he slept and first thing when he woke.

After the party was over, Grace asked Evan what he thought of Rebecca. Evan was almost asleep, exhausted from the day's celebrations.

"She makes my mind quiet and my heart loud," he said, which unsettled Grace Riggs, not simply because it was a remarkably profound thing for a boy of Evan's age to say, but because she knew it was true.

She also noticed that the pocket watch that had survived the First World War now seemed to belong to Evan rather than Carson.

Rebecca Wyatt came over to the Riggses' place three days later. She stood there on the veranda in the sunlight and she was more beautiful than she'd ever been.

Being beautiful meant a different life, a life those without beauty would never understand. Beauty opened doors, alleviated pressures, vanished cares, paid for dinner. Beauty made a path less rugged and challenging. Those fortunate enough to be beautiful would also never understand how it was to be plain and unimportant and forgettable. Those who said beauty was a curse were always beautiful, and they lived in a very different world.

And then there was another kind of beauty, and that was beauty unaware. Even more mysterious and enchanting, even more dangerous perhaps, were those who did not know it. Rebecca Wyatt was one of those, and Grace Riggs knew that through no real intent of her own, Rebecca would break more hearts than ever she would heal.

On Wednesday, January nineteenth, the soon-to-be-sixteen heartbreaker set wheels in motion that would resolutely turn unseen for years to come. Unbeknownst to her, she would establish lines of battle between Evan and Carson sufficient to challenge the ferocity of the Meuse-Argonne Offensive, and it started—as such things so often did—with a kiss.

"Rebecca," Grace said, opening the screen. It was midafternoon, school was done, and this was the third day in the same week that the girl had shown up on the doorstep. Once had been by invitation, but the other two had not.

"Good afternoon, Mrs. Riggs," Rebecca said politely. "I wondered if Carson and Evan would be interested in coming for a walk."

"Carson's away with his daddy," Grace explained. "He's a working man now. Evan is here, but I believe he has homework."

"Maybe I could help him?" Rebecca asked.

"Maybe you could," Grace said. "I know he struggles a little with math."

"Who doesn't?"

"Come on in, my dear. Let's see what he's up to."

Evan was indeed struggling some with math.

"I mean, what the hell would anyone be doing with sixty cantaloupes, each weighing an average of five pounds, anyway?" he wanted to know, and Rebecca said, "That's just math, Evan. It's like life. You don't have to understand why. You just have to figure it out."

They figured it out together, and when the cantaloupe issue was resolved, Evan told his ma that he and Rebecca were going to take a walk out toward the Pecos River.

"Back by supper," Grace said. "You want me to telephone your father and ask if you can eat with us, Rebecca?"

"That's really appreciated, Mrs. Riggs, but I have to have supper with my pa. He says that eating alone is like drinking alone... You wind up talking to yourself out of boredom, and it's all downhill from there."

"Your father has a wry sense of humor, indeed."

Grace stood drying her hands on the veranda as Rebecca Wyatt took off with her youngest son. They were fluid and compatible, those two. There was no awkwardness or irregularity in their body language, as if each knew that there was no other place to be. Even at fourteen, Evan had a sense of grace about him. Nothing less than masculine, but somehow fluently mannered. Together, Rebecca and Carson were different. There was a stiffness about Carson, his actions possessive of some maladroit clumsiness. He was not accident prone, not at all, but his and Rebecca's physicality were certainly not complementary.

Out of earshot, Evan asked more about Vernon Harvey.

"Why do you want to know about him so much?" Rebecca asked.

"It's interesting."

"I got something more interesting," Rebecca said.

"What's that?"

"Got a .22 rifle and a rattler's nest."

"You have not."

"Have too."

"No way, Rebecca."

"Swear it's true. You ever fired a rifle?"

"Sure I have. Pistol, too. With my pa, of course."

"Well, I took the rifle out of the barn, got some shells, hid it down by this place I know. You wanna shoot it?"

"Do I ever! Yeah, sure. Let's go kill some snakes."

They got the gun, fired it a few times at rocks and trees, Evan near flat on his ass one time because he didn't sit it in his shoulder correctly. Rebecca was a better shot than he, but—unlike Carson, who would have been aggrieved by such a detail—Evan merely saw it as an opportunity to learn something.

The snakes' nest was found, but the snakes didn't want to come out and get their heads shot off. Rebecca said they'd been too noisy coming over the rocks, scared the things deep inside, which baffled Evan because he didn't think snakes had ears.

Giving the whole thing up as a foolhardy notion, they walked the rifle to the Wyatt farm, put it right back where it was supposed to be, and went inside for lemonade.

"Where's your pa at?" Evan asked.

"Somewheres," she said, which seemed an adequate answer, because Evan inquired no further.

They sat at the kitchen table, silent for a time, and then Rebecca asked if Evan had ever kissed a girl.

Evan laughed. He didn't seem embarrassed. He just wondered why she asked, and said so.

"Just curious," Rebecca said.

"Can't say I have."

"You want to?"

"Sure. Why...? Who do you want me to kiss?"

Rebecca laughed. "You are a goof sometimes, Evan Riggs. I want you to kiss *me*."

Evan looked serious for a moment. "Now, why on earth would you want me to do that?"

"For the hell of it. To see what it's like. Do you have to have a reason for everything?"

"I guess not," Evan said. "So, when shall we do this?"

"Oh, I don't know. Maybe next Tuesday. I'll have to check my social calendar."

"Well, perhaps I have other girls to kiss next Tuesday, so you should let me know."

"Are there other girls you wanna kiss more than me, Evan Riggs?"

"I don't even really wanna kiss you, Rebecca Wyatt," Evan replied, which was a lie, and he had a tough time keeping a straight face.

"So, are you gonna kiss me or what?"

"Should we stand up?" he asked.

"I guess we should," Rebecca said. "My lips aren't big enough to reach yours from here."

They stood up. They looked at each other and started laughing. It wasn't awkward. It was just kind of dumb, and they both knew it.

Rebecca reached out and took Evan's hand. He took a step or two closer until their noses were no more than four or five inches apart. He closed his eyes and puckered.

"You look like a fish," she said.

Evan frowned. "You want me to kiss you or what?"

"I'm sorry... This is kinda stupid."

"Stoopid is as stoopid does," Evan said. "If you think this is that stoopid, why'd you ask me to do it?"

She leaned forward suddenly and kissed him. Later he would think of it, and though there was no real way to describe the sensation he experienced in that moment, he did see how such a thing might become addictive, how it might prompt people to write songs and poems and suchlike. It was an external action that provoked an internal reaction, and he liked it so much, he kissed her back.

This time she parted her lips a fraction, and when her tongue flickered against his, it was as if he'd been given an electric shock by a butterfly. Most of the sensation he felt, however, was in his stomach.

"How was it?" Rebecca asked him.

"Real nice," Evan said.

She smiled and touched his face. "I liked it, too," she said.

They didn't kiss again, at least not that day, and when Evan headed home, it was already close enough to suppertime for him to go at a run.

When he arrived, his mother, father, and brother were already washed up and hungry.

"Where have you been?" Carson asked.

"Over at the Wyatt place," Evan said, and he smiled a smile that Grace Riggs had not seen before.

She saw something in him, something new, something quite real, that told her that her younger one was closer to a man than her older one might ever be.

TEN

Knox Honeycutt was elbows and knees and little else. The man was a head taller than six feet, and the cuffs of his pants and the sleeves of his shirt were too short by a good deal.

He was friendly enough, though. Said that Sheriff Riggs had just called him, explained someone was coming over who needed a room for the night.

"And you'd be that someone, I guess?"

"Yes, sir. I would be."

"We own the boardinghouse at the end of the street," Honeycutt said. "You go on down there. Can't miss it—white, three-story, flower boxes off the veranda railing. My wife's name is Alice. Tell her I sent you down. You'll be okay for dinner, and she'll make you up a room for the night."

"It's really very kind of you on such short notice."

"Oh, think nothing of it, son. Any friend of Carson Riggs an' all that."

Leaving the mercantile, Henry Quinn was again struck with a sense of something unspecific. He was not a friend of Carson Riggs. Why had Honeycutt said that, if not because Riggs had told him such a thing? And why would Riggs tell Honeycutt that they were friends? Because of Henry's friendship with Evan? Unlikely, if only because there appeared to be no love lost between the brothers. Maybe it was nothing more nor less than Southern hospitality, famous everywhere but the South, for the South was very selective about its friendships and allegiances.

Nevertheless, it was a choice between the Honeycutt boardinghouse and the pickup, and no matter the means by which it was obtained, a bed was better than a bedroll and blanket in the back of a Studebaker.

Henry found the place without difficulty. Alice Honeycutt herself came to the door when he knocked. She was a head shorter than Henry. She and her husband must have appeared an odd pair those times they were seen together.

"Knox send you down?" she asked.

"Yes, ma'am," Henry replied. "Said it would be okay if I stayed over for the night."

"No problem at all, young man," Mrs. Honeycutt said. "And if you're hungry, I can make you up a plate. We sort of finished dinner a little while ago, but there's more than enough left."

"That would be appreciated," Henry said.

"You have a bag or some such?"

"In the pickup," Henry said.

"Well, let's get you fed. I'll get a bed made up, and then you can fetch your things."

Henry was shown through to the dining room. There were a half dozen smaller tables, some of them set for two, some for four, and in front of the street-facing window there was a longer table with eight chairs around it.

"Pot roast," Alice Honeycutt told him. "That's gonna have to do you, because that's all we got."

"That would be just fine, thank you, ma'am."

She left him sitting there, wondering why there had been no talk of money.

Ten minutes, no more nor less, and a young woman came through with a plate. Henry guessed she was in her early twenties. Dressed in jeans, suede moccasins, a cheesecloth blouse, her hair a wild tangle of tight curls corralled with a leather thong, she seemed more suited to a rock festival than a small-town boardinghouse. She was pretty, no doubt about it, and Henry sensed his own awkwardness after three years of nothing but the company of men.

"Hey," he said.

"Hey you," she replied.

"Are you Mr. and Mrs. Honeycutt's daughter?"

The girl sort of half laughed. "I look like the kind of daughter they'd have?"

"Lot of people don't look like their folks," Henry ventured.

"Well, I ain't, no."

"You work here?" he asked pointlessly.

"Nope. I just do this for the hell of it."

"What's your name?"

"You with the cops, or what?"

Henry laughed. "No."

"What's with the third degree?"

"Just being polite. Making conversation, you know?"

67

"My name is Evie Chandler," she said.

"I'm Henry Quinn."

"Good for you," she replied, and turned to walk away.

"Thank you for the dinner," Henry said.

"Think nothing of it," Evie said over her shoulder, and left the room.

While he ate, Henry wondered if Evie Chandler was as abrupt and unfriendly to everyone, or if he'd been selected for some kind of special treatment. Regardless, he couldn't ignore the effect she'd had on him. He guessed any pretty girl would have done the same.

Henry ate. The pot roast was good. He was thirsty, but there didn't seem to be anything to drink.

His dinner finished, he went back out to the front porch of the house, heard nothing, saw no one, and figured he should get his things from the pickup.

Out on the veranda, he found Evie smoking a cigarette.

"So what's your story, mister?" she asked. Her attitude was still brusque and surly.

In the semidarkness, sitting there on the railing, now sporting a denim jacket over her blouse and cowboy boots in place of moccasins, she was West Texas through and through. Her hair, now let down, was a cascading mass of featherweight chestnut curls. She really was a very pretty girl, no doubt about it, but the snarly attitude wasn't doing her any favors.

"Maybe I don't have a story," Henry said.

"Everyone has a story."

"I'm here to find someone."

"You don't say?"

"Too late. I just said it."

Evie smiled. "You think you can win against me?"

"Is there a contest here?"

"Life is a contest."

"Sure it is, but not between you and me, lady." Henry started down the steps toward the pickup.

"That your guitar in the back of that pickup?"

"How do you know I have a guitar in the back of my pickup?"

"I went and looked. Jeez, you ain't so bright, are you?"

Henry laughed. "I am bright enough, I guess. And, yes, it is my guitar."

"You play?"

"Nope."

"Then what you got it for?"

"I use it to beat aggressive, unpleasant girls to death. Weighs ten pounds or more. Hefts like an ax."

Evie smiled. "You wanna go get a beer?"

"What . . . all of a sudden we're friends?"

"Depends how you behave."

"I'll take my stuff in, lock the truck, then we'll go."

"Do whatever. Your truck'll be safe here. No one's gonna steal anything. That's one thing you can say about this fucked-up, shitheel town. Tied up tighter than a . . . well, whatever, you know?"

"Understood, but I'd prefer to see my gear inside."

"You go do whatever you need to do, mister."

Henry, still a little puzzled by this girl, carried his knapsack and guitar into the boardinghouse. Alice Honeycutt was fussing around the place.

"I wondered where you'd gone to," she said.

"Just getting my things, Mrs. Honeycutt."

"Well, you come on upstairs, and I'll show you your room."

It was a perfectly adequate room, a window overlooking the backyard, a narrow bed, a good deal wider than the bunk he'd used for the previous three years.

"Don't know that your neighbors are gonna appreciate that there guitar, Mr. Quinn."

Henry smiled. "Oh, I won't make any noise, Mrs. Honeycutt. You need all sorts of gear to have that make any noise at all. Don't you worry."

"Well, as long as no one's being disturbed, I'm sure it will be fine."

"I wanted to ask about payment," Henry said.

Mrs. Honeycutt waved her hand dismissively. "Oh, I don't deal with any of the business side of this, Mr. Quinn. You'll need to work that out with Knox. Far as I know, you're just a guest here tonight, a favor to Sheriff Riggs. My understanding is that you'll be leaving in the morning anyway."

"Not sure," Henry replied, once again feeling that someone was telling him something without actually saying anything at all.

If Mrs. Honeycutt was surprised by Henry's response, she didn't show it. She simply explained where the bathroom was and that the shower ran a mite hot sometimes so to be careful.

Henry thanked her, said he would be out for a little while.

"Out?"

"Yes, I was just going to have a beer with Evie."

"Oh," Mrs. Honeycutt said. "I see." Merely two words, but they somehow managed to communicate a tone of restrained disapproval.

"Is there a problem with that, Mrs. Honeycutt?" Henry asked, perhaps of a mind to challenge her.

"No, not at all, Mr. Quinn." She smiled, albeit superficially. "It's a free world," she added, her tone suggesting that she believed it was anything but.

Evie was on the street when Henry returned. She was leaning against the pickup as if she were waiting for a ride.

"We need to drive?" Henry asked.

"Nope. We can walk."

They walked for several minutes before Evie said a single word.

"Where you from?" she finally asked.

"San Angelo yesterday, before that Reeves County."

"Where in Reeves County?"

"The prison."

Evie laughed. "You are shittin' me."

"Wish I was," Henry replied, and then wondered if he really did wish that he was bullshitting her. He'd not been out long enough to take stock of how he'd changed as a result of Reeves, the longer-term consequences of spending three years in a cell, but he knew that there had been changes. Beneath the skin, under the fingernails, somewhere in the mind and heart.

"Why were you in Reeves?"

"Shot someone."

Evie stopped dead in her tracks. "You're a murderer?"

"No, not a murderer. It was an accident. They were wounded. I did three years for that and the unlawful possession."

"You are seriously shittin' me, right?"

"I'm not, actually, no. Got out the day before yesterday. Went to see my ma in San Angelo, then drove here."

"For what purpose, exactly?"

"To deliver a letter."

"To someone you know?"

"No, the daughter of someone I bunked with at Reeves."

"And you found her?"

"Nope."

"What's her name?"

"Sarah."

"Sarah what?"

70

"No idea," Henry said. "She was adopted soon after she was born, went to live with another family. She could be anywhere. She could be married, have changed her name again, could be living in Bohunk or Iceland or Panama City, for all I know."

"But you must have had some reason for starting here, right?" Evie asked.

"Sheriff Riggs."

Evie stopped walking. "Meaning what?"

"Meaning the guy I bunked with is Sheriff Riggs's brother, so the girl I am looking for is his niece."

"Fuck," Evie said, and it was a blunt one-syllable gunshot of a word that surprised Henry Quinn a good deal.

"Why fuck?"

"I know that everyone says what a great guy he is and how he's made this town safe an' all, but if you want my opinion . . ."

"I want your opinion."

"There is something wrong with that guy. There is something wrong with this whole place."

"In what way?" Henry asked.

Evie had started walking again, Henry keeping pace, but now she was animated and vocal, so unlike the surly, sassy attitude she'd worn when they'd first met.

"You tell me to name something specific, I can't," she said. "This place is . . . Well, hell, it's like it's never moved for twenty years. I've been coming here my whole life, and it's never changed. He was the sheriff before I was born, and he'll probably be sheriff when I die."

"So you live here?"

"No. I live up in Ozona." Evie pointed to the right of the church. " 'Bout twenty miles that way."

"But you work for the Honeycutts."

"Work for them? Kind of, I guess. I just help out when the regular girl can't come in. Alice Honeycutt is my mom's cousin. My dad drives me down here, and he'll come pick me up when he finishes work. He does a late shift."

"So you live with your folks out in Ozona?"

"Live with my dad. My mom's dead."

"Sorry to hear that."

Evie smiled. "Why be sorry? You didn't kill her, did you?" She frowned. "Hey, wait a minute . . . You shot some woman and went to Reeves. Maybe you have a habit of shooting innocent women and saying it was an accident."

"Yeah, that's what I do."

Evie turned right at the end of the street. Henry had lost track of where they'd been walking, but he saw lights through the trees and figured it was their destination.

"Now this," Evie said, "is about as old-timey as you could imagine, even for Calvary. This is the watering hole for most of the regulars. Good I'm with you; otherwise they'd probably lynch you for the sheer fun of it. They can be a cantankerous bunch of assholes when they see fit."

ELEVEN

The guitar was called a Stella Gambler. It was a good ten years old, and the rosette and playing card decals were somewhat shabby and worn-out around the edges, but it was solid birch and there wasn't a crack in it, and when Evan Riggs held it he felt much the same as Henry Quinn would nigh on thirty years later in that guitar store in Abilene.

There was indeed a gun for every man, a guitar, too, if he was musically inclined, which Evan was.

It arrived for his birthday, and within a week he had a song from the wireless figured out. He was listening to some station out of Odessa that played colored artists like Blind Lemon Jefferson and Son House and a lay preacher called Charley Patton.

Grace thought their names were just the strangest ever, but that guitar and the music he was learning had set Evan on fire, it seemed.

"You done started something here," she told William. "Giving him that guitar. He gets back from school, he eats, does his chores, his homework, and then it's music, music, music. Surprised he doesn't go crazy, playing those same things over and over again."

"Same as anything, I guess. Get as much out of it as you put in."

"Don't reckon Carson is much pleased. Don't think they've shared three words the whole week."

"Carson is doing fine, my sweet. He's out with me, and he's a good worker. Have to stand over him sometimes or he gets slipshod, but he's gettin' the message."

"I know, William. Best thing for that boy is to leave for work at dawn, drag himself home at dusk, and be too tired to eat. He does that for a while, it'll strengthen his backbone, give him some pride in whatever he's doing."

"We'll get there, Grace. We'll get there. I reckon both of them are gonna do just fine."

*

Somewhere inside of a month from Evan's birthday, the first weekend of April 1938, Carson told his younger brother there was something he needed to see.

"What?" Evan asked.

"You'll see when we get there."

"That's just dumb, Carson. Tell me now or I'm not coming."

"Found a rats' nest. A big 'un. Loads of baby rats all squigglin' and squirmin'. It's disgusting. You gotta see it."

"You tell Pa?"

"Not yet, no. Want you to see it first. He's gonna poison 'em, and then that'll be that. It's only a ways down by the river. Rebecca's gonna come, too."

"She walkin' over?"

"Yup."

"Soon?"

"An hour maybe. Told her last weekend, and she said she'd come this morning."

Evan weighed up the Saturday-morning music shows against time with Rebecca Wyatt. The girl won out.

"Okay," he said, not because he wanted to see a rats' nest, but because he wanted to see a rats' nest with Rebecca. Whichever way it went and for whatever reason, she made him feel like no one else.

Rebecca arrived a little after ten. She had on jeans and boots and a blue gingham blouse. Her hair was tied at the back of her head, and she looked like a million bucks.

"You gon' play me a new song, Evan Riggs?" she asked.

"Sure," he said, and started back from the veranda to get his guitar.

"Do that sappy business later," Carson said. "We gon' go see this nest, okay?"

Rebecca looked at Evan, her expression a mite disappointed. Evan smiled at her. "We'll go see this disgusting thing, and then we'll come back and we can listen to the wireless and whatever."

"You really wanna go see a rats' nest?" Rebecca said. "I seen 'em before. Rats is rats."

"Not like this one," Carson said. "You ain't seen nothin' like this one."

Sufficiently intrigued, both Evan and Rebecca came down off the veranda and waited a while for Carson to fetch something from the back of the house. It was a small canvas knapsack.

"What's in the bag, Carson?" Rebecca asked.

"Wait an' see," Carson replied, and there was something

mischievous in his expression that Rebecca—if pressed—would have said she didn't much care for. Carson had a different-colored streak in him, and the times it showed were the times that things went awry and awkward.

"Troubled, troublesome, *and* a troublemaker," Ralph Wyatt had once said of Carson Riggs, echoing a sentiment from the boy's own parents, and when questioned further by his daughter, he had refused to say more.

In truth, Rebecca Wyatt loved both Carson and Evan for their differences as much as their similarities. Carson was very much the man's man, kind of clumsy and bullish, both in manner and mouth. He tried to be sophisticated and sensitive, but it was like trying to train chickens to fly. It just wasn't happening, not in a month of Sundays with an extra weekend thrown in for a last-ditch attempt. But he had his own means and methods, and in some small way his lack of sensitivity was oddly charming. Because he did not really understand the convoluted pathways of human emotion, his attempts to understand were all the more endearing. Carson would be a solid husband, unflinchingly loyal, dependable in all things for which he could be depended upon. A life with Carson Riggs would be a regular life, the kind of life sought by so many women in the Midwest and the South. Pressed for admission, Rebecca would say that Carson held—and would always hold—a special place in her heart. Perhaps he inspired in her some still-unrealized maternal instinct. Perhaps it was something else entirely. She didn't think to question it in detail. She just knew that when Carson was around, she felt safe and substantial, as if anything that came along could be faced, even bested.

Evan, however, was a bird of different plumes. It wasn't just the music, the books, the wireless, the odd comments he made about *why* things were the way they were and *why* could they not be different; it was all of him. Rebecca had turned sixteen in February, and she was already most of the woman she would ever be. Girls grew faster, their emotions and sensibilities matured so much quicker than boys, and already she knew what kind of life Evan would offer a girl. Unpredictable, changing towns as often as they changed shoes, sometimes down-at-the-heel, sometimes affluent, and even when affluent, they would be unconcerned with saving or planning or thinking on tomorrow. It would be a wild life, bohemian perhaps, exciting in some way, desperate in others. Unaware of their fraternal connection, you would never have placed Carson and Evan as brothers. They were that different, and it was as if she possessed no magnetic pole at all and was being pulled both north and south simultaneously.

Wordlessly at first, Evan and Rebecca followed Carson out across the yard and down the driveway to the road. Fifteen minutes and Evan was already asking how much farther, Rebecca inquiring once more as to the contents of the bag. The first question elicited a characteristically uninformative monosyllable, the second another *Wait and see, goddammit!*

They did wait and see, as it seemed there wasn't a great deal of choice in the matter, and within ten minutes Carson was heading left off the main road and down into the scrub. It was there, down in a hollow where the Riggses' fencing walked close to the banks of the Pecos, that they slowed down and approached the quest's objective.

Both Evan Riggs and Rebecca Wyatt had seen enough rats to remain unconcerned by such things, but it had to be said that there was something truly disturbing about the size of this nest. The babies were very young, not more than a week or so, all pink and slippery and squealing. Rebecca counted fourteen of them, and when the mother appeared, distressed and agitated by the presence of outsiders, the noise that was generated by the litter was almost unbearable.

Carson was already laughing when he backed up to the fence and set down his knapsack. When he produced a handful of Globe Salutes, Evan knew what Carson was planning to do. Light those little paper bombs and hurl them in there. It would be akin to putting a hand grenade in your pocket and hoping it didn't hurt.

"What are you doing?" Rebecca asked, perhaps unfamiliar with Globe Salutes to realize how powerful they could be. Carson had gotten some before, and a couple of them dropped into a flowerpot were powerful enough to blow that pot to splinters.

"Gonna blast 'em out," Carson said, and there was a glint in the eye and a crook in the smile that really said everything that needed to be said.

"No," Rebecca said. "You're not..."

"Yes, indeedy, I am," Carson replied, and from within the knapsack he produced another handful of Salutes and a box of matches.

"Where the hell you get those?" Evan asked, caught between a rock and a hard place. He knew it would be carnage and horror, but half of him wanted to see how much carnage and horror it would be. The other half of him would side with Rebecca, the measured and

76

practical aspect that said such things were just downright cruel and unnecessary. Vermin they may be, but there were ways and means of humanely getting rid of them, and detonating them with Globe Salutes didn't figure on that list.

Carson did not say where he got them, and he would not be dissuaded. He was US Infantry. This was as close as he would ever get to the Battle of Meuse-Argonne or Cantigny or Soissonnais et de l'Ourcq.

The first Salute was lit, and even though his aim was wide of the mark, it still was sufficiently ferocious to kick a hole in the ground as big as Evan's fist.

The mother rat, aware now that her nest was under siege, engaged in a futile effort to move her young away from the site of the explosion.

Carson was already laughing like a drunken hyena.

"No, Carson," Rebecca urged him, but he didn't want to hear her. He was set on a course, his blood was up, and there was no way he was quitting. That was a Carson characteristic: stubborn, muleheaded, insistent about his own rightness even when he was plain wrong. Some situations required such an attitude, and some did not.

The second Salute drew blood. A couple of the babies, maybe even three or four, were consigned to whatever hereafter awaited rodents, and Rebecca started screaming.

The mother was aggrieved. She even ventured away from the nest on the attack, but soon realized that she didn't even know what she was attacking. She hurried back to be present as the third incendiary device went off. If this did not kill her, it certainly incapacitated her. The back legs were blown clean off, and she lay there immobile and silent. Rebecca instinctively took three or four steps forward, and even though Evan hollered at her to get back, it was too late. The last Salute landed fair and square in the midst of the remaining babies, and that bomb went off good.

When the smoke and dirt had settled, Rebecca Wyatt looked back at Carson Riggs with a horrified, thunderous expression. Blood had spattered her blouse and jeans, and even as she looked down at her boots, she saw the body of a baby rat there on her right toe. She screamed, kicked it away, and then she did not hesitate. She charged across the short distance between herself and Carson and slapped him across the face.

"Asshole!" she shouted. "You are an asshole, Carson Riggs!"

Carson was stunned. He didn't dare respond, and that wicked glint in his eye was killed as stone dead as the rodents.

Evan didn't know where to look, didn't know with whom to side, and so he did and said nothing.

Rebecca looked at Evan, perhaps waited for him to spring to her defense, but was disappointed.

"Christ Almighty, I don't know why I even visit with you Riggs boys," Rebecca said. "You can both go to hell."

With that, she turned on her heel and stormed away. She headed home to change her clothes, to wash her hands and face and arms, to get the smell of cordite or flash powder or whatever the hell it was out of her hair. What she couldn't wash away, and could not forget for some time, was the sight of baby rats exploding amid clouds of West Texas dirt and the sound of Carson Riggs's laughter as he tossed another Globe Salute into the nest. It had been a wicked sound, both mean and cruel, and she had not heard it before.

Rebecca Wyatt did not visit with the Riggs boys for close to a month, and when she did return, it was to see the younger one, not the elder. There was something she needed to say, and she could wait no longer.

TWELVE

"So he gets up and he says, 'Saved that girl's life, near as damn it. Last time I saw her, I didn't know whether to fuck her or shoot her. I must have figured I was too drunk to fuck her, so that left only one other option.'"

The men around the table laughed. Four of them, seats crossways, elbows touching as if here were some secret redneck conclave. They were fixing to choose the Pope of West Texas, and once done, someone would head out front and light a corncob pipe to alert the world.

"Charming conversation," Evie told the small gathering as she passed. Henry was in tow. He didn't know whether to smile or nod or just keep his mouth shut.

"Well, well, well, if it isn't Princess Evelyn her very self," one of the men said.

"It's Evie, you old goat," was her reply, and then she turned to Henry and said, "These four are why someone should just bomb West Texas and be done with it."

"Careful, now, little lady—"

"Little lady? Really?" Evie said. She looked at Henry, nodded toward the seated foursome. "This here is Clarence Ames. And then clockwise we have onetime Calvary doctor Roy Sperling, next to him, Harold Mills, and George Eakins at the end. They're all here because this is where their wives prefer them to be. Used to be one more, but he up and died a couple of months back."

"Town lawyer," Clarence said. "Warren Garfield . . . a man so bitter he could sour milk at a hundred paces."

Eakins laughed. "You got that right."

"Leave him alone," Evie said. "Disrespectful to speak ill of the dead."

The gathering fell silent, as if a schoolma'am had hushed them. Henry was a little bemused by the level of familiarity so evident between Evie and the four men.

"Anyway," Evie went on, "this is Henry Quinn, late of San Angelo, even later of Reeves County Prison."

Henry glanced at Evie, now ill at ease with the fact that she had told four strangers that he was an ex-con.

Roy Sperling saw that look. "Oh, don't mind her," he said. "And don't mind us. No one here could give a good goddamn where you've come from, son. Besides, you're in Calvary now, and there ain't no such thing as a secret here—right, Evie?"

Evie raised her eyebrows as if some earlier story lay behind the comment. "Don't I know it," she said.

"So, are the princess and the prisoner gonna honor us with their company?" Harold Mills asked.

"We will," Evie said, "but you better not be telling any more filthy jokes."

"Sit yourselves down," Clarence Ames said. "What you drinkin' there, Mr. Henry Quinn?"

"Let me get you gentlemen a drink," he said, and dug his hand into his pocket for dollars.

"Put that away, son. You just got out of Reeves County. You may as well show up with Confederate dollars. Your money is worthless. Now, what you havin'?"

"Bourbon, beer back," he said, "and much obliged."

"Evie?"

"Same for me."

Ames looked at Roy Sperling. "Git, Roy. This 'n' 'd be yours, I reckon."

Sperling rose without complaint, returned soon enough with six of everything.

Once served and seated, Sperling turned the conversation to Henry Quinn's reason for being in Calvary.

"I am here to find someone," Henry said, and nothing more.

"Usually such a statement is followed by a name, son," Ames said. "That's usually the way it goes."

"I know her first name," Henry replied. "Sarah."

"That's all you got?" Sperling asked.

"That's all I got."

"And how do you know to come here?"

"Because of Evan Riggs," Henry said. "I'm here to find his daughter."

In that moment, there was a very tangible shift in the atmosphere.

For a second no one spoke, but it was a long second, and it drew out like a vacuum and seemed to suck every sound out of the room into a pocket of silence.

Harold Mills emptied that pocket with, "Got his record. Killer he may be, but the man can sure as hell sing."

"Let me get this straight," George Eakins said. "You are here to look up Evan Riggs's daughter?"

"Yes, sir, I am," Henry replied.

"And how in hell's name do you happen to know Evan Riggs?"

"Bunked with him at Reeves. Better part of three years."

"Hang fire, Henry Quinn," Evie interjected. "Carson Riggs's brother made a record?"

"Oh, he made a record, all right," Harold Mills said. "I got it, too. Don't know there's anyone in Calvary that didn't buy that record. When was that?"

"Late fall of forty-eight, far as I remember," Roy Sperling said. "Recorded it up in Austin. I remember it being here for Christmas of that year."

"That's right," Eakins said, smiling. "My wife played it over and over 'til I was dead-sick of that thing."

"You never told me you bunked with a recording star," she said to Henry. "And none of you guys ever told me that Sheriff Riggs's brother made this record."

Clarence Ames leaned forward. "We're avoiding the issue, sweetheart. The issue at hand is that your friend, Mr. Quinn, has rocked up here with a view to finding Riggs's girl, and taking into account the fact that there's a great deal of history between them brothers, this is gonna be the cause of trouble, whichever way you look at it. Carson Riggs is Carson Riggs—always has been, always will be. Sometimes you can see that a man doesn't want to be part of his own history, and you gotta respect that."

"Sheriff Riggs said he didn't know nothin' about the girl, that she was adopted right away, that he had no idea where she was."

Again, a tangible silence was present, no less evident than if another person had joined the gathering.

"Is that so?" Ames asked, but it was a question he appeared to be asking himself.

No one answered it, and no one seemed to be able to look at either Henry or Evie. Whatever they knew of this matter seemed to be for themselves and themselves alone.

"So what happened between them?" Henry asked.

Ames frowned. "You spent three years in a box with that man, and he never told you what went down between him and Carson?"

"No. He didn't tell me anything about him at all, 'cept that his brother was the sheriff down here and that he might help me find his daughter."

Again, there was a very awkward hiatus in the conversation.

George Eakins cleared his throat. "So this Sarah..." he started, and left the sentence incomplete.

"Evan told you enough to know that this girl was his daughter," Ames said.

"He did, yes. He asked me to deliver a letter to his daughter, Sarah. Said she was adopted as a baby, that he didn't know what family name she was using, but that his brother had been her legal guardian after he went to jail, and that he might be willing to help."

"And you said you'd met Carson Riggs?" Eakins asked.

"I did, yes... when I first arrived. I went down to his office and spoke with him."

"And what did he have to say about this matter, aside from the fact that he didn't know where the girl was?"

"He asked me why I thought he would be willing to help Evan do anything."

Ames nodded. "Sounds like Carson, all right."

"So tell us the story," Evie interjected. "For God's sake, tell us what happened between them."

"Not me," Eakins said. "I'm stayin' the hell out of this."

"Likewise," Sperling said.

Harold Mills was quick to show his hand, too, and all that Clarence Ames could add was, "See here, this is the thing. Your buddy Evan Riggs has been gone all of twenty years or more. Meanwhile, his brother is back here, has been sheriff in Calvary since old whatever the hell his name was up and croaked—"

"Charlie Brennan," Sperling said.

"He's the one... Charlie Brennan. Charlie was three sips short of a real drink, but he was good enough for a town like Calvary. Carson was his deputy, and when Charlie's heart finally gave out on him, Carson stepped up to the plate, just temporary-like. First election was maybe a year or so later, and Carson walked it. He was the town's best friend, you know? Everyone respected Carson Riggs, and then in the years to come, 'specially after what happened to his wife and his daddy, and then everything with Evan on top of that, it seemed like an unspoken agreement was made. Carson Riggs was Calvary's sheriff, like it was a job for life."

"So he's been sheriff here since the war?" Henry asked.

"Previous sheriff died in November of forty-four," Eakins said. "I remember that because that's when Frances Warner's boy was killed in the Hürtgen Forest."

"And you made yourself ever so available to comfort her in her time of need, eh, Georgie?" Ames said, a crooked smile on his face.

"Man has to do his duty, even when he ain't in the direct line of battle, you know?"

"Oh, you go on telling yourself that, George. And also that Floyd Warner knew nothing about what was going on between you pair."

"So is no one going to tell us anything about the Riggs brothers?" Evie asked.

"Whatever you wanna know, you can ask Carson Riggs yourself," Ames said.

"But surely—" Henry started, and was cut short by a glance from Clarence Ames that left him cold.

"I'm sorry," Ames said. "Did you think this conversation wasn't done?"

"I didn't mean to pry," Henry said. "I apologize."

Ames smiled, and it was as if nothing had happened. "Only thing that needs an apology is that you're still nursing that drink and George here hasn't put his foot on that bar rail once this evening."

"One more drink," Henry said, "which I would like to pay for, and then I'm outta here."

"Me too," Evie said. "My pa's gonna pick me up soon enough."

"If you insist, kid," Ames said.

Henry got up. Headed to the bar.

"I'll give you a hand," Evie said, and followed after.

"What the hell is all that about?" she asked Henry as they stood out of earshot.

"Not a clue," Henry replied. "Was hoping you could illuminate me."

"Can illuminate you like an unlit candle," Evie said. "Seems like they're scared of him."

"But you've been coming here for a good while, right?"

"On and off. Odd summer jobs as a kid. Nothing significant or long term. I'm Ozona, not Calvary."

"Seems like I gotta find this Sarah all by myself," Henry said.

"Seems you do."

"Thought this would be straightforward. Take a trip, ask a couple of questions, find someone, deliver a letter."

"What's the letter about?"

"He never said. I didn't ask. Evan is the sort of guy you don't interrogate."

"Like his brother . . . and like the people who know his brother."

"Don't make sense that Carson Riggs would say what he said about knowing nothing and then these guys pretty much contradict it."

"I didn't hear them contradict nothing," Evie said. "But I sure as hell get the idea you'd have to pull their fingernails to get anything further out of them."

The drinks came. Henry took the beers, Evie the shorts, and they returned to the table.

The conversation had moved to old-timer things—memories of events long gone and half-forgotten—and when the drinks were drunk, Henry thanked them for their company and bade them a good night.

"Was a pleasure to meet you, Mr. Quinn," Ames said, seemingly the spokesman and representative of the little group, "but we shall always remember you as the one who took the pretty girl away."

"You are an outrageous flirt, Clarence Ames," Evie said.

"You go on with your new boyfriend, now," Clarence said.

"This is not my new boyfriend," Evie replied, laughing. "This one'll be out of here before you know it—"

"I'll be out of here when I've found the girl," Henry said.

The laughter stuttered and died.

"Take care with that," Clarence Ames said. "You walk on Carson Riggs's toes, there's an awful lot of bigger shoes you're gonna be muddyin' up."

"Man's got longtime friends," Roy Sperling said. "And that's all there is to it."

Ames looked at Evie. "Give my best to your pa," he said, and went back to his drink. Within a moment, it was as if Henry and Evie had never been there.

Evie grabbed Henry's sleeve and near dragged him to the door.

Neither said a word until they were twenty yards away.

"Thanks for taking me there," Henry said.

"Not that it did you any good."

"Told me I'm gonna be hard-pressed to get any help finding this girl. Told me that Carson Riggs ain't as straight up as he'd have folks believe."

"Seems that way. Looks like you're gonna have to be one of the Hardy Boys all on your lonesome."

"You wanna be my Nancy Drew?"

"I don't think that's a game I wanna play, Mr. Quinn," Evie said.

"I wasn't being so serious. It's nothing that should concern you."

"You're right. It doesn't. However, it does concern me that you have just gotten out of Reeves, you are all alone in the big, bad world, and it looks like I'm the only friend you got in a two-hundred-mile radius."

"Meaning what?"

"Meaning that if you are still here tomorrow, you could come pick me up when I'm done and drive me to Ozona. You can meet my dad. You and he would get along."

"How so?"

"He likes music. Used to play some guitar himself. Has a garage full of old vinyls and whatever. He's a good guy."

"I'd like that."

"But maybe you won't be here, eh?"

"I don't know what's gonna happen," Henry said. "I made a promise, and I have to keep it."

"Lot of people make promises that don't mean shit."

The expression in her eyes told Henry that she was talking about something, more than likely some*one*, very specific. He didn't inquire further.

They were near to the boardinghouse.

"You know the way?" she asked.

"Yeah."

"Maybe see you tomorrow, Henry Quinn."

"Maybe so, Evie Chandler."

She turned and walked away, headed left and across the street to whatever rendezvous point she had agreed with her father.

Henry watched her go. He missed her right away. Considering that he'd not spoken to such a girl for more than three years, it was remarkable to him that they had fallen in with each other so easily. She really was very pretty, and even after she'd disappeared from sight, he could still smell a kind of citrus aroma in the air, perhaps from her skin, maybe her hair, and recall very distinctly the sound of her laughter, which was both liberated and liberating. Until she'd left, he hadn't really thought about those things at all. He had thought about the pledge he'd made to Evan Riggs and how she might be persuaded to help him. That and the evident unease when the name of Carson Riggs was mentioned. Could a town keep a secret? And if so, why?

THIRTEEN

The sun slunk low on the horizon, as if—like a child—it, too, did not wish to sleep.

Dinner was done; William, Grace and Carson were someplace in the house doing whatever they were doing. Evan sat cross-legged on the veranda with his guitar, trying to figure out the closing phrase of "You're the Only Star (In My Blue Heaven)" by Roy Acuff when he saw Rebecca Wyatt standing at the end of the drive that led down to the house.

She was just standing there in a cotton print dress and cowboy boots, her hair tied back, one hand by her side, the other on her hip, and she was looking toward the Riggs house with her head angled slightly to the right. Almost as if she was weighing up the pros and cons of making a visit.

Evan stood up. He set down his guitar and stepped forward to the railing. He raised one hand to acknowledge the fact that he saw her, but she seemed to pay no attention.

Rebecca stayed there for no more than ten seconds, and then she turned back the way she'd come and disappeared into the trees.

Evan opened his mouth, perhaps to say her name. He knew she'd never have heard it, but it was an instinctive response.

Not a sound left his lips, and he stepped back once more and lifted his guitar from where he'd rested it against the wall.

Rebecca appeared again, and this time she was carrying something. A canvas bag, Evan guessed, though he couldn't be sure at such a distance.

Twice she glanced over her shoulder as she made her way down the drive, and Evan sensed that not only was there a degree of urgency, but also some anxiety in the way she was behaving.

Puzzled, he walked down to meet her, but she shook her head and waved him back.

Evan did as she indicated and was there on the veranda once more when she met him.

She handed him what was now evidently something wrapped in a shirt, the sleeves tied to form a handle of sorts.

"Some clothes," she said. "My clothes. I want you to put them somewhere safe, and don't tell anyone."

"But—"

"I am just asking you, Evan. You can do this for me, right?"

"Yes, sure I can," Evan replied.

"Thank you," Rebecca replied, and she reached out and touched his hand. She started to turn, and he grabbed her sleeve.

"Are you in trouble?" he asked.

She looked back at him, that flicker of anxiety so obvious in her eyes. "Not yet," she said. "But I might be."

And with that she hurried away once more.

Evan was left standing on the front steps of the house, a bundle of clothes in his hands, waiting to see if Rebecca Wyatt glanced back over her shoulder at him.

She did not, as if she didn't dare.

As if she didn't want to acknowledge how she'd just drawn Evan Riggs into whatever trouble was on its way.

The trouble went by the name of Gabriel Ellsworth, and—notwithstanding his name—he was certainly no angel.

Cousin Gabe, as he was known by Ralph Wyatt, for he was, in fact, a cousin on his deceased wife's mother's side, was a handful of years younger than Ralph, weighing in at thirty-nine. He was one of the Tecumseh Ellsworths, more a dynasty than a family, for the patriarch—a onetime evangelical minister who lost his faith in the bottom of a bottle and then spent many years vainly looking for it in the same place—somehow managed to sire a total of eighteen children with seven different women. Gabriel was of the same direct line as Ralph's wife, however, and thus Ralph felt a certain obligation to help the man out, to support whatever efforts he made toward a better and more productive life.

Gabe Ellsworth had worked the previous farm back in the summer of 1936. The summer of '37 had been a time of change and upheaval, for that was when Ralph lost his wife and Rebecca her mother. Moving away from Oklahoma had been an effort to escape the past, but—as in most cases—memory was the scenery you found no matter where you were. Things were getting better, a little easier, and Ralph Wyatt had to say that his daughter had shown the most extraordinary resilience and fortitude. Couldn't put it any other way, but had it not been for Rebecca, he might have lost his mind to grief completely.

The untimely death of Madeline Wyatt was still an open wound, and yet the new farm was prospering. He needed an extra pair of hands, and Gabe Ellsworth, sometime drinker though he was, had proven a good worker, accepting a nominal wage alongside room and board. So Ralph made the call, and Gabe set out for West Texas, coming in on the bus to Ozona on Friday, May 13. Portentous the day and date might have been, for it took just one weekend for Rebecca to realize she was in real trouble.

Gabe Ellsworth was a man of appetites, no doubt about it. To anyone with a weather eye for such things, he was a wolf in wolf's clothing, and a pretty sixteen-year-old girl was just about the wrong kind of temptation. Such a morsel was well suited for sharpening teeth as well as wit.

Unbeknownst to most, when Gabe Ellsworth was twenty-two, he did something that meant he could never go home. Not ever. From that point and forever onward, his temper had been volatile, his fuse short, his mouth full of smart one-liners. As if to keep everyone at arm's length, he appeared either unpredictable or infantile, that kind of mischievous bluff and bravado that spoke of a man with unwholesome secrets.

"Hey, girlie," he would say to Rebecca. "You want to come over here and polish Cousin Gabe's trailer hitch," both of them knowing full well that Cousin Gabe possessed neither trailer hitch nor any vehicle upon which such a thing could feature.

The tone was suggestive, the glint in the eye too obvious by half, and the intent of every word slanted toward something devious and unsavory.

On the Sunday just forty-eight hours after Gabe's arrival, Rebecca spoke to her father.

"I don't like him, Pa," she said.

"You don't have to like him, sweetheart. He's here to help me. He don't cost a great deal, and he won't make any trouble."

"I'm not so sure."

"Why'd you say that?"

"The way he looks at me, the things he says . . . not what he says, but what he means."

Ralph Wyatt paused, a flicker of concern crossing his brow like a cloud shadow crosses a field. "He do something to you?"

"No, Pa. He didn't do anything to me."

"Then what's the worry for, Rebecca?"

"What he's thinkin' about doing, I guess."

"Well, I can't really afford not to have him, and until he does something that justifies my lettin' him go—"

The sentence remained unfinished.

Sunday evening Rebecca went straight to her room after dinner. She didn't much care for the furtive glances and sly smiles that now seemed almost without pause.

She heard him in the hallway, and with her door inched open, he said, "You hidin' from me, sugar?"

"No, sir," she replied. "If I was hidin', you wouldn't have found me."

"I do so appreciate the sharpness of your tongue, Miss Wyatt," he crooned, and she could hear the whiskey in his throat, the way it relaxed muscles and morals and good intent.

"Prefer it if you wouldn't behave such a way, Cousin Gabe," she said.

His elbow touched the door, and the gap between door and frame widened somewhat.

Gabe could see a girl alone, pretty as a picture, ringlets like feathered question marks, her teenage breasts so proud and pert, that delicate throat, those honey-tasting lips.

Rebecca could see the shadowed face in the doorway, the way he leaned against the jamb, that dip in his shoulder that made his whole body a question mark. He had his thumbs tucked in his belt, his fingers fanned toward his crotch as if to frame whatever hideous thing lay behind the buttons.

"Why you so mean to me, Rebecca Wyatt?" he purred.

"I'm not mean to you, Cousin Gabe. I just see what's on your mind an' it ain't right an' proper."

"What do you mean? I'm just bein' friendly."

"You know what I mean, Gabe, and what you're thinkin' right now ain't friendly, and you know it."

"So what am I thinkin' right now, sweet pea?"

Rebecca took a deep breath. Beyond the distaste and discomfort, there was now a sense of real anxiety. Gabe Ellsworth's thoughts were so strong, she could feel them pushing right up against her, much the same as what he would do if given half a chance.

"Gabriel Ellsworth," she said. "You are close to my daddy's age. You are also related to my mother. If for no other reason than decency and good manners, I am asking you to leave me alone. I know what you want, an' you ain't gettin' it. Do you understand me?"

"Oh, don't be such a baby—" he started, but was cut short when Rebecca moved suddenly and closed the door.

Gabe Ellsworth pawed the door and whined like a puppy dog. Then he laughed coarsely. "G'night, sugar pie," he whispered, loud enough for her to hear him.

She slept little that night, ever aware for the slightest unfamiliar creak that would forewarn her of Gabe's approach. Visions of him creeping into her room, dressed in nothing but his undershorts, his manhood erect and angry and filled with malintent, haunted her terribly.

Gabe Ellsworth didn't visit with her that night. He sat in his room and drank himself to sleep, and the following morning he looked at her across the kitchen table and smiled his greasy smile.

That was the afternoon Rebecca took her bundle to the Riggses' place and asked Evan to hide it. If she was to make a run for it, then she at least wanted a change of clothes.

Evan didn't see Rebecca again until late on Wednesday. There was no hiding her upset.

"My mama's cousin is here," she told Evan. They were away from the house some distance, Rebecca having found Evan on the stoop playing guitar, asking him to just take a short walk with her so they could speak without being overheard.

"He doesn't mean well," she explained. "He has bad things on his mind, and I think he's set to do them. I don't know how long he can withhold himself."

"Bad things?" Evan asked.

"You know," she said. "He's gonna put the hurt on me. Rape me, I guess."

Evan's eyes widened. Though he'd done nothing more than think about Rebecca Wyatt buck naked and all that this entailed, he also knew that for a man of any age to impress himself on a woman uninvited was a sin against God and nature. It would not be the first time that the color rose in his cheeks when he thought of such a thing, how it angered him, how it stirred some violent shadow in his being. There was rightness, and then there was everything else. This was most definitely part of the everything else.

"What do you think we should do?" Evan said.

The fact that he didn't play it down, question her certainty, the fact that he immediately included himself in the solution to this problem, reminded Rebecca of the fundamental difference between Evan and Carson. She could have taken the problem to Carson, but Carson would have done one of two things: laughed and told her she was foolish for imagining such a thing, or walked over to the Wyatt place, hauled Gabe Ellsworth out from wherever he was skulking, and had a damned good go at walloping some sense into him. That was not what she needed and would certainly cause more trouble than it was worth.

"My pa needs to send him away," Rebecca said.

"Does your pa know what he says to you?"

"I tell him, but I think he wants to read it a different way. He has a problem. He needs help with the farm, but he can't afford anyone but Gabe. Gabe comes cheap."

"Acts it, too," Evan said. "Then we need to prove to your pa that Cousin Gabe ain't no good, right?"

"Right."

"Then we set him a trap."

"That's what I was thinkin'."

"Catch him good when your pa can see it."

"Scares me, Evan."

Evan reached out his hand and took Rebecca's. He squeezed it reassuringly. "I'll be there. If he gets crazy, I'll jump on him."

"He's a big man, Evan. He'd kick a hole in you 'fore you had a chance to take your hat off."

"We shall see," was all Evan said, and there was flint in his expression that reminded her of Carson.

The trap was set for the following Friday. Ralph had business in Sonora, fifty crow-miles east. He'd be gone four hours or more, and Rebecca had known this by Thursday lunchtime. There was time to undertake this thing before Ralph Wyatt departed. At least that was the intent.

Evan told his ma and pa and Carson that he was visiting with Rebecca, that her daddy had some chores as far as he knew, that there was a buck or two in it and he needed new strings for the guitar.

"The way you fuss with that thing, anyone'd think you were gonna marry it and have ukuleles!" Carson quipped.

"Would serve you well to find something to get so interested in," William Riggs told his eldest, a comment that provoked a sulky silence until Grace broached the subject of William's birthday, two months hence, and whether they should all take a trip out to San Angelo for a restaurant dinner.

"We'll discuss it some other time," was William's edict, "when we know better our financial position."

Evan was gone to the Wyatt place right after dishes were washed and put away. He thought to take a weapon of some variety, a baseball bat, at least a sturdy branch, but ultimately decided against it. He hoped that there would not be any violence, for he felt sure that Gabe Ellsworth was not the kind of man to take a step back when tempers flared and fists were drawn.

Evan had never had a fight in his life. Playground scuffles, perhaps, but nothing beyond squinted eyes and flailing hands connecting rarely and with the force of a frightened bird. Cousin Gabe was a traveled man, full-grown, engineer's boots, a good head of steam in him. Evan had recognized his kind from a distance, and recognized trouble.

The plan, if that was its name, was for Rebecca to lure Gabe to the barn nearest the Wyatt house, and here she knew he would set upon her with his seductive lines and molasses charm. Evan would be within earshot and would happen upon a moment of inappropriateness before it became truly threatening, and he would cause sufficient alarm to bring Rebecca's father from the house. Men in their thirties with a mind for seducing teenage girls could only be cowards, and neither Rebecca nor Evan saw him maneuvering his way out of a confrontation with Ralph Wyatt when both his daughter and a witness challenged Gabe with the truth of what had happened.

Would Gabe follow Rebecca out to the barn was the only question, but it wasn't really a question.

Dinner over, Rebecca said she was taking a walk. She walked slowly, knowing that Gabe would require sufficient time to head for the veranda and a smoke, angling to see where she was headed without making it too obvious.

Ralph would be gone soon enough and had his mind occupied with the Sonora drive and whatever business awaited him.

Evan was in the barn already, a split-level affair with a suspended upper hayloft that projected half the length of the building. From this vantage point he could see all below, and he waited patiently for Rebecca to appear, Gabe coming after her with no more than a ten-minute delay.

Sometimes people wore faces that told stories before any word was spoken. Cousin Gabe had one of them faces, and the story was no fairy tale.

Gabe feigned surprise when he saw Rebecca.

"Hey, girl," he said. "Known you was here I'd a left you to your own devices."

Even from twenty feet aloft, Evan could hear the lie in his tone.

"You're not gonna start any trouble, now, are you, Gabe?" Rebecca asked.

"Well, I'll be damned, Rebecca Wyatt," he said. "You certainly have set your mind to disliking me, haven't you? What did I ever do to deserve such a welcome?"

"You are welcome," Rebecca replied. "It's your intentions that ain't."

"And what intentions is they, my sweet?"

"You know very well, Gabe Ellsworth. I know what you're thinking."

Evan guessed she was saying this stuff on purpose, winding Gabe up like a cheap watch. His spring was gonna break, that was for sure, and then he'd do something stupid and irreversible and they would have him run out on his heels and back to wherever he crawled from.

"You do, do you?" Gabe purred. "So, what am I thinking?"

"That maybe you want me to rub your thing for you."

Evan felt sure that Gabe would have heard his intake of breath as he lay there amid the musty hay. Dust filled his throat, and it was all he could do to suppress a coughing fit. Evan was shocked to hear such a thing from Rebecca's lips. But there it was, five seconds of the obvious, and they had both known what they were dealing with before they set out.

"My, oh my," Gabe said. "You do have a wicked mind, little girlie. Though I can't say I am surprised. You always took a liking to me, didn't you? I could tell even last summer that you wanted me to show you a thing or two."

Rebecca didn't reply.

"Why don't you hitch your dress up a little there, sweet pea? Show Cousin Gabe how growed up you is since I last seen ya..."

Evan wanted to gag. After that he wanted to leap from the hayloft and land on the man's head, breaking his neck with one clean snap.

"You better leave me well alone, Gabe, or I'm gonna tell my pa."

"What you gonna tell him, huh? He's gonna be gone anytime now, and then what ya gonna do?"

93

"Don't you come near me, Gabe Ellsworth—"

Gabe took three or four slow steps toward Rebecca. "Oh, come on, sugar pie. Just a little kiss for big ol' Gabe, eh? Gets awful lonely out here, you know? Working like a dog, helpin' out your daddy when he's got no money and whatever. Seems to me you only got food on the table because I'm bighearted enough to work for nothin'..."

Another step, another two, and Gabe Ellsworth was within ten feet of Rebecca Wyatt, and it seemed the man's head was losing whatever fight it may have had with his loins. Seemed he was dumb enough to get frisky before Ralph Wyatt had even left the house for Sonora.

"Seems a man that makes a sacrifice might earn himself a favor. Whaddya say?"

"You want to kiss me?" Rebecca asked.

In that split second Gabe glanced sideways and Rebecca looked up at Evan. There was a fierce and defiant light in her eyes.

"Kiss you, sure," Gabe said, and he took another step.

"Well, if you mean no more than that, Gabe Ellsworth, and you promise that you'll leave me alone, then I will let you kiss me."

"Now we're talkin' the same language, baby doll," Gabe said, and he slunk a little closer to Rebecca, his right hand reaching for her.

Rebecca pushed his hand away. "Don't you get any fresh ideas, Gabe," she said. "You can kiss me one time and one time only, and then we're done with this dumb game, okay?"

"Whatever you say," Gabe replied, but what he said and what he meant were not even close.

Again Rebecca glanced up at Evan, but Evan was already out from under the hay, edging carefully toward the top of the ladder, ready to come down those rungs at lightning speed and start hollering trouble.

"Well, if you're gonna do it, then do it," Rebecca told Gabe, and Gabe came at her with his slick words and his slicker smile, and it was then that Evan Riggs's foot connected with the top of the ladder, pushing it away from the edge of the loft merely a couple of inches, but upon its return it connected with a sufficient thump for Gabe to turn suddenly.

He saw Evan then. His eyes flared. He looked back at Rebecca, and the expression she saw terrified her. There was something inside Gabe Ellsworth that she had never seen before. Unknown to her, unknown to most everyone, it was the same expression he'd worn when he did the thing that got him excommunicated from

94

his hometown, never to cast his greasy shadow over that boundary again.

"Why you—" he started, and with that he raised his hand as if to strike her.

Evan grabbed the ladder, swung his foot over, connected with the second rung, started down with far greater speed than was well-advised.

Gabe turned suddenly, realizing now that this was some sort of honey trap, and there was no way that Rebecca Wyatt and this skinny rat of a kid were going to confound and bamboozle him.

"You little son of a bitch!" he growled, turning his attention from Rebecca to Evan, already reaching out to grab the boy as the ladder started to swing backward.

Evan, arms flailing, lost his footing and dropped to the ground. He felt something twist sharply in his ankle, and he yowled.

Rebecca screamed involuntarily even though Gabe's violent intent was now focused on Evan. On his back now, Evan's eyes wide with fear as Gabe rushed at him, and the ladder still falling.

"Evan!" Rebecca hollered, and Evan rolled sideways just as Gabe dropped to his knees.

The ladder came down with force, landing a good blow on the back of Gabe's head. Gabe flattened to the ground, lifeless almost, no sound but a dull moan escaping his lips.

Evan got up and limped awkwardly to where Gabe lay. He glared down at the man, and then he took a step back and let fly with a good kick to the ribs.

"No . . ." Rebecca said, but she only half meant it.

Evan hesitated, almost as if he were contemplating fetching a rock and bashing Gabe's brains out, and when he looked up at Rebecca, she saw something that chilled her. It was gone as soon as it had appeared, and she shuddered. There was a meanness in that look, and she questioned its source.

They clung to each other then, and Evan was the first to ask.

"Is he dead?"

It was a dumb question, because the moaning was weak but constant, and Rebecca guessed Cousin Gabe was merely concussed.

"Go!" she urged. "Now! Don't be here when my pa comes out."

Evan understood, hurrying away on his bruised and already-swelling ankle, pausing only to look back at Rebecca, in her eyes the unspoken and tacit consent to utter no word of this to anyone.

Whatever they had done, they had done it together.

Rebecca waited until Evan was clear of the bordering field, and then she fetched her pa. By the time Ralph Wyatt appeared, Gabe Ellsworth was struggling to get up on legs as weak as a newborn calf's. The sight of the man, his head already swollen on the right, the toppled ladder, presumed a story that Ellsworth possessed neither the coherence nor the honesty to relay. Rebecca stood back, allowed her father time to check Gabe's condition and then make the judgment that they should take him to the clinic in Sonora. Ralph was headed such a route anyway, and he could take him.

The drive was awkward, Rebecca in back with Gabe slurring out mouthfuls of semi-intelligible words, all the while expecting him to snap to, to start hollering about Evan Riggs and the truth of what had happened. He would leave out the attempted seduction, of course, and Rebecca would be on the spot not only for collusion in the crime, but failure to immediately tell her father what had happened.

But Gabe garbled, and at one point he fell silent and his breathing became shallow, and Rebecca—despise the man though she did—prayed that he wouldn't die right there on the backseat of the truck. Had Evan accompanied them he would have been reminded of a very similar journey the Riggses had made some years earlier with Carson in much the same condition.

Rebecca's prayer was answered. They made it to Sonora, all three of them alive, and the doctor there had Gabe Ellsworth on a bed and under examination pronto, especially considering the hour.

Twenty minutes later the doctor explained that it was a severe concussion, recommended Gabe stay overnight.

"There is no sign of hemorrhaging, no swelling beyond the superficial, and I don't think he needs an X-ray. We'll see how he's doing in the morning, and if he hasn't markedly improved, then we'll ship him up to San Angelo and take a look inside."

The following morning, Saturday the twenty-first, Ralph Wyatt got a call to say that all was well in the Gabe Ellsworth camp. The swelling had diminished significantly, Gabe was lucid and coherent, had demolished a tornado of ham and eggs, drunk a pint of coffee, was even now asking if there weren't any buttermilk pancakes to be had in a place like Sonora. The doctor added that there was no reason not to come fetch him later that day.

Ralph drove out there with Rebecca. Gabe sat up front on the return journey, said nothing meaningful at all, gave no indication that he was going to 'fess up to his part of the scenario and take whatever stripes he got just so he could see Rebecca in trouble.

He went on and stayed the whole summer, wore the demeanor of a kicked cat whenever Rebecca showed up, steered clear of her as best he could.

Saturday nights saw him take off for Iraan, where word had it there was a brothel with two girls, both of whom would do things for five bucks that were probably against the law.

As for Rebecca Wyatt and Evan Riggs, they never spoke of what happened, though it haunted the space between them like a shared shadow. What happened to Gabe Ellsworth they had done together, and that bonded them like bad glue.

However, Rebecca couldn't forget that she'd seen something in Evan Riggs that scared her, like a potential for trouble, and she wondered how long it would be before he did something he'd never forget and forever regret.

She let it lie. Sleeping dogs and sharpened sticks didn't play well together.

FOURTEEN

Alice Honeycutt told Henry Quinn that Sheriff Riggs had been asking after him.

"He was here an hour or so ago," she said, pouring Henry coffee at one of the small tables in the dining room. She had made pancakes and bacon, delivered them as if there were no choice but to eat them, and he'd done so, despite the fact that he rarely ate breakfast.

"Really?"

"Sure. He was here about seven, said that you should go on down and see him at his office soon as you were able. Said he'd be there all morning."

A knot of anxiety started to tighten in the base of Henry's gut. Not a good feeling.

Breakfast done, Henry went back to his room and put on a clean T-shirt. He looked in the mirror and combed his hair. A couple of times he'd been up before the warden at Reeves, once as eyewitness to a stabbing, second time for brawling with a paperhanger from Lubbock who went by the name of Frenchie Robicheaux. His real name was Lyman, and he was about as French as Wyatt Earp. Name aside, he was still an asshole.

This felt the same, as if he had somehow crossed an invisible line, was already in bad with the boss, was about to get striped for something.

Regardless, Henry did not hesitate. Perhaps some degree of institutionalization, perhaps a vague hope that Carson Riggs might have warmed to the idea of giving the estranged brother and his ex-con lackey a helping hand.

Henry remembered the way down to the office, pulled over at the side of the highway to smoke a cigarette and calm his nerves.

He looked out across an all-too-familiar landscape, a landscape merely irritated by something professing to be civilization. Texas, all that was not scarred by human hand, was as old as God and twice as unforgiving. In every stone and tree and handful of red dirt was a certainty that within days of man's departure, this scenery would swallow any sign of his presence. It was a tough place and it bred tough people, and Carson Riggs sure seemed like one of them.

Henry got back in the truck and found his destination.

The Sheriff's Office was open, but there was no sign of Riggs. Deputy Sheriff Alvin Lang greeted him with, "You must be the Reeves boy, I guess?"

"Henry Quinn," Henry said, "here to see Sheriff Riggs."

"Ain't here, but won't be long. Said if you showed up you was to wait. You can sit over there," Lang added, and indicated a couple of plain deal chairs against the wall.

"If it's all the same to you, I'll wait in the truck," Henry said.

Lang looked at Henry dead-straight. He was a lean man with a lean manner, and not once had he cracked that facade with a smile or a gesture of friendliness. In build he was much the same as Riggs, the rangy windswept features pared back to basics by sand and sun and seclusion. This was not a welcoming country, and these men seemed set to remind Henry of this as often as they could.

"You do whatever you wish, Mr. Quinn," Lang said, and went back to filling out paperwork at the front desk.

Riggs drove up within ten minutes. He got out of the black-and-white in slow motion. There was a weight of history in his eyes, in the lines on his face, in the languid gait, moving now as if certain that there was nothing ahead requiring urgency. If it was of any importance, it would wait for him, and he would deal with it in his own time.

He reached for his hat and put it atop his head even though the walk from the car to the office was no more than thirty feet. That was protocol, and so that was what he did. Sunglasses, pressed shirt, high-waisted pants, the crease in those pants so clean it could cut paper. He took one glance at Henry Quinn, nodded in acknowledgment, and walked to the office without a word.

Henry followed on after him, was again greeted coolly by Lang.

"Sheriff will see you shortly," he said. He tipped the end of his Biro in the direction of the plain deal chairs. "You go on and sit there now."

Henry did so, all the while feeling that sense of indignation and ire rising in his chest.

He would carry the mark of a prisoner for the rest of his life, and comments such as that from Evie the night before did not help his cause. In a town such as Calvary, he doubted that anyone was now uneducated as to his past and the reason for his presence.

Sheriff Riggs opened the door to his private office, just there to the right of the reception area, and surveyed Henry Quinn.

"Mr. Quinn," he said.

Henry got to his feet. "Sheriff Riggs."

"I appreciate your swift compliance."

"Not at all," Henry replied.

"You come on in and take a seat, and we'll discuss your business awhile."

Henry started for the door, was halted by Riggs's slowness to move, and then Riggs took one step back and let him pass. That hesitation had been purposeful. *I say what goes here, and when*, that action said. It was clear who was running the show.

Henry took a seat.

"Alvin, fix us some of that good coffee o' yours," Riggs said, and closed the door. He did not close it fully, almost as if he wished to make the point that nothing was sacrosanct here. There was no privacy to be found in the Calvary Sheriff's Office.

Riggs sat down, fixed Henry with that predatory gaze, and smiled like a hungry lizard.

"Hope you didn't say nothin' impolite or out of turn to my deputy there, Mr. Quinn."

"I'm sorry, what?"

Riggs smiled the lizard smile again. "Alvin Lang is a very important person around these parts. His daddy, John, is a real high-up fella in the Texas Department of Corrections, and his granddaddy, Chester Lang, is the lieutenant governor of Texas, no less. May very well be governor one day, though he's maybe a little long in the tooth for that nowadays."

"I didn't say anything to Deputy Lang, Sheriff."

"Well, good enough. You don't wanna be gettin' on his bad side, now, do you?"

"Don't plan to be gettin' on anyone's bad side, Sheriff Riggs."

"Good to hear that, son. Good to hear that. Now, to business. Fact of the matter is that no one ever said I was anything but fair-minded, Mr. Quinn, and no one ever will. Most people aren't lookin' for trouble, and I would consider myself most people."

"Like I said before, I'm certainly not lookin' for any trouble, Sheriff Ri—"

"I ain't done talkin', son," Riggs interjected, and again that smile appeared, right there on his lips without making the short distance to his eyes.

100

"Had some words with myself about this matter here. Whether I should involve you or no. My business head won out. Decided to give you the full truth so you could waste no more time on this matter."

Deputy Lang elbowed the door open and brought in two cups of coffee. He set down Riggs's first, then Henry's.

"You need anythin' else, Sheriff?" Lang asked.

"We're good here," Riggs said, and Lang returned to the front, again leaving the door ajar.

"Now, you may have come down here like Deadwood Dick, scout for General Custer, Indian fighter, Pony Express rider, all fired up to get this matter resolved for my brother, but I have to tell you that it's a fool's errand, boy."

Riggs reached for his coffee, and though it was near boiling, he took a good mouthful as if from a cool stream.

"As far as my brother is concerned, and just so you appreciate my sentiment, I'm after seeing him come here with his hat in his hand, his eyes down to the floor. If not that, then on his knees."

"I guessed there was some friction between you," Henry said, and immediately knew he should have said nothing, especially something so presumptuous and naive.

"Is that so?" Riggs asked. "Well, I don't know what personal matters he may have shared with you at Reeves, but every story has two sides, and most of them have a great deal more."

"I am sorry," Henry said. "I didn't mean to presume anything."

"Well, you went ahead and presumed anyway, irrespective of what you meant," Riggs replied. "Two things you can never take back. Everything you do. Everything you say." Again the smile, and again he lifted the cup to his lips and drank.

"To be honest, I know nothing at all," Henry said.

"Well, son, there isn't a great deal to know, and there sure as hell isn't a great deal of mystery to unravel. It's no secret that my brother and I are estranged. He has been out there in Reeves for a long time. We have never visited, we have never written, we have never spoken, and we never will. That's about as simple as it gets. As to this daughter business, again there is no great secret. He got a girl pregnant, he gave up the child, the child vanished with whatever family took her in, and that is the end of that. I was never her legal guardian, no matter what my brother may have said. Prison may be overcrowded, but I figure it's pretty much the loneliest place in the world sometimes. Loneliness can turn a man's mind. He looks inward too damned much. He gets to thinking things are real when they just plain ain't. Now, if you have some letter that you want me to hold on to in the event that this girl o' his ever shows up, which I think is about as likely as icebergs on the Pecos, then I will do that for you. Beyond that, I don't think there's anything you can do. Sometimes the past is just the past, and best for all concerned that you don't try dragging it into the present."

"I am just trying to help your brother, Sheriff," Henry said.

"Well, maybe my brother doesn't deserve any help, son. You ever think of that? He killed a man in Austin. He beat that poor son of a bitch to death. Facts of the matter are black-and-white. The law is the law. My brother, whatever reason and rationale he may have had, was neither judge nor jury, and he was certainly no executioner. But he went on and executed that man, and now he's paying the price for it. He was a drunk and a violent man, and he done what he did and that's the end of it."

"I have no intent to justify or excuse what he did, Sheriff. He just helped me a great deal, and I wanted to do something in return."

Riggs smiled, and for the first time there was a shadow of warmth somewhere in among the sculpted hardness of his features. "You are young," he said, "and bright you may be, and well-intentioned, but I have seen a great deal of everything and more besides. I have reached a time in my life when the past is clearer than the present. You look back and every decision is easy. The real test of a man is being responsible for the decisions he made in the heat of the moment, even though they might be proven wrong in hindsight. That's where you find real backbone. You made a mistake, and not a small one, but you learned a lesson and now you got a chance to do somethin' useful and constructive with your life. My brother, well, his is a different story, and he don't have a chance to rewrite the end. He's gonna spend his last day looking at the world through bars, and however I might feel about that, there is nothin' I can do to change it."

Henry paused, just to ensure that Riggs was done, and then he said, "I appreciate your candor, Sheriff. If it's all the same to you, I'll hold on to that letter from your brother. Seems only right that I exhaust all possibilities 'fore I quit. Maybe I'll make some inquiries along official adoption channels in San Angelo or San Antonio or Austin. Perhaps there'll be a record of what happened to the girl. The least I can do is my best, right?"

"Whichever way you want it, son, though I reckon you'll be dis-appointed."

"You don't know the name of the family that adopted her?"

"I only know what's already been spoken," Riggs said.

"You were sheriff back then, right?"

"Assumed the post in 1944; been here ever since."

"And Evan's daughter was born in late '49."

"That seems about right."

"Seems odd that you don't remember something so significant as the adoption of your own niece—"

Riggs cleared his throat.

Henry fell silent. He knew then that he had crossed another invis-ible line.

"I guess you have as much a right to your own mind as anyone else. You go on and think whatever you want to think, Mr. Quinn. That doesn't change the facts. I told you what I know. I was suf-ficiently respectful of my brother's troubles to give you the time of day. I know what jail can do to a man. It's my business to know such things. He clings to thin straws. He has desperate thoughts. He regrets his life and tries to change it. Too late, see? His daughter is long gone, and probably isn't even aware he exists. She'll be a young woman now, if she's even alive, and I am sure she has her own mind, too. What right does my brother have to suddenly show up like some uninvited guest? Is that right? Is that fair? What about her feelings? Does she not deserve greater consideration than him? She didn't break the law, did she? She didn't murder someone in a motel room in Austin."

"I didn't think of it like that," Henry replied, which was the truth.

"Well, I did," Riggs said, "and that's how come I said it."

"Rock and a hard place."

"Sounds like a great deal of life, son."

"Now I am uncertain as to what to do for the best."

"Well, there ain't no great reason for you to stay here," Riggs said. "Evan ain't here, nor his daughter, nor anyone who knows the whereabouts of his daughter, so if you want to pursue it, then it seems you're gonna have to go farther afield. Best o' luck to you, but you have to consider the girl in all of this and make a decision about what's right. Gotta put yourself in her shoes, think about being all of twenty-some-odd years old, gettin' on with your life, and then someone throws a rock through the window and you got pieces of glass everywhere. You think she needs to know who her father is, what he done, where he is? You think she wants that hangin' over her?"

"I don't know."

"Neither do I, Mr. Quinn, but right now you're on a mission to throw that rock and you gotta know that no one's gonna get hurt."

Henry said nothing.

"Changes things, don't it?" Riggs said.

"It does, sir."

"Well, that's where we are, son. I got things to do, places to be, people to see, and I can't sit here mindin' your business all day."

"Of course not," Henry said. He leaned forward, took the coffee cup, and drank it down. Though he did not want it, it would have been discourteous to do otherwise.

He rose, shook hands with Sheriff Riggs, thanked him for his time.

"Guess you'll be on your way soon enough," Riggs said.

"Guess I will," Henry replied.

Riggs walked him to the door, watched him cross to his pickup, nodded once more when Henry glanced back.

Back inside the office, Riggs asked Lang if he'd called the saloon.

"Clarence Ames," Lang said. "He and his buddies were drinking with your boy and Evie Chandler last night."

"That's the girl who works for Knox Honeycutt, right? Pretty one from Ozona."

"That's the one."

"Clarence Ames," Riggs said thoughtfully. "Get him on the phone for me, Alvin. Tell him I'll be visitin' with him this evening."

FIFTEEN

By the time war came to Europe, Evan Riggs—despite his tender years—was already earning money as a singer. He played bars and saloons across most of the county, even stretching his legs as far as Loma Alta, Comstock, Langley, and Sanderson. The original songs he was showcasing were those that he would later record on *The Whiskey Poet*. He played the songs folks asked for as well, tunes like "The Convict and the Rose," "Truck Driver's Blues," "It Makes No Difference Now," and "Meet Me Tonight In Dreamland." He put his own twist on them, which listeners seemed to appreciate, and there was no shortage of interest from local radio stations and small labels. But Evan was hungrier than that. He wanted a shot at the big show. It was something that Carson could never understand, and did not seem to try.

"Two types of folks," Carson told him one evening in the summer of 1942. Out on the veranda, Carson and Evan were smoking cigarettes, drinking a glass of whiskey, taking a rare chance to mind each other's business.

"And who would they be?"

"Folks who accept what they have and make the best of it and folks who are restless and will never be happy."

"I guess you're saying you're the former and I'm the latter," Evan said.

"Guess I am," Carson replied.

"You think you're happy?"

Carson smiled and sipped his whiskey. "You out on the road doin' whatever you're doin'. I've been here taking care of everything. Been spending a good deal of time with Rebecca, too, you know? Soon enough, I'll be asking her to marry me."

"You've been saying that for years, Cars. Maybe I'll get there first."

Carson grinned. "She would no more have you than a dose of syphilis. Besides, you may be out there bein' a big ol' country-singin' star, but you are still only eighteen years old."

"Love does not recognize age, dear brother. Besides, the day you ask her is the day I'll know it's true. If I believed you for a second, I might be jealous."

"You are a hopeless dreamer, little man, a hopeless dreamer." Carson smiled; it was nothing more than fraternal banter. They had not shared a cross word for as long as Evan could remember. Somehow, as their childhood years faded behind them, they had straightened out their conflicting angles.

Evan was silent for a time and then said, "I think I'm gonna sign up."

"For what? Dumbass College?"

"The army."

Carson turned and looked at his younger brother as if he had just shit in the soup.

"What the hell?"

"I think I have to," Evan said.

"You are kiddin' me."

"Nope."

"What the hell would you wanna go do somethin' like that for?"

"Not sayin' I want to. Sayin' I should."

"Doesn't change the question."

"Because it will get here soon enough. Because if we don't take some action, then we may find ourselves without any choice in the matter."

"You are talkin' crazy, Evan. That there is some European thing. That is thousands of miles away. Nothin' to do with us, and never will be."

"Everything to do with us, and already is," Evan replied, aware that Carson could not have been reading newspapers or listening to the wireless.

"Well, you go on and do whatever you think is right, Mr. Busy-body," Carson said. "I guess I'll just rest here a spell and see how it all pans out."

"Well, if I get killed over there, then Rebecca won't have to choose between us," Evan replied, knowing such a comment would needle his brother.

"She don't have to choose nothin', my feeble-minded sibling," Carson replied. "She's just waiting for me to make my move, and I have no doubt she will accept me."

Evan smiled but said nothing. He reached for his guitar.

"Shee-it, you gonna start playin' that thing again?" Carson asked. "Sounds like someone choking a cat with five-strand barbwire."

"I wrote a love song for you and Rebecca Wyatt," Evan said. "Callin' it 'Beauty and the Beast.'"

Carson flicked his cigarette butt at Evan. "Prize Number One A-hole," he said, and got up from his chair.

Evan stayed out on the veranda a while, was surprised when his ma came out to join him.

"Pretty," she said. "What was that?"

"Just another tune I'm wrestlin' with."

"Carson says you were talkin' 'bout the army."

"He was right."

"That's a tough thing for a mother to hear, though it comes as no surprise."

"Seems like the right thing to do."

"Which is you all over, Evan Riggs."

"Carson doesn't see it that way."

"Who knows how Carson sees things, sweetheart. He's a good man, an honest man, hardworking and loyal to your daddy, but you and he could not be more different."

"He says he's been spendin' a lot of time with Rebecca."

"Don't doubt it," Grace said.

"Says he's gonna ask her to marry him. You believe that?"

Grace didn't reply for a while. She looked out toward the skyline and sighed. "Out here folks up and marry out of sheer loneliness. Even folks who shouldn't get married do so. All I can say is that Rebecca Wyatt for a wife would be the best thing that could ever happen to your brother."

"You figure she'd take him?" Evan's voice was hesitant, uncertain. He was feeling things he didn't want to feel, but he couldn't bring himself to say them out loud, even to his ma.

"She'll take him if no one else is asking," Grace replied, and they both knew exactly what that meant.

"Carson should stay here and keep the farm going."

"That's the easiest path for him, and so that's the one he'll take."

"And I'll take the hardest one, right?"

"Not necessarily, no. Just a different one."

Evan laid down his guitar. "Joining up . . . I think it's somethin' I have to do, Ma. Otherwise I'll never be able to live with myself. But I ain't scared, because I know I'm not gonna die out there."

"How so?"

"Meant for somethin' else," he said. "I really feel that . . . like I am meant for some other life."

Grace Riggs reached out and took Evan's hand. "You are a special one, no doubt about that," she said, smiling. "Your father says you are gonna conquer the world with your songs. He's mighty proud of you. Maybe he don't show it, but he is. You know that, right?"

"I heard him singin' one of my tunes the other day. He didn't know I was there, but I heard him."

Grace laughed gently. "He was singin' one this mornin'. I asked him whose song it was. He said it was one o' yours. I told him let's leave it that way, okay?"

Evan laughed with his mother, and it seemed that not only was the war a million miles away, but also their wish to discuss it. Same went for whatever was going on between Carson and Rebecca Wyatt.

At last she said, "You do what you feel is right, Evan. You always have, and you always will. I could try to convince you otherwise, but I'm not of a mind to. I know better."

"You don't want me to go, I won't."

"Don't lay that on me, Evan."

"I'm sorry. I just meant that—"

"I know what you meant, and it's appreciated, but this is your decision. Just stay home as long as you can."

Grace rose from where she was sitting and stood beside her son. She put her hand on his shoulder.

"Who knows? You may change your mind," she said, but they both knew he wouldn't.

As fate would have it, Evan Riggs would miss both Thanksgiving and Christmas that year. His decision made, he drove out to Sonora and met with army recruiters there. He signed up for the infantry, was told he should report to the office in San Angelo on Monday, November sixteenth. News of the war in Europe had been filtering through, and for anyone of a mind to garner further information, there were ways and means. The US Marine Corps had landed on the Solomon Islands, taken Florida Island first, then established a bridgehead at Guadalcanal. The advancing German forces had reached Stalingrad, the British Eighth Army had seized key positions near El Alamein, and Himmler had already instigated the wholesale obliteration of the Jewish people. Fifty thousand had been murdered by the SS in the Warsaw ghetto alone. There were rumors that "death camps" had been created for the killing of people on an industrial scale.

On the evening of Saturday, November fourteenth, Evan Riggs walked across to the Wyatt place to find Rebecca.

"You've come to say goodbye, I guess," she said. Her daddy had fetched her from inside, and she found Evan on the veranda.

"I have, yes."

"There's no chance you'll change your mind, then?"

Evan just smiled.

"I knew there wasn't, but you knew I was gonna ask."

"You want to sit awhile, Rebecca?"

"You want me to?"

"Yes, I do."

"You gonna get serious on me, Evan Riggs?"

"Too late," he replied.

Rebecca perched on the railing. She was all of twenty years old, and the age gap between them seemed insignificant now.

"I have always loved you," Evan said. "You know that, right?"

"What's not to love?"

"But . . . well, we never . . ."

"You have kissed me five times," Rebecca said. "Once in the kitchen to see how it felt, twice as thank-yous for Christmas presents, once out of politeness at Thanksgiving, and one time in the barn after Rocket died and I sat with you while you sobbed your heart out. You never really kissed me for love, Evan Riggs."

"I was always afraid that you loved Carson more," Evan said.

"I love you both," she said. "You're different people, and I love you for different reasons. Carson has chased me forever, and I can respect that. He knows what he wants, or at least he thinks he does. It was you I wanted to be chased by, but you no more know what you want than . . ." She shook her head resignedly. "You are an enigma to me, Evan."

"I don't mean to be."

"Sure you don't. You can't help who you are."

"I am sorry if I hurt you."

"You didn't hurt me. You just disappointed me."

"Then I am sorry for disappointing you."

"We are not going to spend this time apologizing to each other."

"I came to say goodbye, but I'll be back."

"You seem very sure."

"I am."

"Lot of boys are getting killed out there."

109

"I'm coming back," Evan said, and there was not a hint of doubt in his voice. "I have things that need taking care of."

"And might I be one of those things?"

Evan smiled. "You read me like a book, Rebecca Wyatt."

"When I can get the pages open, sure."

Evan stepped forward, opened his arms to her, and she came. They held each other for a long time, and when he kissed her, it was neither polite nor a thank-you. It was passionate and heartfelt, and it stirred something within both of them that they had always known was there but had never tried to unearth.

"You do this to me now?" she said. "Before you go get yourself shot in your dumb ass in Italy or whatever?"

"No one is shooting me in my dumb ass in Italy or anyplace else, Rebecca Wyatt," Evan said. "The war will end by Christmas, if I'm to believe the propaganda. Whatever happens, it will end, and I'll make it home."

"Make sure you do," she whispered.

"And I have this for good luck," he said, and from his pocket he took Vernon Harvey's watch.

"Gave that to Carson," she said.

"With your hands yes, but with your heart you gave it to me."

Rebecca pulled him close. She kissed him once more and then stood with her hands gripping the veranda rail as he walked away into the darkness.

Rebecca Wyatt and Evan Riggs would not see each other for nearly three years, and their reunion would be bittersweet for so many unexpected reasons.

William Riggs drove his youngest son out to San Angelo. It was a bright November morning. The sky was crisp cut from blue linen, the sun high and warm and comforting. Carson had hugged him awkwardly, told him he still figured it a dumbass idea, and Grace had tried her best not to cry, yet had failed awfully. By the time the truck pulled away, her handkerchief could have been wrung out for irrigation. She did not want to drive all the way to San Angelo simply because she knew the drive back would be worse than staying behind. Carson tried to comfort her in his own well-meant but clumsy manner, and before William and Evan had even made the highway, she had convinced herself that this was nothing more than a brief separation. Evan's conviction was definitely convincing; she knew in her heart of hearts that she would not be losing her son.

There was a bus awaiting the army's newest recruits, a bus bound for Fort Benning in Georgia. It was a thousand miles or more, all the way through Louisiana, Mississippi, and Alabama. They would stop merely to change drivers in Shreveport and Meridian. They would eat at highway diners, sleep right where they sat, hold their bladders until they were given leave to piss, and pray for the roads to get smoother the farther east they went. They did not. By the time they arrived, many of them felt that they could not have ached more had they endured twenty-four hours in a washing machine.

Within an hour, Evan Riggs met his drill sergeant, a terrier-faced bundle of spite and malevolence called Ronald Curtis. Curtis was a career soldier, and the thought of stabbing Japs with a bayonet fevered his blood. Slipped discs and related complications meant he would never see a frontline, and that challenged him far more than a mess of greenhorns with little discipline and less intelligence. Within days, Evan Riggs would cross him, and yet the resultant barrage of extra duty, additional drilling, and merciless belittlement that Curtis would inflict upon the younger Riggs was perhaps exclusively responsible for Riggs's return from the war. Whatever could be said of him, Ronald Curtis made Evan Riggs a different kind of man. The man who left Fort Benning was equipped not only to survive the Allied invasion of Italy under Alexander and Clark, but also attacks from the twenty-sixth Panzer Division behind the Nicotera defense line, a brief assignment to Molina Pass on the main route from Salerno to Naples, a prolonged exchange as his own unit supported the thirty-sixth Texas Division against von Doering's group, and numerous other frontline skirmishes. The men Evan had trained alongside were no different than he, and yet most of them did not return. Many of them fell right beside him, their blood spilled on foreign soil, their heads and hearts punctured by German bullets, their legs blown clean away by landmines. Perhaps Ronald Curtis had something to do with this, or perhaps it was Evan Riggs's own single-minded determination that he would return from the war that saw him through ... perhaps the same single-minded determination that would see him survive two decades in Reeves without giving up the ghost.

Whatever the reason, Evan Riggs did return, and though he was in no way the same man, he was intact and complete, at least physically, and the Calvary he found awaiting him was not the Calvary he expected.

Carson had changed, too, more than he could ever have imagined, and not for the good.

It would be August of 1945 before the family was once again reunited, and by Christmas Evan knew that he would once again have to leave.

SIXTEEN

Henry's worldly possessions were packed in the truck.

"You're leaving?" Evie asked.

It was a little after eight; she was done at the Honeycutt place, and Henry was driving her home as agreed. They were sitting in the cab, Henry smoking a cigarette and waiting for directions.

"Well, let's just say that there was a very clear message from Mr. Honeycutt that my welcome did not extend beyond one night."

Evie smiled curiously. "What did he say?"

"That Sheriff Riggs said I'd be moving on this evening."

"Really?"

"No different from what the man told me himself this morning."

"He came to see you?"

"Sent for me."

"And what happened?"

Henry's tone was wry and sardonic. "He made a good point, in all honesty. Said that no one had really taken the girl's feelings into consideration. She must be twentysomething years old, maybe doesn't even know she was adopted, has no idea who her father is, and some stranger comes along and tells her that her name ain't what she thinks it is, that she ain't whoever she believes she is, and that her real father is a murderer who is going to spend the rest of his life at Reeves."

"Okay," Evie said matter-of-factly. "That kinda makes sense."

Henry turned and looked at her. His expression was telling. "However much sense it makes, and I'm not denying that it does, I don't believe that Sheriff Carson Riggs is so concerned for the welfare of his niece."

"You think he doesn't want you to find her?"

"My first thought was that he was so pissed off with Evan that he didn't want me doing anything to help him. Second thing, more important, is that Evan was never a liar, not to me, anyway. He said that Carson would know about the girl, and yet Carson says he

113

knows nothing. This morning he said he was gonna give me the full truth, and he ain't given me shit. Third thing, I don't like him."

"Let's go," Evie said. "My dad'll be waiting. We can talk about it on the way."

Henry started the pickup, pulled away from the front of the Honeycutt house, and headed straight.

"Keep going until I tell you," she said. "It's a good way before we turn off."

They didn't speak of Carson Riggs or Evan's lost daughter. They spoke of Evie Chandler and her history. Henry wanted to stay for Evan's sake, to fulfill the promise he'd made, but he now also wanted to stay because of Evie. The more he thought of her, the more he wanted to think of her. Reminded him of a line in one of Evan Riggs's songs from *The Whiskey Poet* album: *She makes my mind quiet and my heart loud.*

"My mom and dad were high school sweethearts," Evie explained. "I was born back in December of forty-nine. I am the first and last of the Brackettville Chandlers." She wound down the window and put her arm out. Even now, close to half-past eight, it was still very warm. "You know Brackettville?"

"Can't say I do."

"Southeast, maybe a hundred and twenty miles or so. Past Del Rio, back end of the Balcones. That's where they were raised, where they went to school, where they met and married, where I was born."

"How'd your mom die?"

"I was a kid. Three years old. She had a brain hemorrhage. Went out like a blown lightbulb right there at the dinner table."

"Fuck."

"Exactly."

"And your dad never remarried?"

"Nope. Don't think he ever will."

"Because?"

"Because he's still of the opinion that he doesn't deserve someone else. He works hard, drinks hard, takes care of me. I guess that's all he expects now. Says change is all well and good, so long as it's not within his lifetime."

"Same as my ma. She's a drinker, too. Has men around every once in a while. But they don't stay long. They remedy her boredom, but then they become part of the boredom and she throws them out."

"Who'd wanna be a grown-up, eh?"

114

Henry laughed.

"So, you get to meet my dad, huh? This is like a proper date."

"You figure?"

"Sure, Henry Quinn. I mean, you're serviceably good-looking, seem like a nice enough guy, gonna be a Grand Ole Opry superstar some way up the road, and if you behave yourself, you never know what might happen..."

Henry glanced right; Evie was pouting at him, batting her eyelids and playing the fool.

"You are a strange one," he said.

"You don't think I'm pretty?" she asked.

"Sure, you're pretty. Very pretty. Hell, what do you want me to say, Evie? I don't know if you're being serious."

"You don't wanna fool around, Henry? You've been in Reeves for three years. You must be so backed up you could drown a girl."

Henry started laughing. It was a truly disgusting notion.

"I don't know what to make of you, Miss Chandler," he finally said.

"You don't have to make anything of me, Henry Quinn," she replied. "I ain't complicated. What you see is what you get. I'm jus' teasin' you because you are the sort of guy who needs to be teased."

"Is that so?"

"It is."

"And why would that be?"

"Because you take yourself too seriously. And you need to turn right down here and take 10."

Henry waited for the turn, got onto 10, and then asked her what she meant.

"Not difficult. You've had a hard time, I guess. You fucked up, you went to jail, and now you think that life is gonna be like this forever."

Henry didn't reply; he was wondering whether or not she was right.

"People make life so much more complicated than it needs to be. Like my dad. Hell, he should just lighten up, find himself another woman, settle down. Sure he can get into a rut, but better to be in a rut with company, don'tcha think?"

"Depends on the company," Henry replied, thinking then of his own mother and Howard Ulysses Morgan.

"See, that's precisely what I mean. With such an attitude, there's always a rider, always a way to twist it to the negative. You gotta stop that kind of shit, Henry Quinn, or you're gonna get ground up in the big ol' machine."

"I'll try, Evie. For you, I will try." He looked sideways. She was smiling wide.

"That's my boy," she said, and winked.

The Ozona trip was brief, forty minutes or so, and the whole time Henry was aware of the tension that now hung between them. She said nothing more that indicated any romantic interest, and he was unsure of whether she'd actually been joking with him. This time, the more he thought about it, the less he wanted to think about it, and yet the more he thought about it, the less he wanted it to have been a joke.

Time with her had merely served to highlight and accentuate everything that was right about her. Where he had considered her pretty, she was now just beautiful. Her sense of humor was sharp and quick. Plain and simple, she was a very special girl, and he wondered whether fate had played some part in this, whether Moirai's spinning threads had drawn them together for some other purpose than mere company and conversation.

By the time they arrived, they were talking like lifelong friends. When he exited the pickup in front of her house, she just sat there. Henry stood on the sidewalk and looked askance at her.

"You darn well come and open the door for me, you ill-mannered son of a bitch," she said. "You take a girl to dinner, you better behave like a gentleman."

"You are so fucked up," Henry said, but still he walked around the car and opened the door.

She got out, hesitated briefly, and then leaned up a fraction to kiss him on the cheek.

"There's a good boy," she said coyly, and took off for the house.

Glenn Chandler was another man with a story on his face. Henry guessed he was in his early fifties, but he carried a few more years in the lines and creases around his eyes. Henry did not imagine they'd been earned by laughing, and when he shook hands with the man, he was subjected to an extended survey that communicated a very clear message: *Can see you, young man; can see right through you; I know you been in prison and want to know what deal you think you're making with my daughter.*

Henry was simply polite, thanked Mr. Chandler for having him over, to which Glenn Chandler replied, "I ain't so much of a cook. Tuna casserole. That's what we got, like it or leave it."

"I'm good with tuna casserole," Henry said. "After Reeves, pretty much anything is the best meal you ever had."

"Evie told me about your troubles. Sounds like you got a raw deal."

Chandler walked through to the kitchen, Henry right behind him.

Evie went to the icebox and took out three bottles of Lone Star. She popped the caps and handed them around. Chandler sat at the kitchen table. Henry and Evie followed suit. The aroma of tuna casserole filled the place. Henry had skipped dinner at the Honeycutts even though it had been offered. Given enough ketchup, he'd have eaten roadkill right off the tarmac.

"You can blame others, even when there's no one specific to blame," Henry said, "or you can just accept responsibility for your own life, regardless of whether or not you really understand what happened."

Glenn Chandler didn't reply. Perhaps he was considering something personal.

"I guess there are those who think everything that happens to them is because of other people and those who think it's all down to themselves."

Chandler smiled ruefully. "So you're not a great believer in luck or coincidence."

"Nope."

"Ever?"

"Can't say that I am," Henry said. "I mean, it depends how long a view you want to take."

"Meaning?"

"Whether we think that a human being came from somewhere, or he's just a mess of chemicals with a street value of about eight bucks."

Chandler shook his head and looked at Evie. "Sober as a judge, haven't even started dinner, and we're already dealing with the spiritual and philosophical. I can see why you like him."

Evie turned her mouth down. "I'm not so sure," she said. "On the drive over, he wasn't as interesting as I thought he'd be."

Henry laughed.

"Let's eat," Chandler said, and when he rose, he gripped Henry's shoulder, and Henry took it as a sign of acceptance. If not that, then at least a heartfelt welcome.

Evie winked at him. Henry smiled. She blew him a silent kiss. He colored up.

The casserole was good. Henry wolfed down a plate, took a second helping. This earned him another brownie point in the Chandler household.

He matched Chandler beer for beer, ever aware that he had no place to go, would more than likely drive half a mile, pull over, sleep in the pickup, and hope he didn't get arrested. He wondered whether Riggs's authority and influence stretched beyond the Calvary town limits. After all, hadn't he said that the entire resources of the County Sheriff's Department were at his disposal? Maybe Redbird was a fiefdom and Riggs the overlord. Maybe he was keeping track of Henry Quinn, making sure that he not only left Calvary but never returned.

"So, Evie tells me you are on a quest to find a missing girl," Chandler said once the dishes had been cleared. There was pie, apparently, but it had yet to show its crusty face.

"Maybe a girl that doesn't even exist," Henry said.

"Evan Riggs's girl, yes?"

"You know him?"

"*Of* him," Chandler said. "Anyone who ever picked up a guitar south of the Mason-Dixon Line has heard of Evan Riggs. Hell of a record he made. Hell of a waste."

"Couldn't agree more."

"And you bunked with him at Reeves."

Henry glanced at Evie. Seemed she had told her father everything.

"No secrets here," she said, immediately understanding the question in Henry's eyes.

"What's to be concerned for?" Chandler asked. "You did what you did, you're all paid up, and if you tell Evie, then you tell me."

Henry smiled. "I'll get used to it," he said. "Prison tends to twist you in strange ways. Has you second-guessing everything, taking care to say as little as possible to as few people as possible. A different world requires a different attitude."

Chandler rose and walked to the kitchen counter. He opened a cupboard and took down a bottle of Old Crow and three shot glasses.

"Drink any of that and I'll be driving sideways," Henry said.

"Bullshit," Chandler said. "You can stay here. Where the hell else you gonna go? Evie tells me you aren't exactly welcome at the Honeycutt place."

"Too true."

"Weird town, if you ask me," Chandler went on. "Don't like it. Never have. And Evan Riggs's brother?" He raised his eyebrows, took a breath. "All I can say is that with friends like that, you won't be needin' too many enemies."

"How so?"

Chandler sat, opened the bottle, filled the glasses, and passed them round.

Evie raised hers. "No strangers here, but friends we've yet to meet."

Henry appreciated the sentiment, yet was still hung up in what was really happening with this girl. He'd been out of any kind of game for three years; his radar was redundant.

"Carson Riggs, from what I understand, has been sheriff over there since the war."

"Since 1944," Henry said, "while Evan was overseas."

"Well, you keep a man in a job like that for that many years, then there's something awry. Either he's the best sheriff anyone could ever wish for—not that I believe there's such a thing—or he has somethin' on folks that makes 'em uneasy to challenge him. I'd lay some money on the latter."

"The guy creeps me out," Evie said. "You saw how Clarence and his buddies were. They don't dare say a word about him. Anytime I'm over there, I'm careful about what I say. Get the impression there are hungry ears around every corner."

Glenn Chandler reached for the bottle and refilled each glass. "Everyone has a history," he said. "Every town, every city as well. Think a great deal of the shadows in that place are Riggs-colored, if you know what I mean. No secret that there was bitterness between Evan and Carson long before Evan went to war and Carson became sheriff. Money-related, as far as I can figure, but I don't know the details. Heard rumor that something happened to their daddy that might not have been so wholesome."

Evie became curious. "What's this about? You never said anything to me."

"What's there to say? I don't know. Rumors are just rumors until something proves they're not."

"But what happened to their father?"

"He died," Chandler said. "Happens to the best of us, or so I'm told."

Evie shook her head resignedly. "He gets like that. A few drinks in him and you start to get the attitude."

"All I'm saying, Evie, is that this is all street-corner gossip. Someone said that someone said that someone said. It's all bullshit. I don't have any time for it."

"But maybe something happened to the father," Henry said. "You heard that much, right?"

"Okay, so what I heard was that he died in a shooting accident, and it was one of those accidents that might not have been an accident. That was all I heard, and I don't know anything further."

Chandler glanced at the clock above the stove. It was past ten.

"One more drink and I am gone," he said. "I have an early start." He refilled the glasses a second time. "Best of luck to you, Henry Quinn, even though you don't believe in it," he said, and downed the whiskey.

He rose from his chair. Henry rose, too, and they shook hands.

"Pleasure to meet you," Chandler said. "Father gets protective when a man comes around after his daughter, but you could be worse." He turned to Evie. "Have fun. Don't get pregnant."

"Go to bed," Evie said, seemingly unconcerned for her father's comments.

Henry was surprised at their transparency. They seemed to hide nothing from each other. Maybe relationships—any kind of relationships—were better that way.

"Did he mean what he said?" Henry asked when Chandler was gone. "That I could stay here?"

"Sure he did."

"You have another room?"

"We have a couch," Evie said, indicating said couch with a nod of her head. "But I have a bed. That is way more comfortable."

Henry frowned. "Are you teasing me again?"

Evie leaned forward, grabbed his hand, and pulled him closer. "Why do you have to make everything so complicated? Seriously, you need to unravel a little, my friend. What's the problem here? I'm a good-looking girl. I can see you think that. You're a good-looking guy. I like you. You like me. Why can't we have some fun together without making it a drama?"

"No reason, I guess."

"So let's get drunk and fuck like the teenagers we wish we'd been."

"I don't think I have ever been seduced, Evie Chandler."

She laughed. "This isn't a seduction, Henry Quinn . . . This is a sexual conquest."

*

120

It was awkward. He knew it would be, but she had anticipated this, and she was assured and sympathetic. The first time happened before he really knew it, but they made love a second time, and it was in slow motion and sensitive, without the frenzied panic that had marked the first time, and she rolled him onto his back, leaning over him, kissing him, touching him, pausing only to smile with such warmth and tenderness that he thought he might cry right there and then.

Despite the proximity of other human beings, Henry knew he had been desperately and terrifyingly alone for more than three years.

They shared a few final words; she asked him about the scar on his torso, and he told her it was little more than a hard-won lesson. Then he held her close, and they fell asleep, their bodies curled in to one another like violin scrolls.

SEVENTEEN

War changes a man. It changes his eyes, his mind, his heart, his soul. It teaches him about impermanence and fragility. It shows him the holes in the master plan, and it questions his belief in God. Most often undermines it as well.

War is for those who have forgotten how to speak to one another. It is for those who have secrets they do not wish to reveal for fear of some penalty worse than war. There is no such penalty, but their blindness and ignorance does not allow them such a rational perspective.

The defeat of the Axis was ultimately inevitable. Evil men unconsciously contribute to their own downfall. They make mistakes; they commit tactical errors. Some believe that such things occur because of the basic goodness in all man, that the criminal seeks to prevent himself from committing further crimes by leaving clues as to identity and motive. *I cannot stop myself. I need someone to stop me.* Perhaps tyrants are merely arrogant sneak-thieves.

Whatever Evan Riggs may have imagined about war, the reality was as far from his imagination as possible. And it seemed that he was alone in his thoughts and feelings, for very few—if any—of Calvary's men had gone to war, and that was something he did not understand. Redbird County had made great sacrifices for the First World War, had even erected a memorial stone naming those who had fallen in defense of freedom, but Evan imagined that no such memorial would be granted for those killed in the war from which he'd just returned.

And the Calvary he returned to was a different place with a different atmosphere, and though at first he believed it was his own eyes and ears that had changed, he began to understand that the changes were real and specific, and most of them were attributable to his brother.

Carson Riggs, by default, by fate, by accident, had assumed the position of sheriff in November of 1944. He was all of twenty-five years of age, the cock of the walk, playing dalliance with self-importance, a gun on his hip, a coolness in his gaze, a sense of assumed authority that belied the truth of his inherent insecurity. Evan had seen such men in the army. Power and money merely exaggerate what is already there. In war, such men got other men killed and then spoke of *collateral damage* and *acceptable losses*. In peacetime, with no war to fight, it seemed such men created skirmishes and smaller wars to keep their uncertain minds occupied.

It appeared to Evan that Carson had become such a man, had perhaps been such a man all along, but the law had now given him an outlet for this predilection. A cruel facet had come to the fore, an aura possessive of cold angles and sharp corners, and the warm reception afforded Evan—the valiant hero, the decorated soldier—was neither appreciated nor condoned. Carson made comments, sly and cool, and it was obvious that envy played a part.

"You couldn't have been more fussed over if you'd been killed out there," he said, and Evan heard something else entirely. Had Evan been killed, there would been a sense of loss, of course, but Carson would have received the attention and the sympathy. Evan would have been forgotten, as was everyone who died, but Carson would carry that burden as if a knapsack of sorrow, and use it to his advantage. Evan could see that in his older brother, and he did not like what he saw.

William and Grace Riggs were not so devout or religiously-minded as to consider that the return of their younger son had much of anything to do with God, but even they bowed their heads and made silent thanks in church. William Riggs knew that war was a crapshoot when it came to who survived and who didn't, and he was just grateful that the dice had fallen in his favor. Grace held her son for a long time that day, seeing him walk down the road in his uniform, the smart snap in his stride, the colors on his breast, aware—as all mothers are—that something had changed in her son. His shadow was more dense, possessive of some immutable darkness that neither time nor love would ever fade. As Plato said, *Only the dead have seen the end of war.*

Where Evan found the most visible welcome was on the doorstep of the Wyatt house.

Rebecca seemed in shock, even though word had gone ahead that he was returning.

"Evan ..." she exhaled, and ran to him, throwing her arms around him, pulling him tight, as if to let go would see her slide right off the surface of the world and vanish into space.

Later she would speak of Carson, the things she'd heard, the things she didn't believe, but for now her thoughts were for no one but the younger Riggs, asking him questions about his campaign medal, his Combat Infantry Badge, what acts of heroism had earned him two Bronze Stars. And Evan made light of it all, saying that his mind had been filled with images of his hometown, of her, of the songs he would write upon his return, of the future he'd planned.

The tension between them was unbearable. The effortless ease with which they had shared one another's company had been replaced by an awkward uncertainty. They were older, perhaps somehow wiser, and—as was the case with all people—the simplicity and innocence of youth had been turned over for self-doubt and shades of cynicism. In different ways, adulthood had shown them that the world was not the magical place they'd believed it to be as children, but an altogether more sinister place.

Later, when the excitement had somewhat exhausted itself, when Evan and Rebecca were sitting out on the Riggses' veranda, William and Grace asleep, Carson attending to some sheriff's business, she gave Evan a reason for some of her reticence.

"He asked if I would be his girl," she said, her voice faltering. "When they voted him in as sheriff. It was that night. He was a little drunk. He asked me if I would be his girl."

"If you would marry him?" Evan asked, unsurprised by this revelation.

"Not in the words, no," she replied, "but in the intention."

"And what did you say?"

"Half of the truth."

"Which half?"

"That I felt it wasn't right to discuss it until after you were home safe."

"Or you heard word that I was dead."

"Yes."

"I bet he was upset," Evan said.

"No, not really. At least not visibly so. I think he wanted to hear a yes or a reason for no that made sense. He got the latter."

"But he didn't believe it."

"I don't know, Evan. He has changed, and not a small amount. He used to be so easy to read, to predict, to deal with, but now he seems to have lost his way."

"Or found a way that winds up somewhere bad."

"You think?"

124

"I think."

"Regardless, I feel for him, and I do love him in my own way," Rebecca said.

"You love everyone, Rebecca," Evan said, and he reached out and took her hand. "That, perhaps, will be your downfall."

She smiled. She knew he was right, but what could she do? She could not change who she was, and the world had yet to hurt her sufficiently to make her be someone else.

"You know that I love you, too, Evan," she said, "but the last thing in the world that I want to do is stand between you and your brother."

Evan smiled and did not speak for a while. What he felt and what he wanted to say were in his heart, but they could not survive the circuitous route to his lips. There was too much pent-up emotion in his chest. He loved the girl, no doubt about it, had carried thoughts of her through Italy and France and Germany and Holland, carried them like a lost man carries water from an oasis. When the battles raged and the bullets flew, he packed them deep beneath everything for fear that they would be shot from his hands, but when he came to rest he found that they were still there, still intact, perhaps scattered with dust, but nevertheless unharmed.

Perhaps it was true that those who survived war were those with the greatest desire to come home.

And yet, for all that he felt, he could see that Rebecca was torn. Perhaps it was inherent in a woman to seek some sense of stability, a sense of firm ground beneath her feet, an inherent wish to raise a family. Carson could provide that stability. He could give Rebecca a home, a place to be, a place where she could raise children and know that tomorrow was within her control. Evan couldn't do that, either, and believed he never would.

"You don't stand between Carson and me," Evan said. "You never have. If anything, you have enabled us to be closer than we would have been without you."

"That is a very sweet thing to say," Rebecca replied, "but I don't know if it is really the truth."

Evan reached out and took her hand. "This is who I am," he said. "I will always be this way, and I have no wish to change. I'll stay in Calvary a while, but I will leave, and I have no idea where I will go. I am willing to let the wind take me, I guess." He smiled, looked away toward the horizon.

"You know that there are disagreements between Carson and your father," Rebecca said. "About the farm ... the land."

"Yes."

"Oil people. You know about that, right?"

"Oil people have been chasing my father for years, Rebecca. They will continue to chase him, but he won't sell."

"He and Carson argue about it."

"So I understand. Right now it is not an issue. My father will stand firm."

"And what about us?"

"Us?"

"Yes, Evan. You and I. What about us? You are going to leave, sure. I have always known that, but isn't there something inside that says you should stay?"

"You are the only reason I'd stay, Rebecca," he said, "but something scratches at me, and it doesn't stop, and the only remedy is to keep moving."

"You are a gypsy."

Evan smiled. "That's what my ma used to say. I was left on the porch and she took me in, said I was her own."

"Wouldn't surprise me. You and Carson are so very different."

"Enough for now," Evan said. "I'm only just back. Let me find my feet, okay? We'll have time to talk, to work things out."

"I hope so."

"Why d'you say that?"

"Because time has a way of running through your fingers. Seems like yesterday we were nothing but kids, and now here we are, making decisions that will affect us when we're fifty and sixty years old."

"I can't think that far ahead. Tomorrow is enough for me."

He leaned up and kissed her on the cheek. She put her arms around him and pulled him close, but she could feel—just like always—that there was something deep inside him that made him want to pull away.

A week later, a cool evening, Evan and Carson on the veranda as the sun glowered along the horizon.

"Sheriff seems to suit you," Evan said. "Youngest in the history of the county, or so I hear."

Carson smiled. "But you are the war hero, brother."

"The war will be forgotten," Evan replied, "as will those who

126

fought it, even though there were so few from Calvary. And it will be forgotten because that's what people want to do."

"I missed you," Carson said, and for a moment everything was forgotten but the fact that they were once as close as brothers could ever be, and this was something that could never be taken away.

"I missed you, too," Evan said.

"A day didn't go by when I didn't wonder if I'd see you again. And it wasn't easy for Ma. She cried a lot. Never seen her attend church so much as when you weren't here."

"Maybe that's what brought me back."

"Bullshit," Carson said. "Prayers and church and whatever . . . all so much nonsense. A man makes his own life. A man makes his own death as well. You came back because you have things to do. Can't say I understand them, but then again, I don't need to because they ain't my things."

"I won't stay long."

"I know."

"A year, maybe two," Evan said.

"That long?" Carson asked, and there was an edge in his tone, as if the earlier moment of fraternal empathy was gone.

Evan turned and looked at his older brother. They had been apart for less than three years, but a world of change had taken place in both their lives.

"You want me to go, Carson?"

"I want you to do what you feel is right for you, Evan."

"Am I in the way?"

"Of what?"

"The oil people. Rebecca."

Carson stepped forward and gripped the veranda rail. "She told you."

"She tells me everything. We are friends, Carson—always have been, always will be. You and I and Rebecca don't have secrets. That's not the way we were raised and not the way we are as people."

"Maybe there are things that are of no concern to you."

"Maybe there are, but I assure you that I have no intention of distracting you from your plans, Carson."

Carson nodded. He inhaled, exhaled. "That presumes that you would have the means to distract me."

Evan frowned. "What has happened to us, Carson? What happened while I was gone? I understand that you're sheriff now, but

127

that doesn't mean you can quit this family or change the way this family cares for one another."

"You and I are very different people, Evan," Carson said, his tone matter-of-fact, businesslike. "Comes a time when you start to think about your future, and how you were as a child bears no relation to how you are as a man—"

"That makes no sense," Evan interjected. "How you are as a man has everything to do with how you were as a child."

"Perhaps for you, Evan, but not for me. What I want and what you want are not the same thing. I don't understand you, and I don't expect you to understand me. That is just how it is, and you can fight it or accept it."

"So what do you want, Carson?"

Carson smiled. "I want everything, Evan." He turned and looked at his younger brother, and there was a shadow in his eyes that was unfamiliar. "Everything I can get, and more besides."

Carson let go of the railing and walked back into the house.

Evan stood there for some time in the coolness of the evening, and he felt strangely and uncomfortably afraid, not only for Carson, but for everyone else as well.

EIGHTEEN

It was hard for Henry not to see his life as a divided thing. The accidental shooting of Sally O'Brien was not so much a semicolon as a full-blown end of paragraph. Life had stopped for three years and had now begun again with the sense that what came before bore no relation to what was now on the way. Paragraphs from different books, the characters anomalous, the dialogue fractured and confusing.

He woke before Evie, slipped silently from the bed, put on his jeans and a T-shirt, and made his way out to the kitchen. Glenn Chandler was gone, presumably to work, and Henry went about the business of making coffee in a stranger's house.

Standing on the veranda, looking out over the flatlands of West Texas, he felt as if this place was no longer his home. The Great Depression had almost killed the spirit of the state, and though oil had brought money, it had never erased the feeling that everything could be swept away in a heartbeat.

Remnants of the past were frequent and varied. Take a drive in any direction, and there were signs of leaving, of giving up, of quitting this godforsaken place for someplace better. A row of eroded fence posts like rotted teeth marking some long-vanished boundary; the stone bed of a redundant gas station, the subterranean tanks nothing more than vast mouths filled with dirt and rust and the bleached skeletons of prairie dogs, jackrabbits, and snakes. Broken-down convenience stores, the once-bright colors whipped by wind and dust into ghosts of former colors. Texas was a cul-de-sac for the westerlies, carrying with them bitterness and aggravation and the memory of failure.

"Hey."

Henry turned and saw Evie standing there in the doorway. She had on nothing but Henry's shirt; she came up behind him, snaked her hands around his waist, and rested her head against his shoulder.

"You left me sleeping," she said.

"You looked happy," Henry replied. "Like you were dreaming."

She sighed gently and pulled him closer. "Did you see my dad this morning?"

Henry turned within her arms and faced her. "No. He was gone before I woke."

Evie leaned up and kissed him. "You wanna hear about how I don't normally do this?"

"I know you don't normally do this," Henry said, smiling. "And neither do I."

"I know *you* don't. You've been in Reeves for three years."

"Still, even if I hadn't . . ."

"Come on," Evie said. "Let's get some breakfast."

She made eggs and rye toast and fresh coffee. Then she asked about Evan's daughter and what it was really about.

"Just keeping a promise," Henry said. "Evan took care of me, saved me from some trouble right at the start."

"The hard-won lesson?" she asked, referencing the scar.

Henry nodded. "The hard-won lesson, yes. So I owe him. He gave up his daughter. I don't really know the details, but I guess that he's got something to say to her and he needs to say it."

"He's never gonna come out of Reeves, is he?"

"Maybe, but if he does, he'll only go someplace else the same."

"How do you even deal with that?" Evie asked. "Knowing that you'll die in prison, that you'll never be free, never drive a car, never make love, never . . ." Her voice trailed away.

"One day at a time, I guess," Henry replied. "Three years seems like forever when you start it. Hell, a week seems like forever on the first night. But you get into a groove, a routine, a pattern of doing things a certain way that uses up the time. You teach yourself not to think. That's the main thing. You teach yourself not to think about the past or the future, just about what's happening right now. It's like being drunk without the liquor. Everything is now—nothing before, nothing after." Henry smiled ruefully. "It's a tough habit to get out of."

"Don't worry," Evie said. "I'm not asking you to think about our future."

"I didn't mean that, sweetheart. I meant with everything. You're eating breakfast, and all you're thinking about is eating breakfast. You're at the gas station, and all that's on your mind is the gas station and filling the tank and whatever. It's not the way you normally think. Your mind is yesterday and tomorrow, you know? Everything is yesterday and tomorrow. You do a few years in a place like Reeves and your mind ain't on nothin' but today."

"So what's happening for you today, then?" Evie asked.

"Figured I'd go stick my nose in some places and see if I get bit."

Evie smiled. "You don't back off, do you?"

"Hey, only thing I've heard is that there's some history with Evan and his brother. Carson Riggs may have himself a reputation as a tough guy, but I'm not breaking the law, and I'm not here to cause trouble. I'm just here to deliver a message."

"Well, you go deliver your message, Henry Quinn, and if someone bites you and you need some first aid, you come on back here and we'll fix you up."

"You got any suggestions as to where I should start?"

"Go on and speak with Clarence Ames, I guess. Seems he had the most to say."

"Also made it clear that the conversation was done."

"Place is full of ears. Man says different things when he thinks he ain't bein' listened to."

"And where's he at?"

"Clarence has a place on the far side of Calvary. Head through town, on past the Honeycutts, keep on that road, and you can't miss it. Used to be white, two stories, round tower on the left-hand side, has a lean-to on the right where he parks his truck. You'll know it when you see it."

"What does he do?"

"Do?" Evie shrugged. "Used to farm, but like all these boys, they sold up for the oil rights. Made a fortune, so I heard. So much money they don't need to work, but to look at them, you'd think they didn't have a dime to share between 'em."

"And what are you doing today?" Henry asked.

"For now I'm mindin' my own business, Henry Quinn, that and waitin' to see how much trouble you get yourself into."

"So I guess I'll see you later."

"I guess you will."

Henry smiled. "Are you really this nonchalant and easygoing, or are you putting this on for me?"

Evie reached across the table and took Henry's hands. She looked him directly in the eyes and didn't crack a smile. "Come back tonight and I'll tell you."

"You are just a little crazy, I guess," Henry said, "but good crazy."

"You hope."

*

Half an hour later he was on the road back toward Calvary. He followed Evie's directions, drove on past the Honeycutt place and kept on going. He found Clarence Ames's place, saw Clarence there at the front window as he drew to a halt. Before he'd exited the pickup, the front door opened and the man himself came out onto the veranda.

"Figured I'd see you again," Clarence said. He raised his hand to shield his eyes from the sun.

Henry walked on up the path to the porch steps.

"You've come with questions."

"I have."

"What makes you think I wanna answer them?"

"I know you don't," Henry said. "Came anyway."

"Evie Chandler put you up to this?"

"Evie said you'd be the best person to start with, yes."

"I'll have words with her, then," he replied, and there was a reconciled expression on his face; the visit was inevitable, and they'd both known it.

"You better come on in, I guess," Clarence said, and unlatched the screen door.

He turned and disappeared into the shadowed hallway. Henry went on up the steps, through the screen door, and followed the man into the house.

"Talk last night got me thinking about Evan," Clarence said. "Went through the records I got and found it."

The room they were in was so much the room of a man living alone. Books and newspapers were piled high left and right. A collection of bottles, some empty, some half full, sat on the floor by the fireplace. Boots, a coat, a pair of gloves, a couple of hats, other things in random places. It wasn't a dirty room, but disorderly, lived-in. Clarence Ames resided here alone—no doubt about it.

Clarence nodded toward the table, and there sat Evan Riggs's record, *The Whiskey Poet*.

Something happened when Henry picked it up. The face that looked back at him was two men—the picture he had seen on the wall at Crooked Cow in Abilene back in 1967 and the friend he'd made in Reeves. They were different men, but even as Henry looked, he could see something in that photograph that he'd not seen before. There was an edge in the expression, something almost cruel in the eyes, and he realized then that Evan Riggs had been the only man in Reeves to never mitigate his actions. Jail was filled with

132

the innocent, the unlucky, the unfortunate, and even in the case of those whose guilt was beyond doubt, their incarceration was still the fault of lawyers and snitches and biased judges with grievances. Friend though he'd been, and a good one, there was no denying the fact that Evan Riggs was more than likely a killer, regardless of his amnesia. Evidence said he'd beaten a man to death with his bare hands in a motel in Austin, and whatever that man might have been guilty of, it had not been Evan Riggs's job to take his life. Simply stated, and if guilt was assumed, Evan Riggs should have gone to the chair.

"You heard it?" Clarence asked.

"Many times," Henry replied. "Had it before I went to Reeves."

"I played it last night after I got back from the saloon. Hell of a singer. Some of it ain't even in tune, but it still makes the hairs on the back of your neck stand up. Outlaw music, I guess."

"I guess."

"You want some coffee?"

"If you're havin' some, sure."

"Tastes like raccoon piss and vinegar."

"Just the way I like it."

Clarence went out back to the kitchen, returned with cups.

He was right: the coffee was awful, but it didn't seem to matter.

"So, I don't know what you think I can do to help you, son," Clarence said.

"I don't know either."

"What's the story here? I mean, really . . . what you doin' this for?"

"Evan stopped me from getting killed," Henry said. "Not that anyone was trying to kill me, specifically, but jail has its own territories, you know? Put a bunch of men someplace, no matter how small, and they all want a piece of it. Instinct, I guess. Anyway, someone upset someone. I don't even know what it was about. But in a place like that, everything gets blown out of proportion. Use a man's soap, and he's gonna take it as an insult to him, his family, his whole world. So one guy wants some other guy dead, and he buys an opportunity by staging a riot. The wardens are occupied on one side of the prison block, some guy gets stabbed on the other, and no one saw anything. I just happened to be on the wrong side of the block. I sort of wandered into the middle of it. There were two or three guys with knives, some other guy on his hands and knees with a hole in his neck, blood everywhere, a hell of a scene, and they took me for his buddy. They came after me and I got myself sliced.

Evan came from nowhere, floored one of them, threw me over his shoulder and ran. Got me into the infirmary before I bled out. Place like Reeves, the wardens'd just as easily let you bleed out as go to the trouble of fixin' you up. A dead man is a man you ain't gotta feed. And that was that. And aside from him being responsible for me still being here, I guess I feel a certain kinship with the man. Live with someone for three years in a room that size, well, you either get on or move out. We got on just fine, talked a lot about music. Evan is the kind of man who doesn't say a great deal, but when he does say something, it's worth listening to."

"Just can't imagine how it'd be to know you'll never be out of there," Clarence said. "He was a young man when that happened, war hero, up-and-coming music star an' all, but a drunk. That was no secret. And he was a bad drunk, I guess. Otherwise what happened would never have happened."

"You think he really did it? Killed that man?"

Clarence shook his head. "I don't know, son," he replied. "One thing that life has taught me is that people are capable of all manner of things you'd never expect. No one's a killer until they kill someone, and from what I understand, he killed a good many in the war."

"But surely war is different—"

"Sure it is, but it's still gotta change a man, hasn't it? Even if you shoot someone from three hundred yards away, you've still taken someone's life. That's gotta do something to your viewpoint."

"Yes, I guess so."

"So what's your story, Henry Quinn? Aside from this thing with Evan's vanished daughter?"

"My story? I don't have one."

"Sure you do," Clarence said, smiling. "Everyone has a story. Everyone has a dream, even a little one. I mean, say you find her tomorrow. Say you track this mysterious girl down and deliver whatever message Evan gave you for her, then what? Where do you go from here?"

"Back home to San Angelo. Have a mother there. She's not doing so good. Drinks too much, hangs out with people who ain't so good for her, far as I can tell. I have a responsibility there. Beyond that, I want to start writing music again. I have a holding contract with a record company in Abilene, same company Evan recorded with, coincidentally. Still owe them five hundred bucks, and that's something that'll need sorting out sooner or later."

"So whatever's going on with your ma and your own life is all on hold until you find Evan's girl."

"Yep, it seems that way."

"That's some promise you made."

"Gave my word."

"And you think I know something?"

"Well, Carson Riggs would be my first choice. However, I get the idea he's not so interested in helping me."

"You got that right."

"So what did happen between them? Why so much animosity?"

Clarence smiled ruefully. "Always the same reasons, son. Money or a woman. In this case, both. I don't know details, but rumor has it that they were both after the same girl, that and the fact that Carson wanted to sell the land for oil rights, and he got involved with people he shouldn't have while Evan was away. And then there was the father's death. Strange circumstance. Folks sayin' that it was not what it appeared to be, that a cloud of uncertainty still stands over it. I say more often than not that things are exactly what they appear to be, but what the hell do I know?"

"But if you don't know what happened and Carson won't talk to me, then what do I do to find this girl?"

"My advice?"

"Yes."

"Drop it like a hot stone, Henry Quinn. Really, seriously, no bullshit. If Carson Riggs don't want her found, then you ain't gonna find her. And if he don't want her found, there's a reason. Maybe it's spite, maybe nothing more than another way to get back at Evan, but if I were you, I would let it go. Can only lead to the kind of trouble you don't want."

"But I promised—"

"Man makes a promise when he gets married. 'Til death do us part. But what happens if she turns out to be a drunk and a philanderer? Does that mean he's gotta keep that promise? I don't think it does. Circumstances change. People change, too. You made a promise in good faith, but you were unaware of the reality out here. You also gotta ask yourself whether the girl really wants to be found."

"Sheriff Riggs said the same thing."

"Maybe he's got a point."

"Maybe he has, but I feel like I haven't even started in on this yet. I'm here, sure, but have I really made any great effort to find her? No, not yet. I can contact the adoption people in Eldorado or

San Angelo. If not there, then there will be records in San Antonio or Austin or someplace. People don't just get adopted and vanish without a trace. There has to be a way to find her."

"And your mind is set on it?"

"Yes, it is."

"Well, I can't help you," Clarence said. "Not because I'm unwilling, but because I just don't know anything."

"I appreciate your time, nevertheless."

"Not at all. Now, do you want some more coffee before you go?"

Henry smiled. "I'll take a rain check. No offense, Mr. Ames, but I have to say it really is the worst coffee I ever tasted. The stuff they gave us at Reeves was better than this, and I think that came off the packing-room floor."

"Well, I'll take that as a compliment, son," Clarence said, smiling.

They shook hands on the porch. Henry drove away. Clarence Ames stood there for a moment and then sighed audibly. He headed back into the house and made a call.

"Sheriff Riggs there?"

Clarence waited while Riggs was fetched.

"Carson. Clarence here. He came down, asked a few questions."

Clarence listened.

"Like you said, not a word. Must say he has a mind to get under this thing, whatever this thing is."

Clarence closed his eyes for a moment.

"I know, Carson. I know. Leave it be, okay? We all know what you want, and we don't even want to know why. You do whatever you have to do. It's none of my business."

Clarence Ames didn't wait for a response. He hung up the phone and stood there for quite some time without moving.

And when he did move, it was back to the kitchen. He half filled his cup with bad coffee and then reached down for a bottle of bourbon and filled his cup to the rim.

Back in the front room, he paused to look at the picture of Evan Riggs on *The Whiskey Poet*.

"Why d'you have to send him down here, Evan?" he asked the picture. "Why couldn't you just leave it all alone?"

NINETEEN

By Christmas of 1945, Evan Riggs knew he could stay no longer. Calvary had become a different place. Even his home was a different place, and there was a dimmed light in his father's eyes that made it clear a fight was not going to happen. At some point William Riggs had decided that Carson as sheriff was a good thing, and now the decision was made, he would not change his mind. He all-too-clearly remembered the sense of nothing he'd felt when Carson was born. Now he could redress the balance. Acknowledge Evan's musical aspirations though he did, his support for Carson was both vocal and unvarying.

"I know you have to go," Grace told her younger son. "Even when you're here, you're always leaving, if not physically, then spiritually. I see it in you, the gypsy blood."

"Same gypsies that left me on the porch," Evan said, smiling.

"Spent all these years waiting for them to return so I can give you back, but have they sent word? Hell, no. Nothing so much as a postcard."

"I'm worried about Carson," Evan said. "I was speaking to Clarence Ames, Doc Sperling, some of the others. They seem scared of him, like he's railroading them into this oil business."

"Carson is headstrong. He'll settle down."

"I think Pa is being too easy about this. I think he needs to tell Carson that the farm is staying a farm."

"And when me and William are gone, what then? You gonna come back and take care of it all?"

"You both have a lot of years ahead of you, Ma. You're gonna be here for a long time. Pa isn't even fifty."

"I know. It's not a matter we have to deal with right now, and we're going to keep this place on for as long as we can. Your father has absolutely no intention of turning it over to the oil people."

"It wouldn't be right," Evan said. "Everything doesn't have to be about money."

"It's a good sentiment," Grace said, "but there's not many folk who have it."

"I would stay and fight with him, but I am not—"

Grace touched Evan's arm. "Evan . . . you don't need to tell me who you are. I know exactly who you are." She smiled, and there was nothing but love and empathy in her eyes. "And even though your father might not find it easy to say, he also understands why you'll never be a West Texas farmer. Only kind of man who can do that has to be more stubborn than the dirt and the weather in this godforsaken place, and your father can be *that* stubborn, believe me."

"I'll stay through Christmas," Evan said, "and then I'm heading for San Antonio. That's the plan."

"You never made a plan in your life, Evan Riggs," Grace said. "And I wouldn't start now."

Evan did stay through Christmas, January, too, and in early February of 1946, he packed what little he possessed into a beat-to-hell station wagon and said his goodbyes.

William Riggs shook his younger son's hand and told him to watch out for three things: women, cards, and liquor. "First will break your heart, second your wallet, third your spirit," he said out of Grace's earshot. "You get involved with them country-singin' fellas, they're gonna have drugs and whiskey and women all around them. You got a square head on your shoulders when it suits you, so you know what I'm sayin'."

"I'm gonna be fine, Pa."

"Famous last words, son. That and 'It'll come out right in the end.' Sometimes it doesn't."

"I know where to come if I get into trouble."

"You do," William said. "Home is home, even when you don't live there no more."

Grace was quiet and tearful. She held him close and didn't want to let go. She wondered if the abiding memory of her life would be that of farewells with Evan. Eventually he whispered something to her and she released him.

"What did you say to her?" his father asked.

"Told her that I survived a war. I can survive San Antonio and whatever else might happen."

"You gonna go see your brother?"

"Sure I am."

"I told him you were heading out today. He said that he still had a job to do, that you could come find him at the Sheriff's Office. Said if he wasn't there, he wouldn't be far."

"I'll find him."

"Don't rile him, okay?"

Evan frowned.

"Don't act dumb, Evan. You know how wound up he can get around you. You were always smarter, and he doesn't care that people know it. If you're gonna part company, then do it civil and pleasant. Don't leave on bad terms with your brother."

"I won't."

"Give me your word, Evan."

"I give you my word, Pa."

"Okay, now git, 'fore your mother starts weepin' and all that theatrical business."

Carson was at the Sheriff's Office. Evan could still not get used to him in uniform. It seemed anomalous.

"So you're outta here, then," Carson said.

"I am."

"Think you're on a fast road to nowhere, Evan, but that's the last time I'm gonna say it."

"I know what you think, Carson. I know we don't see eye to eye on a lot of things, but we ain't ever been enemies and there's no reason to start now."

"No intention of bein' your enemy, Evan. Just think this game you're playin' ain't worth a hill o' beans."

Evan didn't respond. Carson was winding and Evan wasn't going to snap. It wasn't worth it, and he'd given his word to their father.

"So, San Antonio, is it?"

"Yep."

"Safe journey, little brother."

Evan extended his hand. Carson hesitated, and then he grinned like a fool.

"I am just kiddin' you," he said, and opened his arms wide. "Come here."

They hugged, and Carson leaned close to his ear and said, "You are the best brother a man could wish for. I think you is one crazy son of a bitch, but I hope you wind up happy and drunk and rich as a king."

"I appreciate that, Carson, and I wish the same for you. Take care of Ma and Pa."

"Will do."

They parted smiling, which is what William Riggs had hoped for.

Of all the goodbyes, Rebecca was the toughest.

Her father was there when Evan arrived; he shook Evan's hand, clapped him on the shoulder, wished him fair weather and good fortune. He then left the two of them alone, knowing that the words they would share were not for his ears.

"So this is it?" she said, already knowing the answer.

"I'd ask you to come with me, but I know you wouldn't."

"I can't, Evan, and you know it, so sayin' that is just unfair."

Evan looked away toward the horizon, didn't respond.

"You have nothing to say to me?" she asked.

He could hear the break in her voice, the telling edge of loss and anger. She believed he was deserting her, for that's how it felt, like a desertion, some kind of betrayal. It was not, but that didn't change the emotion.

"I can't stay here forever," he said. "You of all people should understand that."

"I do," Rebecca said, "but that doesn't stop me from hating you for going away."

Evan smiled. "You don't hate me, Rebecca. If you hated me, you would feel nothing but relief."

"Why do you have to make my life so complicated?"

"I don't think I am. You are the one who is being unfair now."

She took a step closer, put her hand on his arm. "What would happen if you stayed, Evan? I mean, really . . . what would happen if you stayed?"

"I would die a little more every day," he said, for this was what he believed. "I would drink too much and I would argue with Carson, and I would fight with my father about the land and the work and everything that he wants me to do. I don't belong here . . . and if you want to know the truth, the only people that have kept me here as long as I've stayed is my ma and you."

"Do you love me, Evan Riggs?"

Evan looked at her. "You know the answer to that question, Rebecca Wyatt."

"But are you *in love* with me?"

Evan sighed. "Now it's your turn to make things complicated.

You accuse me of something, and then you do the very same thing yourself. If you have a question, then ask me, Rebecca."

"Could you not bear to stay here if I were by your side . . . I mean really with you, as your wife?"

"Could you not bear to go with me, wherever things took us, if I were beside you as your husband?"

"Is that how it is, then?"

"You know it is."

"Then you are really going?"

"And you are really staying."

Her eyes brimmed with tears. "It isn't right and it isn't fair," she said, and her voice was a cracked whisper, barely audible.

"I think that describes life in general," Evan said. He pulled her close, his arms around her, and he could feel the racing of her heart against his chest.

Everything she imagined he felt, he then felt it a hundred times more. He could not tell her. It would only make things worse. He was caught between one thing and another, and whichever one he chose, he would have to compromise and sacrifice something. But, in truth, the decision had been easier than he would ever tell her, for the pull of his vocation, his music, the desire to travel, to see the world, to find himself in far-flung corners, even the wish to return someday with stories that no one else could tell, was so much stronger than the love he felt for Rebecca Wyatt. Perhaps not stronger, but different. Like a drug. Worse than a drug.

Rebecca pulled back a little and looked up at Evan. "My father says you are irresponsible, a dreamer . . . that you'll come to grief."

"Does he, now?"

"Yes, he does, and I can't say that a little of me doesn't agree with him."

"I don't believe you," Evan said.

"You're calling me a liar now?"

"No, but I know how clever and manipulative you can be, Miss Wyatt."

"To hell with you," Rebecca said, but she pulled him close again and closed her eyes and breathed even more deeply, as if to draw him deep inside through the atmosphere.

"I'll be back," Evan said.

"That doesn't mean anything, and you know it. Of course you'll be back. Everyone comes back. How long? When? Why? You'll come back with a wife and horde of children, or you'll come back in a pine box..."

"Enough," Evan said. "I can't apologize for who I am, and I'm not going to. We meet halfway on so many things, but not this, and that's just the way it is."

Rebecca pulled away. Evan wrested her back, but she didn't want to be held.

"Go," she said. "This is just making it worse."

Evan stood for a moment, and then he reached out and touched her cheek with the fingers of his right hand.

"Until whenever," he said, and then he crossed to the steps and walked down to the car.

"Evan?" she called after him.

He paused, glanced back.

"Will always love you," she said, "whatever happens."

Hindsight, cruel adviser that it was, told him that he should have said something in return. Perhaps then, with some vague hope of being together, she might have made different choices, taken a different path.

A single word and everything could have worked out so very differently.

But Evan Riggs said nothing, and that moment—along with so many others—would haunt him for the rest of his life.

TWENTY

With no certain place to go, Henry Quinn pulled over in front of the Checkers Diner. He went on in, took a seat at the counter, and ordered a Coke, if only to get the taste of Clarence Ames's coffee out of his mouth.

It was here that Carson Riggs found him. It was somewhere not far from noon, and once Riggs had ordered coffee and been served, they had the place to themselves. The woman tending seemed to understand that this conversation was not her business to overhear.

"Seems to me you got a mind to pursue this thing," Riggs said.

Henry nodded, looking straight ahead at the row of flavored syrup bottles against the back wall. "Seems to me I don't have a choice, Sheriff Riggs."

Riggs took a sip of his coffee, set it down again. He reached right and moved his hat along the counter just an inch. Slow motion, every action, as if all the time in the world was available for him to make his point.

"Man can get himself tied in knots if he doesn't have choices. Man can keep walking down a road that just has bad news waiting at the end."

Henry turned and smiled. "You have a way of saying things, Sheriff," he said. "They don't sound like threats, but they sure feel that way."

"I'm just talkin' the way I talk," Riggs replied. "Same way I always did."

"So, what do you want from me? Tell me straight."

"What I want, son, is for you to leave this well alone. This is family business, and you ain't family. Never have been, never will be."

"A promise is a promise, Sheriff Riggs."

"Depends. Circumstances change, son, sometimes as much as the weather. People make decisions based on information that they then discover to be false or misleading."

"Are you telling me that your brother is a liar?"

143

Riggs smiled, but there was no warmth in it. It was the smile of a spider when the web shivers with prey.

"You and I had a civil word about this matter," Riggs said. "From what you said, I believed we had an understanding. Seem to recall we took the girl's feelings into consideration. Also seem to recall that we were of the same mind."

"You recall correctly, Sheriff."

Riggs nodded slowly. He lifted his coffee cup, paused before he drank. "Glad to hear that, Mr. Quinn. Wouldn't want you thinking I was a liar as well."

"And Evan?" Henry asked. "What about him? Do you not think he deserves some real consideration in this matter?"

"I have been giving my brother real consideration for more than twenty years. Our father was dead when this business happened in Austin. Some say that the loss affected Evan, perhaps contributed to his behavior, but his father and my father were the same man, and I was right there when he died. Did I get drunk and kill a man, Mr. Quinn? No, I can't say that I did. You have any idea how it broke our mother's heart? She loses her husband, and then her younger son goes to jail for the rest of his life. People can die of a broken heart, Mr. Quinn . . . far more easily than they can die of a broken promise."

"You want me to leave Calvary, don't you?"

"I have no concern whether you leave or not, son. All I want you to do is drop this little investigation of yours. Whatever consequence you might suffer as a result of failing Evan . . ." Riggs's voice trailed away, and again there was that look in his eyes. The rest of the statement wasn't required for Henry to get the message.

There was no uncertainty now. Riggs really did not want him in Calvary; his mission to find the long-lost daughter was meeting clear opposition. The threat, though not directly stated, was as obvious as daylight. Continue along this line, and Sheriff Carson Riggs of Calvary would be having harsher words with Henry Quinn, late of Reeves County.

Later, after some time to consider how he'd felt in that moment, Henry realized that stubbornness had played a major part. Wherever that stubbornness came from, it was a strong thing, possessed a will all its own. It rose in Henry's blood, and he could not calm it. The determination to defy Carson became as strong as the promise he'd made to Evan. Instinctively, he rested his hand against the scar on his side. He remembered—all too clearly—the certainty that he was going to die, the way his body seemed bathed in blood, how Evan Riggs had shouldered him and crossed one gantry after another to get him to the infirmary.

"I understand," Henry said, which was true. "I will leave it alone," he added, which was not.

Carson Riggs looked at Henry Quinn, and there was a light in Riggs's eyes . . . a light of suspicion, a light of near certainty that Henry was lying, but perhaps an element of doubt borne out of Riggs's self-belief that he could back Henry off with a handful of edgy words. Perhaps he was not used to being contradicted and challenged; perhaps the mere fact that Henry had already spoken with Clarence Ames had set him on an unerring path to Henry's certain failure. There was something about the kid that raised his hackles, and this would not do. Not at all.

This was some kind of standoff, and both were resolute.

"So, where will you be headed?" Riggs asked.

"Back home, I guess," Henry said.

Riggs drained his coffee cup, reached for his hat, put it on. He rose from the counter stool and hitched his Sam Browne. He looked down at his boots as if checking their sheen, and then he looked up at Henry and smiled.

"Been good to straighten things out, Mr. Quinn," he said. "Glad to see that we are not headed in two different directions on this."

"We are not, Sheriff Riggs."

"So this is goodbye, I guess."

"Guess it is."

Carson Riggs extended his hand. Henry got up from the stool, faced the man, and shook.

"Want to believe that I was right to trust you," Riggs said.

Henry said nothing.

Riggs turned and left the diner.

Henry Quinn stood there, believed that never in his life had he felt so set on something. To hell with Carson Riggs. To hell with the veiled threats and menacing intimidation. Fuck him. *Fuck* him.

Henry took his seat again. He looked back toward the wall, through and behind the bottles of flavored syrup to the mirror that sat behind them.

For a moment he did not recognize himself. Was that the expression of a man afraid?

Henry looked away.

What was he getting into? Not only with Riggs and the lost daughter, but also Evie Chandler, her father, the people of Calvary.

He thought of his mother, back there in San Angelo with Howard Ulysses Morgan, drinking a hole through her liver out of which she imagined she'd escape the banal reality of existence. Or the disillusionment of it all.

Henry knew he'd contributed to that disillusionment, her only child little more than a dumb kid with a six-pack and a handgun. What was he thinking? What problem was he solving? Was he no different from her, stumbling blindly from one day to the next in the vain hope that one day he would write a song, earn a fortune, make good his escape? His escape to what?

Was his promise to Evan Riggs nothing more than a means by which he could avoid confronting and taking responsibility for his own life?

No, he could not accept that.

He owed Evan Riggs his life. That was the truth. He owed the man his life, and this was the very least he could do in return.

Carson Riggs was an obstacle, sure, but wasn't the accomplishment of anything merely down to a man's ability to recognize, acknowledge, then surmount whatever obstacles appeared en route?

Henry finished his Coke. He headed back out to the car. He drove in the direction of Ozona. He wanted to tell Evie of his latest confrontation with Sheriff Carson Riggs.

The sense of being watched was there as he headed for the highway. How he knew, he did not question, but he was certain that Carson Riggs knew exactly where he was going and why.

TWENTY-ONE

San Antonio was a kick in the balls. It was a swift right hook into the very substance of Evan Riggs's ego. In San Antonio no one gave a good goddamn about some hick country singer from Calvary with a bagful of old-timey tunes.

Money, lack of it, was the first order of business. Playing juke joints and straw-floored saloons gave him barely enough to cover the rent on a small room in a boardinghouse. Food came second, liquor came third, but it wasn't long before liquor took precedence. It was no consolation, no reprieve, however. It was not a replacement for God or love or anything else. Liquor was a remedy for disillusion and the fear of failure. What he believed he might fail in, Evan was not sure. He didn't even know what it was that he was trying to attain. Fame, money, attention, adoration? He began to question why he was even pursuing this uncertain goal, but any attempt he made to divert his attention to some other plan, same other means of survival, was met with the same feeling: He could not help it. He could not alter his personality. He was who he was, and who he was would never change.

There were girls, of course. There were always girls. Put a good-looking guy on any kind of stage and he became something that he was not. What the girls saw and the reality could not have been further from each other. However certain and confident and charming Evan Riggs might have been with a guitar around his neck, he was a desperate young man with a heavy burden of self-doubt. None of the relationships he undertook lasted long; the veneer wore thin, the drinking became noisy, even violent on one occasion when a woman by the name of Carole-Anne Murphy broke a whiskey bottle over Evan's head, saying, "Lousy good-for-nothin' asshole of a man . . . Christ, Evan, anyone'd think you had some talent, the way you go on . . ."

It was a cutting jibe, and she said it merely to hurt him, knowing that such a line would bury its claws in his skin and burrow beneath the surface. Whatever Evan Riggs needed, it was not further fuel for those fires of self-doubt. It was also clear from the first moment and through every moment beyond that no girl could ever be Rebecca Wyatt. They were substitutes, replacements, stand-ins, and cameos. They would never make the grade. Such a thing was not possible.

Evan stayed in San Antonio for less than a year. He returned to Calvary for Christmas of 1946 and was swiftly reminded of all the reasons he'd left in the first place, so much so that he never even made it to the farm. He sat in his car at the side of the highway and smoked three cigarettes. He then turned around and drove back the way he'd come.

He called his mother the following day.

"Something came up," he lied.

"I don't understand, Evan . . . You said you'd be back for Christmas. We all expected you. Are you coming today?"

"No, Ma. I'm not coming today. Can't make it all. I'm sorry."

She was silent for a while. He could feel the sense of dismay at the other end of the line.

Eventually, "Is everything okay, Evan?"

"Sure, Ma. Everything is fine."

He could hear his own voice. He sounded like the liar that he was. Perhaps not a liar, but certainly a son telling a mother what he believed she wanted to hear.

Her reply reminded him of his complete transparency.

"If you need a little time to get your thoughts together . . . you know, a little break from all the work you're doing, then you could always come and stay for a while. There will always be a bed and a place at the table for you. You know that, don't you, Evan?"

"Yes, Ma. I know that." He closed his eyes and breathed deeply. Not only was he disappointing himself, but he was now disappointing his mother.

"Your father would like to see you. He will be really upset that you won't make it. He worries about you."

"Tell him not to worry. I'm fine."

She fell silent again, waiting for him to say something that would fix things.

"And Carson?" Evan asked, wanting to change the subject, if only to find a reason to get off the phone.

The hesitation at the other end of the line said more than any words. Evan knew then that he should have done as he'd promised and gone back to the farm.

"Carson is Carson," Grace Riggs said. "He has his own way of upsetting things, just like you."

"Who is he upsetting, Ma?"

"Who's he not upsetting?" she replied, and immediately regretted it. "Pay no mind to me, Evan," she added. "Carson is just fine. Carson just has his ways and means, and sometimes they grate on folks."

"You need me to come back and speak to him?"

"I need you to come back and visit your ma and pa, like you were darned well supposed to, Evan Riggs."

"I'll come soon," Evan said. "I promise."

"Well, maybe for the New Year or something, huh? Or even for Carson's birthday in January."

"I'm thinking of moving to Austin," Evan said.

"Things are not working out in San Antonio?"

"Why do you assume that things are not working out, Ma? Why do you fret so much about me?"

"Because you're my son, Evan. It's my job to worry about you. That's what mothers do. Of course, they worry less if their sons come home and visit every once in a while."

"Point taken, Ma. You're starting to sound like a scratched record."

"So, Austin, is it?"

"That's the plan."

"And when are you moving to Austin?"

"I'm not sure. I need to save up some more money."

"Do you need some help, Evan? I can send—"

"No, Ma. I'm not asking for any money, and I don't want you to send any."

"It's okay to accept help, Evan. It's not a sign of weakness."

"It's better to stand on your own two feet. That's a sign of strength."

"Sometimes you are so like your father."

"Is that a bad thing?"

Grace laughed gently. "A terrible thing, Evan, just terrible. After all, he is such a wicked and dreadful man."

"I gotta go, Ma."

"I know you have, sweetheart. So, you're not going to visit anytime soon?"

"Let's see what happens, okay?"

"I think we have no choice, do we?"

"Say hi to Carson for me, and Pa, and I send all my love and everything."

"I'll tell them, Evan. You take care now."

"Sure thing, Ma. Love you."

"I love you, too, s-son."

The line went dead, but not before Evan heard her voice crack on the last syllable. She was upset, no question about it, and he hated to think that he'd made her feel that way.

So how is that different from how you make everyone else feel? he could hear Carole-Anne Murphy saying, and he wondered if he was becoming the sort of man that even he wouldn't much care to know.

His final thought as he walked away from the telephone was that he had sent no message to Rebecca. He wondered if word had gone ahead and she had been expecting him, too. He wondered if he was on some subconscious mission to drive her into Carson's arms so as not to face the reality of what he had done. Make her decide what to do, and he would not have to make the decision. That was the attitude of a weak man. This much he knew.

Evan moved to Austin in January of 1947, and it was the sea change that he'd long hoped for. There was something in the air in Austin, and for a while it suited his mind, his temperament, his mood. Evan Riggs wrote a good deal of songs within weeks of his arrival, as if the change of air released some pent-up creativity within him. He found a residency at a small club on the outskirts of the city, and after three or four months had gathered quite a following. It was at one of these weekly performances that he met Leland Soames. Soames and his younger sidekick, Herman Russell, the pair of them from a small record label by the name of Crooked Cow, came down a number of times to see Evan play. They broached the idea of Evan heading out to their recording studio in Abilene to cut a disc.

"Maybe next year," Soames said. "We have a whole bunch of things on the calendar, and we couldn't really look at it until maybe the fall of next year, but what you're doin' sounds mighty good, and I think you could get yourself some radio play, son."

This possibility lifted Evan's spirits markedly, for he had seen himself tiring of Austin. He'd been playing for six months in the same venue, seeing many of the same faces, and those same faces were now talking through his set. The potential of cutting a disc with Crooked Cow also coincided with a fateful meeting. Her name was Lilly Duval, her mother, Angeline, a French-Creole, her father an itinerant longshoreman who had blown through Angeline's life like a bold and brief squall. Lilly was a handful of years older than Evan, a woman of experience in many ways, and yet possessed of a naiveté and simple charm that belied her appearance. To say she was beautiful would have been misleading. The girl broke hearts crossing the street, married men wondering if they could just shoot their wives right there and claim self-defense. It was Texas, after all.

She did not break Evan Riggs's heart. His heart had already been broken beyond repair by Rebecca Wyatt. However, Lilly Duvall managed to repair it somewhat, papering over the cracks with a deft hand and making the seams close to invisible. At least for a time. The way she drifted across the dance floor in a cotton print dress and cowboy boots, the way she leaned against the bar, one foot on the rail, drinking her drink and watching him sing, making him feel like every song he sang was not only being performed for her, but had been written for her in the first place . . . It was not one thing, but all of them, yet—in truth—one alone would have been sufficient. And when he was done, she kept on watching him, smiling gently, a bemused expression crossing her face when it became obvious that he was walking directly toward her.

They connected in slow motion. That was how it seemed. Or maybe the rest of the world slowed down. Had it been raining, they could have walked between each drop and never gotten wet.

"You play well," she said. "Good voice, too."

"Thank you."

"I've seen you play before . . . a while back, a couple of months maybe."

"I didn't see you."

She smiled. "You were really drunk."

"I used to do that a lot."

"What happened?"

"That made me drink, or made me stop?"

"Made you stop."

"You get up in the night and realize that you actually don't know your own name. I mean, you really have to think hard to remember your own name. Not even kidding. That makes you think about what else you might forget."

Lilly Duvall held out her hand. "I'm Lilly," she said.

Evan took her hand and held it. "I'm Evan."

"I know who you are, but it's a pleasure to meet you anyway."

151

"Can I get you a drink?"

"I only drink with drinkers, and you're not a drinker anymore."

"I drink," Evan said, "but I don't *drink*."

"Then I'll take another Sazerac."

"A what?"

She laughed gently. "Sazerac. It's a New Orleans thing. Bourbon, absinthe, and Herbsaint. Only place you can get it in West Texas is right here, so you picked a good saloon to play in."

Lilly turned and glanced at the bartender. He was elsewhere, but in a heartbeat he was in front of her. Evan would notice that time and again. She got people's attention. Bars, restaurants, clubs, diners, crosswalks, it didn't matter. Lilly Duvall appeared oblivious to it, but she was candlelight and everyone else a moth.

Lilly gave her order, and Evan asked for the same. He put money on the counter.

"So," she said, "how do you wanna do this?"

"Do what?"

"You want to go through the whole 'How are you doing, what's happening in your life,' checking each other out, finding out if we're attached, coming out of something complicated, single, available, all that jazz, or do you just want to give this a go and see what happens?"

Evan smiled. "You're not in the wasting-time business, are you?"

"I haven't got time to waste, Evan. I don't mean the 'Life is too short' stuff, but sometimes you meet someone and you think something good could happen, and most people are too afraid to say or do anything about it. The epitaph for most peoples' lives is 'What if?' Wouldn't you say so?"

The drinks came. It was a good cocktail. Evan Riggs never thought he'd say such a thing, but he did.

"New Orleans was my mother; still is," Lilly said. "French-Creole."

"And your father?"

She shrugged. "Who the hell knows? Who cares? These things happen, right?"

"They do. And you live here now, in Austin?"

"Staying with friends. Came here for a week or so ... oh, I'd say three months back."

Evan laughed. "So, let me get this straight. Your friends have had enough of you. They are kicking you out, and you need somewhere to stay. So you're not actually looking for a boyfriend. You're looking for free accommodation?"

"Boyfriend? Really? You wanna be my *boyfriend*?"

"You are teasing me, Lilly. I'm an outlaw. You tease me, I will shoot you and throw you down a dry well for the rattlesnakes."

"Well, I am French-Creole in my blood, and I will do some fucked-up hoodoo on your skinny white ass and then you'll be sorry."

Evan Riggs lost close to half his drink.

"See?" she said. "The spell is working. You are already losing control of your limbs."

"I think I did that the first time I saw you," Evan said.

Lilly smiled. "Is that what you call outlaw charm?"

"Maybe," Evan said. "Why, is it not working too well?"

She reached out and touched his hand. "It's working just fine, Evan . . . working just fine."

Evan Riggs looked at Lilly Duvall. Somewhere, deep within the recesses of his mind, a light had been switched on. Felt like he could see the way to himself for the very first time since Rebecca. Felt like he'd found a girl who could not make him forget, but make him unafraid to remember what it was like to fall in love.

Before their second drink, he'd fallen. No doubt about it. Fallen like a stone.

153

TWENTY-TWO

Evie was not home. Without a clue as to her whereabouts, Henry was painfully aware of the tenuous and uncertain nature of his situation. He neither belonged here, nor in San Angelo with his mother. He felt rootless and transient. He even considered going back to visit Evan at Reeves, if for no other reason than to establish the motivation for Carson's evident unwillingness to assist in any way. It seemed now that it was less a case of Carson not wishing to help Evan and more a case of Carson not wanting Henry to find Sarah. The question begging for an answer was why.

Glenn Chandler showed up first. Henry had waited a good two hours. It was close to three in the afternoon. The sun was high and bold, and sitting in the truck, he felt like he'd done an overnighter in the Reeves' sweatbox. That was a memory he didn't want to be reminded of, but was reminded anyway.

"Hey, son. What's up?" Chandler asked him. The tone was warm and amicable. Glenn Chandler seemed to Henry to be a good man.

"Just waitin' on Evie," Henry said.

"You're gonna be waitin' a while longer, then," Chandler said. "She's up in Big Lake. She has a cleaning job in a hotel up there."

"Any idea what time she'll be back?"

"If she comes on the bus, she'll be back by six or thereabouts. She finishes up at five, so maybe you wanna go up there and fetch her. She'd appreciate that." Chandler smiled. "She's always asking me to come get her. I tell her get the bus. She says some folks was born to be chauffeured."

"It's not so far," Henry said. "I can go up, sure."

"Well, come and get a cold one and shoot the shit for a while, unless you got someplace else to be."

Henry shook his head. "Only other place I could go is Calvary, and I ain't so welcome there."

"Sheriff Riggs run you out?"

"As good as."

"Best excuse for an asshole that ain't actually the thing itself,"

Chandler said. "Never liked the man, never will. Coupla things happened I didn't tell of last night. Not so polite for dinner conversation, and I ain't a man to talk of others out of school. For Carson Riggs, however, I'll make an exception."

Chandler turned and walked to the porch steps. Henry took this as a cue to follow him.

"One time," Chandler explained when they were seated at the kitchen table, "there was a kid got clipped by a car on one o' them narrow roads out here. This was, I don't know, maybe four or five years back. It was an accident, plain and simple, and I don't believe the driver of the car was even aware that it had happened. It was evening, pretty dark, and he come around a corner and the kid was in the road and that was that. Kid wasn't killed, but he got his legs busted up and suchlike. Anyway, no one is sure of the whys and wherefores, if the driver knew what had happened or what. You drive these roads at night, you clip all sorts of things, animals and whatever, and you don't think to stop. What you gonna do?"

Chandler reached for his beer and took a drink.

"Riggs set himself to finding out what happened. Kid himself remembers it was a dark car, out-of-state plates or somethin'. I don't know the details, but three days later, there's this guy found tied to a bed in a motel room up near Barnhart. Someone has gone to work on his legs with a tire iron or somethin'. Busted 'em to pieces. From what I heard, they were busted so bad he wasn't gonna walk again. There's an investigation or whatever, and they find evidence on the front of his car, a scrap of fabric, a ding, I don't know, that suggests he's hit somethin' with the car. Word had it that Riggs found him and done that to him. Eye for an eye an' all that. Figured he didn't have a hope in hell of proving that he hit that kid, but he was gonna get the kid some justice anyhow."

Henry had listened silently. He had no difficulty imagining Riggs tying some poor unfortunate son of a bitch down to a bed and going at him with a tire iron. The man had a look about him, the kind of look that said such a thing was well within his capability.

"First time I met him, I walked away unsettled," Henry said.

Chandler smiled sardonically. "There are some people you decide to stay away from, or at least don't make a fucking enemy of them, and he sure as hell is one of them."

"You have any further notion of what went on between him and his brother? Why he doesn't want me to find the daughter?"

"Secrets," Chandler said. "That's what it's always about. Basic problem with families is that you don't choose who you get. That's the fundamental flaw right there. You don't choose 'em."

Henry thought of his own father, Jack Alford, gone before he even knew that Nancy Quinn was pregnant, unconcerned regarding the consequences of his own action, and Nancy now drinking herself into an early grave, already losing her grasp on whatever fragile threads tied her to the same world as Henry. His expression gave up his thoughts.

"You got 'em, too, right? The ones you don't know what the hell to do with, the ones you invite and then sorely regret it when they turn out to be just as plumb crazy as you remembered 'em to be." Chandler laughed. "When I was a kid, my folks had a cousin used to come over for Thanksgiving. Drunk from dawn to dusk, telling the kids the worst jokes, teachin' 'em the worst language ... laughing like a hyena when some five-year-old he'd coached said *Fuck you, Mommy* at the dinner table. Real asshole. Anyway, it's the same with all families. Doesn't matter who they are, where they're from, if they're dirt -poor or they shit in high cotton. We all got 'em. Now, whether Evan is the crazy one or it's his brother, or maybe both of them, I don't know, but if there's something serious going on between those two, I sure as hell wouldn't want to get involved."

"I think it's too late," Henry said. "I already dug the hole."

Chandler paused for a moment and then leaned forward. "My girl is a smart one," he said. "I trust her judgment about people, and she says you're a smart one, too. She doesn't fall easy. I'll tell you that much. But she seems to have fallen for you. If I had my choice, I wouldn't have her take up with an unemployed ex-con who's gotten hisself into a scrap with Carson Riggs, but there's no explaining the human heart, is there, Mr. Quinn?"

"No, sir. There isn't."

"Well, for whatever reason, you and she have wound up together, and whatever trouble you're getting' yourself into, she's more than likely gonna get into it, too. She's like her mother that way, you know? She sees a door, she wants to know what's on the other side, especially if it's locked. She sees a dark hole, she wants to climb down it, see if the monsters are real. Some of us choose the safe option, my friend. Chandler girls ain't those people."

"I'll take care of her, Mr. Chandler," Henry said.

"You can't say that, Henry," Chandler replied. "You can't say that without knowing what you're dealing with. And you are evidently the kind of man who makes a promise with the intention of keeping it. Besides, if and when there's trouble, then she's more 'an likely gonna be the one takin' care of you." Chandler gave a wry smile and added, "And if you're plannin' on pursuin' this thing, whatever this thing might be, then I think it's more a question of *when* than *if*."

"Can I ask about Evie's mother, Mr. Chandler?"

"Why so?"

"I am just curious. What happened to her, why you never married again."

"Ain't none of your business, son," Chandler said. "You may be in Evie's good books, but you ain't family. If you ever get to be family, then I'll have that conversation with you, but until then I'll just politely decline."

"I apologize if—"

Chandler smiled, and it was sincere and genuine. "You don't got nothing to apologize for, son. I ain't bein' ornery about it, and I ain't offended. And I sure as hell ain't concerned if Evie tells you whatever she wants, but family is family, and you ain't there yet."

Henry understood; seemed that when it came to Glenn Chandler, there was what you saw and what you got and they were invariably the same thing.

"So, you gon' go get her, or what?"

"I'm gonna go get her," Henry said.

"I'll give you the address where she's working. She finishes up at five, so if you're outside o' there, you'll surprise her."

Chandler scribbled down the address. "You won't have any difficulty findin' it. It's on the main drag."

"Appreciated."

"You comin' on back here for dinner?" Chandler asked.

"I don't know. Figured maybe I'd take her out or something."

Chandler looked thoughtful. "Ah, well, this here's where you and I are gonna have to have words, son. You start taking her out, then I'm gonna be sat here with a knife and fork and little else in front of me."

Henry opened his mouth to speak.

Chandler smiled, laughed a little. "Go," he said. "I'm yankin' your chain. You ain't back here by seven or thereabouts, I'll take care of my own dinner."

Henry finished his beer, thanked Chandler, shook the man's hand.

"This thing with Riggs," Chandler said as a final comment. "You hear a rattler, first thing to know is where he's at—if he's behind you, if you're in his line of sight. Sometimes running is the worst thing to do, you know? Sometimes you just stand your ground and let him pass by. Main thing is not to give him cause to take a snap at you. Know what I mean?"

"I do, yes."

"I hope so, son. 'Cause if any harm comes to Evie and it's of your doin', there'll be a standoff. And I ain't gonna be like Carson Riggs, I assure you. I ain't comin' around corners when you least expect it. I'm comin' at you dead square, and I'll be carryin' a thirty-aught-six. Maybe somethin' bigger."

Henry nodded, didn't say a word. One thing he'd learned at Reeves is that sometimes any word was a word too many.

Evie's surprise pleased him. She was genuinely shocked to see Henry standing there at the side of the pickup across the street from the hotel.

"Holy crap, Henry Quinn. What the hell is this?"

"Saw your pa. He told me where you was at, and I figured I'd come get you."

She threw her arms around him and kissed him hard on the mouth.

Henry was a little taken aback himself, but in a good way.

"So what's the deal?" she said once she was in the cab and the engine was started.

"Can go on back home if you want, or I can take you someplace for dinner."

"Someplace sounds good," she said.

Henry put the truck in gear and pulled away from the curb. "I had a talk with your pa."

"Uh-huh?"

"He told me about Riggs. Something that happened a while back." Henry repeated the story of the busted legs, then added, "Dangerous man, potentially, and he has warned me off again. He really don't want me lookin' any more."

"He told you that already, Henry. How many times do you need to be reminded?"

"Enough times to get it through my thick skull, I guess."

"Is it through yet?"

"Don't reckon it is."

"That's what I figured." Evie put her heels up on the dash, took a cigarette from a packet in her jeans jacket pocket, and lit it. "So what you gonna do?"

"Gonna keep asking questions 'til I get some answers."

"Or he ties you to a motel bed and breaks your legs with a tire iron."

"I guess so, yes."

"So why do you owe so much to Evan Riggs, Henry? What is the deal there? I get that he dragged you out of a fight an' all, but that kinda thing has gotta happen plenty in jail. You got something going on with Evan Riggs that your girlfriend doesn't want to know about? Was Henry Quinn a cute little prison wife, maybe?"

Henry laughed. "Sure. That was it right there. You got me, baby."

"No, seriously. Why do you have to find this girl?"

Henry took Evie's cigarette from her, took a drag, handed it back. "Sometimes you cross paths with someone," he said. "There's something there. You can't name it or label it. It just is. Evan Riggs is me, you know? Bad decisions, moment of weakness, moment of stupidity, and I could be there. Evan's gonna die in Reeves. He knows he's got one shot at leaving something of value behind. At least that's the way I believe he thinks. His daughter, for better or worse, is his daughter, and maybe he's not taken into consideration that she might not want to be found, I don't know, but he has his mind set on this one thing, and I made a promise I would see it through." Henry looked sideways at Evie and smiled ruefully. "I didn't think there was anything to it but delivering a letter. I didn't know that Evan's brother was going to get in the road like a fallen telegraph pole, but he has, and now I have to deal with it."

"So you're gonna keep looking for her no matter what Carson Riggs does?"

"Well, I can only look so long, but yes, I guess I've made that decision."

"Only look so long?" she asked. "Meaning?"

"Meaning that if he kills me, then the game is over, ain't it?"

"You think it's that serious?"

"Sweetheart, I don't even know what the *it* is, let alone whether or not it's that serious."

"He's warned you off twice now," Evie said. "Looks serious to me."

"Well, right now there's no law against trying to find Sarah Riggs or whatever the hell name she goes by, and the more people tell me to be careful, the less careful I want to be."

"Regular kind of man, then," Evie said, lowering the window an inch or two further.

"And if you want to stay out of this, I understand completely."

Evie laughed. "You don't know me at all," she said. "You may have fucked me, but you don't know me, Henry Quinn. Nope, I'm in this 'til the bitter end. I'm like you, I guess. Someone tells me not to fetch down the cookie jar, then not only am I gonna fetch it down, but I'm gonna eat every damn cookie in there even if it makes me sick as a dog."

Henry laughed, and then he glanced sideways at her. She had a smile on her face, but there was a coolness in her eyes, a flicker of anxiety perhaps.

"Bring it on, Carson Riggs," she said.

So now he knew. Whatever they were cooking up, they were in it together. Okay, so they weren't on some wild spree of robbing banks and shooting folk, but there was trouble up the line. Five days out of Reeves, and there was something going on. Henry could feel it in his bones. Bonnie and Clyde, Dillinger and Billie Frechette, Starkweather and that poor dumb teenage girlie he dragged along for the ride. Not such good precedents.

"Now you gotta feed me," Evie said, interrupting his thoughts. "Hungry enough to eat shoelaces and bottle caps."

TWENTY-THREE

Lilly Duval: muse, inspiration, lover, friend, the beginning and end of so much.

Love changed the world, both for those who were in love and those who were not. Determining when loving someone became being *in love* was indeterminable. Something they said, something they did, an idiosyncrasy of character that was theirs and theirs alone? The simple fact that such an idiosyncrasy became achingly endearing, that you were the only person in the world who could see it, and thus you somehow became more special in your own eyes. Loving someone helped you love yourself a little more, perhaps. That was how it worked for Evan Riggs. Loving this girl made reality more real. He wrote more, more than he'd ever done, and not just songs of love. He wrote from the gut as well as the heart, and sometimes he would find lyrics that surprised even himself. "Lord, I Done So Wrong." "I'll Try and Be a Better Man." It was during this time that such plaintive expositions of the soul were penned, and few were the times he dared to ask if she could ever mean as much as Rebecca. He knew she could not, that no one ever could, but Lilly somehow consumed his thoughts and emotions so as to leave room for little else. Rebecca, at least for a while, was a ghost of something that might have been but never was.

There was an edge to the woman, a spectrum of colors that erred toward the dark and shadowed. Perhaps there was just a greater part of everything, the ability to love and to love life matched by an ability to hate whatever opposed her. She fought, and fought with ferocity. She railed against conformity, acceptance, banality, against that which she perceived as *safe* and *normal*. She was bohemian, a firebrand, a wire so live that the very air around her seemed to crack and snap with electricity. Against her, Evan knew that he did not possess anything like the gypsy blood his mother had jokingly suggested.

And yet, as with all people, Lilly was a contradiction, sometimes spending days in bed, wishing to do nothing, seemingly exhausted with the effort of forcing life to be interesting. Perhaps she believed that merely being alive entitled her to something, that she should not have to work so hard, that there should not be so many reasons and obstacles and deprivations.

"Why is it all so shit?" she would ask Evan, and yet be unable to define what *all* actually was.

A month, seeing her every day, almost every hour of every day, made Evan aware that a life with Lilly Duval would be no ordinary life. Everything was drama. There was no middle ground. It was extravagant and wild, or it was nothing, and the nothing was to be challenged and argued with and defied.

Perhaps he began to better appreciate the decision Rebecca had made in letting him go, how her refusal to follow him was more to do with saving herself from something almost destructive in its intensity than any real measure of her love for him.

Three months with Lilly and the edges were wearing thin. Even sex seemed driven by some other purpose, as if fucking each other was an act of revenge against something or someone unknown.

Nine months in and Evan felt himself start to disconnect. Just a little, but he did disconnect. He watched himself as if from a distance, finally refusing to become embroiled in the furor of her emotions. There were no half measures, no respite, no breathing space, and where he had at first found her passion and hunger for life somehow energizing, it was now enervating. The attention that had once seemed so perfectly validating of everything that he was, now felt claustrophobic and oppressive. A fight with Lilly about some meaningless detail left him exhausted, not only mentally and emotionally, but spiritually.

Close to Christmas of 1947, the train came off the rails.

Evan played a bar in Round Rock, night of Friday the twelfth of December. Just a small place, maybe thirty or forty regulars, but it was a good set and he was well received, hollered at for three encores and a crowd at the bar waiting to get him drunk. And he got drunk. So drunk he did not make it home until the following day.

"I was here all night waiting for you," she said.

"I know, and I'm sorry," he replied.

She stood in the kitchen doorway. She had on her fighting face, the eyes that said *I'm winning this one, asshole,* and Evan was hung-over and tired and he'd driven back as early as he could, and his mouth tasted like a goat had bedded down in there, and he didn't need it.

Hand on her hip, that sass in her stance that said she wasn't moving until there was an explanation that would satisfy, forgetting—as always—that there was no such thing as a satisfactory explanation.

"Sorry isn't gonna be enough, is it?" he asked.

She smiled, and there was a cruel flash in her eyes. He had left her behind. That was the point. It was not that she suspected the attention of other women. Nothing like that. It was simply that something had happened, something that might have relieved her boredom, and she had been excluded. It would only be later that Evan would begin to understand this state of mind, the sense that whatever was happening now, however good or exciting or new or fresh or interesting it might have been, there was always the chance that there was something better going on elsewhere. It was an inability to *be* in that moment. People could spend their whole lives elsewhere, all the while oblivious to the wonders right before their eyes. Had he understood that at the time, he might have been able to do something about it, but he did not, and thus was impotent.

"It's not a matter of sorry, Evan. It's a matter of thoughtlessness. You could have called me, told me you were going to stay. I could have driven over there. It's twenty miles, goddamnit. I could have stayed overnight with you, and we could have had breakfast together and whatever."

"You're right," Evan said. "I didn't think."

"Is it because you didn't want me there?"

"No."

"Then why?"

"Because I didn't think. Because I played a set, I had a drink, then another one, and the more I drank, the less I thought. That was all there was to it. There is nothing else to it. There is nothing else to read into it or try to understand. I fucked up. I am sorry. I apologize. I will do my best not to be so thoughtless in the future, okay?"

"The sarcasm isn't appreciated, Evan," she said, and she glowered at him.

"I wasn't being sarcastic."

"Sounded sarcastic to me."

"Okay, well, it wasn't meant that way. What I am saying and what you are hearing are not always the same thing."

"Meaning what?"

Evan stood facing her, his hand on his guitar case, his mind slipping its moorings.

"I know that look," she said.

"Do you, Lilly? Do you really? Well, enlighten me, sweetheart. Why don't you tell me what my face is telling you right now? I would love to hear it."

"Sometimes you are such an asshole, Evan Riggs."

"Sometimes you are such a bitch, Lilly Duvall."

"Is this the way it's going to be?"

"Is this the way *what* is going to be?"

"Our life together. You forget me and I get angry, and then we fight, and then we fuck, and then we wait for it to happen all over again."

"Is that how you think our life is?"

"That seems to be how it's going, Evan."

"You are fucking crazy sometimes, Lilly. In fact, no, you are not crazy. You are driving *me* crazy. This is bullshit. This is just wild. I don't know where the hell you get these ideas from, but they seem to be based on nothing that I can even see, let alone anything that I think is actually happening. Seems to me you are angling for a fight, and I am wondering why—"

"I could say the same about you ... leaving me back here on my own."

Evan fell silent, inside and out. He was exhausted. He didn't want the battle. He sighed quietly and then turned and headed back toward the door of the apartment.

"You're leaving?" Lilly asked.

"Yes, I am, Lilly."

"Asshole."

Evan turned back. "Enough now," he said.

"Meaning what?"

"Meaning nothing more nor less than that, Lilly. I love you, but this is driving me crazy. I don't know how to make you happy. I don't know how to make you stop fighting the world—"

"I am not fighting the world," she interjected.

"You *are*, sweetheart, and you know you are. I have lived with you for a year, and I see it every day. I even see it when you are enjoying yourself. There is always some tiny facet of you that wants something better or different. You know what it's like? It's like talking to someone who's always looking for someone more interesting to talk to, and it wears me out."

"You're leaving me," she said matter-of-factly.

Evan smiled. "I am not leaving you."

"But you want to."

"No, I don't."

"You've stopped loving me," she said, as if whatever now passed her lips was an undeniable truth.

"It's not a question of how much I love you, Lilly, but *who* I love. I don't love the person you are being right now, not the person you believe you have to be in order to get what you want."

"That doesn't even make sense," she snapped.

"Yes, it does. And you know it makes sense, and that is why you are getting defensive."

"Fuck you, Evan."

Evan smiled again, which aggravated her further.

"You can't just walk up to someone and tell them what to think about who they are," she said.

"Yes, you can," Evan replied. "And I just did."

"Well, you're wrong."

"I am always wrong, Lilly, even when I'm right. That's the point."

"I can't talk to you. You contradict yourself and you make no sense."

"Okay," Evan said resignedly, and once more he headed for the door.

"You really are leaving me, aren't you?" Lilly asked, and in her voice there was a slight shadow of anxiety, as if she was wondering if she had pushed him too far.

"Yes," Evan said, "I am leaving you for about fifteen minutes. I am going to the store to get some cigarettes and some beer, and then I will come back. Do you want me to get you anything?"

Lilly looked at him wide-eyed. There was an emptiness in her expression. He felt something then, some strange sense of uncertainty, but he did not trust his intuition. He let the moment go.

His hand on the door, Evan glanced back at her and smiled. It was an artless, simple smile, an effort to lighten the mood, to relax her, to make her feel at ease, but she did not smile back.

He should not have gone. He knew it in that second. It was the same as that final moment with Rebecca, knowing he should have said something but staying silent.

Evan Riggs left the apartment and walked to the store. He bought cigarettes, half a dozen bottles of beer, and a box of Ritz crackers.

As he'd told Lilly, he was gone no more than fifteen minutes, but a quarter of an hour was all it took.

By the time he got back, it was too late.

TWENTY-FOUR

That which had been suspected was proven out, at least by intuition and observation, that evening at the saloon in Calvary.

Ames, Sperling, Mills, and Eakins were present, and when Henry Quinn and Evie Chandler starting plying them with drinks and questions, the seams began to unravel. For there *were* seams, pulled tight from one to the other and back again, and there were moments when one would look to another, and both Henry and Evie knew that some unspoken agreement was in force. *Someone speak first, then I will speak; until then I am silent.*

"I am not saying that Carson Riggs's continued presence as sheriff is incorrect," Harold Mills ventured, "but Warren, being a lawyer an' all, said there might have been questions asked about the veracity of those elections ... whether or not the votes placed and the votes counted were one and the same thing."

"Isn't there some kind of limit as to how many terms someone can serve as sheriff?" Henry asked. "I mean, from what I can work out, Riggs has been sheriff for the better part of thirty years. That can't be right."

"Garfield's the man who'd have known," Sperling said. "But he up and died at the end of May."

"How did he die?" Evie asked.

"Heart gave out," Ames said. "Right there at his desk."

"And no one has ever really challenged Riggs for the position?" Henry asked.

George Eakins leaned forward, his elbows on the table, his hands nursing the glass of whiskey before him. "This isn't San Angelo, kid," he said. "Life in a city and life in some small backwater town are not the same thing at all. Here you say something, everyone knows it in an hour. Everyone is living out of one another's pockets. That's the way it is, the way it's always been, probably the way it will always be."

"Things are the way they are because no one changes them," Evie said.

Clarence smiled. "The voice of youth."

"The voice of truth," Evie said. "Seems to me you guys are frightened of Carson Riggs. You flinch every time his name is mentioned."

There was a definite cooling of the atmosphere then. Henry sensed it, felt it, looked at each man in turn and knew that Evie had voiced something that none of them had wanted to hear.

"Careful now, young lady," Roy Sperling said, almost under his breath. "You don't go saying things like that if you want to keep your friends."

Evie Chandler smiled, started to laugh. It broke the tension. "Oh, come on, guys!" she said. "You know what I mean. Hell, this guy backs everyone off. Henry's here trying to find something out, trying to help a friend, and all he gets is brick walls and bullshit. Someone must know something about what happened between Evan and Carson."

"Their mother," Harold Mills said, and if there had been a cooling of the atmosphere in the saloon before, it then became positively icy.

Ames looked at him, Sperling, too, and there was an unspoken hostility in their response. It was unclear who wished for this history to be revealed and who wished for things to remain unquestioned.

"Their mother?" Henry said. "She's alive?"

Clarence Ames looked away and down, shook his head in seeming disapproval. Something was definitely not right. Some line had been crossed.

"Hey," Evie said. "What's the deal here? Carson's and Evan's mother is alive?"

Harold Mills nodded. "She's alive, yes."

"Where?" Evie asked.

"Someplace out in Odessa, far as I know," Mills said.

"Enough, Harold," Ames said. "You can't send these people out there . . . harassing some old woman who can barely remember her own name."

"Old?" Harold said. "Grace Riggs is not so much older than you. And maybe they should go out there. Maybe they should start some trouble, Clarence. Been a long time since there's been any real trouble in Calvary. Warren said it a few times, didn't he? That we should all tell him to go fuck himself, and to hell with the consequences."

"You're drunk," Ames said. He turned to Henry and Evie, smiled somewhat resignedly. "Pay no mind to him," he told them. "He's drunk." It was clear that Mills was not drunk, clearer still that Ames was angry with him for speaking of Grace Riggs.

"I am not drunk, Clarence," Mills said. "Nothing to do with liquor. Hell, maybe it is . . . If I had a good deal more, I might open my fucking mouth and never shut it."

"You go ahead and do that, Harold. See what the hell happens," Ames said.

"You think I wouldn't?" Mills retorted, his voice edged with animosity now. "You think I wouldn't say to hell with all of this . . . all of you. Take one last stab at that—"

"Enough!" Roy Sperling said sharply, cutting them all dead.

Silence hung awkwardly in the middle of the room. There was no going back. Words had been spoken that could neither be retrieved nor forgotten.

Henry Quinn and Evie Chandler perceived a sense of quiet terror. It was tangible; the air was cold and electric.

Henry got up from his chair. "We're going," he told Evie.

Evie got up without a word.

"Thank you for the drink, gentlemen," Henry said. "Next time it's on me."

He turned and started toward the door. He reached out his hand behind him, and Evie took it.

"Mr. Quinn."

Henry stopped, turned back, and looked toward the small gathering.

"Man digs a hole, he better shore up the sides," Clarence Ames said. "Last thing he wants to do is go and bury himself."

Evie opened her mouth to respond, but Henry squeezed her hand and she said nothing.

They left the saloon and walked back to Henry's truck, and neither of them said a word.

An hour later, sitting beside each other in the Chandler house, *McCloud* on the TV with the sound turned down, Evie's father evident in his absence, the conversation could not have been about anything but what they'd witnessed and heard that evening in the saloon.

"He's got something on them," Evie said.

"All of them," Henry replied, "and maybe not the same thing. He has been sheriff for nearly thirty years, for Christ's sake. Every misdemeanor, every wrongdoing, every fuckup . . . It's a small town. He must know everything that happens, every little secret."

"And he keeps them in check and he keeps getting voted in."

"And the mother," Henry said. "Evan never said a thing about her. I never even suspected that she was still alive. I want to go to Odessa and talk to the mother."

"We have no idea where she is, Henry. Odessa ain't Calvary. I don't think you can stop the first person you see in the street and they'll tell you."

"We ask Harold Mills," Henry said. "There's a man who wants to talk if ever I saw one."

"Tonight? Tomorrow?"

"Tomorrow," Henry said.

"And tonight?"

"I wanna get drunk and do stuff to you that's nearly illegal," Henry said.

Evie laughed. "Hell, soldier, why stop at *nearly* illegal?"

TWENTY-FIVE

The apartment entrance was off a walkway. At the end of the walkway there was a flight of wrought-iron steps down to the street. It was one flight, maybe twelve or fifteen feet. By the time Evan returned to the lower step of that flight, he knew something was awry.

A gentleman dances with the one that brung him.

Someone said that to him one time. He couldn't remember who or when or why, but it had stayed with him. It meant so many things, and all of them were about loyalty.

Later he would ask questions that could never be answered, and there would be so very many of them.

Later he would turn all of it back upon himself, and she would be blameless and perfect, and he would be the worst kind of man for any woman, and there would be nothing right about what he had said or done. He had broken promises. He had lied. He had deserted her. He had made her life a misery. He had used her to fill a vacuum left by Rebecca, and that—in itself—was the greatest lie of all. He had told Lilly that he loved her so many times, and yet he didn't even know the meaning of the word.

This was his penance. Of course it was. If not, then how could this have happened?

Halfway up the stairs, he set down the bag he was carrying. Why did he set it down? He did not know then, and he could not explain it in hindsight.

He just *knew*.

He would write a song about this moment. It would be called "No Time Left." He would never perform it. He would never even sing it after the day it was completed.

As he reached the end of the walkway and started down toward the door of the apartment, a quiet feeling of panic started in his lower gut. He had felt this before. Stronger then, walking down to the barn and finding that Rocket had vanished. He remembered it vividly, the sense that something was so terribly, terribly wrong, and

170

one thing could never be wrong by itself . . . There would be other things wrong, things spiraling out of control, one small catastrophe somehow drawing other greater catastrophes and disasters into its orbit. Eventually it would all be a black hole of despair and panic and horror . . .

Evan Riggs forced such things out of his mind.

He reached the apartment door. He pushed it, but it did not give. He had neither closed it nor locked it. He turned the handle. Again, the door did not give.

His heart skipped.

Evan raised his hand and knocked. He waited no more than five seconds and knocked again.

"Lilly?" he called out. "Lilly, open the door, for Christ's sake. This is just dumb."

Nothing.

He knocked again. Clenched his fist and pounded. Heart matching rhythm, but pressure inside now, like something coming to the boil.

He looked left and right as if to find someone or something that would tell him what he didn't know.

Was she just being mischievous? Was she meting out a little punishment for his failure to come home, his failure to call, his failure to inform her? For all his little failures.

Was this all that it was? Or was there something else happening? Was there something more serious?

"Lilly? Sweetheart?" he called, louder this time. There was no way she would not have heard him. The apartment was small. Four rooms: bathroom, kitchen, bedroom, a narrow living room where they would sit and talk and watch TV and sometimes he would read lyrics and sing melodies to her and she would say, *That is so beautiful, Evan . . . That breaks my heart . . .*

And now the pressure he feels is breaking his heart. Surely a heart cannot survive such a thunderous assault . . . panic swelling up like some dark spread of blood in water, like a black flower of despair that buries its roots deep into the very core of self, the petals filling the chest, the odor rank and fetid and poisonous.

This is not happening.

Evan remembered thinking that. He was behind himself. That's how it felt. As if he were right there on the walkway watching himself as he beat on the door, having to step aside as other people came out of their apartments, people he knew, people saying, *Is everything okay, Evan? What's happening, Evan? Jeez, Evan... give it a rest, man,* until they understood that this was real life, that this wasn't Evan once more drunk and raging, that this wasn't Evan drunk and fighting with Lilly or Lilly mad with Evan yet again and trying to break down the door to get to him and rail at him for some other foolish stunt he'd pulled...

This was life in its realest form, and it did not look good.

People came to help.

Evan was back inside himself. His shoulder was against the door. Couldn't have been more than a minute since he'd first knocked, and yet it seemed as if he had been prevaricating for an hour.

What would have happened if he had acted immediately?

What might have he been able to do had he gotten through that door without delay?

In truth, nothing, but rationality and logic parted company as soon as panic and fear showed up for the party.

The door went through on the third attempt.

He *knew* then without doubt.

There were people behind him as he rushed through the living room, the kitchen, the bedroom, all the way to the bathroom, where he had lain beside her in the overflowing tub, a tub too small for two, but both of them drunk and laughing and so very much in love, candles lighting the room with a multitude of halos, late nights beside each other, talking of things that they wanted, things they would do together, things they could never do with anyone else... traveling the world and seeing wonders and making friends and gathering into their collective experience those things that only they and they alone would fully understand and appreciate. That was the life they had planned. That was the life that should have happened.

The blood spooled through the water like clouds being born. Scarlet, slow-motion clouds.

She had cut her arms from elbow to wrist, the full length, the full nine yards. Her veins had opened up without resistance, given her an irreversible escape route out of whatever desperate unreality within which she imagined she was living.

What she believed and what actually was could never have been the same thing.

Anything can be changed.

Tomorrow will always be different.

Most things come easier after a good sleep and a long laugh.

Not this time.

Evan dropped to his knees at the side of the tub.

Fifteen minutes, maybe less. He grabbed her arms, and the blood filled the spaces between his fingers as he lifted her from the tub.

Evan could not speak. But he could scream, and the sound came from deep inside him, somewhere primitive and ancient, and he pulled her close and held her so tight, and she looked back at him with that unmistakable deadlight in her eyes.

Standing then, he turned, and there were people crowding the bathroom.

His voice returned. "Get back!" he shouted. "Get out of the way! Goddamn you, get out of the fucking way!"

The huddle parted, and Evan staggered through into the bedroom, the living room, out onto the walkway beyond the front door of the apartment, and Lilly seemed to weigh nothing at all, as if every drop of blood within her had now been emptied out.

He kicked over the brown paper bag on the way down the steps. The bottles of beer he'd bought bounced down the steps. Two of them broke, and beer spilled out into the dirt. He would have opened that beer with Lilly. He would have opened a bottle of cold beer and passed it to her, and she would have smiled the way she always did after they'd fought, after the emotional dust had settled, and he would tell her she was no good for him, and she would tell him how he couldn't live without her, and then she would laugh and tell him he was more of an asshole than she was a bitch, and then he would pull her close and they would stay like that for some endless time, and he would tell her once again that he was sorry, and he would mean it with every atom of his being, and then everything would go back to battery until the next time.

Now there would be no next time.

Now there would be nothing.

Evan dropped to his knees in the dirt at the bottom of the steps. He cradled her in his arms, and he knew she was dead.

He'd known that from the first moment he'd seen her lying there within a scarlet, slow-motion cloud of her own blood.

To Evan, in that moment, it all seemed to have been borne out of a lie. If he had stayed back in Calvary, this never would have happened. If Rebecca had left with him, this never would have happened.

But it happened, and it happened in a heartbeat.

All done and over with: the passion, the promise of the future, the life they would have created together.

The end of one thing is not always the beginning of something else; sometimes it is just the end.

It was twenty minutes before an ambulance showed up.

The attending medic was named Don Halliday, and he'd seen it all before.

TWENTY-SIX

Henry Quinn woke beside Evie Chandler and wondered what he had done to bring all of this upon himself. He believed he had lost all connection to whatever his life might have been before Reeves.

For a short while he lay there as Evie slept, her father making the sounds of someone trying not to make a sound, and then he left the house, the banging of the screen perhaps an accident. Evie stirred, but she did not wake, and Henry slid out from beside her and put on his jeans and T-shirt.

He did not leave the room but took a chair from near the wall and set it in front of the window. Sunday morning, the sky bright, the breeze uncharacteristically fresh for West Texas, as if the arid wind that so often drew everything from you had now acceded to the notion of giving something back.

Henry thought of Evan. He missed the man, and though un-afraid to voice his feelings, he perhaps missed him more than he would have been willing to say. And even if he chose to speak of it, what would he say? That one of the most important people of his life was a killer he'd known for less than three years? It made no sense.

Henry thought of his mother, too; if she and Howard Ulysses were drunk and fighting or drunk and getting along great. Or just drunk.

If he was completely honest, he cared more for what was hap-pening with Evan than he did for what was happening with his mother. They were mother and son, sure, but they had never con-nected. He was, after all, an accident, and though she had never said or done anything intended to make him feel that way, it was still an inescapable truth that sat between them like an unwanted member of the family. They both were aware of it, but never said a word. That was how they dealt with it.

That morning, the morning he got drunk and fired the handgun, the morning he nigh on killed Sally O'Brien and simultaneously fucked his own immediate life beyond repair, was perhaps the single most complete expression of his own desperate frustration. It begged the question: How much of what happens to us is determined by a single, nonchalant thought? That carefree, throwaway *I wish*... becomes the force majeure, and then everything changes, perhaps rapidly, even more likely in increments and inches, sometimes so slowly you don't even notice... and then you're looking back and wondering how the hell you ended up here.

Started with a thought, and that was all that was needed.

Henry glanced back as Evie stirred.

She stretched, opened her eyes, saw him sitting there, and smiled. "What you doin'?"

Henry smiled back. Sometimes she surprised him with her beauty. "Just thinking."

"Surgeon General health warning against that," Evie said. She leaned up, the sheet falling from her and exposing her throat, her breasts, her stomach.

"Dad gone?"

"Yes."

"Every Sunday he goes out to put flowers on my mom's grave."

"Where is she buried?"

"Hundred and something miles away," Evie said. "Done it for years, no matter the weather, no matter what else is going on."

"True love, huh?"

Evie frowned. "I don't know, Henry... Maybe it's just that he can't let go. Sometimes I wonder if he does it out of guilt."

"Guilt... for what?"

Evie shrugged, brushed her bangs from her eyes. "Christ knows, Henry."

She slid from the bed, sat naked on the edge of the mattress. "We gonna go to Odessa and find Grace Riggs, right?"

Henry nodded. "Go see Harold Mills first and ask him if there's anything else he wants to tell us."

"You think he'll talk?" Evie asked as she tugged a T-shirt over her head and fetched clean underwear from the drawer against the wall.

"Seems like he wanted to last night," Henry said.

Evie smiled knowingly. "The previous night and the following morning can be a thousand years different, right?"

Henry nodded. "Yep."

She made eggs. Henry wasn't so hungry, but he ate a few mouthfuls out of courtesy. He drank three cups of coffee, though, and asked

Evie if her father had given any indication that Henry's presence might be a problem.

"My dad is a *What you see is what you get* guy," she said. "Maybe the last of a long line. If there's a problem, he'll tell you. He'll tell you nice, but he will definitely tell you. Besides, he likes you."

"He does? How can you tell?"

"Has he told you to get the fuck out of his house?"

"No."

"Then he likes you, Henry. Don't sweat it. Sometimes you are too well-behaved for your own good."

"Meaning?"

"Meaning that you're not in Reeves anymore. You don't always have to color inside the lines. Most of the time it's perfectly okay to be nothing but yourself."

"And the rest of the time?" Henry asked.

"Be someone better."

Henry laughed. "Where the hell did you come from, Evie Chandler?"

"Fell from heaven, didn't I?" she said. "Isn't it obvious?"

Henry drove. Evie knew where the Mills house was, but she suggested they park up the block and walk down. It was a little after nine. If the Millses were heading to church, they would be going soon enough.

Harold Mills was sitting out on the veranda. He was smoking a pipe, perhaps forbidden to do so indoors, and when he saw Evie Chandler and Henry Quinn turn the corner, there was a definite shift in the atmosphere. For a moment it seemed he was going to stand and greet them, but he went right on sitting there, his back against the front wall of the house, his feet outstretched. He was dressed smart—a shirt and tie, his pants pressed, his boots polished.

"Wondered if you'd show," he said when they were within earshot.

"Harold," Evie said. "You okay?"

"Could be better," he replied, "but isn't that always the case?"

Henry didn't speak. He waited for Mills to broach the subject that they all knew was coming.

"Sometimes a man opens his mouth when he should just keep the darn thing shut," Mills said.

"Last night," Evie replied.

"Last night, last week, last year, it don't matter when," Mills went on. "But what a man says is nowhere near as important as what he does. And what he does is sometimes far less important than what he doesn't do." Mills drew on the pipe, using the moment to consider what he was going to say next. It very much seemed that way to Henry, that Mills was choosing words carefully, considering what to say, how best to say it.

"If you want to go out and see Grace Riggs in Odessa, I don't believe anyone will stop you," he said. "From what I hear, she's as crazy as a shithouse rat. Can't imagine she'll be able to help you better understand much of anything, to be honest, but you never know. Sometimes the crazy ones went crazy because they saw more truth than anyone else."

"What happened with that family?" Evie asked.

Mills looked momentarily surprised. "You think this is about the family, sweetheart?" He smiled resignedly, shook his head. "This isn't about a family, my dear. This is about a whole town, maybe a whole county. Sometimes you don't ask a question for the sole reason that you know how bad the answer's gonna be."

"And this all has something to do with Evan's daughter?"

Harold Mills shrugged. It was not the shrug of a man who did not know, but that of man who did not *want* to know. Everything about him said that forgetting, perhaps even pretending to never have known in the first place, was sometimes so much more preferable than reality. Reality meant responsibility; responsibility meant confronting the fact that there were things that should have been done that were not.

"Where is she?" Evie asked.

"Odessa, like I said," Mills replied. "Some nuthouse out there. They call it a rest home or some such. You want to find it, you'll find it. They don't say so, but it's part of the Ector County Hospital. Like most things, they dress it up as something it ain't."

"Did Carson put her there?" Henry asked. It was the first time he'd spoken, and it was a question that raised a knowing smile on Harold Mills's face.

Mills paused for some time before he said anything, and the silence became tangibly uncomfortable. When he did finally speak, it was to Evie, almost as if the question had arrived from the ether and Henry was not there at all.

"I've said all I'm gonna say, and if you want to go digging holes and looking for stuff, then you knock yourself out."

He turned then, suddenly, and walked back into the house. The door slammed shut behind him like a gunshot.

Evie looked at Henry. Henry looked back at Evie.

"Fuck," she said, and that, too, was like the sound of a gun in the still morning air.

TWENTY-SEVEN

Evan Riggs's life did not modulate gracefully into a minor key; it dropped with all the force of gravity.

Like a cold stone from a great height, Evan's emotional state plunged into the deepest reaches of despair and self-hatred. He could not have believed himself more guilty for what had happened to Lilly Duvall. Perhaps he did not wish to believe himself anything other than solely responsible, looking to punish himself for so many things that may have led to her suicide: the small betrayals, the lies, the deceptions, the times he ignored or neglected or set aside her importances in place of his own. These were things of which all humans were guilty, an incumbent and inherent aspect of all relationships, but some believed themselves more culpable than others. Looking to punish self for both the real and the imagined, any motivation would serve. Evan believed himself the guiltiest of all. Perhaps it was his nature to be melodramatic, to be the artist, the tortured poet; perhaps he was looking to fuel the fires of creativity with something dark and possessed. Whatever the rationale, it was a heavy coat he cut for himself, and he wore it irrespective of the weather.

Never once in those initial weeks did he consider the possibility that he may not have been complicit. Never once did he look beyond himself for the cause of her death. The truth, in fact, was that Lilly Duvall had been on a self-destruct mission for years, her suicide the final act of a performance lasting more than two decades. Perhaps she had merely become exhausted with remembering lines, writing new scenes, recognizing that those who shared the stage with her were not there of their own volition. That last vain declaration of abandonment had been her curtain call, an invitation for an encore that never came, and so she bowed out in the most dramatic way she could imagine. History would write her as some tragic Shakespearean character, a Lavinia, an Ophelia perhaps, but history was as good a liar as any Machiavelli. In the final analysis, the facade stripped away, the scenery taken down, Lilly Duvall's suicide was an act of selfishness. She died to make others feel guilty for her own inherent shortcomings.

Evan did not write for a long time, and then the songs he wrote were moody and somber. Those songs he had earlier created now became something else, something so much darker and more introspective. The people who came to hear him changed, too—no longer the lovers of classic country melodies and soulful ballads, but those also seeking some kind of tacit consent and agreement that life was forever tinged with sadness and desperation.

And Evan drank. He did not drink to quench some physical thirst, but to douse some inner fire that raged unseen. However much he drank, the fire raged on, and the violent shifts in temperament became too much to bear. Those around him either escaped, or they were drawn into this dark orbit and turned inside out.

The decline of Evan Riggs did not end in a fall. A woman had sent him into a tailspin that lasted for the better part of six months, and he finally reached a point where he knew he would have to level out, climb once more, or keep on heading down until he crashed for good.

Morning of Sunday, March 21, 1948, Evan Riggs woke on the floor in the back room of a bar. He had evidently collapsed dead drunk, been locked inside, and everyone had gone home none the wiser. He went into the bar itself, found a glass, headed for the first bottle of bourbon. He poured a good three inches, raised it to his lips, and stopped. There was a mirror behind the bar, and he could see himself as clear as day. That—it seemed—was enough, for he tipped the bourbon back into the bottle and put the empty glass in the sink.

He could hear his mother.

Show me anyone who ever got anything done by being weak and I'll be weak, Evan. You show me one person who hasn't made a mess of things. It happens. It's called life. You get past it. You deal with what happened.

The choice was there, plain as day.

Evan started cleaning the bar. He swept; he washed glasses; he straightened chairs and tables and cleaned the windows. He worked hard. By the time the owner turned up at four, Evan was flat-out exhausted.

"Hey, what the hell is this?" the guy said. "What you doin' in here?"

Evan smiled. "Got locked in here, woke up, figured I'd clean the place up a bit."

The man came forward. "What's your name?"

"Riggs. Evan Riggs."

"You didn't drink nothin, rob the till?"

Evan laughed. "No, sir, I did not."

"So, what's your business, son?"

"Don't have one . . . not exactly."

"You want a job? I got a bunch of places, all need to be taken care of. I got cleaners, but they rob me blind, steal liquor, you know?"

Evan shook his head. "To tell you the truth, I'm a musician."

"Is that so?

"Yes, sir."

"That what were you doin' when you got locked up in here? Being a musician? Seems more likely you were sleepin' off a drunk."

Evan didn't reply.

The man extended his hand. "Name's Lou Ingrams."

Evan Riggs and Lou Ingrams shook hands.

"You look like you need a job, son. You can take it or not. You show up here Monday at noon, I'll know I got a supervisor. You don't, I know I ain't. Not complicated."

Lou Ingrams let Evan out of the bar. Evan went back to the apartment and surveyed the devastation of empty bottles, dirty laundry, unwashed cups and plates.

He got to work. Three hours. Then he bathed, shaved, and put on clean clothes.

He looked in the mirror and was reminded of a man he once knew.

Monday at noon he went back to Lou Ingrams's bar.

"I got five bars, one club," Ingrams said. "I'm gonna show you where they are and what I need."

Evan worked the day. He worked the week. By the start of April, he was a different man. He wasn't drinking. His apartment was clean, and it stayed that way. He took his clothes to the Laundromat. He showed up on time for work and he went home exhausted.

One time he asked Lou Ingrams why he had given him the job.

"Because I done the drunk thing," Ingrams said. "You got locked in a bar all night and didn't kill yourself with bourbon. Where you were was the same as me. That's no place for anyone. You get back on the horse, you know? Even if he gets a leg up from someone, a cowboy gets back on the horse and gets himself home no matter what."

"I appreciate what you done," Evan said, and they never discussed it again.

In July of that same year, Evan Riggs contacted Leland Soames at Crooked Cow in Abilene and asked whether there was still an opening to go on up there and make a record. Soames said he would get back to him, and Evan felt it was a brush-off. Soames, however, was good to his word. Called him three days later and said there was a week in August if Evan could make it.

"I can make it," Evan said.

Evan then told Lou Ingrams about it.

"So, you gonna be the new Hank Williams, then."

"What, get so drunk that they won't have me on the radio?"

"Some sense of humor you got," Ingrams said. "Don't let them music business people take it off you."

"I won't."

Evan Riggs and Lou Ingrams parted company on Sunday, August 1, 1948. Evan was taking a Greyhound up to Abilene early on the following day.

Ingrams told him to make a good record and to send him a copy when it was done. He promised he would. He said he would bring one back and deliver it personal.

Just a week later, August eighth, Lou Ingrams was shot dead in a failed robbery at his club. He died right there on a floor that Evan Riggs had cleaned a hundred times.

Evan Riggs heard about it more than a month later. The funeral had been and gone.

Evan went to a bar and drank himself senseless. He spent the night in a jail cell and was bailed out by Herman Russell the following morning.

Leland Soames thought nothing of it. He'd recorded too many people and spent too much time with too many musicians to see Evan Riggs's behavior as anything but standard. You took the rough with the smooth. The kid was young. He'd get over it, whatever it was.

Evan Riggs wasn't so sure. Life had beaten him hard with Rebecca Wyatt, beaten him some more with Lilly Duvall, and now—with the untimely death of Lou Ingrams—it seemed intent on undermining every ounce of faith he possessed in the universal balance of all things. It wasn't right. It was further confirmation that life was skewed in favor of someone other than himself.

And that was when Evan Riggs decided to quit Abilene, to quit his plan of returning to Austin and head home to Calvary. Maybe to lick his wounds, maybe to try to gain some perspective, he didn't know. Intuition told him that going back for a while was the right thing to do.

In truth, he couldn't have been more wrong.

TWENTY-EIGHT

Henry and Evie followed the Pecos up to Iraan, took 349 to the intersection of 67 and headed west. They made Odessa by eleven. Henry had been in Odessa just five days earlier, had stayed overnight on the day of his release. Five days. It was hard to believe. This was the journey now: his experiences in Calvary; the run-in with Carson Riggs; meeting Evie Chandler, a girl who had so effortlessly worked her way into his heart and seemed set to stay there; the time spent at the Honeycutts', the words he'd shared with Evie's father, with Clarence Ames, Roy Sperling, George Eakins, and finally, with Harold Mills. All of it in five days. It seemed surreal, and yet it stretched out behind him in slow motion. Time was relative to nothing but itself. This he had learned in Reeves. Boredom was nothing more than an inability to occupy each moment as if it were the only moment that existed, agitation and frustration nothing more than an effort to slow it down. Time just was, and if you did not let it be what it was, it became an endless source of trouble.

"I want a cup of coffee," Evie said. "Let's find someplace and ask where the County Hospital is."

It was Sunday morning; finding someplace wasn't as easy as would have been the case in Austin, but a small diner downtown was serving late breakfasts and strong coffee for those who weren't in church.

Henry and Evie took a corner booth at the back, asked the waitress for directions to the hospital when she brought their order.

"Easy enough," she said. "Go right, keep on going, and don't stop until you see it. Big building. Ugly, too." She smiled and left them to it.

Ector County Hospital was big, and it was ugly. It seemed intent on spoiling the view with its dingy concrete mass. The design was cumbersome, as if additional wings and blocks had been nailed on as afterthoughts and addendums. Frank Lloyd Wright would have refused even to be sick in such a place.

"So, we have a plan?" Evie asked.

"Tell them you're her sister's niece or something," Henry said. "Her granddaughter, maybe? I don't know."

"Let's go see what happens," Evie said, and took off up the main steps of the facility and went through the heavy glass doors.

It was far easier than either of them had imagined. Hospital policy seemed welcoming of visitors, and inquiries were not made as to who Henry and Evie were or how they were related to the patient they were asking after.

"Grace Riggs, yes," the woman at reception said, having consulted a typed directory of names. "She is in the Andersen Wing. Third floor, turn left out of the elevator, go all the way to the end of the corridor, turn right, and then follow the signs."

They did as they were told, the size of the building evident only as they walked. It must have taken them ten minutes to find their destination. The Andersen Wing was some sort of psychiatric facility, perhaps a final repository for the unsalvageable and terminally ill. The atmosphere was foreboding, as if to find yourself here was to know that all hope had been abandoned.

The ward nurse did ask who they were, their names, who they had come to visit.

"John Wilson," Henry lied, "and this here is my wife, Mary." He smiled guilelessly. "Mary is Grace Riggs's niece's cousin," he added.

The nurse looked surprised. "Well, if ever there was a distant relative contest, you'd more 'an likely win a prize, my dear," she said. "However, I am sure that Grace will appreciate your makin' a visit. She's been here a long time, and aside from her son, she don't get no one comin' down here."

"That'd be Carson, right?" Henry asked. "The sheriff."

"He's a sheriff?" the nurse asked. "Who woulda known, eh? Saw him just the once. That was a long time back, though. Like I said, she don't get no visitors."

"How long has she been here?" Evie asked.

"Oh, Lord, I have no idea," the nurse said. "I've been working on this wing for fifteen years, and Grace was here long before me."

"She hasn't told you?"

The nurse gave a weak smile. "You go visit her now," she said. "Let me introduce you."

The nurse left them standing there at the edge of a bed, within which was a frail and distant woman, a woman representing nothing more than a rough sketch of the person she'd once been.

Evie looked at Henry. Henry looked back at her. Their expressions

185

were the same: a sense of disbelief, a sense of guilt, as well, as if they were bringing bad news to the doorstep of someone who had already received far more than any human being should have to bear.

Evie pulled up a chair and sat down. She reached out and took the pale and fragile hand of Grace Riggs.

"Grace," she said, and Grace turned her head and looked back at her through milky eyes.

She smiled faintly, as if there were some sense of recognition, and she said, "We had angel food cake at the party. I made it myself."

Henry stepped up behind Evie and placed his hands on her shoulders.

"We came to visit you, Mrs. Riggs," he said. "We wanted to talk to you about Evan and Carson, you know? We wanted to ask you about Evan's daughter . . . your granddaughter."

Grace looked surprised for a moment. "She was only here for a little while," she whispered, as if some secret was being divulged. "I saw her before she died." She smiled then, heartfelt and sincere, yet with a shadow of poignancy. "I came to visit her, but Carson was so angry. He told me never to come again."

"Sarah was here?" Evie asked. "And she died?" She turned and looked at Henry, and there was a visible sense of distress in her expression.

"Sarah?" Grace asked. "Who is Sarah?"

"Your granddaughter," Henry said. "Evan's daughter."

"No, I didn't see her today," Grace said. "Is she here?"

"Who died, Mrs. Riggs? Who was here that died?" Henry asked.

"Why, Rebecca, of course. Sarah's mother. I came to see her here. Carson told me not to come again, so I didn't. I should have defied him."

Grace Riggs looked away for a few moments, and then she turned back. She smiled at Henry, at Evie Chandler. "We had angel food cake at the party," she said. "I made it myself, you know?"

Evie squeezed Grace Riggs's hand gently. "Is that right, Mrs. Riggs? Rebecca was Sarah's mother, and Rebecca died here at Ector?"

The look in Grace's eyes was so very distant that Evie knew she was gone. Where she had gone, Evie had no idea, but she certainly wasn't in the Andersen Wing of Ector County Hospital talking to her visitors.

Evie sat there a while longer. Henry didn't say a word. When they finally got up to leave, they found the nurse again and told her they were leaving.

"She was lucid?" the nurse asked.

"A little."

"Less and less frequently now," she replied. "Six months, a year perhaps, and she might not even recognize me, and I see her every day."

"Thank you for letting us visit," Evie said. "And thank you for taking such good care of her."

"Someone has to, eh?" the nurse said, smiling. "Most of these old 'uns have been abandoned and deserted by family, you know? Terrible shame, but that's life, isn't it?"

Outside, they sat in the truck. Both of them were silent for a while, but Henry broke that silence with something they had both been thinking.

"You reckon Rebecca was the mother?"

"I do," Evie said. "She wound up here, died here. Grace winds up here, too, and Evan ends up in jail. The father is dead, as well. Is it my imagination, or does everyone around Carson Riggs get completely fucked-up?"

"Not your imagination," Henry replied.

"That was really sad. Seeing that woman like that. Carson doesn't come out here and visit her. However, I can't say that's so bad, all things considered. She can't see Evan . . . probably doesn't even remember what Evan looks like. She's been there—what?—twenty years, maybe?"

"Fifteen at least."

"No life, is it?"

Henry shook his head.

"So we need to find out who Rebecca is, if she ended up here, if she died. We find some record of her, we might get a little closer to Sarah."

"Interesting, huh?"

"Which bit?"

"Looking for someone no one wants us to find."

"Except Evan," Evie said. "Wouldn't be here if it weren't for Evan, right?"

"Right."

"You ready to quit, Henry?"

"Hell, no."

Evie smiled. "Me either. More I hear about Carson Riggs, the less I like him. The less I like him, the more I want to see him get fucked-up, too."

"Remind me to stay friends with you."

"Oh, I think you'd make a pretty good enemy, Henry Quinn. I think you're a much darker horse than you let on."

"Oh, you're so right there, sweetheart," Henry said, a smile in his eyes. "All hidden currents, me. Black water. Deep, too. So very deep."

"Idiot."

Henry started the engine and they pulled away, both of them making a point of not looking back at the dark, angular shape on the horizon.

TWENTY-NINE

The album sold, and sold well. Some of those tunes on *The Whiskey Poet* got more airtime than Leland Soames or Herman Russell could have hoped for. Herman had questioned the tone of the thing, said that the lion's share of those songs were pretty downbeat and morbid.

"Sounds like a man who knows he's lost," he told Soames.

"We're all lost, Herman," Soames replied. "Believe it or not, folks like to know that they're not alone, especially when they're at their lowest. It's called human nature."

Seemed Leland Soames had his finger on the pulse, however weak that pulse might have been, and Evan Riggs's record matched the rhythm.

Evan didn't change his mind about going back to Calvary, but when he arrived in January of 1949, he arrived as a small star in the country music firmament.

His parents could not have been happier. Carson could not have been more jealous. Just as had been the case when Evan got back from the war, Carson was in the shade while Evan hogged the limelight. Evan didn't see it, but then Evan never did. He was not plagued with the same insecurities as his older brother. He had his own monkeys to carry, and jealousy was not one of them. Seemed like a week of parties, and every party he was invited to, people played his record, and some of those people remembered the words better than himself. Everyone had an explanation for what such and such a song meant, and it was always to do with Calvary and something that had happened there. No one was right, save Rebecca Wyatt.

She came the first night, just to say hi, and then she returned the next day, and she found Evan on the veranda, his head a little swelled and hungover, and she sat with him quietly and waited for him to tell her something of the time he'd been away. It had been three years, pretty much to the month, and though he'd forgotten the last words they'd shared, she had not. She had professed to hate him for making her life so complicated, how he knew that was not true, and then those final words—*Will always love you . . . whatever happens*—to which he had failed to reply.

"I listened to your record," she said that morning on the veranda as he smoked his cigarette and drank his coffee and looked out across a horizon that was awkwardly familiar, "and those songs are way too sad to be about you and me."

She waited for a response that never came.

"So I know you met someone else, Evan."

Evan nodded slowly, but he did not look at her.

"What's her name?"

"Was," he replied. "She's dead."

Her face and tone of voice communicated genuine shock and distress. "Oh, Evan . . . my God . . . what happened?"

Evan turned and looked at her. His expression was strangely implacable, as if whatever he was feeling was buried so very deep.

"She killed herself," he said. "I went to get cigarettes and beer, and she killed herself."

"Oh, Evan," Rebecca echoed. "I am so sorry . . . I had no idea . . . I don't even know what to say."

He smiled resignedly. "There's nothing to say, sweetheart, and nothing needs to be said."

"When did this happen?"

"An earlier life," Evan said, "but that life is done with, and this here is a different one, and it's good to see you."

She reached out her hand, and though she expected him to be unresponsive, perhaps even to withdraw, he did not. He returned the gentle expression of affection and looked at her directly.

"It really is," he said. "No bullshit. It's good to see you. Of everything here, you're the only real reason to ever come back."

She glanced away. Had he not been looking at her, he perhaps might have missed it.

"I know about you and Carson," he said. "I'm not stupid."

She turned back. "Carson . . . he . . . well . . . you went away, Evan. You really went away. Three years. I told you I would always love you and you said nothing, and then you just disappeared. I was supposed to wait for you?"

Evan shook his head. "No, Rebecca, not for me, but for someone else."

"Carson is a good man," she said. "Headstrong, a little arrogant sometimes, but he's young. He'll settle down. Besides, there's a lot to love about your brother, regardless of what you think."

"And you love him?"

"Yes, Evan. I love him. I really do."

"You gonna marry him?"

"I don't know," she said, but the hitch in her voice said that such a decision had already been made.

"I can't tell you what to do, Rebecca. Hell, I'm the last person in the world who has any right to tell you what to do. I deserted you—"

"You didn't desert me, Evan. You never made any promises to me."

"Maybe I should have."

"Is that what you think?"

"I don't know what I think. Lilly . . . that was her name . . . she died more than a year ago. December 1947. Life just vanished for a while. I drank a lot." Evan smiled, almost to himself, and then he turned to Rebecca. "A lot," he repeated. "Like I saw the sign DRINK CANADA DRY and thought it was an instruction."

Rebecca laughed.

"Anyway, I drowned myself in liquor for a while, and then I met a man who made me clean bars and saloons for a while, and then I went out to Abilene and made the record, and now I don't know what to do with myself."

"Keep on making records," Rebecca said. "What else is there to do? You're a country music star now, Evan Riggs. People are buying your record, and they're gonna want to buy more."

"I guess."

"There's no *guess* in it," she said. "This is what you've always wanted, isn't it? I can't understand why you would even think about this as anything but good."

"Because success does not vanquish demons," he said, and he really meant it.

"You puzzle the crap out of me sometimes, Evan Riggs," she said.

"That's nothing," he said. "I sometimes puzzle the crap out of myself."

The tension was there. It was unspoken, but it was there. That day, those final words uttered, he should have responded in kind. He should have told her he loved her. She might have waited for him. She might even have gone with him, and had she done so, there might never have been a Lilly Duvall. But Lilly Duvall starred in most of the songs on that record, and those in which she did not star, she was a walk-on, a cameo, or somewhere in the scenery directing the emotion of the thing. And had she not been there, he may never have sold so many, because whatever he was feeling when he stood in front of that microphone connected with real people who had real lives who had felt similar things themselves. Later he would understand that those emotions were already there because of Rebecca, that Lilly had merely brought them to the surface and given them words.

As Leland Soames had opined one drunken night in Abilene, "It ain't so complicated, son. You live life, you write some songs, and people recognize their own lives in the words and music, and they feel like you're cut from the same cloth. You explain how they feel in ways they never could."

That had made sense to Evan while he'd recorded those tunes, but now—in hindsight—it seemed like that had been some different man, some other life he'd lived, some other story that was no longer his own. His emotions now belonged to the wider world, and he wasn't so sure how to feel about that.

Evan stayed through January of 1949. He slept a great deal, as if exhausted from the three years he'd been away. He gave money to his ma, knowing his father would never take a cent from him, and for no other reason than pride. Fathers supported sons, not the other way around, no matter how growed-up those sons were.

Carson was here and there. He came for dinner every Sunday, stopped by now and again as he was making his way from someplace to someplace else. He had an apartment close to the Sheriff's Office, slept there most nights, and planned to buy a home once he and Rebecca were married.

He had asked her several times. She'd never said yes, but—yet again—she'd never declined. To an outsider, someone who didn't understand the dynamics of her relationship and history with Carson Riggs, it may have seemed cruel and unkind, but it was not. These were people who had grown up together. Evan had always been there, but Evan had gone to war, Evan had gone to San Antonio, to Austin, to Abilene. Rebecca Wyatt and Carson Riggs had stayed back in Calvary, and that fact alone gave them something that Evan would never possess. Rebecca might never have admitted it, even to herself, but there was something that drew her to the safety and predictability of whatever life was represented here. She was only part gypsy, whereas Evan merely had to stay a month or two in one place and the inner nomad started scratching on the walls of his soul. Evan knew better than to unsettle her with choices. He stayed in the wings, he watched, he listened as she went on convincing herself that marrying Carson was the right choice.

Evan knew that there was no such thing as the *right* choice. What was right today was wrong tomorrow, and vice versa. Given his time again, more than half of the decisions he'd made would be reversed.

Whereas Rebecca was evidently pleased to see Evan, Carson was far more unpredictable. There was something about Carson that made every conversation ambiguous and vague. Carson's character was made of mercury. As soon as you put your finger on something, it slid from beneath you and became something else.

"You here for keeps, then?" he asked Evan one evening a couple of weeks after Evan's return. They were out on the veranda together, the setting sun nothing more than a ghost haunting the horizon, the sky over their heads a rich midnight blue that seemed utterly without stars.

"You know I'm not here for keeps, Carson," Evan replied. "Why do you ask questions that you already know the answer to?"

"Just want to be sure, brother."

"Of what? That I am not here to capsize your plans?"

"What plans would they be?"

"Your plan to marry Rebecca, to settle down, raise a family with her."

"Are you here to do that, Evan?"

"You know the answer to that question, too, Carson."

"Do I?"

Evan turned and looked at Carson. There was a flinty hardness in his eyes and his manner, even more so than when they'd last spent time together. "Yes, you do, big brother. Yes, you do."

"She ain't said yes to me."

"She ain't said no neither."

"You think she's gonna say yes?"

"I don't doubt it, Carson. I think she's making you work for it, is all."

"I ain't been nothin' but a gentleman," Carson said. "In every way."

"Does that mean what I think it means?"

Carson paused, as if now he was once again explaining something very simple to a slightly backward child. "A man has his own standards and attitudes, Evan. You should know that, you bein' all

193

perceptive and sensitive and artistic and whatnot. I see it enough, you know? The way men treat their wives. I see them get violent, and I hear about them doing things that surely don't seem right and proper, and I choose not to be that kind of man. I wasn't raised that way, and neither was you, but you choose to live your life a different way from me and I don't have any right to judge that."

"What the hell is that supposed to mean, Carson?"

"Well, the drinkin' and the women you been involved with and whatever."

"The drinking, sure. What the hell, you know? I had a problem with drinking. I got over it. You should get over it, too. Shit, Carson. It wasn't even your problem! And as for women, there was one woman, one woman who really meant something to me, and now she's dead, and if you're asking me to consider what you think and feel about something that's personal, then you can shut the hell up about that right here and now. You go on and say whatever the hell you like about me, but you keep your words in your mouth when it comes to her, if only out of respect for the dead."

Carson Riggs was quiet for a moment, and then he said, "I guess we both know where we stand, then, little brother." He smiled like a rodent. "I'm glad we had this little talk," he added. "We should talk more often, don'tcha think?"

Evan opened his mouth to speak, but Carson turned and walked back into the house before he had a chance.

At the end of January, Evan told his parents that he was going back to Austin.

"It's where I should be," he explained.

William, routinely laconic but periodically eloquent, said, "We understand, Evan. We knew you were only here for a short while. You have the whole world out there waiting for you now, and we couldn't be more proud. We couldn't be more proud of both of you, to be honest."

Grace took Evan's hand. "We shall have a party," she said. "Friday evening. Everyone should come. Let's make it a dance. We could use the old barn, put some lights up, and you could sing for us."

"Oh, Ma, really? You don't want me singin', surely?"

"Why the hell not?" William said. "You're a singer, ain'tcha? Damned fine one, if that reccud o' yours is anything to go by."

"One song," Evan said.

"To hell with that, boy," William said. "You can sing at least two

194

or three. I'll get them boys over from Ozona, them fiddle players, that fella with the stand-up bass. You can make a band and do some real entertainment."

It was the expression on his mother's face that sold the deal: excited anticipation with a real potential for disappointment if he refused.

"Okay," Evan said. "Let's have one hell of a party."

When Carson heard about it, he was uncertain.

"Maybe there's an ordinance about public performance and the consumption of alcohol and whatever," he said at Sunday dinner.

"I am sure there's gonna be an ordinance about everything somewhere," his mother said, "and every single one of them designed to stop people enjoying themselves. Fact of the matter, Sheriff Riggs, is that we're having a going-away party for your brother, and there's nothing you can do about it. You got a problem, then the first two arrests will be your father and me."

Carson smiled. "Looking forward to the party," he said, which was not at all what he meant.

Had the party been derailed, a great many things might have been a great deal different. But it wasn't. It was a done deal. Invites went far and wide, and those musician boys from Ozona agreed to come on over the Wednesday beforehand and rehearse up some numbers with Evan. They were proud to be asked and said they could gather up four fiddles, two more guitars, a couple of washboards, and a double bass. Grace and Rebecca were in charge of the food, William Riggs and Ralph Wyatt in charge of the liquor. Carson was given the job of fixing up lights and power supplies and whatnot for the old barn, that same barn where Evan had once kept Rocket, same barn out of which Carson had scared the poor thing. But that had been a different age, the better part of nineteen years before, and to anyone beyond the immediate confines of the Riggs family, the resentments and petty jealousies that had plagued them as children were a thing of the past.

If only that had been the case, then the events of the early hours of Saturday morning, February 5, 1949 might never have taken place.

But they did take place, and—in hindsight—it was doubtful that anything could have been done to stop them.

THIRTY

"You done poked a hornet's nest, son," Glenn Chandler said as Henry got out of the truck in front of the house.

Evie walked to the porch steps and looked up at her pa. He had on a face that she rarely saw.

"Sent one of his boys out here to warn you off."

"Warn us off?" Evie asked. "Who was it? What did he say?"

"It was Alvin Lang, Carson Riggs's deputy, and he said that Henry should find his way home right about now." Chandler looked down at his daughter. "And you, my sweet, should be a mite more careful about the company you keep; otherwise there mightn't be work for you in Calvary."

"What did you say?" Henry asked.

Chandler smiled. "I said I didn't know what the hell he was talking about, and that if he had business with you, then he should take it up with you. I told him I wasn't no messenger boy for the Redbird County Sheriff's Department."

"Go, Daddy!" Evie said, laughing, but her father didn't join her in the laughter.

"I don't know what the hell you're digging up, but what I do know is that Carson Riggs ain't happy about it. These are people you don't want to upset, for a great deal of reasons."

"We went over to Odessa," Evie said.

"What the hell for?"

"See Carson and Evan's ma in the psych place they got up there at Ector County Hospital."

Glenn Chandler seemed to take a step back, though in truth he didn't move an inch. "You did what?"

"We went on out to—" Henry started.

Chandler raised his hand without looking at Henry. "I'm asking my girl, son," he said, his tone direct, unflinching.

"Pa?" Evie said, her voice tremulous.

Chandler took a moment and then came on down the porch steps. He waved at the pair of them. They came around the front

196

of the trunk and stood before him as if scolded kids. Henry had his hands clasped behind his back, just as he'd been required to stand when being addressed by a boss at Reeves.

"People's lives are people's lives," Chandler said. "Now, I don't know what kind of deal you had with Evan back there in Reeves, son, but Evan ain't Carson, that's for sure. Seems to me that whatever you tryin' to dig up is something he wants to stay buried. He lost his father, his mother's out there in Ector, his brother's in jail for murder, and now some ex-con snot-nosed punk comes sniffin' around his personal affairs like a hungry stray in the yard. Maybe they's all dead bodies up in that man's yard, maybe not. I don't know, and I don't care to know. What I do care about is that I got a sheriff's deputy, in uniform, mind—Sam Browne and .44 to boot— over my place on a Sunday morning, telling me that Carson Riggs don't much care for my daughter getting herself up in his business. That's gonna give a father some cause for concern."

"Daddy, I'm more than capable of takin' care of myself, and Henry hasn't gotten me into anything that I didn't want to get into."

Chandler smiled. "So tell me, sweet pea, what is it *exactly* that you pair of busybodies have gotten yourself into?"

Evie glanced at Henry. They both knew the answer to the question, as did Glenn Chandler.

"'S what I figured," he said. "In fact, I'd go so far to say that if you took everything you know between you and put it together, you wouldn't even reach half a clue."

"Pa... Henry made a promise. He gave his word to Evan."

"I understand that, sweetheart, but that is between Henry and Evan, and it doesn't include you. I find out that whatever is going on here is jeopardizing your safety, then I am gonna get concerned, and I am going to dissuade you from pursuing this. I am your father, Evie, and that is my instinct. And your mother would say the same thing."

Evie shook her head. "No, she would not."

Chandler looked momentarily surprised. "You're telling me what my wife would have thought?"

"I'm telling you what you know she would have said about this, Pa. Last-chance saloon for the lost and lonely. That's what she used to say, right? This house is the last-chance saloon for the lost and lonely. You told me that. You told me that she never backed off, that she always spoke her mind, that she always had something to say about the things she disagreed with. You told me that she was the toughest woman you ever met."

"Well, she ain't here now, Evie, and you are, and that's what I have to deal with."

"No, Pa, what you have to deal with is that she and I are the same . . . at least in that way, and I have made a decision. I want to help Henry keep his word to Evan, and you have to accept that I am not a child no more, and that's just the way it is."

"Is that so?"

"Yep. End of discussion."

Chandler turned to Henry Quinn. "And what do you have to say about all of this, Henry Quinn from Reeves County Prison?"

"I don't have anything to say, Mr. Chandler. I understand what you're feeling, and I understand that Carson Riggs sent his deputy over here to warn us off, but I guess I'm as stubborn as your daughter. I made a promise to a man who saved my life, and I reckon that until I've done what he asked me, this is not really my life. That may sound crazy, but it's the way I think. If I were up there in Reeves and I knew I was never gonna get out, and this girl was all I had in the world, would I want to say sorry? Would I want to make some kind of reparation? I think I would, sir. Evan Riggs can't do that, but I can, and I said I would, so I'm going to."

"And if folks get hurt in the process? People who have no right getting hurt?"

"I don't intend that, sir," Henry said. "Least of all Evie. And she can quit right now, and if she does, I'll be sorry about that, but it won't stop me."

Chandler smiled. "Jeez, you pair are so alike, it's painful to watch."

"No one is gonna get hurt, Daddy," Evie said. "I mean, what's he gonna do? Kill us?"

"He's the law, sweetheart. Don't be so naive. Fifteen minutes and he could have Henry here back in Reeves for another half dozen years. He's been sheriff in Calvary since the war. You don't think that says something about the sway he holds over there? Whatever the deal is with Redbird County Sheriff's Department, I am thinking that Carson Riggs is the grand dragon of all that and more besides. He'll find out that you went up to Odessa. You think he won't? Christ, Evie. You went to see his mother in the hospital. What were you thinking?"

"We were thinking that his mother might be able to shed some light on where Evan's daughter is," Henry said.

"And?"

"She has pretty much lost the plot," Henry said. "She's been up there at least fifteen years. She's an old woman. She didn't make a great deal of sense, but she spoke of someone called Rebecca, and from what we can guess, Rebecca was up there at Ector County, too. Seems that Grace Riggs visited her, and then Carson told her not to visit anymore. Anyway, from what she said, it seems that this Rebecca is dead, may even have died in Ector itself."

"The girl's mother?" Glenn asked. "Is that who this Rebecca is?"

"That's what we think," Evie said.

"And the daughter's name is Sarah, right?"

"Right," Henry replied.

"And you didn't think to ask them if this Rebecca died in their care, seeing as how you were already in the building causing trouble?"

Henry looked at Evie. Evie looked right back.

"Not exactly Holmes and Watson, are you?" Chandler said, to which neither of them had an appropriate answer.

"Easy enough to find out, I guess," Chandler said, "but the more people you speak to, the more questions you ask, the more certain Sheriff Carson Riggs will know what you're doing."

Glenn Chandler took a step forward and put his hands on Evie's shoulders. "If I lose you . . ." He hesitated, then shook his head and sighed deeply.

"Pa—" she started, but her father raised his right hand and placed it against her cheek. He kissed her forehead, and then he turned to Henry.

"I said it before and I'll say it again. Anything happens to her, Mr. Quinn . . ."

"Nothing's gonna happen, Pa," Evie interjected.

"I'll take care of her, sir," Henry said. "I give you my word."

"So be it," Chandler said, and with that he turned and walked back to the house.

Henry reached out his hand. Evie took it.

"He sent Alvin Lang out here," she said.

"You know him?"

"Some."

"I met him when I arrived," Henry said. "When I went down to Riggs's office. He's a big guy, and like Riggs said, he's the grandson of the governor or whatever."

"Big guy with a small dick, I reckon," Evie said.

"You know this from personal experience?"

"Fuck off, Henry Quinn."

Henry laughed.

"So where now?"

"Calvary cemetery first, then Clarence Ames," Henry said.

"Last thing Clarence said to us was something about buryin' ourselves. You think it was a hint?"

"No idea, but I want to see if there are any Riggs graves out there, or graves for anyone called Sarah who could be the right age for Evan's daughter. If not, I want to go back to Ector and get into their records office."

"You ain't quittin' 'til you know for sure what happened, are you?"

Henry nodded. "Here until the last dog is hung, little lady."

Evie laughed. "Who the hell talks like that, Henry Quinn? I mean, really? 'Til the last dog is hung. You are *such* a loser."

"Enough of that there mouth, woman," Henry snarled. "Ain't you got some cleanin' to do?"

She swung her hand backward and connected with his shoulder. "Just get in the car, will you?" she replied. "Christ, sometimes you are fuller of shit than a Christmas goose."

200

THIRTY-ONE

The world came to see Evan Riggs. At least that's the way it seemed.

It had to be said that Carson held up his end of the deal, and the old barn where Rocket once lived was transformed into something special. Carson and a handful of men from town—George Eakins, Warren Garfield, Roy Sperling among them—took one side off the building and created an open stage. They set a platform for the band inside, hung lights all over, pulled hay bales out and covered them in tablecloths where food could be set down. Though it was February, it was temperate, somewhere in the late sixties; it was warm enough for folks to be out there in shirtsleeves and cotton print dresses, cool enough to dance and not have folks passing out from heatstroke.

And the boys built a dance floor, as well; they dragged a couple of dozen rail sleepers down from the lumberyard, set them in front of the barn to the right, laid floorboards over and nailed them fast. It was a sight to see, watching them put it all together like a Swiss chronometer.

Carson ran the whole thing like a site foreman, barking orders, telling Roy Sperling to "heft it like a man, not a schoolgirl," to which Sperling recommended he "go soak your head in a bucket of bullshit, Carson . . . I'm a doctor, not a goddamned longshoreman." It was good-humored, and Evan made a point of getting out there and pitching in.

"Stay out of it," Carson told him. "Know you can drag sleepers and nail down boards with the best of us, but what would happen if some darn fool like Warren Garfield dropped a hammer on your hands, eh? The man's a lawyer, not a carpenter. You stick to your rehearsals; we'll build you your Grand Ole Opry."

For the first time in as long as Evan could recall, there seemed to be no tension between them. It was a good feeling. Maybe Carson was mellowing. He was twenty-nine years old, had been sheriff for five of those years, and perhaps the simple fact of having to deal with real peoples' lives day after day had settled him somewhat. Carson had never been the soul of patience, but a law-enforcement job demanded a good deal of patience, if only to contend with the utter stupidity and ignorance of some folks. Other than that, it required more than enough sensitivity, delivering up bad news about car wrecks, arms and legs lost in agricultural machinery, the mess left behind after a once-in-a-decade homicide. Such business as this was all sheriff business, and Carson appeared to have grown into it without the expected awkwardness that folks had predicted. Maybe, after all was said and done, Carson was the better choice for Rebecca. Evan could see that, and he loved her so much that he couldn't find it in himself to resent her for loving someone else, even if that someone else was Carson. Part of being human seemed to be reconciling oneself to the fact that one could not always have what one wanted. As with Lilly, so with Rebecca, but for different reasons. Lilly denied herself the world. Rebecca just denied herself the limits of human experience.

By late afternoon on Friday the fourth, the Riggs farm was already like the scene of a wedding party. There was an excitement in the air, perhaps nothing more than the thrill of having a real-live celebrity music star in Calvary, perhaps for reasons known only to those attending. Whatever the motivation, it didn't matter; the atmosphere was everything, the hubbub and the noise, the flowers, the food, the plates of baked goods and cured hams and pitchers of home brew that were endlessly ferried from the backs of cars and trucks and station wagons. Clarence Ames and his wife, Laetitia, showed up with a whole hog—head, tail, and all in between—and William Riggs and George Eakins helped him rig up a spit. They had that thing turning by four in the afternoon, and by six the smell was sufficient to draw even greater crowds from Lord only knew where.

Grace Riggs watched her son take the stage at eight, and the roar of voices must have come from nigh on three hundred throats. She didn't know for sure, and she sure wasn't of a mind to be doing any counting, but that was the way it seemed. A sea of smiling faces right across the front yard and all the way down to the barn.

William stood beside her, snaked his arm around her waist.

"Our boy done good," he said.

"They both done good," she replied, and was about to say something further when she was interrupted by Evan and his pickup band breaking forth into "One Has My Name (The Other Has My Heart)." Evan and the boys had worked up a number of covers, some of the recent hits from Ernest Tubb, Tex Williams, and Bob Wills, but it was Evan's songs that the people of Calvary, Ozona, and Sonora had come to hear, and when he hit the opening lick of "I'll Try and Be a Better Man" the place went crazy. Double bassist fell apart in the middle eight, but no one seemed to notice, and if they did, they didn't care. The dance floor looked like it would drop right through the sleepers, but people kept on dancing. Evan was grinning like a fool, making quips about the folks he knew, telling tales of how such and such a line was inspired by some darn fool stunt he and Carson had pulled when they were kids, and it seemed like the world that had showed up was a world owned outright by the Riggs brothers.

After a soulful rendition of "Lord, I Done So Wrong," Evan made Carson come up on stage and take a round of applause.

"Our one and only Sheriff Riggs!" he shouted, and the place erupted. "Just wanna say that all of this could not have been possible without my big brother here . . . finest brother a man could ever wish for."

Grace Riggs shed a tear.

Rebecca Wyatt watched from the left side of the stage and didn't know which brother she loved the most.

William stood between George Eakins and Roy Sperling, a glass of ten-year-old bourbon in his hand, and he felt his heart swell like a balloon.

Carson took his applause and the hollering with good humor. He made a joke about illegal drinking and live music and how he had a couple of his men taking notes of all the license plates. Someone threw a bread roll. Carson saw it coming and kicked it back high over the crowd. Everyone fell about laughing. Evan and Carson hugged each other, and then Evan strapped on his guitar and tore the place apart with a version of "Cigareets and Whusky and Wild, Wild Women" that The Sons of The Pioneers would never have recognized.

Evan came off the stage at ten. He had three encores, and then he asked them if they didn't have homes to go to. He was done, drenched in sweat, face redder than a beet, hair like damp string. He went inside and washed up, was back out by half past to a crowd of folks waiting with handshakes and backslaps and a seemingly endless supply of liquor.

Carson was dealing with some drunken squabble between two girls who should have known better when Rebecca cornered Evan near the smaller of the sheds beside the barn.

The pickup band were playing slow dance numbers for those whose feet could still support their weight, and Evan was soaking it all up like it was Christmas, Thanksgiving, and some kind of anniversary tied together with a bow.

"You done so good," she said, and Evan could see she was almost drunk. She looked more beautiful than he'd ever seen, and he knew that she would marry his brother.

"I have to say goodbye, Evan. You know that, right?"

"Not tonight you don't," he said.

"You know what I mean," she said, and she raised her hand and touched the side of his face.

Evan tilted his head as her fingers touched him. He closed his eyes, and he inhaled the smell of her perfume, no perfume that ever came from a bottle, and he felt for a moment that this symbolic goodbye was, in fact, a farewell to everything that Calvary was, everything he had been before this night, as if playing his songs for these people was his way of bidding adieu to the world that had made him who he was.

In truth, she was the main part of it all. Rebecca Wyatt. Skinny girl who rocked up a thousand years before with bangs and pigtails and a sass all her own.

"Remember this?" he said, and from his vest pocket he took the pocket watch.

She smiled, reached out and touched it. "You recall the stories I told you?" she said.

"Corporal Vernon Harvey from Snowflake, Arizona, got his darn fool legs blown off in the Argonne Forest," Evan said.

Rebecca raised her eyebrows. "You impress me, Evan Riggs."

"He didn't save no children from burning farmhouses, did he?"

She smiled. "I doubt it, no."

"Nor did he track no German sniper for three days and then kill him stone dead with a bullet to the heart."

She shook her head.

"Loved those stories," Evan said. "Used to lie awake looking at that watch and wondering what the hell really happened."

"I'm sure nothing quite so dramatic as what I told you."

"I'm gonna go on believing every word of it," Evan said.

Rebecca looked away for a moment, a wistful expression on her face. "That was always the difference between you and Carson, wasn't it? He always asked *Why?* and you always asked *Why Not?* You wanted to believe everything was possible."

"Still do."

"Guess it comes down to which of us forget we were all children once upon a time."

"Maybe," Evan said. "I don't know." He put the watch back in his vest pocket.

Rebecca touched his shirtsleeve, her fingers just glancing off it tentatively, almost as if she didn't want to risk any real physical contact. "I am staying, you know?"

"I know you are."

"And I will marry Carson."

"I know that, too."

"Are you mad at me for that?"

Evan shook his head. "Nope."

She laughed. "That's a telltale Evan *nope*," she said. "That's a *nope* that means *yes*."

Evan took her hand and walked away from the edge of the barn to a table someone had set over behind the hog roast.

He was quiet for a time, just looking at her, perhaps soaking up whatever he could of that moment because he knew he would never be able to look at her in such a way again, and then he said, "You want to know what I want? What I really want, Rebecca?"

"I don't think I do," she said. "Not if it's gonna hurt."

He smiled, closed his hands over hers. "I want to hear that your kids are doing good in school, that Carson is the best sheriff in the county, that your pa is gonna be a grandpa, that you still listen to my records, and that you don't hate me for leaving you behind."

"You're not leaving me behind, Evan," she said. "I could come if I wanted to."

"But you don't want to," he said.

"Not that I don't want to, but that I can't. It's a life, Evan. You know that. Some people can do that; some people can't. I gotta have foundations somewhere or I start seeing things all wrong, you know? I gotta know where I'm gonna be tomorrow and which horizon I'm looking for; otherwise . . . well, you know what I mean. That's the way it is, and I don't see that you can shoehorn one into the skin of another and make it work."

"You can't," Evan said. "I seen people, good musicians, great songwriters, and they get off at the first bus stop and head back home. It's a shitty life, that's the truth, but I gotta do it."

"I know you have, and you will find someone who can do it with you."

"I'll find someone," Evan said, "but she won't be you."

205

"Don't say that."

"It's the truth."

"I know, but you don't need to say it. I can feel it. I can see it written all over your face. Just hurts me, you know? I don't like it."

"I'm sorry."

Rebecca shook her head. "No more sorry, neither."

Evan smiled. It was a smile of philosophical resignation.

"Walk me back?" she said.

"Be a pleasure, ma'am."

Evan told his ma that he would be back in half an hour or so, that he was seeing Rebecca home.

"Well, you make sure you get on back here pronto," she said. "This party's for you, and you can't be missing any of it, okay?"

Evan kissed his mother on the cheek. "Thanks for all of this, Ma," he said.

"I didn't do much o' nothin'," she said. "You got Carson to thank for this."

"I know," Evan said. "He done good."

By the time they reached the Wyatt place, the sights and sounds of the party were distant ghosts. They stood on the veranda together, Rebecca's hand on the railing, Evan's hand over hers, and when she turned and looked up at him, he could not stop himself from kissing her. It was a goodbye kiss. That's what he told himself. He had not kissed her since he'd left for the war. This time it was different. This time it was fueled by loss and sadness and a pent-up wave of feelings that were all some variation of *missing you already*.

She turned toward him then, pressed her body against his as he put his arms around her and tried to pull her even closer.

"Oh God . . . Evan . . . no . . ." she exhaled, but she didn't mean a word of it, and he couldn't stop himself, and didn't want to, and then they went through the screen door and down the hallway to the stairs and hesitated before climbing, and she led the way, her hand out behind her, and he took that hand and followed her to her room, and even as they passed through the doorway, it was as if he were watching himself from the downstairs hallway . . . as if he had let her go up alone . . . as if he had steeled himself resolutely against all temptation, as if the head had won over the heart and he had indeed let her go.

But he had not, and he did not, and the door closed behind them. Evan Riggs and Rebecca Wyatt showed each other how things would have been if Moirai and the spinning of threads had not woven their lives apart.

Their lovemaking was furious, perhaps angry, each convinced to show the other what each was being denied, as if here was a way to release something that could never truly escape.

And when they were done, they said nothing. Evan merely rose from the mattress, got dressed, and left the Wyatt house.

A hundred yards away, he glanced back, but he did not see her watching him from any window.

Evan had been absent for close to an hour, but if anyone thought something was awry, they did not speak of it.

THIRTY-TWO

If nothing else, walking between the gravestones and markers in Calvary's only cemetery served to strengthen Henry Quinn's resolve. Many was the time he and a crew of other inmates had been dispatched to clear stones and weeds from the further reaches of Reeves's own makeshift potter's field, an ignominious final resting place for those society no longer cared for. Simple wooden markers gave a prisoner's name and number, no birth date, no date of death. Perhaps, somewhere within Reeves's administrative system, there was a record of who they were, the term they'd served, their cause of death, their next of kin. Perhaps not. And that same scrubbed and featureless acreage would be where Evan Riggs would finally wind up; his marker would crumble and degrade in time; the records he'd made would be scratched or lost or forgotten, and there would be nothing remaining to remind the world of his existence. Except his daughter. Perhaps his daughter. Granted, it may not be fair to tell her now of her origin, but there was always the possibility that she knew, deep down, that she did not really belong to the family that had taken her in. Could such a thing be known by instinct, by some deep-rooted knowledge that those surrounding you were not of the same blood?

Just inside the entranceway was a memorial plaque to those of Redbird County who had fallen in the First War. Just as was the case with so many of the stones, it was covered in moss, its letters almost unreadable. There appeared to be no such memorial for those who had fallen in the Second.

"Hey," Evie called from the far corner of the cemetery. "I've found the father."

Henry walked across to meet her, stepping carefully between the stones and crosses, one or two of them draped with faded and weatherworn Confederate flags. Dead flowers lay everywhere, their blooms devoid of color and life.

Evie stood looking down at a moss-covered stone, the ground around it unkempt and neglected. There was no doubt as to who was buried there. WILLIAM FORD RIGGS, the stone read. BELOVED HUSBAND TO GRACE: DEVOTED FATHER TO CARSON AND EVAN.

Dates of birth and death were respectively given as July 8, 1896 and August 8, 1949.

"Short life," Evie said. "Fifty-three years old. Fucking sad."

"Accident, right?" Henry said. "That's what your dad said . . . some kind of shooting accident."

Evie didn't reply. She was down on her knees, tugging clumps of weed from around the gravestone.

"What are you doing?"

Evie looked back at Henry. "Doesn't seem right to just leave it such a mess," she said. "Looks like no one's been here for years."

"Only person who could come is Carson," Henry said.

"Another reason not to like him," Evie said. "As if we needed one."

"Come on. Let's see if we can't find anything about Sarah."

Evie got up. She took a step forward and touched the uppermost edge of William Riggs's gravestone. Henry didn't ask, but he was sure she mouthed a couple of words. It was a touching moment, and it said something very clear about Evie's sensitivity and compassion.

"So this girl," Evie asked as she walked away. "She was born when?"

"November of forty-nine," Henry said.

"She never met her grandfather, then," Evie commented.

"Seems not."

Had the girl died, and had she, in fact, been buried here, then hers would be one of the more recent interments. It seemed futile, so unlikely as to be beyond the bounds of reasonability, but it wasn't long before Henry found something.

"Here," he said. He knelt down, rubbed moss and lichen away from the letters.

"Wyatt," he said. "Ralph Wyatt, loving father to Rebecca."

He looked up at Evie.

"Look at the date of death," Evie said. "August 8, 1949 . . . Same day as Evan's father."

Henry rubbed further, his hands now filthy, and there was no mistaking it. Ralph Wyatt, whoever the hell he might have been, had been born on the eleventh of November, 1892, and had died on the same day as William Riggs.

"Rebecca's father?" Evie asked.

Henry shook his head. "Lord knows, but if so, then both of

Sarah's grandfathers died on the same day. That seems altogether too coincidental."

"The shooting accident," Evie said.

"Seems there's a good deal Evan could have told me that he didn't."

"Seems there's a good deal a number of people could have told us that they haven't," Evie said.

They kept on looking, wending their way back toward the crumbling stone arch that marked the entranceway of the cemetery, every once in a while pausing at some lichen-clad marker, kneeling to look closer, to ascertain whether or not their search for Evan's daughter would end there. In some strange way, Henry half hoped that they would find something, if only to resolve the question of her whereabouts, but it was a wish without real substance. He did not want to disappoint Evan. He wanted to do what he said he'd do.

By the time they reached the last handful of stones, they were certain that there was nothing further to be discovered there.

"Time to head back to Ector," Henry said. "We need to know for sure if the Rebecca that Grace spoke of is this Wyatt girl. If she is, then it looks like we've found Sarah's mother."

"Who is also dead, right?"

"Died at Ector."

"We only have Grace's word to go on."

"Most certain thing she said, though, wasn't it? That she went up to Ector to visit Rebecca, that Carson got mad at her for visiting, and that Rebecca died."

"I don't know," Evie said. "I don't know what to make of any of it. I just know that the more we look, the more questions we find."

"You gonna come with me?" Henry asked.

"What the hell you gonna do? Break into their records office?"

"I am gonna ask, that's all," Henry said.

"And if they won't tell you?"

He shrugged. "Hell, I don't know, Evie. Break into their records office, I guess."

Evie hesitated for no more than a second. "Let's go," she said.

They followed the same route they'd taken only that morning. En route they stopped at a gas station and convenience store, bought flowers and a box of pastries. The receptionist was surprised to see them back, asked why they had returned so soon.

Evie smiled so sincerely that the woman couldn't help but smile with her. "We just felt awful," Evie said. "I mean, with no visitors for such a long time and Grace up there all by herself. It just seems so dreadfully sad, you know?"

The woman concurred. It was dreadfully sad, yes.

"I can let you up for a while," she said, "but doctor's rounds will start in half an hour, so you don't have long. Then they'll have lunch. Might be better if you came back in an hour or two, and then you could visit for longer."

"What's your name?" Evie asked.

"I'm Anne," she said. "Anne Regis."

"Well, Anne, we just wanted to bring some flowers," Evie said. "And some pastries."

Henry held up the box as evidence.

"Brighten the place up a little," Evie went on.

"You are very sweet," Anne said.

"I did have a question," Henry said. "When we were here earlier, Grace mentioned someone called Rebecca. Said that she was here, and that she died. My wife and I were talking after we left, and her grandmother used to speak of another cousin called Rebecca." Henry turned to Evie. "You never did meet her, did you?"

Evie shook her head, leaned closer to Anne. "Said she wasn't well, you know? Hence, we wondered whether or not she might have ended up here at Ector."

"I wouldn't have the faintest idea," Anne said. "Of course, all of that kind of information would be in records, but that's confidential. I don't go in there. That's just for the doctors and the consultants and the directors and whoever."

"Is there someone we could speak to about it?" Henry asked.

"Today?" Anne asked. "It's Sunday. There's just the medical and psychiatric staff here today, my dear. None of the senior people come in on a Sunday."

"And how much trouble would we cause if we just went and looked?" Evie asked.

"Oh my," Anne said. "You can't do that. Those are peoples' confidential medical records. I couldn't possibly let you do that."

"From what Grace told us, Cousin Rebecca died here," Henry said. "Is there a record of deaths in the facility?"

"Well, yes, there would be," Anne replied. "Again, somewhere in the same department, I guess."

"And if that's just a record of people who have died, then there wouldn't be any harm in having a look for our cousin, right? I mean, it's not going to tell us anything that isn't on public record elsewhere," Henry said.

"And if we found out that she did die here, then maybe we have a hope of finding out what happened to her, where she was buried and all that."

"Do you think she might have been buried here?" Anne asked.

Henry frowned. "Here? What? At the hospital?"

"No, I don't mean in the hospital grounds themselves," Anne said, "but if someone dies in the hospital and there is no family to take care of everything, then they are given a plot in the county cemetery."

"Which is where?" Evie asked.

"Well, the cemetery itself is about twenty-five miles away, but the administrative facility and the crematorium is about five miles west of here, right along the highway," Anne said. "I've never been there, but I know that's what happens when we have someone die and they've got no relatives."

"That's really good of you, Anne," Evie said. "We're gonna go see right now."

"You're not going up to see Grace again?"

"Maybe not such a good idea, seeing as how the doctors are going on their rounds," Henry said.

"Could you see that she gets these things?" Evie said.

"Flowers, yes, but pastries I'm not so sure," Anne said. "I know they don't much care to have their diets varied."

"Then the pastries are for you," Evie said, and she set the box on the reception desk.

"Er . . . er, thank you," Anne said, somewhat surprised, by which time Evie and Henry were halfway to the door.

"Appreciated," Henry called out to her, and then both he and Evie were gone.

The county cemetery facility was exactly where Anne Regis had told them it would be, little more than five miles west along the highway. Notwithstanding the fact that it was Sunday, it was staffed and receiving visitors.

Henry and Evie parked and surveyed the scene in front of them. A narrow path dissected a neat lawn, at the end of which sat a low-slung white stone building, the legend over the door reading ECTOR COUNTY CREMATORIUM. Beneath that it said COUNTY RECORDS DEPARTMENT and gave the opening hours.

Once inside, they were greeted by a dour-looking man in a charcoal-gray three-piece suit. His face was white and pinched, as if he and sunlight had been strangers for years. A brass plaque on the desk gave his title as chief registrar, his name as Mr. Langford Crossley.

"And how might I assist you?" Mr. Crossley asked Henry and Evie.

"Hello," Evie said, and shot him her best smile.

Mr. Crossley didn't respond in kind. Apparently, it was neither his job nor his predilection to demonstrate any degree of friendliness.

"We wondered if you might be so kind as to help us," she went on. "We are trying to locate some details concerning a long-lost relative whom we think might have passed away at Ector County Hospital some years ago."

"Her name?" Mr. Crossley asked.

"Rebecca," Evie said.

Crossley smiled, as if humoring a child. "That's very good," he said. "And her family name?"

Evie laughed, somewhat embarrassed. Henry realized then that she was putting it on, giving Crossley the opportunity to assist this slightly backward young woman. "Oh, I'm sorry, yes. Wyatt. Rebecca Wyatt."

"And your names?"

"Mary Wilson," Evie said. "And this is my husband, John."

Henry stepped forward, extended his hand. "How do you do, sir."

Crossley merely grazed Henry's hand with his own, as if the prospect of shaking hands with strangers was just a little too much to bear.

"And your relationship to Rebecca Wyatt?" Crossley asked.

"Well, it's kind of complicated," Evie said.

Crossley gave a weak smile. "I have time, my dear."

"She was the daughter of my grandmother's niece on my father's side."

"Very good. And when did she die?"

Henry stepped forward. "Well, we're not exactly sure," he said. "We're sort of on a mission to find out whatever we can, and we're following little snippets of information. So far we've learned that she might have died at Ector County Hospital, but her father was already dead, you see, so we thought that maybe everything was taken care of by the county. That's why we've come to see you."

"Why, indeed," Mr. Crossley said.

"So can you help us, do you think?" Henry asked.

"I can do my best, Mr. Wilson. If you would care to sit, then I shall consult the ledgers and see if there is any record of your grandmother's niece on your father's side." Once again, the slightly ingratiating smile, and then Crossley retreated through a door behind the desk and his footsteps receded into silence.

"Is it just me, or do you want to slap that smug expression off of his face?" Evie asked. "I mean, the guy sits in an office and checks records of dead people, for Christ's sake. What the hell is the attitude for?"

Henry smiled. He reached out and took Evie's hand, squeezed it reassuringly. "The less important you are, the more important you pretend to be. That's just the way some folks are. Had it the same with some of the wardens in Reeves."

"Asshole, plain and simple," Evie said.

They waited in silence, and they didn't wait long. A handful of minutes, and the footsteps could be heard once again. Crossley came through the door, in his hand a thin manila folder.

"Are you aware of any other details regarding the family?" he asked Evie. "Just as a matter of security, you understand. Though we are dealing with those who have passed away, there is still a certain degree of privacy and protocol that we have to maintain."

"Well, Uncle Ralph was her dad. I mean, whether he really was an uncle or not is a different matter, but his name was Ralph, and he died . . ." Evie turned to Henry. "When was it, sweetheart?"

"When what?"

"Aren't you listening to me and Mr. Crossley?" Evie turned, rolled her eyes at Crossley. "Never listens," she said. "When Uncle Ralph died. Forty-nine, right?"

"Yes, 1949. August, as far as I remember."

Crossley opened the file. "Rebecca Wyatt," he said. "Daughter of Ralph and Madeline Wyatt, née Ellsworth. You are right, Mrs. Wilson. Rebecca Wyatt passed away in care at Ector County Hospital in June of 1951."

"Oh my," Evie said, feigning something akin to shock and sadness. "Oh dear."

Henry stepped forward, put his arm around her shoulder. "There, there, sweetheart," he said. "We kind of knew, didn't we? It isn't exactly a surprise, is it?"

"I know, John, but nevertheless . . ."

Crossley closed the file. "Is there anything else I can assist you with?"

"I assume she was cremated here," Henry said.

"That is correct, Mr. Wilson."

"And her ashes?"

"Would more than likely have been interred at the county cemetery. Precisely where . . . well, they would have that information at the cemetery itself."

Evie continued to play her part.

Henry smiled, extended his hand to have it grazed once more by Crossley's pale fingers, and said, "You have helped us enormously, but I think I better take her home."

"I understand completely," Crossley said. "I am pleased to have been of assistance."

They left the building, certain now that Sarah's mother was dead, that her grandfathers had died on the same day, and that both Evan and Carson Riggs knew a great deal more about these events than either of them had communicated.

As they pulled away from the side of the highway, Henry said, "Let's go upset Clarence Ames. Seems to me that there's a man who knows a great deal more than he's letting on."

THIRTY-THREE

Grace Riggs knew her sons better than she knew herself. She knew when things were right and when they were awry.

When Carson came to her on the Sunday afternoon after Evan's farewell party, he was damn near bursting with excitement. She had not seen him so uplifted since . . . well, since she did not know when.

"She said yes, Ma . . . She said yes."

Grace knew who had said yes and what she had said yes to. More important, she knew why—after all these years—Rebecca Wyatt had finally consented to marrying the eldest of the Riggs boys.

Grace called William down from upstairs. William shook Carson's hand, slapped him on the back, pulled him close, and hugged him half to death.

"I couldn't be happier, son," he said, which was the truth. Friday night had seen him on fire with pride for Evan, and now his eldest was to be married, and as far as William was concerned, there was no better girl in the world for him. Rebecca Wyatt was an anchor, a stabilizing influence, possessing not only a wealth of feminine sense, but also sufficiently strong a personality to never be overwhelmed by Carson. There was a great deal of Grace in Rebecca, and that was precisely what Carson needed.

However, William was a man, and thus he saw only what was in front of him. He did not look left, nor right, nor behind the thing. He saw what he wanted to see, and that was just fine.

Despite the fact that she'd said nothing, Grace knew how long Evan had been away that night. She guessed—and guessed rightly— that something had happened between Evan and Rebecca, that they had said their goodbye in the most personal and intimate way, and she hoped—for Carson's sake, for everyone's sake—that it never came to light.

In that moment, she allowed herself to be as happy as the event befitted, but there was a shadow behind her smiles, the very same shadow she saw lurking among Evan's features when Carson told him of the news.

216

Outwardly, Evan was overjoyed; inwardly, his mother knew he was heartbroken.

Like oil and water, Evan and Rebecca would not mix. Had Rebecca merely permitted herself to be who she really was, then she and Evan would have had the kind of marriage, the kind of *life*, of which most folks could only ever have dreamed. But the vast majority of people spend their lives being not who they are, but the person everyone else requires them to be. Rebecca was no different; by denying what she felt for Evan, she was also denying herself.

Grace let it be. Carson could not have been happier. Evan would live the life that only Evan could live. She and William had to accept that the lives of their sons were not theirs to dictate, direct, or control. At least they had raised boys possessed of their own minds, and neither would be swayed by the opinions of others.

Sunday supper done and dusted, out on the veranda as the sun slipped away, Evan told his mother that what had happened was inevitable.

"I don't know that anything is inevitable," she said.

Evan did not reply, merely stood looking out toward the horizon as if some answer lay there.

"Do not let her break your heart," Grace said. "I understand how you must feel, Evan, but feelings are transient. Just because you feel this now does not mean you have to feel it forever."

"I won't feel it forever," he said, "and regardless of what anyone may say or do or think, I couldn't be happier for Carson."

"I know you couldn't," Grace said. "You are not a selfish man, Evan. I know that. At least that much, eh?"

"Meaning what?"

"Meaning you know what exactly."

Evan laughed. "Meaning you think I am a troublemaker."

"I don't *think* you are a troublemaker, son. I *know* you are."

"Well, some of us have to cause trouble, or life would just be ... well, you know."

"I do, and I don't disagree. You're plenty capable of causing trouble for yourself, and that's all I'm asking you to be mindful of."

"I can take care of myself, Ma."

"I don't doubt it, and I know you can take care of others as well ... but ..."

"But what?"

She shook her head, smiled in that philosophically resigned manner that was so much Grace Riggs. "A son will never understand

217

a mother's viewpoint, Evan. You have to appreciate that Carson was not . . . well, he was neither expected nor accepted at first. Your father had great difficulty coming to terms with the fact that he was a father. He managed it, eventually, but that had more to do with you than anyone else. Fatherhood . . . the *responsibility* of fatherhood scared him, I guess. Maybe it's the same with all men. Maybe they just fear that they won't make the grade. Anyway, he managed as best he could, but he and Carson never really bonded. And then you came along." Grace smiled nostalgically. "Your father changed. His attitude toward Carson changed. Even his attitude toward me. Of course, this is all distant history now, but still the fact remains that had you not come along, things might have been very different indeed for all of us."

"Do I make you happy, Ma?" Evan asked.

The surprise in Grace's expression was impossible to misinterpret. "Happy? What a question, Evan. Of course you make me happy."

"Do you worry about me . . . what will become of me?"

"Every mother worries what will become of her children."

"You know what I mean, Ma."

Standing beside him, Grace reached out and closed her hand over his. She looked out toward the darkening horizon as she spoke.

"You are different, Evan. I don't mean different from Carson. I mean different from everyone. The whys and wherefores are unimportant. It just is. You have a gift to do something, and that gift is important. Look at Friday night, the happiness you brought to people, how much you made people smile. As far as I can see, the ability to do that is kind of magical, you know? People who can do that are rare. But it carries a price, I guess. I can see it, and I have heard about the kinds of difficulties people like you experience—"

"People like me?"

"Artists, musicians, singers, poets, actors, the Hollywood folk you hear about with their drinking and their . . . well, their other vices, you know?"

"What have you been doing? Reading gossip magazines in the hair salon in Sonora?"

"Well, you hear things, and sometimes you hear them enough to think there might be some substance to them."

"You're worried I'll be a drunk and a womanizer, Ma?"

"No, son. I'm worried that there's a fire inside you that won't be lit by anything but attention. That's the addiction that worries me."

"I think you see something inside me that no one else sees."

218

"Rebecca sees it. That's why she doesn't dare follow you."

"Rebecca doesn't dare follow me because she loves Carson and wants to settle here and raise a family."

The silence was a punctuation mark in the conversation, obvious enough to be unmistakable for anything but Grace's lack of concurrence.

"You don't think she loves Carson?" Evan asked.

Grace reached out her hand and gently touched Evan's face. "Sometimes I wonder whether your blindness is selective, or if you are, in fact, a little dumber than we give you credit for."

" 'Preciated, Ma."

"You really don't see it?"

Evan was silent. He turned his face away slightly. His ma could read him clearer than any sign of changing weather.

"I know, Evan," she said eventually, and her voice was barely a whisper. "I know, and I have always known, and you have known, too. Rebecca convinces herself that she is making the right decision, and perhaps she is. Perhaps following you around the country would bring her nothing but unhappiness, but she will never know. Therein lies the danger. It will haunt her forever, and she knows it. Carson can't see it. Carson doesn't want to see it. Your father just wants the best for you both, and he ignores anything that falls into the category of feelings or intuitions. But you and I know better, and we have always known better."

"Ma—"

"I know what happened Friday night, Evan. I could see it painted as large as life on your face. Maybe that's all there is to it. Maybe it has all ended here, and I hope for the sake of both your brother and his wife-to-be that it has ended here."

Once again, Evan opened his mouth to speak, but Grace cut him short with, "Enough now. What's been said is all that needs to be said. No amount of words can turn back time."

She moved sideways and put her arms around him. Evan pulled her close and hugged her.

"I'm sorry, Ma," he said.

"Not me you need to be saying sorry to, son. If anyone, it's Carson who needs an apology, but Carson would never take an apology from you, so best not give him a chance."

Grace leaned up and kissed Evan on the cheek.

"Goodnight, Evan," she said.

She let him go and disappeared back into the house, leaving Evan in silence.

He stood there for a while, wondering what kind of man he really was and if what he'd done had consigned them all to disaster.

The following morning, Monday the seventh, Carson asked Evan to take a walk with him.

"Some things I just want to talk to you about," he said.

Evan went, no fear that the matter for discussion was Rebecca Wyatt, but concern that it was something else just as significant. He had sensed it in Carson for some while, and he knew it related to their future.

They walked a good quarter mile before the subject of interest was broached.

"Pa's not getting any younger," Carson said. "I know he's only in his early fifties, but this life has taken its toll on him physically. Mentally, as well. Farming is unpredictable, dictated by weather, other things you can't understand or control, and it wears a man down. I could never do it, and I know you couldn't, either."

"Could never see myself staying here, let alone farming," Evan said.

"I have my job now," Carson went on, "and I guess this is what I'll always do. Idea of being sheriff of Calvary, marrying Rebecca, raising up some kids an' all . . . well, I have to say there's little else that I could ask for."

"You are a lucky man, Carson. Not many men who could say that they have their life mapped out the way they want it before they've even hit thirty."

"And I want to take care of Ma and Pa," Carson said. "I want to make sure they have enough money to never have to worry about things . . . to never have a concern for where the next meal is coming from—"

"We have never had to worry about where the next meal is coming from, Carson," Evan interjected. "I think that's a little melodramatic, wouldn't you say?"

"How would you know, Carson? You've not been here. Things have been tough sometimes. Winter before last, you know? You wouldn't know what was going on. You've never stayed long enough to get into the grain of the thing."

"I'll give you that, Carson, but I'll not give you the fight you're spoiling for."

"I'm not spoiling for a fight, Evan. I'm trying to have a real, honest-to-God conversation with you about our responsibilities here."

"And what responsibilities would they be, Carson?"

"See," Carson said. "Just like always, you assume I have some other agenda here. I have no other agenda. I am trying to do what is best, and the reason I am talking to you about it is that you are heading off again, no doubt, and there ain't no clue as to how long you'll be gone or what's gonna happen to you, and—just like always—I'll be the one left behind to take care of everything. Now, we can either have this conversation, or you can agree to stay behind and take care of the farm and everything else with me. It's your choice, Evan."

Evan conceded. "I am sorry," he said. "You're right. I will leave, and you will stay behind, and I will hear you out."

"Okay, good," Carson said. He took a pack of cigarettes from his vest pocket and lit one. "So, here goes . . . I have been approached by a representative of the US Navy. More accurately, the Naval Petroleum Reserves Department. They are very interested in test drilling on our land, seeing if there's oil here. If so . . . well, if so, you can just imagine the kind of money we're talking."

"You want to sell the farm," Evan said matter-of-factly.

"I want to look at the possibility of subleasing the land to a petrochemical firm that processes fuel oils and suchlike, Evan. I want to give us and our parents every opportunity to succeed in this life. I want Ma and Pa to have some real financial stability and freedom in their later years."

"And what does Pa say?"

Carson hesitated.

"He doesn't know, does he? He doesn't know that you've been talking to the navy people, right?"

"Ha! You make it sound like some sort of conspiracy. People come to me. I can hear them out, hear what they have to say, make a decision to discuss it with you, and then if *we* decide it's a good idea, we can go to Pa together and see what he thinks."

"If *we* decide?" Evan said. "I get the idea you've already made a decision, Carson."

"So, what are you telling me? That you won't even consider such a thing, even though it might give Ma and Pa a quality of life that they could never have even dreamed of?"

"I am telling you that this discussion, as you call it, is not for you and me to have. If we have this discussion, then Ma and Pa are right here... unless you don't want them here."

"You don't change, do you?" Carson said. "You were always a selfish son of a bitch, always thinking of yourself before anyone else. Everyone running around pandering to your every wish, Ma and Pa doting on you, spoiling you, giving you whatever you wanted. Hell, you couldn't deliver up an honest day's work if your life depended on it."

Evan didn't respond. There was no point. Carson was going to be pigheaded and opinionated, and once he'd taken a stand, there was no shifting him. Changing his viewpoint was tantamount to admitting he was wrong, and that was something he could never do.

"I am going to leave for Austin soon," Evan said. "I won't mention to anyone that we had this conversation, Carson. If you want to raise the issue with Pa and include me before I go, then so be it. If you act behind his back, then I will speak to Warren Garfield and stop you dead in your tracks. Sheriff you may be, but that does not give you license to do what you want. You say you're acting in Ma's and Pa's best interests, but I think you're acting in your own. You want to accuse me of selfishness, you go right ahead. Looks to me like you're just after painting me the same color as yourself."

"Fuck you, Evan," Carson said. "You are narrow-minded, self-centered, and an asshole, to boot."

"You were first of the line," Evan said. "Seems to me you got the lion's share of all those things."

Carson just looked at his younger brother, and there was a defiance in his eyes that Evan knew all too well.

What Carson would do in his absence he could not predict, and he knew that he should stay. He should stay, but he could not. Not after what had happened with Rebecca on Friday night, not to see her marry his older brother, not to see Carson manipulate and maneuver his way around everyone, tying them up, getting them convinced that whatever he was doing was for the best. No, he could not stay for that.

Evan Riggs knew he was relinquishing his responsibility for the family as a whole, and perhaps that was selfish and uncaring, but the pull to leave was far greater than any force of familial gravity. His mother and father had always taken care of themselves. His ma would see something she didn't like long before it even happened, and she would prompt her husband to act. Together they would effortlessly subvert and derail any attempt on Carson's part to do

222

something with which they did not agree. And then there was the law. Sheriff he may be, but Warren Garfield, the family lawyer, would have access to any and all paperwork and documentation relating to land, leases, mortgages, ownership deeds, and suchlike, and Carson did not have the authority to act as proxy for their father. The farm was safe. Evan felt sure of that, and if he was not sure of it, then he would work on convincing himself so as to justify his departure.

Evan stayed a few more days, and then he made preparations to leave. Carson did not broach the matter with their father, and William Riggs showed no sign of anything that gave Evan cause for concern.

William and Grace were sorry to see their youngest leave once more, but they knew better than to try and stop him.

And so Evan left Calvary for Austin. Morning of Monday the fourteenth, he pulled up stakes once more and left the Riggs farm behind, Rebecca, too. Carson was stoic and mannered, evidently suppressing what he really wanted to say for the sake of their parents. He shook his younger brother's hand, wished him well, but his tone was guarded. No doubt Grace was aware of it, but she said nothing.

What she did say unsettled Evan, and it was a mere whisper as he hugged her.

"Let's not see you back here with anything but good news, eh, son?"

He did not reply. The implication was that he was more capable of returning with bad news than anything else, and in his very being he knew this to be true.

Perhaps he was—after all was said and done—nothing but a magnet for trouble. Carson's fall from the hayloft back in thirty-seven, the incident with Gabe Ellsworth, the death of Lilly Duvall, this most recent matter with Rebecca and his betrayal of Carson, the potential conflict about the oil people.

Was he a harbinger of trouble and bad news? Was that the kind of person he was? Someone whose passing could be proven by the wreckage he left behind?

Driving away, the farm once again disappearing in the rearview, Evan Riggs hoped he would not return with bad news, caused either by himself or his older brother.

Carson Riggs was an arrogant man, a man of fixed opinions and vested self-interest. He had not really settled, nor had he really learned a great deal from his work. Evan had tried to convince himself that Carson had mellowed, but he had not. Now Evan was not only leaving the family farm once more, but also leaving Calvary in his older brother's hands. Those hands were more than capable of stirring up a great deal of trouble.

Evan turned a blind eye, as he was wont to do, as he had so often done before, and that was perhaps his greatest sin. The last person to admit cowardice is the coward himself.

It had been said that all it took for evil to prosper was that good men did nothing.

Carson was not evil—far from it—but he had a mind of his own, and that mind formulated intentions that perhaps did not serve everyone else as well as they served himself.

Was Evan now also painting Carson the same color as himself? Perhaps so. They were brothers, after all.

What would happen now, he could not predict; events would play out, and only time would tell.

THIRTY-FOUR

Marriage hadn't worked for Clarence Ames. He had a taste for liquor and cards; she had a manner of making her disapproval clear without ever saying a word. Her name was Laetitia Redmond, one of the Langley Redmonds from over the Pecos. Langley women said Calvary men were all hat and no cattle. Calvary men said that Langley women were two shovels short of a bucketload. Within a week of marrying her, Clarence Ames knew he'd picked a sour 'un, and there wasn't no way to take her back and pick again.

Emotionally speaking, Laetitia Ames was as cold as a fish. Had a face on her like a well-worn shoe. Not the well-worn that comes from fondness, but the kind that comes from wearing them in all weathers or wading through the deepest shit. Pinch-faced is how you might call it, *like a bloodhound chewing a wasp*, Roy Sperling said, but never to Clarence's face. There were two things you never ran down to a man: his choice of handgun and his taste in womenfolk.

When all was said and done, the marriage was over before it started. Laetitia returned to her ma and pa in Langley, thus precluding the hope of any progeny. Once bitten, twice shy, Clarence said, and never considered another marriage. The Ames line would die with Clarence, and he knew it. In truth, there was a deep and ingrained sadness in the man, and over time that had soured to a vinegarish resentment toward those in love, those married, those with children, and pretty much everyone else who wasn't Clarence Ames. He tolerated the saloon crowd—Doc Sperling, Eakins, Mills, even Warren Garfield when he'd still been alive enough to drink with them—but that was simply borne out of a sense of responsibility for the community as a whole. Lord knows what they would have gotten up to without someone to keep an eye on them, and he had assigned himself this supervisory duty.

Henry Quinn and Evie Chandler were—additionally—a cause for civic concern. A small social environment such as Calvary possessed a natural balance, and that balance was maintained by knowing what worked, knowing who did what and when, by following tacit agreements and consents, some of which didn't even need to be directly communicated. Some things were just *understood*, and that was enough.

Like Carson Riggs. As a result of Carson's post and functions as sheriff, there was almost nothing in the way of crime in Calvary. Bums and hobos showed up every once in a while. They didn't stay long. Itinerant workers came in from the east and south in the hope of farm work at harvest time. Where they were needed, they stayed. Where they were not, they were moved on quickly. If they drank too much, got troublesome, harassed the womenfolk, made trouble of any kind, they spent a night or two in Carson's office basement, and then they were gone. First train, first bus, Carson even going so far as to drive them thirty or forty miles back the way they came and bidding them adieu personal-like. Of course, there were rumors, hearsay, some story about a hobo being found dead out near Stockton Plateau, both his arms snapped jagged and drag marks behind him for a quarter mile, but rumors and hearsay could go to hell in a handbasket. Calvary was safe and quiet and settled. Calvary was everything that it needed to be, and Evan Riggs, and everything that had taken place all those years ago, was a thing of the past. The past was full of different people, and they had no place in the here and now.

What Clarence had heard of Henry Quinn didn't sit well with him. He had gotten drunk and shot a woman. Carson had told him so. Carson had access to prison records, police records, any kind of record he wished. He done looked the boy up, and there he was in black-and-white. Grievous assault, unlawful possession of a firearm. Probably other stuff. Drugs, no doubt. Evie Chandler was a sweet enough kid. Had a mouth on her, for sure, but nothing malicious. They flirted with her in the saloon, but then, who wouldn't? She was a pretty girl, and even if they were old enough to be her granddaddy, they weren't queers, were they? It was a little fun, harmless enough, and it never went beyond that. But now this boy had showed up and she'd fallen in with him. An ill-advised course of action, if Clarence had ever seen one.

Clarence was in his kitchen when Henry Quinn and Evie Chandler showed up at his door.

He saw them standing there through the screen from the end of the hallway, and though his initial feeling was one of aggravation and ire, he quickly recognized the potential for defusing what could be a volatile situation. Carson had made it very clear that he did not want this Quinn boy snooping around in Calvary business. And so it was with a calm sense of self-assurance and moral rectitude that Clarence Ames opened the screen door and greeted his visitors.

"Mr. Quinn," he said politely. "Evie."

"Hey, Clarence," Evie said. "Wondered if you had some time for us."

"Sure thing," Clarence said, and stepped aside. "Come on in."

Moments later they were seated at the kitchen table. Lemonade had been offered and accepted, and Clarence awaited the questions that he knew were forthcoming.

"Maybe hard to understand," Henry began, "but I really feel a sense of obligation and duty to do this thing for Evan . . . to find out about his daughter, you know?"

Clarence nodded, took a sip of his lemonade. He glanced at Evie and smiled patiently.

"I did a really stupid thing, Mr. Ames, getting into trouble and winding up at Reeves an' all, and had it not been for Evan, I might still be there. I got into some scrapes. That kind of thing can happen in places like that, and Evan sorted it out." Henry smiled. "Might sound foolish, seein' as how I was there an' all, but there's a lot of people in a place like Reeves who you wouldn't want knowing where you live."

"I can imagine so," Clarence said.

"So, Evan helped me out, and then he asked me to deliver this letter to his daughter, and I thought it was just a straightforward matter of comin' on down here and finding out where she was at. But it's not turned out to be as simple as that."

"No, evidently not." Clarence raised his glass and sipped his lemonade again.

"So, I need some help, you know? Evie here has been good enough to sort of get involved, but she's Ozona, not Calvary, and she doesn't really know much about the Riggs family and everything that happened in the past."

Henry paused, as if he expected Clarence to speak. Clarence remained silent.

"But you've been here as long as Carson, longer maybe, and I wanted to ask you about some of that history."

Clarence set down his glass. He was calm and measured in his response.

"I have to tell you, Henry, that Carson and I have discussed this matter. Not at length, of course, but the bare bones. Carson raised a good point, and I know he raised the same point with you. Carson even understood that you and he agreed on this particular detail."

"That the girl might not want to be found?"

"Precisely."

"I understand that, sir, but—"

"But nothing, Henry. There is no *but* here. One thing you learn with age and experience is that there are two things you cannot take back."

"I know, sir . . . everything you say and everything you do."

"You sing the tune, son, but you don't really *know* the words. I do know that Sheriff Riggs was certainly of the understanding that this matter was closed. Though you may have shared a cell with Evan Riggs, you are nevertheless a stranger here, Mr. Quinn, and I don't believe you will ever be anything but a stranger."

"This is all getting a bit heavy and serious if you ask me, Clarence," Evie interjected.

Clarence turned toward her slowly. He didn't crack his face with a smile. "I didn't ask you, Evie."

"Whoa, what the hell is this?" she asked, her tone one of indignant surprise.

"I'll tell you what it is," Clarence said, looking first at Evie, then turning back to Henry. "It is none of your business."

"But—" Henry said.

"But nothing," Clarence said. "You are from Ozona, Evie, and Mr. Quinn here is from Reeves, and before that who knows where. You are not Calvary. Never have been, never will be. Evan was once Calvary, but he killed a man in Austin, and now he will die in Reeves. That is the way it is, and there is nothing you can do to change it. Evan may very well have asked you to come on down here to deliver some letter to his daughter . . . a daughter he has never seen, a daughter that should never have been his in the first place. You don't know what happened back then, and I am not going to explain it to you. All I know is that the past stays where it is, and that's all there is to it."

"But Evan—"

"Evan Riggs killed an innocent man. He got drunk and he beat that man to death. Evan had talent, he had a career ahead of him, and then he betrayed his brother, betrayed the Riggs name, and he became a drunk. More than likely it was the guilt of what he did that drove him down the neck of a bottle. Well, look where it got him, why don'tcha?"

"What did he do, Clarence?" Evie asked.

Clarence turned and looked at her. He was silent for a few moments, and then he said, "He didn't mind his own business, sweetheart."

Evie took on a look Henry had seen before. She had been pushed, and she didn't like it.

"You threatening me, Clarence Ames?" she said.

"Nothing of the sort, my dear."

"Sounds like a threat. You done wrapped it in pretty paper and tied me a bow, but I know what's inside."

"Well, if you already know what's inside, then there's no need to unwrap it further, is there?"

"You always have been a sour old goat, Clarence Ames."

Clarence smiled. "I know your pa, Evie. He's a good man. I also know that he and Alvin Lang shared a few words."

"Do you, now?"

"Yes, I do."

"And how is that, Clarence? How do you know that Alvin came over and talked to my daddy?"

"Very little escapes me, Evie. You should know that by now."

"Well, if there's very little that escapes you now, that tells me that you know exactly what the deal is with Carson and Evan Riggs, that you know exactly who the daughter is and where she lives. I bet you even know her name."

"Not a betting man, Evie," Clarence said. "Only betting man I know is Carson Riggs, and I wouldn't advise wagering on anything with him."

"I have to say that I am beginning to dislike you, Clarence Ames."

"I have to say that I don't much care whether you like me or not."

"So, you're not gonna help us?" Evie asked, almost as if she was giving him one last chance.

"I have given you all the help you need right now," he replied.

"Mr. Ames—" Henry started.

"Leave it, Henry," Evie said. "He's not gonna help us. He's on Carson's payroll."

Clarence Ames walked the pair of them to the front door without a further word. He let them out and watched until they reached the street. He had intended to defuse the situation, but it was obvious from the get-go that this pair were not seeing sense, likely never would.

As soon as they were beyond the bounds of his property, he turned back down the hall and went for the telephone.

He dialed a number and waited.

"Sheriff... it's Clarence Ames... We need to meet..."

He paused, inhaled slowly and closed his eyes.

"No, Carson... all of us..."

The journey back to the Chandler place was made in silence.

Henry tried talking, but Evie said, "I'm wound tight, Henry. Let me unwind or I'm likely to snap your head off."

Henry let her unwind, and all seemed to be settling just fine until they turned off the highway and the house came into view.

Carson Riggs stood beside his car, hat tipped back, thumbs in his Sam Browne belt, cigarette parked in the corner of his mouth. He had on sunglasses, and as Henry Quinn pulled up, Riggs took off those glasses and smiled.

"Fuck," Evie said under her breath.

"Fuck," Henry echoed.

Hesitant then, Henry let the engine idle for a moment before he turned it off. He got out of the truck slowly, paused for a moment, and then closed the door.

Evie reached for the handle on her side, but Henry shook his head. "Stay in the truck," he said.

"To hell with that, Henry Quinn," she replied, and got out.

The smile never left Sheriff Riggs's face, even as he stood straight and said, "Heard you went on up and made a visit at Ector County Hospital."

Henry didn't reply.

"Maybe you're surprised how I know so much so fast, huh?"

"Never meant to be a secret, Sheriff Riggs."

"Is that so?"

"It is."

"So tell me this, son... Why the hell do you go on digging around in this business? Straight up, no bullshit."

"Like I done told you and anyone else who asked, I just made a promise, Sheriff. Gave my word, is all."

"Okay, so we have what they call a stalemate, don't we? I'm asking you to back off. You're saying you're gonna do whatever the hell you want regardless of what I say."

"I don't think I'm doin' whatever the hell I want, Sheriff Riggs, I think I'm doin' what is right."

"Sometimes the person who's doin' ain't the best judge of what's right."

"I can see that."

Riggs nodded slowly. He took off his hat and scratched his head. "Say I decide to help you."

Henry frowned. "Come again."

"Say I give you a helping hand. Say I point you in the right direction, help you out some."

"And why would you do that?"

"Because I am not a selfish man, Henry Quinn. Because I got to thinkin' about my dumbass brother up there in Reeves and how he's been there all these years. Okay, so he killed a man and screwed up his life, but I seen his daughter one time, and she was something special. Bright, you know? Pretty as a picture. If God, in his wisdom, decided to get one good thing out of Evan's life, then it's gonna be that girl. And you know, I ain't so sure that she wouldn't want to know who her father was . . . who her father is. Maybe she's aware of something missing. I don't know if her folks ever told her that she was adopted. I don't know much of anything, to be honest. Anyway, I got to ponderin' all of this, and I figured that maybe I was wrong to get in the way of this. Maybe this is one of those things that's meant to be."

Henry listened to Riggs, his mind turning over rapidly. What the hell was this? Was this sincere, or just another misdirection?

"So," Riggs went on, "I had Alvin look up some of this stuff, and he has a name and a town for you. Dates way back, ten, fifteen years, and maybe it ain't gonna get you to her, but it's something more than the nothing you've got right now. You go on over to Alvin's place and he'll give you what he found."

"Seriously?" Henry asked. "You're really giving me a hand with this?"

"No, son. I ain't helpin' you none. If I'm helpin' anyone, it's Evan."

Riggs looked at Evie. "You know where Alvin lives, right?"

"Yes, sir. I do."

"You go on over there now. He's got the information I told you about."

"That's much appreciated, Sheriff," Henry said.

"We shall see what happens, eh?" Riggs said. He put on his hat, his sunglasses, and he opened the door of the car. He paused, turned back. "Actually," he added, "you can save me a journey." He reached in through the window and took out a package.

"Just old parking tickets and whatever, all expired, but we gotta store 'em for two years. Old Alvin has a mountain of the things in his garage. Don't have room for them in the office."

Riggs tossed the package to Henry and Henry caught it. It was as it appeared—just a stack of tickets, all bound together and bagged in plastic.

"You just give that to Alvin for me, would you, son?"

"Sure thing, Sheriff," Henry said.

Riggs got into the car and started the engine. He backed up, paused to look out the window at Henry.

"Too many years have gone by for me to stay angry, I guess," he said. "Just the thought of it wears me out."

Without another word, he turned onto the street and drove away.

"Something is fucked up," Evie said. "I know it."

"Let's go see what Alvin Lang has to say for himself, then, shall we?"

"I don't like it, Henry," she said. "Somethin' really ain't right here."

"So, what do you want to do? You want to quit on me now?"

"Not sayin' that, and you know it," she said. "Just sayin' that it seems mighty strange for him to be doin' the Mr. Helpful thing all of a sudden."

"Maybe it's one of those times when what someone says and what someone means are actually the same."

Evie frowned. "Are you just dumb or naive or both, Henry Quinn?"

"Both, I guess," he said, smiling. "It's all part of the charm, you know?"

"Get in the car," she said. "Let's go see how deep this shit goes."

Alvin Lang was on the porch when Henry and Evie pulled up in front of his house. He was in jeans and a T-shirt, seemed incongruous out of uniform, as if his head no longer suited his body.

"Howdy there," he called as they exited the pickup.

Evie raised her hand in greeting. Henry picked up the package of spent tickets and walked up the drive. When he reached the steps, he said, "Got a package here from Sheriff Riggs."

"That them tickets?"

" 'S what he said."

Alvin nodded at a small table beside the swing hammock. "Set it down there, son," he said.

Henry did as he was asked.

"So, Sheriff Riggs asked me to make a few phone calls and check a few things out on this here Evan's daughter business," Lang said. "Said I should give you what I got, let you take it from there."

"Did you find out her name, where she lives now?" Henry asked.

"Her name? Nope. Didn't find that. However, I did find something. Doesn't harm to have your granddaddy be the lieutenant governor of Texas. People tend to jump when you play that card." He gave a self-satisfied smile, as if he had been personally responsible for his grandfather's election success. "Anyway, it seems she went out to some place in Menard, far as I can figure. Some kinda orphanage, I guess. Whether it's still there, where they kept records of where she went once she was growed up, who knows? But that's what I got for you."

"Is there any paperwork?" Henry asked.

"There is some paperwork, sure."

"Can we look at it?"

Alvin smiled, shook his head. "We got ourselves a misunderstandin' here. When I said there was paperwork, there *is* paperwork, of course, but ain't no kind of paperwork we're s'posed to be lookin' at. This is confidential stuff, you know? Hell of a thing Sheriff Riggs done for his brother here, and if someone found out that he was snoopin' around in stuff like this . . . well, let's just say that it might compromise his pristine service record with the Sheriff's Department. You just take what you got and be grateful, son. Orphanage in Menard, like I said."

"That's very much appreciated, Deputy," Henry said.

"Nothin' at all to me, Mr. Quinn. Like I done said, Sheriff Riggs had a change o' heart. After all that happened between him and that crazy son-of-a-bitch brother o' his, I think that shows the kind of forgiveness you rarely see in a man."

"What—" Henry started, and knew immediately that it was one question too far.

"Conversation's done, Mr. Quinn. You go on about your business. Oh, and if you want a word of advice, I wouldn't go drivin' on up to Menard today. It is Sunday, after all, and some folks don't take too kindly to unexpected visits on a Sunday."

"Understood," Henry said. "And thank you."

Alvin Lang merely nodded, turned, and went back into the house.

Henry and Evie got back in the truck.

"I don't like this even more than I thought," Evie said. "Somethin' seems really fuckin' out of whack here."

"We'll find out soon enough," Henry said, and started the motor.

THIRTY-FIVE

Despite strenuous efforts to locate Evan Riggs, he could not be found. His mother, ever the wisest of the Riggs clan, suspected this was due to the fact that he did not wish to be found.

"To hell with him," was Carson's response when—two days before the wedding—he was informed that the likelihood of his younger brother being there was growing ever more unlikely.

"Warren can be best man," Carson said.

"Warren Garfield?" his mother asked.

"Sure, why the hell not? He's a good man. Reliable, you know?" Carson seemed settled on the idea. "I'm sure he'll do it," he added soberly, as if what was being proposed was a posse heading for the Diablo Plateau after cutthroats and brigands of the worst kind.

"Town lawyer seems an odd choice," Grace told William.

William shook his head. "Garfield's a little man trying to be bigger," he said. "He'll do whatever Carson tells him to do—always has done, always will. Not a good situation for the sheriff to have the law in his pocket like that."

"You don't think Carson's doing a good job as sheriff?" Grace asked.

William smiled wryly. "I have no doubt that he's doing a good job, my sweet. My only concern is that he's doing *too* good a job."

"Meaning what exactly?"

"Man thinks he's being done a favor when the sheriff lets the odd traffic ticket slide, when some complaint about steer grazing where they shouldn't is overlooked. Sometimes things a little more serious, you know? All well and good until the sheriff comes asking for a favor in return."

Grace frowned. "In plain English, if you don't mind, William Riggs," she said, but William would not be further pressed for details.

She wondered if there wasn't some sort of small-town conspiracy going on, her sense of unease precipitated more by ignorance than indirect involvement.

Thus it was: Warren Garfield was asked, and Warren Garfield

accepted. It was a substantial wedding by Calvary standards, and after word got out that Grace Riggs would not be pleased to once again be asked as to the whereabouts of her youngest, the subject was no longer raised. Truth was, Evan knew all about the wedding, had received at least two of the telegrams, but the prospect of watching his older brother marry Rebecca Wyatt could not be faced. On the day in question—Saturday, March 12, 1949—Evan could have been found in a bar near the junction of Red River and East 7th, and though he did raise a glass to his brother and new sister-in-law, it was his fifth or sixth glass, and he would have happily raised a glass to the revocation of American independence. Their marriage was a fleeting thought; the memory of that night with Rebecca was not.

Evan was alone again, and Evan did not believe he was at his best when alone. That was a viewpoint unshared by those who considered him a friend. When Evan was in love, he was besotted. When Evan was angered, he was, in fact, outraged and terrifying. When Evan was morose or nostalgic, he was closer to abject depression. Evan Riggs did nothing by halves. Just as when he drank, everything was in doubles and triples, sometimes forgoing the glass altogether and swallowing life straight from the bottle.

He made money, but he just as quickly lost it. He was not extravagant, just irresponsible. He bought guitars, pawned them, retrieved them only to pawn them again three days later. He slept on couches, floors, one time in a doorway and was tanked for the night by the cops. That he had made a moderately successful record counted for nothing. It was Austin; everyone and his cousin had made a moderately successful record. *The Whiskey Poet*, though acknowledged as an adequate representation of a more-than-adequate talent, was six months old, and that flurry of excited sales right before Christmas had tailed off. Herman Russell and Leland Soames were after him for another record. Crooked Cow was not a sufficiently established label to survive on back catalog alone. They needed new material, and if that material wasn't coming from signed names, then it had to come from new blood. Only so many times would Herman drive from Abilene to Austin to drag Evan Riggs out of some drunken self-loathing funk. Soon that gas would be put to better use taking him to those selfsame county fairs and talent shows where Henry Quinn would later be discovered. There were new singer-songwriters everywhere. Texas was good for oil, good barbecue rubs, longhorn steers, and balladeers. That's what it did best, and Herman was a hound for the latter.

Back in Calvary, the newly-married Riggses were spoiled for choice. There was ample space at both the Riggs and Wyatt spreads, and then there was Carson's place in town. Alongside the badge and the salary, the sheriff was afforded a comfortable two-bedroom apartment in Calvary center. It was here that Rebecca chose to live, excited at the prospect of furnishing it the way she wanted, having her own place away from home, she and Carson maintaining their own schedule, eating at their own table, waking in their own bed. Carson gave her what she wanted. There was no doubt in anyone's mind, least of all Carson's, that he had secured himself the best wife a man could have wished for east of the Pecos. He was not infatuated or smitten; he was not Evan when it came to such matters, but he was altogether satiated with love for the girl. See him on the street, he in uniform, she in whatever finery he had paid for, and he was big boss with the hot sauce. All that Calvary was waiting for was news of a baby, and that news came soon enough.

Rebecca told Carson that he was going to be a father in April. He lit up like a Roman candle and whirled through Calvary in pretty much the same fashion, telling everyone who crossed his path that he was going to be a daddy, and those who didn't cross his path as well.

They headed out to see her father, dragged him along to the Riggs farm, and there they made the announcement. William, old-school when it came to such things, saw the Riggs name passing down the line with the farm. Had he ever doubted that Carson would give him grandchildren? No, he had not. Had he doubted Evan would do the same? Most definitely. He was reassured, at least, that neither the county nor the state would be selling his farm and donating the proceeds to some so-called community purse.

"Couldn't be more proud of you, son," William told his eldest. They stood on the veranda together, smoking a ritual cigar. William had kept a box for such occasions, though knowing nothing about the correct manner in which to store good cigars, they had dried out. Tasted like maize stalks rolled in damp newspaper, but neither uttered a word of complaint.

"She's a great girl," Carson said. "Love her dearly, Pa. I really do. And she's gonna be an excellent mother."

"No doubt about that," William said. "Heart the size of Texas and then some."

"You heard word from Evan?"

"Not a sound," William said. "But that don't trouble me none.

Evan is Evan. He's his own start and finish, and no one knows how he gets from one to the other."

"He wasn't here for the wedding, and now he's not here for this."

William turned to Carson. "You worried about him?"

Carson smiled. " 'S what brothers do, Pa. Worry for one another even when there's no reason for it. Just sad that he ain't as close to the family."

William shrugged. "You don't choose family, son. Family gets chose for you. I know he loves us just as much as we love him, but that don't mean he's gotta see us three times a week."

"I know, Pa. I know. Just a shame that he ain't here, that he don't know he's gonna be an uncle."

"Oh, I'll guess we'll get word to him soon enough, and I am sure he's gonna be overjoyed. He was always good with the little 'uns. Kids always gravitated to him for some reason. Maybe 'cause he has some kinda artistic thing, you know?"

"Sure he'll be overjoyed," Carson echoed, and the conversation drifted away in some other direction and Evan was not mentioned again until later.

"You will tell Evan, won't you?" was the next time his name was raised, and it was raised by Rebecca as she dried dishes with Grace in the Riggses' kitchen. Dinner had been nothing but smiles and laughter, and had anyone missed Evan, they did not show it.

"Of course we'll tell him," Grace replied. And then with a know-ing smile, she added, "Once we manage to track him down."

"I'm still sad that he didn't come to the wedding."

"No need for that," Grace said. "What's done is done."

"I guess I'd just like to know why."

Grace turned and looked at her daughter-in-law. "If you are trying to draw me into a conversation about you and Evan, then it ain't gonna work, girl," she said. "And if you really don't know why he didn't come, then you're a great deal dumber than you look, and I'll be advising Carson to divorce you as soon as he possibly can."

Rebecca colored up.

Grace handed her another dish from the sink.

There were words on Grace's lips that she couldn't bring herself to utter, and so she did not.

There was a fear in Rebecca's mind—more than a fear, a terrifying certainty—and she would no more have voiced it than she would have told Grace Riggs what happened between herself and Evan that night of the party. The fact that the one might have led directly to the other was the issue, and she hoped against all odds that this was not the case. However, whatever she might have wished for, there was a line in one of Evan Riggs's songs that was coming back to haunt her like a ghost. *Even if no one else ever knows the truth, I still know I done you wrong.*

Like someone would later comment, *Take those pretty tunes away and you may as well have called it a confession*. Not solely for the singer, but for the listener as well.

By the time the first trimester came up, Rebecca was already talking nursery colors and Carson was doing his damnedest to appear enthused. To be frank, he didn't see a great deal of difference between *sunshine yellow* and *French marigold*, but he tried not to make his limited spectral differentiation skills become a topic for heated discussion. He was excited, yes; he was nervous, of course, but the color of a nursery wall seemed relatively insignificant in the face of the pregnancy itself. He wanted Doc Sperling to do all the checks he needed to do and tell them that there was a baby in there and that everything was A-OK.

Doc Sperling did the checkup. It was Thursday, July twenty-first, and Carson translated Rebecca's nervousness as only natural considering what was going on. He was anxious, too, but for the right reason; he just wanted to know that everything was as it should be, that there were no *complications*. He had heard this word in such a context before, and to him they sounded less like *complications* and more like natural disasters.

Doc Sperling said nothing beyond the routine as the examination was undertaken, but Rebecca sensed there were questions unasked.

"What?" she eventually said.

Sperling tried to look surprised, but he was no natural-born liar.

"Seriously, Roy . . . You look like you got a fly in your ear. What's bugging you?"

"I gotta ask, Rebecca . . . I just gotta ask, but I don't want to."

Rebecca's color visibly paled. Had she said she didn't know what was coming, she would have been lying.

"I need to ask whether you and Carson were . . . well, whether you were intimate before you got married."

Rebecca closed her eyes. Her heart deflated like a slow-punctured balloon. That feeling in the pit of her stomach, a feeling that had sat there like a cold stone ever since that night with Evan, suddenly became burning hot, hot enough to sear right through her and kill her where she sat.

"W-w-why d-d'you ask, Doc?"

"You gonna answer the question, Rebecca?"

"Tell me why you're asking, Roy . . ." she said, her voice faltering at the end, because she knew well enough why he was asking. She prayed that what she feared most and what he was about tell her were not one and the same thing.

"You're into your second trimester, my dear . . . no question. I'd say you were not so far from the start of your third."

Rebecca didn't speak.

"So, my question stands," Sperling said. "Do we got a problem here?"

It was a long time before she responded, and when she did, it was a barely noticeable nod of the head.

"Evan?" Sperling asked, to which Rebecca said nothing, and Sperling merely repeated Evan's name, this time as a statement rather than a question.

"Night of the party," Sperling said, almost to himself. "When was that? Start of February. That would put you at about twenty-three weeks. Makes sense, from what I can see."

"Oh, God—" she said.

"Calm yourself," Sperling said. "Let's work this out now, my dear. There's no need for Carson to know—"

"What do you mean, there's no need for him to know?" Rebecca said, suddenly coming to life. "I'm going to have his brother's baby. And to answer your question, no, we were never intimate before we were married. I am two months further along than I should be, Roy . . . How the hell do you hide something like that, and what kind of wife would I be to have such a secret? He has to know." And with that she got up, almost as if marching out to the waiting room and announcing this revelation was her immediate plan.

"Sit," Sperling said, and grabbed her arm.

Rebecca sat.

"Listen to me, Rebecca. You have more than yourself and your husband to think about now. You have to think about your father, Carson's folks, the entirety of Calvary, if you want me to be brutally honest. Carson is the sheriff here. He has a certain position, a certain reputation. You have any idea of the damage that could be done if this comes out without some sort of strategy?"

A sense of numbness was overtaking Rebecca's emotions. Not knowing what to feel beyond utter terror, she had perhaps decided that the safest option was to try to feel nothing. Maybe there was no conscious decision at all, her mind just shutting down on her like a worn-out engine.

"Of course he needs to know, Rebecca," Sperling said. "But I don't think you should be the one to tell him, and I don't think he should know now."

Rebecca just stared blankly at Dr. Sperling. Whatever life she thought she was going to have had just ended. The future was some wild unknown, and she was scared beyond belief.

"Let me give you something to calm your nerves," Sperling said, and from a small cupboard against the wall, he produced a pill bottle, tipped out two, handed them to Rebecca with a glass of water.

She took them without thinking, without even asking what they were, and Sperling sat with her until a dazed and slightly disconnected sense of unreality overtook her thoughts.

She smiled at the doctor, and when she asked him what they were going to do, he simply said, "I don't know, Mrs. Riggs . . . To be honest, I really don't know."

THIRTY-SIX

Henry and Evie had sat up late the night before. Glenn Chandler had sat with them, too, drank a couple of beers, talked of nothing significant, and the sense that Glenn was avoiding the issue at hand seemed as real as anyone present. It was the elephant in the room. Evan Riggs's daughter. Carson Riggs's change of heart. The reason for Henry's presence in Calvary. Of course, Evie herself was now rapidly becoming just as good a reason to be there. Henry watched her laugh with her father, caught the odd moment as she turned and looked at Henry, her eyes flashing with humor. He felt a very tangible connection, a sense that she—above and beyond everyone else—truly understood what he was doing and why. He hoped that their partnership would last so much longer than the search for Sarah.

Later, lying beside her, those few minutes before he himself drifted into sleep, he questioned his own motivation. Had it now become a matter of stubbornness, the unwillingness to back off, the blunt fact being that he would not be swayed by Carson Riggs? Having spent more than three years doing exactly what he was told, had this now become his way of fighting back? Carson Riggs was a figure of authority. He was a man of the law. Fuck the law. Fuck Carson Riggs. *I will find what I want, and I don't give a damn what you do to stop me.* Was that all it was now?

It didn't matter. He had set himself on a course to do this thing, and regardless of any additional reasons he might find to do it, his promise to Evan was enough. It was with this certainty that he slept, and when he awoke the certainty remained.

They set out right after breakfast. The featureless road gave onto an all-too-familiar landscape. West Texas had no dearth of towns that looked much as the one left behind, identical to the next you'd happen upon, no matter the direction taken. The flat horizon was punctuated with grain towers, water towers, irrigation pivots and pumps, all evidence of folks trying to give the land what it did not have, or prevent the weather taking it away. Dusty caliche roads ran away left and right, took you out through fields of bluestem, buffalo grass, Indian stem, every once in a while a grove of cottonwood or willow to break up the monotony.

They spoke little. Henry drove while Evie smoked, careful to ensure each butt was thoroughly extinguished before flicking it from the pickup. Prairie fires had taken lives and livelihoods with less than a thoughtless cigarette.

It was a little after nine when they arrived, and when Henry Quinn and Evie Chandler pulled into the main drag on Monday morning, it felt more like a ghost town than the end of Henry's quest.

They were looking for an orphanage, maybe some kind of fostering home, and, with a population exceeding little more than one and a half thousand, they figured it shouldn't be too hard. A town like this everyone would know everyone, and if they didn't, they'd know someone who did.

They asked first at the post office.

"Orphanage?" the woman asked. She shook her head. "Never been no orphanage here, son."

"Maybe some kind of fostering place?" Evie asked.

The woman frowned. "How far back you talkin'?"

"Would be twenty years, maybe," Henry said.

"Well, I don't know whether it's gonna be of any help, but there was a family called Garrett who used to look after some strays. That was years ago, though."

"They still here?"

"He is, she isn't, far as I know."

"You know where he lives?"

"I do, yes," the woman said, and gave them directions.

The house to which they were directed did not seem at all like the place Henry had expected.

Close to ramshackle, whoever lived here could not have possessed a shred of domestic pride. Little more than a wood-built lean-to crudely appended to an almost-derelict single-wide, the roof of both structures a patchwork of exhausted felt, corrugated sheeting, random boards, and a length of threadbare carpet upon which was growing some sort of bright-colored moss. The steps up to the front door were lengths of railway sleeper, as far as Henry could guess, and when he approached and knocked on the door, it felt as if the whole structure reverberated sufficiently to risk collapse.

"This is bullshit," Evie said as they waited. She wore an expression like some bad smell had assaulted her nostrils.

Henry said nothing. What could he say? He knocked again and stepped back as he heard movement.

Predictably, the man who appeared from the side of the building was carrying a shotgun.

"Hell do you want?" he said.

"Sorry to disturb you, sir, but we were told to come looking for you by a woman at the post office," Henry said. "Got word that you used to run some kind of orphanage or somethin'."

The man shook his head. "Hell, that's all history now, son. That was a good deal o' years ago."

"We just came to ask about someone that may have stayed with you," Evie said. "That was all."

"Lot of kids stayed with us," Garrett said. "That's what we did. Looked after kids no one wanted until they found a home. Thankless task, if you ask me, but that's what we did."

"There was a girl," Henry said. "Born in late forty-nine. Mother was from over Calvary way; father was a singer called Evan Riggs."

The man smiled a crooked smile. "You'd be speaking of Sarah."

Henry felt an unexpected rush of emotion bloom in his chest. He felt light-headed for a moment. He looked at Evie. Evie opened her mouth to speak but said nothing.

"Sarah, yes," Henry said. "That was her name. Sarah."

"She be dead," Garrett said. "Good while now."

Henry's eyes widened. His intake of breath was audible. He looked back at Evie once more. She looked stunned, her brow furrowed, her shoulders sagged, as if those three words meant everything and nothing at the same time.

"Dead?" Henry asked.

"Dead is what I said, boy."

"But . . . but how? When? What happened?"

"She died. That's what happened," Garrett said. "Ain't no point to dress it up fancy. She got the pneumonia when she was all of seven or eight years old. Killed her stone dead. Had a rash of them here, Calvary, too. Whole bunch o' kids. Adults, too."

"She's dead?" Henry asked Garrett, as if repeating the question would somehow change the answer.

Garrett looked at Evie. "He a bit simple-minded or what?"

Evie shook her head. "He's just shocked, Mr. Garrett. He's been looking for her, and we never expected that she'd be dead."

243

"Well, in my experience, what you expect and what you get is rarely the same thing, miss. Life is pretty much rough corners an' sharp angles. That's a fact right where it stands."

"I can't believe she's dead," Henry said.

Garrett took a step closer toward them. "Seems our business is done, eh?"

Henry was still in disbelief. He kept shaking his head and sighing. He thought about Evan, about what he would say, about the defeat such a thing would bring to the man. The weight of this was sufficient to crush him, Henry believed, considering then that the idea of one day seeing his own daughter had been the sole motivation for Evan's staying alive in Reeves. Take this away, and what did he have?

"Are there any records, any documents, any pictures of her?" Evie asked.

Garrett shook his head. "You wanna know the history, look elsewhere, girlie. My wife done raised up that girl only to see her die. And she wasn't the only one. Boys, too. Broke her heart. Broke her mind. She up and burned everything . . . clothes, shoes, toys, pictures, everything. Done killed herself a year later. Been livin' alone with naught but conscience for company ever since."

"Oh, Christ . . ." Evie exhaled, and even though it was not her loss, she looked close to tears. "I'm sorry," she whispered, her voice cracking.

"Gotta be sorry for? You didn't kill her. Only thing you done is remind me of it."

"Well, then, I am sorry for that, Mr. Garrett," she said.

"No need for sorry, sweetheart. What's done is done."

Evie turned to Henry. "Let's go," she said. "Let's not trouble Mr. Garrett any further."

Henry nodded but said nothing. She stepped back, took his arm, steered him toward the pickup, and opened the door for him.

"Start the engine, Henry," she said, and he complied.

Pulling away, she waved back at Garrett, and he raised his hand in response.

"She's dead," Henry muttered to himself as they reached the main drag of Menard.

"Sad fucking business," Evie replied, and yet she could not shake that ghost of doubt at the back of her mind. Something was awry. She knew it. Knew it in her bones.

They drove back to Ozona in near silence, Evie wanting to say something, anything, but there were no words. The atmosphere in the car was as if packed tight with thunderclouds. Henry started to say something a couple of times, but then his thoughts fell short of verbal realization.

Both of them spoke when they turned down the drive toward the Chandler place.

"Oh, hell," Evie said.

"What the fu—" Henry started, but left it unfinished.

Alvin Lang stood beside his black-and-white outside her house, a smug grin on his face, and they knew then that whatever trouble they had started into had only just begun.

"Mr. Henry Quinn," Lang said as Henry exited the pickup.

"What the hell you doin' here, Alvin?" Evie asked, at once challenging and aggressive, though beneath the bravado there was a clear tone of anxiety.

"Attendin' to some business that don't much concern you, Evie Chandler," he replied.

"You have business with me?" Henry asked.

"Reckon I do, son," Lang said.

"Concerning what? This business with Evan's daughter? If it's that, then it's finished. We went out to Menard, found out that Sarah is dead."

"That so?" Lang asked, seemingly disinterested.

"You aren't surprised, Alvin?" Evie asked. "Or did you already know she was dead before you sent us?"

"Didn't know nothin'," Lang replied. "And I don't care to know much of anythin' now. Not here to talk about that. Here to talk about something a good deal more serious."

Henry knew that. He felt it in the pit of his gut.

"What *are* you doing here, Deputy?" he asked.

Lang reached into the car and took out a brown paper bag. From it he withdrew another bag, clear plastic, and within that was some kind of parcel, again wrapped in clear polythene.

"This here belongs to you, I guess," Lang said.

Henry frowned. "What is that?"

"Some kind of unlawful substance, I figure," Lang said.

"The hell you talkin' about?" Evie said, her expression already giving up her anxiety.

"Like I said, Miss Chandler, this ain't none o' your business. This here is business between Henry Quinn and the Redbird County Sheriff's Department."

"So I'm asking," Henry said. "What the hell are you talking about?"

Lang smiled like a lizard. "Seems we got some marie-joo-ana here, son. A good deal of it. All wrapped up like a Christmas present and your fingerprints all over. That's what we got, son, and that's what's gonna git you right back in Reeves. Correct me if I am wrong, but you're on parole."

Henry knew then what they'd done. Riggs had sent him over to Lang's with the parking tickets. Lang never took that parcel of tickets off of him, asking him to set it down on the table. Used that wrapper to bundle up some weed, and now they had him.

The world closed in a little. Lang was right; Henry was on parole; one violation and he was back at the county farm for another year, and then whatever they could slap on the tail end for possession, maybe intent to supply.

"Now, seein' as how you been stayin' here, you'll find that I done searched the house for more drug evidence," Lang said. "You may find things a little all over the place, so to speak, but you have to be thorough, you know?"

"You son of a bitch, Alvin Lang," Evie hissed. "You goddamned spineless asshole son of a bitch."

Lang frowned, though the expression was mocking. "You be careful with that sharp tongue, there, missie," he said, "or you're gon' find yourself with a charge o' complicity to sell and supply this here primo numero uno Mexicana weed.

"Now all that remains is for me to search your vehicle, Mr. Quinn, and you can either let me do that right here and now, or I can send for a truck and we'll get it towed in and taken apart."

"What the—" Evie started, but Henry grabbed her arm.

"Do it," he told Lang. "I know what you're looking for, and you ain't gonna find it."

Lang didn't hesitate. He took his time, and he was thorough, and when he was done, he looked at Henry Quinn and they both knew what the search had really been about.

"I know what Sheriff Riggs wants, Deputy . . . I just don't know why. Did he kill the girl? Is that what happened? Did Sheriff Riggs kill his own niece?"

Lang shook his head. "I have no clue what you're talkin' about, son," he replied.

"What is he hiding, Deputy Lang? Why is he so afraid?"

"Afraid? Carson Riggs afraid? Is that what you think?" Lang

laughed dryly. "Day I see Carson Riggs afraid of anything is the day I know the whole world is done for."

Henry nodded slowly. "You got what you wanted," he said. "I ain't goin' back to Reeves. Not for nothin'. You tell Sheriff Riggs that we is all done and dusted on this business. I'll be stayin' a while, I guess, over in Ozona, but let's call it a little postrelease R 'n' R. Then I'll be on my way and you won't ever hear from me again."

Lang smiled. "Knew you weren't dumb, Henry Quinn, and Sheriff Riggs ain't a man to bear a grudge. However, things will stay just as they are until we see you're gone for good. This ain't a game, Mr. Quinn. We ain't friends, and we ain't never gonna be friends." Lang took a step forward, looked at Henry, turned and looked at Evie. "You make your own bed, you gotta lie in it. You been told a coupla times to mind your own affairs and not be concernin' yourself with anyone else's, but you saw fit to keep on kicking the dog. Well, even the most patient dog is gonna get up and bite you, you know? This one's got big teeth, bigger than you think, and this dog has been around a long time and has gotten himself some mighty important friends. Are we seein' eye to eye, Henry Quinn?"

"Tell you the truth, Deputy, I was of a mind to give up anyway," Henry said. "This is some harebrained scheme that ain't gonna come to any good."

Lang nodded. "Sheriff Riggs said you would see sense. Said you had your head set the right way." He tossed the bag in through the window of the car and opened the door.

As a parting word, he added, "Sometimes a man gets bullheadedness confused with keeping his word and suchlike. They ain't the same thing, I assure you. Smart man is the man who knows when to quit."

Evie stepped forward, once again intent on making a speech.

Henry grabbed her hand and once again shook his head. "No, Evie."

Lang smiled. "Listen to the man, Evie Chandler," he said. "And listen good . . . Pushin' on this thing ain't gonna serve no one no good."

Lang put on his sunglasses, got behind the wheel, and slammed the car door behind him. The engine kicked into life, and he cut out of the drive and started down the highway.

Evie stood silent for a moment, and then she turned to Henry with a look of disbelief on her face.

"You are not the man I thought you were," she said.

247

"How so?" Dav's face was a frightened of surprise.

"Quittin' like this . . . givin' up on this thing."

"Who's quittin'?" he replied. "He came here to find Evan's letter. They can look for a month of Sundays. They ain't never gonna find it. However, now they've made me angry."

Evie smiled wryly. "Let's go see what kind of mess Alvin Lang has made, eh?"

THIRTY-SEVEN

The truth—hard like a bullet—came out. Inevitable it may have been, but the way in which Carson became apprised of it could never have been predicted.

Doc Sperling and Warren Garfield, Calvary's only lawyer, were thick as thieves. Drunk one night, Sperling let it slip. Ida Garfield, chairwoman of the church committee, overheard. Fact was that she didn't so much overhear as eavesdrop. To say she was interested in the business of others was an understatement of significance, and being married to a lawyer gave her all manner of opportunity to inveigle her way into the unsuspecting confidences of those who would have preferred her to remain ignorant. She knew, for example, that misdemeanors were perpetrated by all and sundry, everything from Clarence Ames's multiple parking and speeding violations to George Eakins's impropriety with a young woman from Sanderson who'd been hired by Mrs. Eakins to assist with the school bake sale. Girl said that George Eakins was drunk and put his hands someplace where they really shouldn't have been; Carson Riggs calmed the whole thing down, convinced the girl there was nothing to pursue in the way of legal action, sent her packing, never to be heard of again. Nevertheless, there was a conversation in the Garfield kitchen a day or two later. Present were Warren, Sheriff Riggs, and George Eakins. Ida did not catch the details of the discussion, but bade George farewell when he left. To say he looked sheepish would have been putting it mildly; the man looked positively crestfallen. Ida Garfield guessed that Sheriff Carson Riggs went on being Sheriff Carson Riggs for a very simple reason: He knew what he knew, and—most important—he kept records.

One time Ida asked her husband if he and Carson Riggs were in collusion, if they were in fact keeping the collective menfolk of Calvary in their sway with a litany of unexposed crimes, all of which could become public knowledge in the event of a betrayal.

"Where you get these ideas from, I do not know," Warren told his wife. "Guess you've been reading those trashy *True Detective* magazines in the hair salon."

Dismiss it he may have done, but Ida read her husband far more closely and with far greater interest than any *True Detective* magazine, and he was no gifted liar. He and Carson Riggs were up to no good. She knew it in her bones.

Thus, when she got wind of Rebecca Riggs's pregnancy being something other than it was, she could not withhold herself from having a quiet word with Grace Riggs when next she saw her. Take three yards of bull-hide rein and lash Ida Garfield's tongue to a hitching post and still she'd find a way to gossip.

Grace had known all along. Grace had known it from the moment she saw Evan return from the Wyatt farm that night of the party. Had Rebecca Wyatt wanted a parting gift from Evan Riggs, something personal with which to remember him, she could not have asked for something better or more permanent. Maybe it was female intuition, maybe simply because she was Evan's mother, but a sense of quiet and certain anxiety had been present among her thoughts since that fateful February night.

Sunday, July twenty-fourth, the vast majority of Calvary's women-folk huddling for postchurch chatter while the men smoked cigarettes and discussed whatever men discussed, Ida steered Grace aside and cornered her.

"I got the notion there might be some awkwardness on the way," Ida said.

Grace frowned. At that point she could not surmise what Ida was implying. Ida was always rooting for scents like some sort of tactful bloodhound.

"Word has it that the new Mrs. Riggs—"

Grace knew then. How she knew—more to the point, how Ida knew—was irrelevant. She cut the woman short. "Ida," she said, doing all she could to maintain an implacable composure, "if you concerned yourself with your own affairs with the same diligence as you concern yourself with the affairs of others, then your stoop would be a great deal cleaner."

"Well, I don't know what on earth you mean by that, Grace Riggs," Ida Garfield retorted. Her indignation was not feigned; as with all hypocrites, her hypocrisy was unknown to herself, the suggestion of any such thing met with nothing but dismay and disbelief.

"I mean nothing by it," Grace said, "save that Proverbs tells us that whoever keeps their mouth and their tongue keeps themselves out of trouble."

"You are quoting Scriptures at me, Grace?" Ida said, this time feigning hurt.

"Ephesians, chapter four, verse twenty-nine, Ida. Let no corrupting talk come out of your mouths, but only such as is good for building up, as fits the occasion, that it may give grace to those who hear."

Hindsight told Grace Riggs that she had perpetrated an act of aggression tantamount to declaration of war. Hindsight told her that she should have bitten her tongue. Her wish to reprimand Ida Garfield had been nothing more than defensive, a knee-jerk response to the threat of discovery. It has been said that emotional responses to criticism are merely efforts to obscure the fact that the criticism is justified. So it was the case here, for the sharpest spike of hindsight, the one that drew blood, was Grace's knowledge that she could have dissuaded Evan from walking Rebecca home that night and she had not. In truth, perhaps she had made some subconscious wish for something such as this to happen. Secretly, Rebecca's acceptance of Carson's proposal had troubled her more than she had ever let on, even to William. Rebecca should have married Evan. Evan needed someone like Rebecca far more than Carson ever did or ever would. Unanchored, Evan was a ship adrift, the kind of ship that gravitated toward rocky outcrops and hull-shredding reefs as if a magnet for such things.

"Your response tells me all I need to know," Ida Garfield said, and the impulse to knock the woman on her ass was almost overwhelming.

Grace withheld herself, not only because it was Sunday, the minister and Calvary's entire congregation in hailing distance, but because she didn't wish to give Ida Garfield the satisfaction of proving herself superior.

Grace let it go, at least for that moment, but when dinner was done, she took Rebecca aside and told her that she knew.

"Know what?" Rebecca asked, her cheeks already colored, her eyes deer-in-headlight wide.

"Let's not play games, my dear," Grace said. "What's done is done. There's no going backward. No one, least of all you and Evan, can undo what happened that night."

There was a moment of stunned silence, and then Rebecca Riggs, married little more than four months, broke down. She sobbed like a spring runoff, and Grace merely held her.

Carson appeared at one point to find out what in tarnation was going on out on the porch, but Grace waved him away with three words sufficient to communicate that not only was his presence unwanted, but he wouldn't understand it anyway.

"Just woman things . . ." she whispered, and Carson vanished like a ghost.

Grace held her new daughter-in-law for a long time. She even cried herself, for she knew that whatever would unravel now would unravel their lives completely. They were in this together, neck-deep, no hope of rescue, and what transpired was dependent exclusively upon Carson's reaction to the news. A fuse had been lit, but the power and consequences of the explosion were utterly unknown. This was no Globe Salute. What it actually was, they had no inkling, save that it would be bad. That much they knew for sure. It would be bad.

An hour or so later, Grace told William to drive Rebecca over to her father's place. She told him not to ask questions of the girl.

"Just take her, William," she said. "Just take her home and we'll talk when you get back."

Carson was in the kitchen.

"What the hell is going on, Ma?" he said.

"She's pregnant, Carson. Get used to all manner of things you don't understand."

"But she's my wife. She should stay here with me."

"Well, what you think she should do and what she wants to do are not always going to be the same thing, son. It's called marriage. Deal with it."

"But—"

"The conversation is done, Carson. You go on to bed. Let me deal with all of this."

Carson kissed his mother good night and went to his room, a room still decorated with Carson's childhood and teenage years, a room he and Rebecca used when they were staying over at the Riggs farm. He could have headed back to the apartment in town, but he was not of a mind to. He was of a troubled mind, to be honest. Blessed with little more than his limited male intuition, he still knew something was awry.

It was past midnight when William Riggs returned home to find his wife still dressed and wide-awake in the kitchen. On the table in front of her was a bottle of whiskey and two glasses. William knew from experience that here was the clearest sign he could ever get that trouble was afoot.

"Sit down," she said. "I already had a drink. You better have a couple."

She told him then, straight as could be.

"Rebecca is going to have Evan's baby. Night of the party before Evan left, that's what happened and this is the result."

William Riggs sat and looked at his wife without comment, without the slightest change of expression.

"Did your heart stop, William?" she asked.

"Yes," he replied. "But it'll start again in a moment."

"So we need to make some decisions."

"Yes," he replied. "Some decisions."

"You just sit there awhile," she said. "Let me know when you're ready to work on this."

"Evan knows?"

Grace shook her head. "No. Only people who know are Rebecca, me, you, Doc Sperling and the Garfields."

William's eyes opened wide. "Ida Garfield knows?"

"She made it clear that there was something awry in the Riggs household. You know how she is, William."

"So if she knows, then the whole of Calvary knows."

Grace nodded. "And if they don't, I give it a day before they do."

"And how is Rebecca?"

"I don't know, William, and neither does she. To have done that and then married Carson is as wrong as it gets, but there's no use beating her to death about it. People make mistakes. Adults are no different from kids. No matter how bad the decisions they make, the reason is always the same. It seemed like a good idea at the time."

"If we don't tell Carson, he will find out from somewhere else. If we don't tell Evan, then Carson will tell him. What will happen, I don't know, but my fear is that one or both of them will wind up dead." He paused for a moment, then added, "There is no way to hide this, is there?"

"If it were just us, if there were no one else involved . . . if it had been someone other than her husband's brother, then maybe we could hide it. Premature births happen all the time. But it *is* her husband's brother and there are other people who know. Doc Sperling, Warren Garfield, his wife . . ." Grace sighed, shook her head resignedly. "Lord knows who else by now."

William Riggs closed his eyes and inhaled deeply. His insides felt hot and twisted. "Christ Jesus Almighty on a bicycle," he said under his breath.

"This is what they call life," Grace said. "There's no accounting for it. No one ever told us it'd be easy."

"No one told us it'd be this tough."

"Are you mad with Evan?"

"He's my son, Grace. Drives me crazy, want to knock his silly head off, but no, I can't be mad with him."

"So what do we do?"

"We find a time to tell Carson and we tell him."

"There is not going to be a good time for that, William."

"I know, my sweet, but there are going to be times that are worse than others."

Neither of them spoke for a little while, and then William Riggs reached for the whiskey bottle and filled both glasses.

"Girls would have been less trouble," William said.

Grace gave a wry smile. "Knowing us, we'd have had two girls just like Rebecca Wyatt."

"Or worse."

Grace laughed, William laughed with her, and thus they did not hear the retreating footsteps of Carson Riggs as he made his way back from the shadowed end of the hallway to his room.

THIRTY-EIGHT

It was Glenn Chandler they approached, and though unexpected, there was a certain inevitability to it. At least that's how he felt.

Returning to the house, seeing the disaster zone that it had become—books pulled from shelves, clothes turned out of drawers, boxes of private papers spilled left and right, mattresses upended, cupboards emptied, their contents left strewn along the landing—Chandler knew that Riggs had sent a very clear message. Where the hell Evie was, he did not know. No doubt somewhere with Henry Quinn, and that was the man Chandler needed to talk to.

And then the visitors came—before he'd even begun to straighten up the mess—and the three of them sat and talked for a while, and then the visitors left and there was nothing but silence and disarray.

Glenn Chandler sat in his kitchen and wondered what the hell to do. Obligation played a part in it, of course, but it also walked around the edges of duty, even justice. He had been drawn into it by default, but he was pragmatic enough to understand that luck and coincidence were merely attempts to rationalize those things for which people were not prepared to take responsibility. He was responsible for his own daughter, and whether he liked it or not, she had gotten herself into a situation with this feller from Reeves.

Riggs was desperate to find his brother's letter, and where else would they look aside from where Henry Quinn was staying?

Those thoughts were summarily interrupted by the sound of Henry Quinn's pickup as it pulled to a halt outside the Chandler place.

Glenn didn't move. He sat there waiting for them both to appear, and when Evie came into the kitchen, she and Henry were carrying paper sacks of groceries.

"Hell of a mess," Chandler said.

"Alvin Lang," Evie said. She walked to her father, leaned down, and put her arms around his shoulders. "I am so sorry, Pa. I don't know what to say. We started getting it sorted out, and then we went to get some groceries. We will straighten everything out. I promise."

255

"There's a trail of photos across the landing," Chandler said. "Most of them are of your mother."

Evie hugged her father.

Henry stood there in silence.

"And while you were gone, I had a couple of visitors."

Evie stood up, took a step back. "Lang?" she asked. "Did Sheriff Riggs come, too?"

"Not Riggs and Lang, no. But it was about them."

"So who came?"

"Roy Sperling and George Eakins."

"And what did they want?"

"Wanted to let me know how much trouble you were in."

"We know how much trouble we're in," Henry said. "Riggs and Lang have cooked up a possession beef for me. Told us to back off or I go back to Reeves for a year."

Chandler nodded, didn't speak for a moment, and then he said, "And they did this to me, too. Trashed my home. Emptied boxes of my private papers, my photos, everything..."

"He searched Henry's car as well," Evie said.

"This isn't about delivering a letter anymore, is it?"

Henry looked at Evie, back at her father. "I don't think it was ever about delivering a letter, Mr. Chandler."

"So what did Roy and George want?" Evie asked. She took a seat facing her father.

Chandler raised his eyebrows, exhaled slowly. "To be honest, I am not really sure. They talked a great deal and said little of any real sense. All I could gather was that there is some wealth of history between them and Carson Riggs, and they don't want it coming out."

"Seems everyone in Calvary has secrets," Evie said. "Never been anywhere like it."

"All comes back to Riggs," Henry said. "And if you want my opinion—"

Chandler cleared his throat, interrupting Henry. "To be completely truthful, son," he said, "I'm not sure what to think or feel about you at all. I don't know what the hell you've gotten my daughter involved in. Now I'm involved, too, if only from the viewpoint that my home is being searched by the cops."

"I got myself involved, Dad," Evie said. "We've already talked about that. If Mom were here—"

"If Mom were here?" Chandler said. "Well, she's not. She died,

Evie. She died, okay? I lost her, and I sure as hell don't have my heart set on losing you."

Evie laughed nervously. "You're not gonna lose me, Dad. Carson Riggs is not gonna kill us."

"Maybe he will," Chandler said. "Hear what Roy Sperling and George Eakins have to say about it, and maybe there wasn't so much of the natural causes going on when Warren Garfield bought it."

"They said that Riggs killed Garfield?" Henry asked. "He was Calvary's lawyer, right?"

"He was, indeed," Chandler said, "and no, they didn't say that Riggs killed him. They said that people who start turning rocks over tend to find rattlers. Rattlers like the cool and the shade. They don't like to be disturbed."

"Then they told you that Garfield was turning over rocks?" Evie asked.

"In so many words, yes. That was definitely the message I got from . . . well, what I can only describe as a slightly surreal one-way conversation."

"I am thinking we need to talk to one or both of them," Henry said.

"How did I know that that was going to be your next plan of action?"

"Because he's like me, Dad. That's why. That's exactly what I would do right now, and I am going to go with him."

"My sweet, naive daughter . . . Everyone has more going on than they're prepared to say. You've just gotten yourself wound up in the rightness of it all, and you think that backing off will say something about your integrity or your human decency or whatever." Chandler looked at Henry Quinn. "Okay, so you shared a cell with the guy, and maybe he did help you out some, but if it came down to it, then would you risk your life to get this message delivered to his daughter?"

"I would, yes," Henry replied, and he replied without hesitation.

Chandler seemed surprised at the speed and certainty of Henry's response. "And why, might I ask, are you so indebted to the man?"

"Because he did the same for me, Mr. Chandler."

"He risked his life for you?"

"Yes, sir, he did. Twice, if not three times."

"And he did this because?"

"It may seem crazy to anyone outside of someplace like Reeves, but it's a world all its own. There's a way that things are done, and they've been done that way for a long, long time, and no one explains these things to you, and sometimes you cross a line that you didn't even know was there. Before you know it, there's word out that you probably ain't gonna make it to the end of the week."

"And you crossed some lines," Chandler said.

"I did, yes."

"And Evan Riggs took care of it so you made it to the end of the week."

Henry nodded, walked from the door to the kitchen table and sat down facing Glenn Chandler.

"You are how old?"

"Twenty-one."

Chandler sighed. "Jeez," he said. "Twenty-one years old and you're already in shit so deep most people'd have drowned by now."

"What did you always say, Dad?" Evie asked. "No one should ever aspire to a normal life?"

"Not exactly what I meant, Evie. Gettin' yourself killed at twenty-one wasn't the kind of thing I had in mind."

"I don't really think Carson Riggs is gonna kill anyone," she said.

"You don't know what he's gonna do," Chandler replied. "And the reason you don't know what he's gonna do is because you don't know what he's hiding. Whatever the hell he has under his bed might be big enough to justify anything you can imagine. Say that whatever he's done, or whatever he knows, is gonna put him in Reeves for the rest of his life, maybe even send him to the chair. You don't think a man like that would be prepared to do whatever it took to protect himself from such an eventuality? The bottom line here is that you pair don't even know how deep the hole is or what's at the bottom, and you might go on falling forever before you find out."

"Jeez, Dad, where the hell do you get this thing about people being killed from? What the hell is this? You honestly believe that Carson Riggs has murdered people? That he's trying to hide something like that?"

"The point, my dear, is that we don't know. This is West Texas. Normal-people rules don't apply here. Even East Texas rules don't apply here. Head out to the plateau and the Davis Mountains and there's an awful lot of space to lose a couple of bodies."

"Since when did you get so paranoid?" Evie asked.

Chandler shrugged. "Hell, I don't know . . . Maybe since I came home and found out that the Sheriff's Department has searched my house, looking for something I haven't even seen." He nodded at

Henry. "Maybe since this joker came along and got me to thinkin' about losing my daughter."

"You're not gonna lose me, Dad," Evie said, "but I'm not going to let this lie. I'm just not. I can't even explain why not, but that's just the way it is."

Chandler smiled, a moment of recognition, almost as if he'd heard that kind of line delivered just that kind of way many times before. "You want my advice?" he asked.

"Sure."

"Roy Sperling. Calvary's doctor for however many centuries. If he doesn't know stuff, then no one does."

"We need to get him out of Calvary," Henry said. "I go back there and I might as well drive myself straight to Reeves."

"I can call him, see if he's willing to meet someplace," Evie said.

"I think he'll come," Chandler said. "Got the feeling that there was a man who wanted to get something off his chest. Eakins did all the talking. Sperling looked like he had a ghost inside him just desperate to get out."

Evie got up, walked out to the hallway.

Henry Quinn and Glenn Chandler sat in silence, heard murmurings of whatever conversation Evie was having. She was back within a couple of minutes.

The expression on her face was telling.

"He'll meet us," she said. "A diner just off 10, about twenty miles east of here. An hour from now."

"What did he say?" Henry asked.

Evie shook her head and frowned. "He said the weirdest thing... that we didn't have the right to judge him. That no one but God had the right to judge him."

"What the hell does that mean?"

"Means he wants to confess," Glenn Chandler said. "Means he's an old man, and he ain't as strong as he used to be."

THIRTY-NINE

The world fell quiet for a little while. Rebecca stayed at the Wyatt place. Carson went about his sheriff business, called on his wife a couple of times, and from all appearances she seemed to be all right. Subdued, a little quiet, but all right. Carson spent a night in town, another at the farm with his folks. The third night he drove out to see her, took her into Calvary, and they stayed together in the apartment.

In the morning Carson drove her to the Wyatt farm once more, knew from his wife that Ralph would be gone for the afternoon.

"I'll come over for lunch, if that's okay," he told her as he left the house.

She stood on the veranda and watched him drive away.

If there was anything unusual in his manner, Rebecca didn't notice it. She went about the business of cleaning up for her father, gathering up his laundry, taking care of those things she had always taken care of. She forced herself to think of anything and everything but what was set to consume her completely. In the odd moment that she caught her own reflection in a mirror, she saw a frightened and lost woman. For Carson, her face was brave and resolute, but the facade was wearing thin. Hiding the truth was exhausting beyond anything she could imagine.

Just after eleven she made a telephone call to Doc Sperling. She needed someone to talk to, someone who had some inkling of what she was going through. There was no answer, and Sperling's receptionist said he was up at County Hospital, wouldn't be back until late afternoon.

Rebecca thought of walking over to see Grace Riggs, but she couldn't bear the idea of seeing so many reminders of Evan.

She was torn in two. Not until now had she ever really grasped the conflict that had always been present. Carson and Evan. Evan and Carson. When they were kids, it was no big deal. The snake hunts. The rats' nest. The incident with Gabe Ellsworth. The foolhardy stunts they had worked up together. Three of them, always three of them, and it wasn't until this moment that she understood the ultimate inevitability of choosing between them. It had always been inevitable. Life was not fair. Life was not just. However, it could not be lived backward, and things done could never be undone. At least not this.

For the hundredth time since her conversation with Doc Sperling, she found herself truly overwhelmed. Cleaning the tub on her hands and knees in the bathroom, she just leaned forward, rested her head against the cool edge, and sobbed. She made barely a sound, and the tears ran down her face and dampened the front of her apron. After a while she got to her feet and washed her face, sat there on the rim of the bathtub and took as many deep breaths as she could. A sense of dizziness filled her mind, but it passed soon enough.

She went back to cleaning the tub. It was another half an hour before she started crying again, this time on the back veranda as she hung her father's work shirts up to dry.

This is madness, she told herself. *This is getting me nowhere . . .*

Nevertheless, she could not stop herself. The tears came, and there seemed to be an unlimited supply.

She needed to speak to Evan, but she knew she could not. They had not been able to find him for the wedding, and in some small way she had been glad of it. Knowing he was Carson's best man, standing right there beside her husband-to-be as she made vows that she could so easily have made to Evan, would have been worse than . . . No, she corrected herself, nothing could be worse than what she was facing right now.

Evan did not know he was going to be a father. Carson believed he was the father, but soon enough he would understand otherwise, and then what?

She could not hide; she could not escape; she could not run away or desert Calvary and her husband. She could not leave her father behind; she could not vanish into thin air. She could do nothing but wait for that inevitable moment when Carson was informed of the truth. He was not going to be a father; he was going to be an uncle.

And had she known she was pregnant right away, would she have aborted the child? That was a question she could not answer. As of tomorrow, she would be six months pregnant. Abortion was now impossible, and thus it would serve no purpose to further cloud her mind with considerations of it.

Close to noon, Rebecca heard the sound of a car. She was cried out, at least for the moment, and thus there were no further tears to be hidden as she went to greet her husband. She'd made a chicken broth, sandwiches, too, and a pot of fresh coffee was even now brewing on the stove.

Seemed he was not alone, for following his was another car, behind that a white vehicle she did not recognize.

It was only when Carson drew to a halt in the yard that she realized that Doc Sperling had come, too.

Her heart stopped.

Had he told Carson? Was this the moment he'd chosen to tell Carson what was going on?

Carson got out of the car. He did not smile at his wife. He reached back into the vehicle and took out his hat. He put it on.

The white vehicle drew to a halt behind Sperling's car. A man and a woman emerged, both of them dressed in hospital uniforms.

"Carson?" she said, her voice faltering. "What's happening?"

Carson looked back at Sperling. Sperling looked crestfallen, as if even now he was bearing the very worst news a man could ever bear.

"I never said a thing—" he started, but Carson said, "Shut the hell up, Roy," and then looked back at his wife as she came down the steps from the veranda and into the yard.

"What's going on, Carson?" she said, even though she understood full well.

"You know what's going on, Rebecca," he said.

Her eyes wide, blood draining from her face, she looked and felt no more than a ghost.

"Carson, I beg of you—" Sperling said, and the expression on his face said that anywhere in the world would be a better place than where he was in that moment.

"Enough, Roy," Carson said. "Don't say another word."

"Sweetheart," Rebecca said. "Tell me what's happening? Who are these people?"

"They are from Ector County Hospital," Carson said. "They are here to take care of things."

"Take care of things?" she asked. "What things, Carson? What are you talking about?"

Carson sneered at her. "Why are you doing this to yourself?" he said. "You know why I'm here. You know what's going on. You know exactly what's happened... and no, Roy Sperling didn't tell me about it. I heard it from my own mother's lips. I heard what you did, and I know that the child you're carrying isn't mine, and there

262

is no way in the world I am going to let you live under my roof with my brother's child, Rebecca—"

"Carson . . . Carson, please . . . You can't take away the baby. No, you can't do that. Please, please, you must forgive me . . ."

"Forgive you? You want me to forgive you? And how would this work, Rebecca? I should just make believe that the child you're carrying is mine?" Carson shook his head in disgust. He looked back toward the medical orderlies. "Take her," he said.

Rebecca rushed toward Doc Sperling as if there were some chance that he might come to her aid.

Sperling stepped back. Simultaneously, he lowered his head and looked down at the ground. "It is out of my hands, Rebecca," he said, and Rebecca understood all too clearly that Sperling would not help her.

The woman grabbed Rebecca's arm. "You need to come with us, dear," she said.

Rebecca pulled back, turned to run, but the woman was fast. The man joined her, and within a heartbeat Rebecca had her arms pinned on either side.

"Carson!" she cried. "Carson, stop them! Carson, you can't do this!"

Carson Riggs looked back at his wife, his expression harder than flint. "You want me to be a better husband, do you?" he asked. "Perhaps you should have considered how to be a better wife."

"Carson . . . no . . ." Rebecca pleaded, but there was nothing.

The orderlies marched her back to the white car and bundled her inside, the woman in the rear of the vehicle holding her down as the man stepped around to take the driver's seat.

The engine gunned into life, but—even above this—Doc Sperling could hear Rebecca Riggs screaming at the top of her voice.

Roy Sperling looked at Carson Riggs as the car reached the end of the Wyatt driveway, in his expression some last desperate hope that Carson might find compassion in his heart.

"We're done here," Carson Riggs said. "And I have nothing else to say."

Sperling stood in shocked silence as Carson Riggs got into his car, started the engine, and then headed back toward town.

FORTY

It was the kind of place where the blue-plate special had been special for way too long. Low-slung, flat-roofed, dusty windows, one of which wore a spider's web of fine cracks, Lonny's Roadside Diner was more in need of demolition than a bucket of soapy water and a lick of paint.

The absence of clientele within was testament to the success of the uninviting facade, and when Henry stepped up to the counter and asked for coffee twice, his order was met with a hint of resentment by a greasy-aproned short-order cook who seemed to consider customers an interruption of what he was really supposed to be doing.

The coffee came, predictably overboiled and bitter, and Henry carried the cups to where Evie sat in the farthest booth from the door. Through the window was a bare red-dirt lot, the pickup sitting there like a lost and patient dog.

"You think Carson Riggs had anything to do with Warren Garfield's death?" he asked her.

Evie shrugged. "Hell knows."

"What was he like, this Warren Garfield?"

"I didn't really know him so well," Evie replied. "He used to hang out at the saloon with the rest of them. He was a lawyer in Calvary pretty much his whole life. Had a wife, no kids. Wife died a good while back. One of those old Texas boys who just do the same job forever, end up widowed, never remarry, retire, don't believe they're lonely, but die of it anyway." She smiled ruefully. "I reckon that's the way my dad'll go."

"He's a good man," Henry said.

"He is. You're right there. Breaks my heart that he'll carry the ghost of my mom for the rest of his life. Thinks it'd be a crime to let go of her, but I think that's the first thing she'd ask him to do."

"A while ago," Henry ventured, "after we left the saloon that first night, you said that it was a good thing for people to keep their promises. You said it like someone broke a promise they made to you."

Evie sighed and shook her head. "I was young and innocent and he was a cruel boy and he broke my heart and it will never mend and I will never love again."

Henry smiled. "Seriously, what happened?"

"A different story for a different day," she said, her attention distracted by the sight of a car pulling into the lot beside Henry's pickup.

They watched without comment as Roy Sperling got out, as he went through the routine of checking each door was locked before he walked to the diner.

Sperling stepped into the shadowed entranceway of Lonny's and glanced around. He seemed both troubled and relieved, the latter perhaps attributable to Henry Quinn and Evie Chandler being the only people in the place, the former due to the reason for his own presence.

The short-order cook appeared through the multicolored strip curtain, his expression one of mild irritation. *And what the hell is it that you want?*

"Coffee, please," Doc Sperling said.

"That all?"

"For now," Sperling replied, and walked down the room to the far booth where Henry and Evie awaited him.

"I have no idea why I am here," was his opener.

"To try the worst coffee in West Texas," Evie said.

Sperling smiled, glanced at Henry. "Son, if you got this girl's heart, then you must be doing something right."

"Is that a compliment, Roy?" Evie asked.

"It is, Evie."

"Then I shall graciously accept it. I have to say that of all the crazy old fucks who hang out in the Calvary saloon, I like you the best."

"Aw, shucks, lady," Sperling said. "You're just saying that."

Sperling's coffee arrived. Sperling took a sip and grimaced. "Jeez," he said, "last time I had that taste in my mouth, I was heavin' up a half pint of bad bourbon."

Sperling slid along the seat and faced Henry and Evie.

"So, why are you here?" Henry asked. "Why did you agree to speak to us?"

Sperling shook his head resignedly. "I am older than Carson Riggs by a good fifteen or so years," he said. "I don't know about anyone else, but you get to the point where you realize that pretty much everything in your life is now behind you, and your attitude starts to change."

Sperling reached into his jacket pocket and took out a hip flask. He unscrewed the lid and added a half inch to his coffee. He did not offer any to Henry or Evie, perhaps of a mind that he might need all of it to get him through the meeting.

"Conscience?" Evie asked.

"Doesn't have to have a name, does it?" Sperling asked. "Your boyfriend here done three years in Reeves for getting drunk and shootin' some poor woman in the throat. Can't say you're too proud of that, eh, son?"

Henry shook his head. "No, sir, not too proud."

"Grown-ups ain't so different from kids," Sperling said. "I never had none myself, but I doctored enough to get an idea. Most everyone in their thirties and forties came through my surgery as a little 'un. Seen and heard it all, and some of it is the dumbest shit you ever did hear. Fool stunts, accidents, pranks gone wrong, you name it. Broken bones, broken teeth, bullet holes . . . hell, anything you can think of. Ask a kid how the hell he ever thought that leaping off the roof of his house into a water barrel was gonna wind up with anything but trouble, and the answer is always the same. Some eight-year-old thinks that gittin' his daddy's sidearm and takin' a potshot at the neighbor's cat will be nothin' but shit an' giggles, little girl gets pissed with her brother and sets his comic books on fire, both of them wind up at the clinic in Sonora with the nastiest burns you ever did see . . . always the same answer. It seemed like a good idea at the time." Sperling shook his head, took a healthy swig of his bourbon-laced coffee. "Guess you never think any other way, no matter how old you get."

Henry watched Doc Sperling. He was winding himself up for a confession. That was how it looked. Detail the justifications before you start, and you temper the severity.

"What happened, Roy?" Evie asked, highlighting once again that she was a straight shooter. The more time Henry spent with her, the more he understood that what you saw was what you got. Just like her father. Seemed there had been too few such people in his life. Even now, looking back at the time he'd spent with Evan Riggs, he was aware of how little the man had actually told him.

"A lot of things, Evie," Sperling said, "and I can't think of a single good reason to tell you any of it, save the simple fact that Carson Riggs is starting to grate on my nerves."

266

"He certainly seems to have the place in his pocket," Henry said.

"Son, you have no idea. There is a lot of history here, and there's no way to explain or understand much of it, except that everything we did, every decision we made . . . well, it seemed like a good idea at the time."

"This is about Sarah, right?" Evie asked.

"You don't know anything about Sarah," Sperling said, "and Lord knows if you ever will. Sarah doesn't even know about Sarah. I doubt she has ever heard the name 'Riggs,' and she sure as hell wouldn't know her parents. Her father is in jail and will never see the light of day as a free man. Her uncle Carson is a crazy fuck, her maternal grandmother is in the same nuthouse where we put her mother, and her granddaddy . . ." Sperling sighed.

"The same nuthouse . . ." Evie prompted. "You mean Ector County, where we went to see Grace Riggs?"

" 'S right. Me and Warren Garfield and Carson Riggs put that poor dumb pregnant girl in a crazy house, and then we took her baby off of her. We took her baby off of her and gave it to some strangers."

Sperling lowered his head, as if in shame, and when he looked up again, there were tears in his eyes.

"Why?" Henry asked. "Why did that happen?"

"Because Sarah's mother was Carson's wife. That's why. Rebecca Wyatt. That was her name. There was a party, all the way back in February of 1949, and right after that party, Evan done slept with Rebecca when she was already kind of promised to Carson. She'd never said yes, but the very next day, maybe out of guilt or shame or whatever, she went on over to Carson and agreed to marry him. Carson was lit up like a jack-o'-lantern. Never seen a man happier. Evan left for someplace, Austin, I guess, and he went on doing whatever Evan did best—getting' drunk, bein' an asshole, the usual thing—and Carson and Rebecca got themselves married and settled down. That was until she came to me pregnant, and I knew from the get-go that something was awry. She was *too* pregnant. Carson had his ways, always considered himself a churchgoin' man and whatever, but he was of a mind that sex was something you did after you got married, not afore. So she's a good deal more pregnant than she should be, and Garfield's wife . . ." Sperling smiled nostalgically. "You never did see ears so big on a woman. Only thing that matched the size of her ears was the size of her mouth. She overheard something, said something to Grace Riggs, and before anyone could say or do anything, Carson knew what was going on. His wife was carrying his brother's child."

"Christ Almighty," Evie said.

"Goes a way to explainin' the bitterness between them," Henry added.

"Hell, if Carson Riggs knows how to do something, it's hang on to a grudge," Sperling said, "though I have to say that when it comes to upsetting your brother, fucking his wife and getting her pregnant is pretty high stakes."

"So he had her committed and took the child away?" Evie asked.

"He did," Sperling said, and then he looked away through the dusty window as if the past was right there in the parking lot. "Actually, he didn't commit her . . . We committed her. Me and Warren Garfield and Carson Riggs. We consigned that poor girl to hell, and she never came back. She died in there. June of 1951. Little girl o' hers wasn't even two years old, her mother was dead and her father was in jail for the rest of his life."

"How did Rebecca die?" Henry asked.

"Same way we all do, son. Short of breath and brokenhearted."

"Did Evan know she'd died?" Evie asked.

"I don't know, Evie. I just know what I did and what I didn't do. I just know that I made some bad decisions, and somehow, some way, I'm gonna end up payin' for them."

"So why did you agree to commit her?" Henry asked. "You and Warren Garfield . . . Why did you let that happen?"

Sperling's expression was then one of reconciliation, as if he'd known this moment was coming for a very long time.

"What you're asking, Henry Quinn, is how was Sheriff Carson Riggs able to blackmail Calvary's doctor and Calvary's lawyer into falsifying documents so as his wife could be consigned to Ector County Hospital Psychiatric Facility and his bastard niece could be handed over to strangers, never to be seen again. Correct me if I'm wrong, but is that what you want to know?"

"Yes, Dr. Sperling, that's what I want to know."

Sperling smiled sardonically. "Regardless of what anyone might think or believe or suspect, there are only four people in the world who know the answer to that question. Two of them took it to their graves, the third is Carson Riggs, and I am the fourth. And I have the same plan as Garfield. That is going to my grave with me, and that's all there is to it."

"Two of them took it to their graves?" Evie asked. "Garfield and someone else."

"That's right, sweetheart. Garfield and someone else."

"And the someone else—"

"This is not twenty questions," Sperling said, cutting her mid-flight.

"And you don't know which family Sarah went to?"

"I do not."

"But Garfield knew, right?" Evie said. "He must have handled the adoption."

Sperling nodded, glanced at Henry. "This one's dangerous," he said. "Smarter than all of us put together."

"So the only person who now knows where Sarah went is Carson Riggs," Henry said.

"That's right," Sperling replied.

"I have one more question," Evie said.

"Which does not mean I have one more answer, but you go ahead and ask me."

"Warren Garfield," Evie said. "Did he die, or was he murdered?"

Sperling laughed. "Murdered? My, oh my, you do have an overactive and excitable imagination."

"I wondered," Evie said.

"So did I," Henry added.

"Well, if you are wondering whether Carson Riggs is capable of such a thing, then I think you already know the answer. However, I attended the autopsy. Warren Garfield's heart quit on him—no question about it. Maybe holdin' on to all them secrets finally killed him, and maybe Carson Riggs had something to do with the stress that was brought to bear. It's all supposition. There was no smokin' gun in Carson Riggs's hand, if that's what you're asking."

Henry leaned forward, elbows on the table, voice lowered. "What do you think is really going on here, Dr. Sperling?" he said. "Why do you think Sheriff Riggs is so afraid that we will find Sarah?"

Sperling smiled knowingly. "Oh, I think you are looking at this the wrong way around, son," he said. "I think you should be wondering what Sarah will do if she finds Carson. What would happen if that girl knew where she really came from? Seems to me that a number of pertinent answers might be revealed if you took a look at that letter of Evan's, but from what I understand, you are not going to do that."

Henry shook his head. "No, sir. I'm not. Just doesn't seem right. Private business is private business, and he asked me not to read it."

"Well, that's mighty noble, Henry Quinn. Seems like such a lesson might have been of use to Ida Garfield, God rest her soul. Carson Riggs, too, I guess. Carson's had his nose in everyone's affairs and his hand in everyone's pocket for the better part of thirty years, and it seems about time someone cut it off. Maybe you're the man to do that, eh?"

"I have no beef with Carson Riggs," Henry said. "I only came here to—"

"Doesn't matter whether you have a beef with him or not," Sperling said. "As is all too obvious now, he sure as hell has a beef with you." Sperling raised his cup, drained it, wincing at the taste. "What we did was wrong. There's no other way to dress it up. We sent that poor girl to her death, and it has kept me awake more nights than I ever care to recall. Maybe you can do something to fix some small part of this. I don't know. Maybe you pair are gonna wind up lost somewhere in the Davis Mountains, never to be heard of again. My sole interest here is not what Evan Riggs may or may not want, and to be honest, I don't much care to know what's in that letter that you are protecting so fiercely . . . What I want to see is the expression on Carson Riggs's face when he realizes that you can't get away with this kind of thing forever. Some say he's done more good than bad, and maybe that's the truth. Calvary is a safe place to live, quiet, peaceful, sure, but at what cost? We are all getting old now. Me, Clarence Ames, George Eakins, Harold Mills, and maybe it's time to man up, deal with the consequences, let Calvary drag itself up out of the past and get on with the future. Carson Riggs has controlled that town for way too long. Time for new blood. Time for change. Time for the truth, I guess is what I'm saying."

Sperling made as if to get up to leave.

"Doc?" Henry said.

Sperling looked back at him.

"Where do we go now with this? Give us something. Please."

"If I were you?" he asked. "Where would I go if I were you? Hell, son, that's a good question. Heard Sheriff Riggs sent you on some wild-goose chase out to Menard."

"He did, yes."

"Someone told you the girl was dead."

"Yes."

"Well, that's a lie, for sure and certain. Warren told me three weeks before he died that Sarah was alive and well and living not so very far from here."

"I knew it," Evie said. "I fucking knew it."

"Did he say where?" Henry asked. "What her name was?"

"He told me she was alive and well and living not so far from here," Sperling repeated, "and would say nothing further. Whatever he knew, and I am sure he knew a lot, went with him to the worms."

"Records?" Evie asked. "Adoption records, maybe. Something in writing somewhere."

"I couldn't swear on it, but I doubt very much that anything was on official lines. Carson Riggs is a good tracker, always has been. Good trackers don't only know how to follow tracks, but also how to cover 'em up. Anyway, you now have an answer to that all-important question—why Carson Riggs is so pissed with his brother. Sarah should have been Carson's daughter, but she wasn't. Rebecca should have been Carson's wife, but she was Evan's sweetheart all along. At least that's the way Carson sees it, and I don't disagree with that. It was enough to break any man, but Carson got vicious—"

"Did he frame Evan?" Henry asked.

Sperling paused. He looked away for a moment and then turned back to the pair facing him. "I think Evan Riggs was always more than capable of getting into the worst kinds of trouble all on his lonesome. Evan was a firework, you know? He was a bomb just waiting to go off. Rebecca Wyatt was a hell of a woman, but I don't know that even she would have corralled that boy any. Some people just deal with today and that's fine an' dandy. People like Evan always think that tomorrow is gonna be so much better, and they smash today all to pieces trying to get there."

"So, do you think Carson framed Evan for that murder in Austin?" Henry asked again.

"You're gonna get the only answer I can give you on that, son. I don't doubt that Carson would've been more than capable of something like that, and he sure as hell was pissed enough to do it. Did he frame his kid brother and put him in jail for the rest of his life? I guess only Carson can answer that question because, as far as I've heard, Evan doesn't remember a good goddamned thing about it." Sperling sighed audibly. "Evan was a drunk, not a good one at that. And he was a musician, too, and they're always hightailin' it toward crazy."

"Thanks for the heads-up on that, Doc," Evie said, "now that I got myself all involved with one."

Sperling smiled. "You wanna know something, Evie Chandler? I'll tell you now, and there's been a couple others who've commented on it ... You got the same kinda spirit as Rebecca. You don't look like her. You don't act like her. But there's something about you that seems kind of similar. And whatever she may or may not have done, and however much she betrayed Carson, what he did to her was not right, and we let him do it. There are only a couple of things I've done in my life that I'd take back, and that's one of them."

"So help us take it back," Henry said. "Help us find her ... if not for Evan, then for Rebecca."

"You got all you're gonna get outta me, son," Sperling said, and then he hesitated for a second, his expression thoughtful. "I don't have the same sensibility as you. I would open that damn letter and see what the hell Evan thinks he needs to say to a daughter he never met. Maybe Carson is right, though. Maybe telling her is exactly the wrong thing to do. Who knows what kind of whirlwind you'll let out of the box. All I can tell you is that whatever this is about, you got Carson Riggs badly rattled. Don't see him backing down, do you? Don't see him giving you anything but heartache. He's a tough son of a bitch, has a real mean streak, and I wouldn't choose him as an enemy."

"I think it's a little too late in the game for that," Henry said.

"I'm no lawyer," Sperling said, "but Garfield was my best buddy for years. Old legal adage he used to quote: Set the rules of the game, and the game's already won. Seems he's got you on the back foot. Always has had. However, every man has a weakness, and Carson Riggs is not the only officer of the Redbird County Sheriff's Department."

"Alvin Lang," Evie said.

"Redbird County is a real small county, and the sheriff has a great many responsibilities, everything from catching escaped felons to assessing local taxes, collecting past dues, seizing property, all sorts of things. It's a political function as much as anything. Man with that much authority and influence, hell, even after the voting is done, the sheriff has to be approved by higher powers. Gotta make sure they don't got some crazy son of a bitch runnin' around with a six-shooter, right? Degree of scrutiny is applied to anyone in that job, and unless he does an awful good job of hiding his skeletons, then they can come out to haunt him." Sperling smiled conspiratorially. "Sheriff has the power to deputize anyone, however. Same degree of scrutiny does not apply to a deputy. That's the sheriff's job, and the buck stops with him. You tell Alvin Lang that you know why he will never make it to sheriff, even after Carson Riggs is long gone, and he may be more help than you think."

"But we don't know—"

"In my time I have taken care of a great many improprieties," Sperling said. "As a doctor I am bound by oath not to divulge the details of my patients' concerns. However, let's just say that Alvin Lang came to me for some advice maybe half a dozen years ago. He didn't come as a patient, but as a confidant. He knew to come to me because of some things that happened back before Carson Riggs became sheriff of Calvary. He knew I would keep my mouth shut. It was May of sixty-six, to be exact. Seems he had been involved with someone he really shouldn't have been involved with . . . a married woman, no less, and she needed a certain procedure very quickly, very quietly. Far as I know, that procedure was carried out in Nueva Rosita, a good place, a place where they don't ask too many questions. But they do keep records. Dumb son of a bitch didn't have the sense to get a fake ID, something he could so easily have done from his position as deputy. Carson knows, as do I, but the husband never found out. He's still in West Texas, the wife as well, and though whatever indiscretion that took place is now over, it is still very present in Deputy Lang's thoughts."

"We're going to blackmail Lang into helping us," Henry said. "This is really looking up, isn't it?"

"Fight fire with fire, son," Sperling said. "Doesn't seem to me that Lang would miss a second's sleep if you wound up back in Reeves with your good ol' buddy Evan Riggs."

"Thank you, Roy," Evie said. "We really appreciate this."

"Well, that's me done and gone," Sperling said. "Anything else you need to know, then I have no idea what you're talking about."

Henry and Evie watched Sperling leave the diner and drive away in silence.

"The more we dig, the deeper it gets," Henry eventually said.

"You scared what we'll find?" Evie asked.

Henry shook his head. "Nope," he replied.

"Good. So let's go rattle Alvin Lang's cage, huh?"

FORTY-ONE

"My affairs are my affairs," Carson Riggs told his father.

"That is just bullshit, Carson, and you know it. That girl is part of this family."

"That girl slept with my brother the night before she agreed to marry me, and now she is pregnant with his child."

"I am not saying that she didn't do a terrible thing, son. And if you want to know the truth, it probably had more to do with Evan than Rebecca. But sending her up to Ector is just plain wrong. That is just the worst thing I can imagine. I may as well have found out that you killed her with your own bare hands—"

"Don't think I didn't consider it," Carson replied.

"You are letting your heart rule your head, son. Sometimes you gotta love someone even though they let you down every imaginable way."

There was a heartbeat's pause, and then Carson said, "The way you love me, despite the fact that I have always been a disappointment to you? Is that the kind of love you're talking about, Pa?"

"Carson . . . Carson . . ." William Riggs said, but he was stalling for time, and Carson knew it.

"You have no idea how obvious it has been all these years. You have no idea how it feels to stand in the shadow of your golden boy, Pa. Even with Rebecca . . . Hell, I knew what was going on. I knew the only reason she married me is because she was too damn scared to marry Evan. You don't think I knew that? Well, Evan may be bright and brilliant and a fucking musical genius, but he's also a drunk and a liar and he fucked my wife and got her pregnant, and then he disappeared and he doesn't even know what the hell is going on."

William Riggs stood on the veranda of his house, a house he'd built, a house that had seen him raise up a family, where he and Grace had tried to create the best life they could for the past thirty years. He was fifty-two years old, but he felt like a hundred. Was it better to stop loving someone suddenly, or—even when they were blood and kin and all that such entailed—to just never really love them at all? Who had committed the greater crime here? Evan, Carson, or himself?

"Son, no matter what's happened in the past—"

"The past matters, Pa. I used to think otherwise, but now I see it's true. The past determines everything. The past is where we all came from, good, bad, or otherwise. Even Evan used to tell me that. People tell you to forgive and forget. Well, I can't. You don't think I thought about it? You don't think I wrestled with this? You don't think I tried to find some way around this? Well, I did. I thought about tracking him down, wherever the hell he is, and telling him what happened. I thought about letting him take her and the child, about just giving her up." Carson shook his head. "I have been married five months. To be honest, I have never really been married. That wedding was a sham and a lie. You can't build a life with someone when there's a secret that big right at the start of it. It doesn't work."

Carson backed up from the railing and sat down in one of the veranda chairs. The sun was setting. The shadows were deepening, and from where William stood, he could barely see his eldest son's face. His voice came out of the gloom, and there was a chilling clarity and decisiveness in his tone.

"You don't think I thought about killing her? You don't think I thought about killing the pair of them? I want them to hurt for what they did to me, and killing them just seemed too darned easy. Now, to take her child away... That's a different story. Take away that bastard child and make sure she never sees it. That seemed like a much more fitting kind of justice. And Evan? Never tell him. He'd find out where she was in time, and then maybe he'd find out that she'd had a child... and he would always wonder, wouldn't he? He would forever be haunted by the ghost of doubt. Hell, if he learned when she had the baby, then it would all make sense, but there'd be no way to get to her and no way to find that child. I will make that child vanish forever, and my lying son-of-a-bitch brother and his whore mistress can tear the world apart looking for it and—"

"Carson," William said, interrupting his son. "Carson, you're starting to sound like a crazy man. What you're saying is wrong, just plain wrong, and I cannot let you do this—"

Carson laughed softly. "You cannot let me do this? What do you mean, you cannot let me do this? It's done, Pa. It's all done and dusted. Rebecca is up at Ector. She ain't never comin' out. Soon as that bastard child is born, it will disappear. Doesn't matter what you or Evan or Ma or Ralph Wyatt or anyone else says or does; it is over."

"I know where your mind is at," William said. "I know you've been talking to those oil people. You think I don't know what you're cookin' up? You do this . . . hell, Carson, you go through with this and—"

"And what? You'll cut me off? Write me out of your will? Give the farm to Evan so he can cut it up and sell it, pour the proceeds down his throat while we all go to hell? I made my decision, Pa, and there ain't nothin' gonna change my mind."

Carson rose from the chair, stepped out of the ever-deepening shadow, and faced his father.

"You think you have the right to tell me what to do, how to live? You expect me to treat you like a father when you never treated me like a son? Think again, Pa. The past catches up with you."

Carson took a step forward with such suddenness that William Riggs had to move rapidly to avoid being knocked on his ass. It was a physical challenge, and one that he did not rise to. William Riggs knew that he'd lost his son to whatever vengeful passion now coursed through his blood. He knew that Carson was stubborn enough to smash everything to pieces as long as he got his own way in the end. He had seen it before, all the way back to his childhood. The same fierce drive that made him sheriff at twenty-five years of age was of sufficient force to bulldoze everyone and everything that he considered contrary to his intent.

William watched as Carson got into his car and pulled away from the Riggs place. It was a symbolic departure. William felt it in his bones and his blood. He had lost his eldest son. Yet, even as the taillights disappeared into nothing, he had to ask himself whether he'd ever really been a father in the first place.

On the morning of Friday, August fifth, William Riggs sat outside Warren Garfield's office until Garfield appeared. He did not challenge him right there on the street, but marched the man inside and closed the office door behind them.

"If you say a word to Carson, I will have you ruined for what you did, Warren Garfield."

The words left William Riggs's lips like bullets. His anger was not only audible in his tone, but visible in the coldness of his eyes, the tension in his face.

"I have no idea what sway he has over you people," Riggs continued, "and I don't want to know. Whatever leverage he has brought to bear upon you and Sperling is none of my concern."

"William . . . you have to understand—"

"What, Warren? What do I have to understand? Very little, as far as I can tell. The girl done wrong. I understand that. Goddamnit, Warren, there is also no doubt in my mind that Carson and you and Roy Sperling done plenty wrong in your lives as well. Tell you what. Every time anyone ever does anything that upsets Carson Riggs, let's throw them in the crazy house and lose the key. How about that for a grand idea?"

"William—"

"To hell with you, Warren Garfield. Only reason I come over here is to deliver these documents. As far as business is concerned, that's you and me done."

William Riggs handed a bundle of papers across the desk to Garfield, and then he rose to his feet.

"William . . . come on. Let's talk about this. Let's be reasonable here—"

"Reasonable? Are you out of your mind, Warren? You talk about being reasonable? The same degree of reasonable you and Roy Sperling applied to my daughter-in-law? That kind of reasonable?"

"You don't understand, William—"

"I understand plenty good, Warren. I know what goes on up at that place . . . and she is pregnant, for God's sake, man. The girl is pregnant and you sent her up there to satisfy Carson's vengeful nature. They are gonna kill her, Warren, and her death will be on your hands. Roy Sperling's, too. As for my son, I will deal with him, and what I have done here today is the first step. What I have delivered to you is legally binding, and if you tamper with it or destroy it, I will see you ruined. I will see you absolutely and completely ruined. You understand me?"

Warren Garfield just looked back at William Riggs. The blood drained from his face, his eyes wide.

"I will take your silence as the answer I want, Warren. You file those papers I gave you, you understand?"

"Yes, William, I understand."

William Riggs glared at Warren Garfield for a moment longer and then turned and left the office. He slammed the door shut behind him, making Garfield start.

Garfield stayed motionless for a good minute, and then he reached forward and lifted the telephone receiver.

"Roy, it's Warren. You had a visit from William Riggs yet?"

Garfield closed his eyes as Sperling replied.

"Well, you're gonna get one. Man's blood is up. He's on the warpath."

Silence for a moment.

"Hell no. Don't call Carson. Jeez, we got ourselves into this, and no one but us is gonna get us out of it."

Garfield leaned back in his chair, shook his head. "No, Roy, leave it be. What's done is done. You don't think Carson'd fall on his own sword to see us done for? He's crazy, and that's a fact. We always knew it'd come back to this. I just never guessed it'd be so soon. You do nothing and maybe we got a chance. You go turnin' rocks over, you're gonna wake up more snakes than we could ever run from."

A moment's hesitation.

"We are not doing anything, Roy. No matter what you do, the past always catches up. You think I want to be in this position? We helped each other, remember? An opportunity presented itself, and we took advantage of it. We made a lot of money, you and me and Carson Riggs. You don't think it's haunted me, too? Well, this ain't no different, Roy. I'm asking for you to stand by me the same way I stood by you. That's all I am asking of you, and you cannot deny me that."

Garfield gripped the receiver. He closed his eyes and inhaled slowly as if everything was now testing him.

"No, Roy. You listen to me now. As long as that girl stays up at Ector, we have a hope of keepin' ourselves out of Reeves County Farm. Piss off Carson Riggs, and he's gonna get his high-an'-mighty friends to use whatever influence they got to see us burn in hell. That's the beginning and end of it, and I ain't hearin' another word."

With that, Garfield leaned forward and hung up the phone.

He rose from his chair, walked to the window of his office, and looked down the length of Calvary's main drag.

"Lord Almighty, what have we done?" he asked the empty room. He did not expect an answer, did not need one, for he knew it well enough already.

FORTY-TWO

They sat side by side in Henry's pickup outside the Chandler place. They'd killed the brights so as not to disturb Evie's father. It was getting late. Evie was tired, said she was burned out with everything.

"It's like untying one knot, only to find there's another knot beneath that, and then yet another," she said. "And Evan? You think Carson framed Evan?"

"I think Evan is just as likely to have done that all by himself."

"You said he remembered nothing."

"*He* said he remembered nothing. Wakes up after drinking himself blind, there's blood on his hands, and in the hallway outside his room there's a dead guy with his brains beaten out. Circumstantial maybe, but . . . Jesus, how do you even defend yourself against something like that?"

"You don't," Evie said. "Wonder if he knew about the kid by then."

"Maybe not," Henry said. "Rebecca got pregnant in February of 1949. Had the kid—when?—November sometime, right? Evan killed the guy—if he did, in fact, kill him—in August. He may have gone to jail knowing nothing about it."

"I wonder when he found out that Rebecca had died," Evie said.

"He didn't really speak of her. He only told me about the daughter right toward the end of my sentence. Way I'm thinking right now is that he told me only enough to get my word. I don't think Carson was ever Sarah's legal guardian . . . maybe in name, but certainly not in any other capacity. I think Evan told me that because he knew Carson would contradict it. He wanted to put me in enough mystery so I wouldn't quit."

"He knew you well enough to know how stubborn you'd be."

"Maybe so," Henry said.

"And you're really not gonna open that letter, are you?"

Henry shook his head. "Nope."

"Because?"

"What if there's something in it that changes my mind, Evie?

What if there's something that makes me not want to deliver it? Regardless, what Evan wants to say to her is none of my business."

"Seems to me you've been manipulated by one brother and framed for something you haven't done by the other. I could say you were dumb as milk, sure, but I actually admire you, Henry Quinn."

"Fuck off, Evie Chandler," Henry said, laughing.

"No, seriously, I really admire you. You ain't a quitter. You got some backbone. You are an idiot for that stunt with the gun that put you in Reeves, but you saw it through and you got out, and I know you ain't gonna go back."

"Hell no, not a chance."

"There's some kind of girls who could fall for a man like you."

"Is that so?"

"Sure there are. I mean, a couple of cans short of a six-pack, maybe. You don't like to say 'mentally defective,' right, but you know the kind of girl I'm talking about. Pops bottle caps with her teeth, eats off the kitchen floor."

"You are such a dumb fuck," Henry said. "Christ in hell knows what I am doing hangin' out with you."

"It's because you love me, Henry Quinn, but you're too proud to admit it."

"Pride is not one of my primary faults, I assure you," Henry said.

"So you don't love me?"

"I didn't say that."

"So you *do* love me?"

"Didn't say that neither."

Evie laughed. "Asshole."

"Fuck you very much."

Silence reined for a minute, and then she said, "Carson Riggs scares me, Henry. He's a bad fucking guy. I just feel it."

"I know he's a bad guy, and he scares me, too."

"Maybe he framed his brother, maybe he killed Warren Garfield . . . and he had something on Doc Sperling and Garfield, something that got them to do whatever was needed to get that poor girl committed to Ector Psych. And then he sent his mother there as well. Carson Riggs is the kind of family everyone could do without."

"And there was a fourth one, Sperling said . . . someone else who knew what Riggs had on him and Garfield."

"Yeah, someone else who's dead."

"You seein' a pattern here."

"Everyone we need to talk to is dead."

"Apart from Alvin Lang, grandson of the fucking lieutenant governor of Texas, for Christ's sake. And that's who Sperling said we should talk to."

"I need to sleep. I don't even want to think about Alvin Lang until tomorrow."

"Talking to the guy isn't the problem, Evie. Who's to say that this affair, the abortion in Mexico, whatever the hell happened, is even something that he's concerned about? Maybe he couldn't give a damn about being sheriff. Maybe he doesn't even want to be sheriff. And if Carson knows about this, what's to say Lang won't just hightail it over there, tell Riggs that we're trying to blackmail him, and all of a sudden I'm back in Reeves trying to explain to Evan why the hell his daughter never got the letter."

"They'll cut my head off and drop me down a dry well."

"Could be worse ways to go."

"Fuck it," Evie said. "Let's go inside and drink bourbon 'til we puke."

"Sounds like a plan," Henry said, and opened the car door.

They did drink bourbon, but not so much as planned. Glenn Chandler was sleeping, and so they stayed quiet, hung out in the kitchen for a while, and then went to Evie's room where they lay side by side and looked at the ceiling and talked about what would happen when the letter was delivered, or not delivered, and this was all done and dusted. The real possibility that it might be never be done and dusted was not broached.

"I gotta go make some records," Henry said.

"You're gonna have to sing me a song one of these days, Henry Quinn. For all I know, you might sound truly awful."

Henry smiled. He didn't know what he'd done to deserve her, but Evie Chandler just pleased the hell out of him. In that moment, he could not think of anyone with whom he'd rather be.

"So say it all settles down. Say you get your letter delivered, or maybe we find out that she really is dead, then what? You gonna go back to your ma in San Angelo?"

"I'll go see her, sure," Henry said, "but I have no plans to stay. Me and my mother sort of hang together more out of necessity than design."

"You have no desire to find your father?"

"None at all. Far as I understand, he didn't even know that my ma got pregnant. I don't think he knows he has a son. Guess he's alive somewhere, maybe has a family now, and the last thing in the world he'd want is someone he'd never even been aware of showing up and claiming to be his son. Wouldn't be right to do that to someone."

"That's a very compassionate viewpoint. If it were me, I'd wanna go over there and collect up on all the past birthday and Christmas stuff."

Henry laughed. "What's done is done; that's the way I see it. He didn't break any promises because he didn't make any in the first place. People do impulsive things, and sometimes there are consequences. Doesn't mean you have to beat them to death for it."

Evie pulled herself closer to Henry. She liked that feeling of warm solidity beside her. Her hand on his chest, feeling it rise and fall as he breathed, feeling sleep stealing her words away even as she tried to speak to him.

"You're making no sense now," Henry said. "Sleep, why don'tcha?"

" 'Cause I wanna talk to you."

"We got plenty of time to talk," he whispered. "Like Louis said, we have all the time in the world ..."

"Don't make promises you can't keep, Henry Quinn."

"I don't," he replied, but she didn't hear him. She had already slipped out of wakefulness into a deep and undisturbed sleep.

FORTY-THREE

The sermon on Sunday, August 7, 1949, struck a chord with William Riggs. The words that got his attention were: *Whoever spares the rod hates his son, but he who loves him is diligent to discipline him*. It was from Proverbs, and the minister went on with further verses from the same book, saying such things as *The rod and reproof give wisdom, but a child left to himself brings shame to his mother*, and *Folly is bound up in the heart of a child, but the rod of discipline drives it far from him*.

Since his confrontation with Garfield, William Riggs's attention had been completely bound up, tied tight like some Gordian knot. Grace had seen it clear as day. "You're wearing your troubles like an overcoat," she said.

"You aren't troubled?" he asked her, a question that provoked an expression of dismay.

"Of course I am troubled, William. Lord, what would you have me think about this? That poor girl is up in that crazy hospital, and our son put her there. I understand that she wronged him terribly, but I never thought him so vindictive and heartless."

"Can't help but think that had I loved him more . . . or at least demonstrated some greater degree of affection when he was a little 'un . . ."

"Enough of that sort of thing," she said. "That's all just so much supposition and nonsense. You think they arrive like a blank slate and we get to write their personality? Children have a mind of their own before they even learn to walk."

"You think so?"

"I know so."

"Still, it is difficult not to think that—"

"That what? That had we done something a different way, he might not be the man he is now? You're forgetting Evan in all of this. Evan was the one who done slept with his brother's girl, William. How is he blameless in all of this? Way I see it, Evan is the one who's responsible for this trouble, but we long ago accepted that he was a troublemaker, and so that makes whatever he does forgivable."

"I'm not saying that."

Grace smiled. "You don't know what you're saying, William Riggs."

William paused, smiled in self-recognition. "You're right there."

"If all the energy we spent worrying about how something might have been different was devoted to dealing with what is actually there, then half the problems we have would no longer be problems."

"That's a very wise observation, my dear."

"Well, what do you expect? I am a very wise woman."

"That you are," William replied. "So, I seek your counsel. What do you think we should do?"

"I think that this will settle. I think that his blood is up, and he is driven by little but anger. The anger will dispel, he will remember how much he loves her, and he will start to forgive her."

"You think he will ever take her back?"

"No, I don't believe he will. Had there merely been an indiscretion, a dalliance, then perhaps. But a child? Carson's wife carrying Evan's child, and everyone knowing, thanks to Ida Garfield and her storm drain of a mouth, I don't think so. I think that would be too great a burden to bear."

"It troubles me greatly that he was able to influence Garfield and Sperling so easily. Without their medical and legal authority, he could never have done this."

"Warren Garfield and Roy Sperling have a great deal to answer for, William, and I doubt it is merely this business with Rebecca."

"What do you mean?"

Grace sighed and shook her head. "Why didn't they tell him to go to hell with this notion? How did he convince them to fall in with this?"

"Leverage," William replied.

"Leverage, indeed. But time unties all knots, no matter how well tied."

"Well, whatever befalls that pair will be no less than they deserve."

"Don't let your mind turn against them, William," Grace said. "That serves no purpose but to make you bitter."

William heard what his wife said, and even though he agreed, he could not feel anything but resentment toward Garfield and Sperling. No one deserved the fate that had befallen Rebecca. And Evan did not know. William felt it his duty to alert his younger son as to what was taking place here, if for no other reason than to make him aware of what he'd done. Not for punishment; it was not his task to punish his son, for Evan—being Evan—would punish himself

284

more than anyone else could, but for didactic reasons, perhaps. Evan needed to understand this lesson: life did not go easy on the shirkers. A man makes a decision, he then acts, and the consequences spread out like ripples from a stone tossed into a lake. Those ripples would fade before they reached the shoreline, or caught by wind and preexisting currents sometimes became waves sufficient to drown someone. Rebecca, if not helped in some extraordinary manner, would drown, and that was something William had no wish to see.

"I need to speak to Evan," William said.

"Well, you will need to find him first," Grace said. "Lord knows where he is these days."

"I will find him," William said. "And he can help me deal with the trouble he's caused."

Morning of Monday the eighth, William Riggs rose earlier than usual. He'd not slept well, his mind occupied with possibilities, very few of which were good. Last word of Evan he'd been Austin-bound, and that was where William figured he'd begin the search. Needle in a haystack came to mind, but he was intent on delivering the news to Evan.

"And if you don't find him?" Grace asked.

"I'll just keep on looking," William said, hefting a bag of clothes in the back of his truck. He then proceeded to kick the tires in turn, perhaps determining air pressure, roadworthiness, something else known only to himself. Stalling, Grace thought, as if William knew his only destination was disappointment. Fact of the matter was that Evan could be anywhere. He was probably still in Texas, for Evan was Texan through and through, held within the border as if drawn by some preternatural magnet, its pulse both hypnotic and unrelenting.

"Austin ain't Calvary," Grace said, stating the obvious.

"Evan is a big enough personality for folk to remember him," William said. "It's a music town. Someone'll know him."

"You've got a picture?" Grace said, herself now stalling. She had a bad feeling, had pushed it aside, but it kept coming back again and again like a bad taste.

William just smiled. He didn't need to answer. They both knew this was some fool's errand, that this was no organized and calculated strategy, but merely a matter of doing something rather than nothing. Only way William's mind would rest was if he acted. That was his nature. Only real regrets were those things left undone.

"Find a good boardinghouse," Grace said. "Somewhere clean. Make sure you eat properly."

William laughed. "Yes, dear."

She walked around the truck and opened her arms. He met her halfway, and they held each other for the longest time.

"This is a rare business," she said.

"Our sons' business," William said, "and thus our business, too."

"Travel safe. Telephone me. Let me know what's happening," she said, and kissed her husband.

"Of course," William said, and with that, he relinquished her and got into the truck. He started away, the window wide, waving back at her from the end of the drive before he turned onto the highway.

Before Grace had a chance to turn and walk back inside, Carson's car appeared at the end of the drive and wound its way up to the house. She stayed there in front of the steps, wondering what had prompted a Monday-morning visit.

"Ma," he said as he climbed out of the car. He was in uniform. Maybe he'd just been passing and thought to stop in.

"Carson," Grace said. "Brings you here?"

"I need to discuss things with you," was his answer, and there was a dryness and a formality to his delivery that did not sit well with her.

"Things?" she said.

"What has happened with Rebecca and what is going on with Pa."

"You want to come on in the house, son?"

"I don't have time to make a visit," Carson said, "but I wanted to give you a heads-up. I have been talking to the oil people—"

"Carson," Grace said, interrupting him. "I've heard enough already. We've talked about this before, and I reckoned we'd agreed on it. Evidently not—"

"Listen to me, Ma—"

"No, you listen to me, Carson. Your father has gone off in search of your brother. Knowing your father, he will find Evan, and he will haul him back here, and we will start making this thing right. I know what Rebecca did, and maybe there ain't no forgivin' her, but what you and Roy Sperling and Warren Garfield have done is ungodly. I ain't makin' no bones about it. That's my viewpoint, Carson. What you've done is wrong in every way something could be wrong. I don't care whether you are the law. You are still my son, and I am telling you right here and now that you have to set this right—"

Whatever was happening in Carson's mind made little evidence in his expression. He seemed calm and self-assured, as if what he was hearing were of no concern to him at all.

Grace saw the child that had let Rocket out of the old barn and scared him away. There was something cruel and vindictive in her eldest son's eyes, and for a moment she was afraid.

"You're right on one count, Ma," Carson said. "There ain't no forgivin' her, and there never will be any forgivin' of her. She couldn't have done worse. Evan, too. Evan's gonna drink himself to death or get hisself stabbed in some bar someplace. I don't give Evan a second thought. Rebecca is my business, however. Mistake to marry her it may well have been, but she is still my wife, whether I care for it or not. She is being punished, and that punishment will stand whatever you or Pa might think or do or say. And you're right on another count, too. I am the law, and what I say goes. That's the end of this business, and I ain't sharin' another word with you about it."

"You think we can't do anything about this, Carson?"

Carson smiled. "I *know* you can't do anything about it. She is crazy—no argument—and she's up there in Ector for the duration. After that baby done gets itself born, I'll be filing for divorce and she will have no right to contest. And those head-peepers up there can do whatever the hell they like with her, because she will no longer be my responsibility."

"And the baby? What's to be done with your brother's baby?"

"Hell, I couldn't care a single good goddamn, Ma. Pa finds Evan and drags him back here, then he's gonna be comin' back under duress. Evan don't want a wife, and he sure as hell don't want a kid. The man's a drunk and a bum and a transient. You see him draggin' a kid around the saloons and bars of Austin?" Carson snorted derisively. "I don't think so."

Grace knew that Carson was right. What was she dealing with here? A bullheaded tyrant and an irresponsible drunk. Said a great deal about how they'd been raised. Not such a good testimonial for their parenting skills. However, as she'd pointed out to William, children came personality intact, and no matter what they might have done, these boys would have gone the way they were going. She told herself this, tried to believe it, but it lacked conviction. She was not convinced that they hadn't just flat-out failed, that what was now transpiring was a result of their own mistakes.

"Evan and the girl smashed everything to pieces, Ma," Carson said, and there was a ghost of sadness in his tone. "I loved that girl from the day I first seen her, and you know it. Took me more 'an a decade to win her over. Well, to *believe* I'd won her over. But I never did, did I? She loved Evan more than she could ever love me, and that is something I can't abide. You wanna know the truth? It's not the infidelity. It's not what they did. It's not that she got herself pregnant and is carryin' my brother's child . . . It's that she came to me the very next day and said she would marry me. She knew exactly what she'd done, and she went ahead and accepted my proposal. Whether she knew she was pregnant is not the issue here. It's that she went behind my back with my brother, and she was all set to marry me the very next day. She would never have told me, would she? She and Evan would have held on to that dirty little secret until the end of time, and I would be there, the good husband, the dutiful father, and she and Evan would be sneaking looks and sharin' something that only they knew about right under my nose. That is what I can't forgive, Ma."

"Oh, Carson, I'm sorry . . ."

Carson shook his head. "You ain't got nothin' to be sorry for, Ma," Carson said. "Pa neither. You done good by both of us. Okay, so maybe we ain't all you wanted us to be. Maybe we're a disappoint-ment every which way you could imagine, but whatever you might think about me, I am not one to betray my brother or my wife. Bad things I may have done, but not to my family. Family is different, Ma, and you well know it."

With that, his tone and expression evidence enough that he didn't want to hear another word, Carson opened the car door and got back in.

He accelerated away, kicking up a cloud of dust behind him.

Grace stood there, her heart racing, her whole body taut.

Bad things I may have done, but not to my family.

Was this what she'd been afraid of? That Carson had been involved in something terrible, something involving Roy Sperling and Warren Garfield, something that tied them all together in such a way as to never be untied?

Grace hurried back into the house. She wished she'd gone with William to Austin, ludicrous notion though it might have been, but the very last thing she wanted to be was alone.

FORTY-FOUR

"For a man who's been here all of five days, you sure have caused some trouble, ain't ya?"

The expression on Alvin Lang's face was of a man assaulted by a malodorous scent. Something rank had invaded his nostrils, and the sense of displeasure it gave him was writ large on his features.

Henry and Evie had driven over to his place. It was early, a little before eight on Tuesday morning, and in the light of day, it seemed that this was akin to sharpening a stick with which to wake a slumbering wolf.

"I didn't plan to cause any trouble, Deputy Sheriff Lang," Henry said.

"Oh hell, you just go on and call me Alvin," Lang said. "I ain't even had time to get my uniform on."

"You gonna ask us up for coffee?" Evie said.

Lang smiled. Many was the time he'd thought about what he would do with Evie Chandler. After all, he wasn't so many years older than her. He was single, had a couple of little intrigues going on here and about, but nothing serious.

"Sure, Evie," Lang said. "You can come on up for coffee, but I gotta be away in a while. Got work to do, places to go, people to see."

Lang led the way, Evie and Henry following on after. Once in the kitchen, Lang busied himself setting out cups and cream and sugar.

"So you got Sheriff Riggs madder 'an a shithouse rat," Lang said. "He sure as hell don't appreciate you snoopin' around in his family business, my friend." The communication was directed at Henry Quinn, and Lang made a point of making *my friend* sound like a couched threat.

"Just wanted to deliver a letter," Henry said.

"Sure you did," Lang replied. "Just like you wanted to play dumbass with a pistol back in San Angelo, and look where the hell that got you."

"Don't need to be reminded about that," Henry said.

"Well, maybe you do, Henry," Lang said, "because you sure as hell don't seem to have learned your lesson."

"I think this is a little different," Evie said.

Lang poured coffee for all three of them, passed around the cups and sat down. "Circumstances are different, sure, but that don't mean that whatever Henry Quinn is doin' is any less foolhardy."

"What you did was wrong, Alvin Lang," Evie said. "That stunt with the package. That was a setup, and it was plain wrong. Searchin' my pa's house, Henry's car an' all. You don't think you're gonna get away with something like that, do you?"

Henry reached out and touched Evie's arm. "Hey," he said. "Let's not get into a fistfight here."

It seemed that Henry's physical gesture, perhaps the fact that he was familiar enough with Evie to tell her to back down, irritated Alvin Lang. Perhaps he felt challenged by Henry. This was his territory, and he had known Evie Chandler a great deal longer than Henry, after all. Regardless, this ex-con troublemaker had somehow secured her attention and affection.

Evie—being Evie—acted as if Henry hadn't even spoken.

"People screw up, Alvin. Everyone fucks up one time or another, and you got no right to—"

"Well, you can stop right there, Evie Chandler," Lang said. "You are in no position to be telling me about what I do and do not have a right to do."

"Alvin, you know what I mean—" she started.

"Evie, seriously—" Henry interjected, but Lang raised his hand and silenced him.

"Let her talk, boy," Lang said.

Henry felt tense, as if waiting for news that could only be worse than expected.

"You set him up, Alvin, you and Carson. You got Henry all wound up in a knot with another year in Reeves hangin' over his head. What for? Because he wants to get a message to Evan's daughter. Seems to me that this is a very strange response to a very simple situation."

Lang shrugged. "Carson says he don't want to help out his brother. Isn't that enough for you to leave well enough alone? Evidently not. You wanna keep stickin' your fingers in the socket to see if the shock feels the same. Sometime soon you're gonna get burned real bad."

"Are you threatening us, Alvin?" Evie asked.

Henry leaned forward. "Evie, enough." His tone was firm and certain.

"You her keeper all of a sudden?" Lang asked. He looked at Evie. "He responsible for everything that comes out of your mouth now, girl?"

"Like I said, I didn't come here for a fistfight, Alvin," Henry said. "I never intended to upset anyone."

"Well, you walked into it blind, didn't you?" Lang said. "Or you done got yourself set up by Evan Riggs. Seems to me he's the cause of what's happening here, eh? The real problem here is between them brothers."

"So what is the problem between them?" Evie asked. "You must know."

"What I know and what I discuss with you are two very different things."

"Never known so many people with so many secrets," Evie replied.

Lang sighed. "Hell, you're beginning to irritate my nerves, little lady." He looked at Henry. "Maybe you *should* take charge of what comes out of her mouth, because it sure as hell is gratin' on me right now."

"I am perfectly capable of takin' responsibility for what comes out of my mouth, Alvin Lang," Evie snapped.

Lang sneered, looked sideways at Henry as if conspiratorially masculine. "I don't know that any woman can say that with a clear heart," he said.

"Christ Almighty, you really are as much of an asshole as I thought," Evie said.

Lang laughed sincerely, heartily. He believed her antagonism a source of real humor.

Looking at Henry, Lang said, "Tell her to shut her chatter, boy, or I'll quiet her down some myself."

"Fuck you, Alvin Lang," Evie said.

"This is bullshit," Henry said. "You're as bad as each other. I don't know what the hell is going on here, but we were supposed to be having a perfectly civil conversation about this situation. This is fucked-up, and I am really getting to the point where I don't want anything more to do with it."

"You should listen to your man here," Lang said to Evie. "Walk away. That's what we've been telling you, and that's what we're gonna keep on tellin' you."

For a few moments there was an awkward silence in the small kitchen.

"Why you so scared, Alvin?" Henry asked.

Lang turned slowly and looked at him unerringly. "Who said I was scared?"

"Writ all over you," Henry said. "Secrets. That's what we've got here. Evie is right. Never been anyplace where there's so many people who are afraid to open their mouths."

Lang laughed dryly. "What the fuck is this—some kind of bullshit backwoods psychology? Oh sure, I'm afraid to open my mouth." He shook his head. "Like hell I am. Go fuck yourselves, the pair of you."

Neither Evie nor Henry responded.

"Maybe it's time to leave," Lang said, and leaned forward as if to rise from his chair.

"What happened to you?" Henry said.

Lang looked at him askance, his expression one of immediate suspicion.

"Heard word you used to be a straight shooter, Alvin. Heard word you were on the up-and-up. Knew where the lines were, knew when you were over them. What the hell happened to you?"

"What the fuck are you talking about?"

Henry shook his head. "Was it the thing with the woman?"

Lang bluffed it, but the color draining from his face was something that would have been visible from the end of the street. "Wh-what are you talking about, boy?" he said, doing all he could to sound as controlled and direct as possible.

"You know, Alvin . . . all that trouble that went down a few years ago. Is that what Sheriff Riggs has over you?"

Alvin Lang was white, not only with shock but with anger. "You haven't got the faintest fucking clue what you are talking about," he said. "You have no idea who you're dealing with. This has nothing to do with Sheriff Riggs—"

"What doesn't, Alvin?" Evie asked. "Are we talking about what happened in May of sixty-six, or are we talking about something else?"

Lang said nothing for a good ten seconds. Those seconds stretched and distorted as he looked at Evie, then to Henry, and back to Evie again.

From Henry's viewpoint, Evie's expression was implacable, yet he knew a deep and profound panic simmered beneath the surface. She was terrified. He could feel it there in the room, something almost tangible.

"You just crossed the line," Lang said, and his voice was gentle, almost sympathetic, and—as a result—altogether disturbing. "You open your mouth about whatever you have heard one more time, and—"

"And what, Alvin?" Henry said, feeling now that it had gone far beyond any point of retraction. The wound was opened, it was bleeding, and nothing would cauterize it. "Your daddy works up in the Department of Corrections, I hear, and your granddaddy is the lieutenant governor of Texas. You got stuff buried here that's gonna upset them real good, I guess..."

Lang seemed to slip into some sort of slow-motion reality, a reality unrelated to that within which Henry and Evie existed.

Evie looked at Henry. Henry shook his head. He didn't know what was happening. He didn't understand what they had done here, and he had no inkling of the consequences.

"You people are as good as dead," Lang said, and even as the words left his lips, he rose from the table, pushed the chair back, and walked to the kitchen counter. From a drawer beside the stove, he produced a .38 revolver.

"Jesus, Alvin, what the fuck are you doing?"

"I d-did what Evan should ha-have done," Lang said, his voice kind of slurring, as if he were drunk, losing control of his faculties. "Oh, fuck," he said. "He told you, didn't he? He's gonna tell everyone. I knew it. I knew it would come to this. Oh, Jesus Christ Almighty..."

"Alvin, seriously, put the fucking gun down," Evie said. She looked utterly aghast, didn't know whether to stay seated or get to her feet, then decided on the latter but rose slowly, her arms out toward Lang as if entreating him to set the .38 aside and not do whatever the hell he was thinking of doing.

Lang pointed the gun at Henry. Even as the barrel was aimed unerringly at Henry's heart, Henry could see Lang's hand shaking. Lang wasn't even looking directly at Henry, his gaze flitting back and forth between Henry, Evie, and some vague middle ground that may very well have been nothing but a thought.

Lang smiled then, and the expression was unsettling.

"All comes back, doesn't it?" he said. "Past is the landscape that follows you no matter where you go."

"Alvin," Evie pleaded, her voice edged with real panic and distress.

"For God's sake, nothing is worth this. Please . . . please don't shoot him . . ."

Lang just looked back at her and smiled. The smile was almost peaceful. "All of this because of shame," he said.

"But it doesn't have to be this way," Evie said, her tone was pleading, desperate.

Henry couldn't move, his gaze fixed dead ahead, watching Lang's ever-shifting expression as he wrestled with the reality and possible consequences of what was happening. If he shot Henry, he would have to shoot Evie. If he was to commit murder, then there could be no eyewitness.

Alvin seemed to look right through Evie, and then he turned back to Henry. He held Henry's gaze for a good fifteen seconds, then looked down at the gun as if it were being held there by some force he could not control. He sighed audibly, the sound like something deep inside him as it collapsed in slow motion.

"Only shame for me is that I won't see Carson's face when it all falls apart," he said, his voice barely a whisper.

The hand tightened on the gun.

"Fuck it," Alvin said.

"Alvin, no . . ." Evie gasped.

Alvin gave one last vacant smile, turned the gun around, aimed it at his own heart, and pulled the trigger with his thumb.

The sound wasn't anywhere near as loud as Henry Quinn had expected it to be. Compared to the sound of the gun with which he'd wounded Sally O'Brien, it was nothing at all. A firecracker, a punctured tire, a hand clap.

There was no drama, no blood, no agonizing death throes. Alvin Lang just slid to the floor, his hand releasing the pistol as he hit the floor. It skidded across the linoleum and stopped against the baseboard.

The only sound, in fact, was Evie's screaming, and to Henry it seemed the most deafening thing in the world.

FORTY-FIVE

Morning of Monday, August eighth, Ralph Wyatt rose early. Seemed the hours he slept and the hours he lay awake restless and agitated could no longer be separated. For the previous weeks since Rebecca had been up at Ector County Hospital, his daily visits had become ever more difficult and exhausting. It was like watching his wife die for a second time. He was losing his mind, and there seemed to be nothing he could do about it. Physical and mental exhaustion assaulted every sense. He found himself mumbling and then turning suddenly to hurl expletives at someone existing only in his mind. The law was down on him, medical opinion, too, and now the psychiatrists at Ector had their claws into his daughter, and it seemed that she would never come home. And if she did, well, he didn't believe that she would really be his daughter anymore. Already she was vacillating between periods of intense introversion and wild excitement. They had given her medication. He didn't even know what it was. He worried not only for her but for the child inside her; any kind of medication surely couldn't be right for an unborn baby.

Ralph had started drinking. He had drunk as his wife died, seeming to find some brief solace in the oblivion that liquor gave, and after her death had sworn off the stuff for life. That oath had now been broken, and broken far too easily. There was a thirst inside him that could not be quenched, an emptiness that could not be filled, and it was all because of Carson Riggs.

Work on the farm had gone undone. He had thought to call Gabe, but had decided against it. He was not of a mind to supervise anyone. He was not of a mind to engage in anything but the rescue of his daughter from the clutches of Ector County Hospital, and after that the clutches of Carson Riggs and his scheming family. William and Grace Riggs must have known what Carson was going to do. By doing nothing, they had in fact colluded, wittingly or unwittingly, and now, even now—Ralph Wyatt watching his daughter fade before his eyes—they could have stepped in, could have insisted that their son relinquish whatever obsession he felt to punish her so severely.

295

Rebecca was their daughter-in-law, after all. They were duty-bound to help, if not from any sense of loyalty they might feel toward Rebecca, then because their younger son had been the one to create this situation in the first place.

Ralph Wyatt was not so narrow as to consider that Rebecca bore no responsibility for what had happened. The girl was a wild one—always had been, always would be. Took after her mother in that respect. Both she and Evan were as moths to flames. Ralph saw that, had been aware of it since they first met as children. They had grown up together, both Riggs boys and his daughter. He'd known that there would be a problem at some stage, that one of them would lose out, but if he'd been told that this would be the outcome, he would never have believed it.

On a couple of occasions Ralph Wyatt had considered marching over to the Riggs place and confronting Carson, William, Grace. He had practiced his speech, the vehemence pouring out of him as he paced the kitchen, in his mind's eye the Riggs family standing in front of him, all of them stunned into shamed silence as he told them exactly what he thought of them, as he demanded they do whatever was necessary to see his daughter out of that terrible place. But the words had stayed in his kitchen, and they had echoed back at him and lodged in his mind until they became bitter and twisted. He was aggrieved, distraught, wound tighter than a watch spring, and the thought to go on over there and vent his anger, to demand immediate action, just grew ever stronger. His daughter had to be out of that place, and if neither her husband nor the father of her child wanted her, then so be it. She would stay with her father, and as soon as was feasible, they would move away from this godforsaken place and disappear forever. He could help her raise the child. He would be the best grandfather a child could ever wish for.

The thought to kill Carson Riggs came like a bolt out of nowhere. It came with the force of a truck, and yet it arrived silently, almost gracefully, and it sat in and amongst Ralph Wyatt's dark and twisted thoughts as if it had been there all along.

It hung there like a second shadow. Take a thirty-aught-six over there and kill the son of a bitch. So he was sheriff. What did that matter? If he was going to kill Carson Riggs, then Ralph himself would be done for anyway.

A little after eighty-thirty, Ralph Wyatt took a bottle of bourbon from the kitchen counter and poured a good slug. He drank it down. He went to the back of the house and fetched down a Springfield.

Had it for years, kept it cleaned and oiled, rarely used it. He loaded the rifle, went out to the truck, and set off for the Riggs place.

As he drew close to the turnoff for the farm, he saw William Riggs heading off in the direction of Calvary. He guessed that he was en route to see Carson.

Ralph Wyatt floored the truck and overtook Riggs as the dirt track reached the highway. He came to a staggered halt, Riggs swerving off the track and slamming on the brakes before he hit a tree. The front passenger-side wheel wound up in a rut.

William Riggs got out, his blood up, and stood there for a moment as Ralph Wyatt got out of his truck.

He saw the rifle immediately.

"What the hell are you doing, Wyatt? You damned near drove me off the road into that there tree. Christ, man, what are you thinking?"

Ralph Wyatt looked like half the man Riggs knew. Hair all mussed, eyes wide, black beneath them as if he hadn't slept for a week. He was unshaven, his clothes disheveled, and he carried a Springfield. He took a step toward Riggs, and Riggs recognized the lack of sure-footedness that came with drink or physical exhaustion. The man appeared to be on the edge of collapse.

"Ralph," Riggs said, almost as if Wyatt needed a reminder of his own name. "What's the deal here, Ralph? What you doin' with that gun?"

"Where's your boy at, Riggs?" Wyatt said.

"Ralph, calm yourself. Christ, man. I don't know what's gotten into your head, but it can't be right. You look like hell. Come on back to the farm with me. Let's get you fixed up, get some clean clothes, get you some breakfast, some strong coffee, eh?"

Wyatt raised the gun. He held it at waist level, cradling it in his nervous hands. He caught flashes of bright light out of the corner of his eye.

"Now, look here, Ralph. This is just plumb crazy. You and I have things to talk about, sure . . . Maybe we got trouble, you know? We need to work this thing out. Carson done her wrong, man. I get that. But she done him wrong, too, and we gotta take responsibility for our kin and help them sort out their troubles."

"Gon' ask you one more time, Riggs," Wyatt growled. The lights in his eyes were fiercer. He raised one hand as if to shield himself from a sun that wasn't there. "Where's your boy at?"

"You want Carson? You want to talk to Carson? Is that it?"

Wyatt sneered. "This here Springfield got everything in it I wanna say to Carson Riggs."

Riggs backed up a step. There was a .45 in the glove box of his truck. He couldn't even remember if it was loaded. It had been there forever. Longer than forever.

"Ralph . . . seriously, my friend—"

"Friend?" Wyatt laughed cruelly. "This from a man who sees his own daughter-in-law in that place? Don't know what the hell Carson has going on with Roy Sperling and Warren Garfield, but they cooked up all manner of deceit and labeled her crazy. You coulda done something, Riggs. You coulda dealt with your boys, but you didn't. Now I gotta take care of it, and it ain't right. You call me a friend? We known each other all these years. Our kids done growed up side by side all these years, and this is what we got now, man. This is what we got and it needs to be dealt with . . ."

Riggs took another sideways step, but it was unsubtle and awkward.

"Back the hell away from there, Riggs!" Wyatt barked. "What you got in there? You got a pistol? You gon' get a pistol outta there and shoot me? Is that what you're plannin' to do?"

"You got your rifle there, Ralph. You gotta rifle aimed right at my heart."

"I ain't gonna shoot you, Riggs. Christ, what kinda person you think I am?"

"I think you've lost your mind, Ralph. I think you done lost your mind some, and you need to come on back with me and get some rest and some food and whatever, and then we can sit down and talk this out."

"Your boys is the ones you need to talk to, William. Both of them. They done a bad thing here, and it's too late to fix it, isn't it? She's gonna have this baby, and neither one of them is gonna want it. But I want it, Riggs. I will take her away and look after her and the kid, and I hope to hell that kid don't look like a Riggs, 'cause you people done me enough hurt to last a lifetime already."

"I understand, Ralph . . . I understand how much you're hurtin' . . ."

"You don't understand nothin'," Wyatt said, "and after I'm done with them, your boys gonna understand nothin', too."

"Meanin' what?"

"Meanin' I'm gon' find the pair of them and kill 'em stone-fucking dead."

"Can't let you do that, Ralph."

"Can't do squat to stop me, William."

Riggs went for the gun. He believed he didn't have a choice. He moved quickly, but Ralph Wyatt was just as quick, and even as William Riggs turned back out of the car and looked back at Ralph, that Springfield barrel was pointing right at his head.

The .45 was loaded, even chambered, and William Riggs acted out of nothing but instinctive response when he saw Ralph Wyatt's finger tighten on the trigger of the Springfield.

Two gunshots went off as one.

Grace Riggs heard it. Wondered if that troublesome old truck was misfiring again.

Wyatt took a bullet in the throat, fell back into the ditch.

Riggs was jolted with the recoil of the pistol. He hadn't fired it for a long time, and it sure had a kick. He saw Wyatt go down, knew there was every possibility the man was still alive, still clutching that Springfield, and he made a cautious approach.

He saw the soles of Wyatt's boots. Those feet weren't moving. Riggs's heart was running like a train, adrenaline coursing through him, and he didn't know whether to feel relief or terror or both. He was alive—that was the main thing—and he had acted in self-defense. There was no one who could question that, even taking into account the fact that his son was the sheriff.

It was as he looked down at Ralph Wyatt's lifeless body that William Riggs felt something in his side. His arm felt weak, and for some reason the gun slipped involuntarily from his fingers. He looked down as a wave of nausea and light-headedness overtook him, and there was blood on his hands, his arm, blood down the front of his pants. He frowned. He had not touched Wyatt. Where had the blood come from?

Something kicked him in the right side, something hard and sharp, and it was only then that he understood that Ralph Wyatt's bullet had found a mark.

A weight dropped on him, and he went to his knees.

With a sense of disorientation flooding through him, he pulled back his jacket, saw the red rosette of blood blooming out through his undergarment, his shirt, his vest, and he knew that there had to be some hole in him to be leaking that much.

William Riggs felt as if he'd been kicked in the back. He went forward onto his hands and knees, and an unearthly pain ripped through him. It was like being struck by lightning. Maybe things weren't so good. Maybe he wasn't going to walk away from this.

He could hear himself then. It was a terrible sound, the sound of a man running out of air awful fast. His only thought was to make it back to the house. He started moving, and with each staggered motion, the pain tore through him again. Blood on the leaves beneath his hands, blood in the dirt, his own blood, and every foot he made felt like a mile.

Stubbornness alone got him twenty yards. How long it took, no one would ever know. He fell facedown in the mud within sight of the house, but there was no one there to see him.

William Riggs spent his last seconds wondering why the Riggs family had been dealt such a losing hand.

It was Carson who arrived first at the scene, not because it had been reported, but because he was on his way back home to relay one last thought to his mother.

The message with which he'd driven over and the message he then delivered were not the same thing.

He came up on the house with blood on his shirt and blood on his hands and a look in his eyes like God had punished him good.

FORTY-SIX

The urge to run was overwhelming.

Henry held her down, but Evie fought back like a wildcat. She scratched his face. She was out-and-out hysterical.

Alvin Lang sat slumped against the kitchen cabinets, an expression on his face like relief and disappointment all rolled into one. Whatever guilt had burdened him was a burden no longer. Now he just had his Maker and the afterlife with which to contend.

Ten minutes, fifteen perhaps, and Henry managed to get Evie to her feet. Hauling her out of the kitchen and getting her into the front room was a Herculean task, as if she believed that staying in the kitchen would somehow enable her to turn back time. She held on to the frame of the door, still crying, still hyperventilating, looking at Henry with wide-eyed horror and abject disbelief.

She didn't speak for another ten minutes after that, and then it was some kind of shocked rambling monologue about Alvin Lang and Carson Riggs and what the hell were they going to do.

"We are calling the Sheriff's Department," Henry said. "We have no choice."

"Let's j-just g-go," she said. "Let's j-just go... No one knows we came here... No one know we're h-here. Let's just g-go." And with that she started for the front door. Henry had to grab her and haul her back and sit her down and hold her shoulders so he could get her focused and talk directly at her.

"Evie!" His voice was like a whipcrack. "Evie! Stop! Quiet! That's enough! Listen to me!"

She sort of snapped to, and then she was gone again, trying to get out of the chair. Henry held her down and she started crying.

Henry slapped her face hard, the sound as sharp as his tone.

Evie started hyperventilating once more, and then she kind of hitched her knees up toward her chest and held on to them, turning on to her side and lying there in the armchair.

Henry walked through to the front hall and called the operator.

"Put me through to the Sheriff's Office, please," he said.

He held on for just a moment.

"This is Henry Quinn. I am over at Alvin Lang's place. He just shot himself. He's dead. You better send over whoever the hell deals with this shit."

Henry hung up. He went back to Evie and got a number for her father.

Henry called it. There was no answer. He went back to the living room and lifted Evie out of the chair. She walked with him to the front of the house, and he sat her there on the porch steps. It was a matter of minutes before Carson Riggs's car drew to a halt outside the Lang house.

Riggs got out and stood on the sidewalk. He looked at Henry Quinn, at Evie Chandler sitting there beside him on the steps, and he said, "Now what the fuck have you done, boy?"

"Done nothin', Sheriff Riggs. Came over to talk to your deputy, and he done shot himself."

"Is that so?"

"Yes, sir, it is."

"Well, I'm gonna go on in there and take a look. You stay right there, both of you. You move a goddamned muscle and I'm arresting both of you, you understand?"

"Not going anywhere, Sheriff. I called it in. You got nothin' on me."

Riggs shook his head and started toward the front door. "I wouldn't be so damned sure of yourself, Henry Quinn. Can have you back in Reeves in a heartbeat."

"Is that so?" Henry said, feeling the color rise in his cheeks, feeling his heart start to race.

"It is, boy. It sure as hell is."

"Well, you know what I think you should do, Sheriff Riggs?"

Riggs hesitated, standing now no less than six feet from Henry and Evie.

"I think you should go fuck yourself."

Riggs laughed. "You really got a bad mouth, son. Mouth like that winds up swallowing teeth."

Henry didn't rise to the bait. "Your deputy said something very odd just before he turned his gun on himself, Sheriff."

"And what might that have been?"

"Said he done what Evan should have done. You know what that means?"

"No idea what he was talking about."

302

"Maybe something to do with May of sixty-six and what he had to take care of down in Nueva Rosita? Take care of an unwanted child, maybe..."

Riggs's face changed. Implacable superiority was replaced with something bitter and enraged. Henry could see it in the man's eyes.

"You don't talk about my deputy. You don't talk about my brother. You hear me, boy? You've done enough damage here. This ain't your town. It's my town. This is my territory, and I control it. I don't need the likes of you comin' down here and stirrin' all manner of private business up. You know nothing about Calvary or the Riggs family. It ain't none of your damned business, and you'd best be leavin' 'fore I do whatever the hell I have to do to see you back in Reeves or six feet under."

Riggs pushed past Henry and went on through the screen door. He was not gone long. When he reappeared, he merely glanced at Henry Quinn and Evie Chandler, an expression of disdain on his face. He went to the car and called it in, asked for the coroner, told the woman at the desk to call in a couple of special deputies, have them bring the necessaries to close off the scene.

"No doubt that he killed himself, is there?" Henry said. "Make it look whichever way you want it to look. You and I still know that your deputy shot himself in the heart rather than deal with whatever you people are fuckin' hiding down here. What's so big that people are gonna die for it, Sheriff Riggs? What's so big a secret that you're gonna threaten folk, run this place like it's your own little county farm, stop me gettin' Evan's message to his daughter, even try to put me back in Reeves? What the hell is really going on here, Carson?"

Riggs turned suddenly. His face was red, his eyes wide, his lips white as he gritted his teeth and leaned close to Henry Quinn. His face was inches from Henry's, his words a hissed threat.

"Don't use my name," he said. "Don't ever use my name, boy. You have no right to use my name—"

"Carson? What's the problem with that? Carson Riggs. Asshole sheriff of Calvary. What the hell is wrong with you? What the hell did you people do? You and Roy Sperling and Warren Garfield? What was so bad that you had to hide Rebecca up in Ector, that you had to put your mother there, that you had to blackmail and threaten everyone into silence? Did you kill Warren Garfield, Carson? Is that what you did? Did you ki—"

Henry never finished the word.

Riggs's first strike hit him square in the face. Henry had never had his nose broken before, but that didn't alter the certainty with which he knew it had just been broken.

He went down like a tenpin, and Riggs was over him, fists flailing, and then his sidearm was out and he was beating down on Henry with the butt of the gun, and Henry just rolled on his side and got his hands up over his head, and his knees were tucked up into his chest much the same as Evie had done in the house, and he kept his mouth shut because that's what Evan had told him to do the last time he'd taken a beating like this in Reeves.

The beating didn't stop.

Henry remembered Evie screaming once more, but he couldn't connect her screaming with what was happening to himself. He remembered thinking that they needed to get things under control. But they were out of control. Completely.

Henry was unconscious before Evie managed to drag Carson Riggs off of him. Riggs was still a whirlwind of thrashing fists and kicking feet. He caught Evie Chandler broadside and floored her. She went down, too. And then it was all over. Sheriff Riggs stood breathless over the broken body of Henry Quinn, Evie Chandler unconscious at his feet, and an ever-increasing crowd of people gathering in the street, each of them asking what the hell was going on, what had happened, where was Deputy Lang, why were two people on the ground in Lang's yard, one of them spattered with blood.

Was he dead?

Had Sheriff Riggs killed someone?

What the hell was going on?

And then the special deputies arrived, two of them, their names being Lucas Wright and Donny King. Wright, ironically, was distantly related to old Ralph Wyatt. He'd heard word of the daughter who went crazy and died up at Ector, but he never followed it.

Special Deputies Wright and King took one look at the situation and knew it was as good a mess as either of them had ever seen. Then Wright went on in the house and realized there was a dead deputy sheriff in there.

By the time he got back out onto the front yard, Sheriff Riggs was sitting on the ground. King had taken the blood-spattered pistol off of him with no resistance. Had he understood something of what had happened, he might have decided to handcuff Riggs, but he did not know the details. Riggs was sheriff. Riggs was still the boss. King saw no guns or weapons in the hands of the girl and the guy. There appeared to be no other weapons on the veranda, in the yard, or in the front of the house. Wright told King about Lang. King wanted to go take a look. Wright told King there'd be plenty of time for that.

Wright called for both an ambulance and the county coroner. He went on in to look at Lang's body again. He got down on his haunches and stared at that dead face for the longest time. He'd seen dead animals, sure, but this was different. This was altogether creepy. It made him feel a little sick, but he would never have admitted it.

He shouted for King, told him he could come on in and take a look. King didn't say much of anything. He was surprised that there was so little blood. He asked Wright what he imagined might have happened here, but the question sort of hung in the air and Wright didn't reply.

And then there was hollering in the street, and Donny King and Lucas Wright—as familiar with police procedure as they were with Wright's family tree—hurried back out to the yard to discover that Sheriff Carson Riggs had gotten to his feet and taken off.

Bystanders across the road were shouting and pointing, indicating the direction Riggs had taken.

Both Wright and King could hear the engine, but they did not see the car.

Caught between a rock and a hard place, Lucas Wright told Donny King to stay with the injured folks, and then he ran down to the street, got into his car, and took off after Riggs.

King went to speak to the girl, but she was talking crazy, made no sense at all, and she wouldn't let him see to her friend. King was worried about that one, the way his face was all smashed up, the blood around his eyes, the fact that he wasn't moving at all. He tried to remember what he should do from first-aid classes, but nothing came. He hoped to God that the kid didn't die before the ambulance got there. The girl was getting kind of wild, too, shouting at the people gathered across the street, telling them that Riggs had done this, that Riggs had to be stopped, that Riggs was *a fucking crazy motherfucking son of a bitch*.

Donny King, a churchgoing man, told her that that kind of language wasn't necessary. The girl told him to go fuck himself. He wanted to handcuff her, simply because she was annoying the hell out of him, but then the ambulance arrived and people who seemed to know a great deal about what to do were all over the scene.

Donny King stepped out of the fray and let them go on about

their business. The coroner arrived, too, another car from the Ozona Sheriff's Department, and Donny felt like a spare part.

The whole scene was surreal. Lights, crime-scene tape, gurneys, people shouting, sawhorse barriers erected and ropes strung between them to cordon the Lang place off from the street.

The ambulance peeled away, presumably to the County Hospital. For triage and surgery and suchlike, it was the closest and largest facility, and that boy sure as hell looked like he needed something more than a doctor's clinic.

Lang's body was taken away, and then it all went quiet, and Donny King sat in his car and watched as the crowd of onlookers dispersed. He wondered where the hell Lucas was, if he'd caught up with Sheriff Riggs, and what the hell was going to happen next.

FORTY-SEVEN

It rained, and rained good. A couple of pickups got jammed in muddy ruts, and Carson Riggs organized other pickups to drag them out. Seemed like the world and all its relatives descended upon the farm that Wednesday afternoon, grim-faced, sodden through, tracking footprints across the veranda, down the hall, right into the front parlor where Grace Riggs held court like the bereaved matriarch that she was. William Riggs was dead. Ralph Wyatt was dead, too, but with Rebecca up at Ector, her doctors unwilling to release her for her own father's funeral, the Wyatt occasion had been organized by Ralph's sister. A handful of cousins, news of an aged uncle who ultimately never showed, and now the Wyatt place was as still and silent as Ralph's grave. Word was that the sister would take over the place. Time would tell, as it always did.

The Riggs gathering was different. William had been settled in Calvary these past three decades. He knew everyone, and those he did not yet knew of him, if not through Carson, then through the country-singing son. He was fifty-three years of age, no age at all, in fact, and here he was laid out in his Sunday best in a handmade coffin from a funeral place in Ozona.

Grace Riggs had told Carson to find Evan. Carson gave his word and was good to it. Evan was found just three days after the shooting, drunker than a second-rate actor in a third-rate play, all set to fall into the orchestra pit and break his darned fool neck had someone not been there to catch him.

And so it was that the Riggs boys were having to bury their differences along with their father, at least for the duration of the funeral itself and the gathering that followed. They stood side by side at the end of the hallway, shaking folks' hands, accepting condolences, directing the mourners through to the parlor where women from Grace's church group had laid out potato salad and honey-baked ham, King Ranch chicken casserole, a bucket of spaghetti for the kids, assorted sandwiches and sheet cake and an endless supply of lemonade and hot coffee. The menfolk huddled awkward and silent, discreetly passed around a bottle with which to fortify the aforementioned coffee; the women gathered around Grace as if their presence alone would somehow serve to offset the imbalance occasioned by William's absence. Absence did not and never had made any heart grow fonder. Absence was absence, nothing more nor less.

Carson appeared stoic, Evan merely stunned. Nevertheless, he was sober for the first time in months. The shock of his father's death had been complemented by the shock of all that had transpired between Carson and Rebecca. It was his mother who had told him about the pregnancy, about Carson's decision to send the girl up to Ector County, and yet no one had possessed the courage to tell him the real truth: that Rebecca was carrying his child, that he was—in fact—a father.

Carson said nothing. It would have been an admission of utter failure. To stand in the shadow of a brother was difficult; to stand in the shadow of a younger brother was nigh on impossible. To know that you played second fiddle when it came to the affections of your parents was one thing; to know that you played the same part when it came to the life you'd subsequently created for yourself as an adult was another level of failure altogether.

Carson simply said that the pregnancy, as was sometimes the case with women, had unsettled her, not only physically but emotionally, and her needs were being best served by the professionals up at Ector. Not only that, but she was now contending with the loss of her own father in such dreadful circumstances. Psychiatric opinion, according to Carson, was that her attendance at the funeral could only make things worse, and protest though she might have done, what they were doing was for her own good. Could Evan visit with her? No, not yet. Could Evan perhaps send her a note to let her know that he was here in Calvary, that he was thinking of her, that he wished her a speedy recovery? No, it was best not to do that right now. Let her concentrate on getting herself well.

Perhaps Evan's deep-ingrained guilt regarding what had happened between himself and Rebecca the night of the farewell party made him take a step back. Unaware that it was his child she was carrying, Evan acceded to Carson's dictates and decisions. He had no right to challenge Carson's authority when it came to his own wife.

With all that was needed for their own father's funeral preparations, Carson insisted that Evan spend time with his mother, that he be appropriately attentive to his own family. Perhaps Evan was a little shamed. He had been found drunk; he had been hauled back to Calvary, had barely realized what was going on until he'd been there a good twenty-four hours. As was always the case in such situations, those left behind believed that had they been present, perhaps they could have done something to avert whatever inevitability had struck. Evan could no more have prevented the strange series of events that resulted in the deaths of both William Riggs and Ralph Wyatt than he could have left a bottle of rye unopened. Life, in truth, was not there to be challenged. It was there to be lived, and it possessed more than enough force and unpredictability to remind you who was in charge if you ever believed yourself capable of besting it.

Life and circumstance had bested William Riggs, and the brothers were reunited to bury him. Grace told them not to fight, and so they did not. Not until later. Not until the last of the mourners and well-wishers had traipsed through the red Texas mud back to their respective pickups and cars and buggies. It was late afternoon, the sun aiming for its usual spot beyond the horizon, and Evan stood looking out from the west-facing veranda at a view he barely remembered. Carson came up behind him, carried a bottle and two glasses, told his brother that they should share a drink and a few words.

Evan took his first glass of the day, drank it down, had it refilled before Carson had taken his first sip.

"Bad business all round," Carson said.

Evan merely nodded.

"Changes coming, and fast."

Evan drank, listened, didn't have much to say.

"You gonna stay for a while, Evan?"

"Long as Ma needs me," he said, holding out the glass for a third go at the bourbon. The shakes were settling, his stomach untying from whatever Gordian arrangement had tangled his innards.

"I'm here," Carson said, which was as good as telling Evan his presence was no longer required.

"You are, indeed," Evan replied, which was Evan's way of telling his brother that the whole of Calvary now seemed to be in the thrall of Sheriff Riggs.

"I'll speak to Warren Garfield in the morning," Carson said.

"About what?"

"What do you think?" Carson said, a note of disbelief in his tone. "The will. The land, the farm . . . what we are going to do. Everything will be in Ma's name, but she'll want us to sort it all out. She won't want to be dealin' with lawyers and whatever."

"You been talkin' to them oil people still," Evan said. "Ma told me. She ain't happy, you know? Not what Pa wanted, and not what she wants."

Carson smiled imperiously. "Sometimes you gotta make a decision for someone, Evan. Sometimes you gotta do what's right for someone even when they don't know what's right themselves."

"Like what you done to your wife?"

Evan felt it rather than saw it, as if the very spirit of his elder brother took an angry and defiant step forward. Fists were raised, figuratively speaking, and Evan knew that he should back off or face the music here and now.

"You're not to speak of my wife, Evan," Carson said, his voice a snarling hound on a leash.

"Your wife, my friend," Evan said.

"Hell of a friend you are. Deserted her, deserted Ma and Pa, went off to Austin to drink yourself stupid."

"Least I had stupid to get to, Carson. You been livin' there for years."

"Sometimes you are such an asshole, Evan."

"Beats being an asshole all the time, Carson."

"We gonna do this now?" Carson asked.

"When did we ever not do it?" Evan asked. "You always been down on me. You always had a sharp word and a bitter comment in your mouth when it came to me. You ain't much of a brother by any standards. Doesn't look like you're much of a husband, either. Ain't right that you got her up at Ector. She should be here, being looked after by kin."

"Don't see you have any right to tell anyone how to behave, little brother. You're so courageous, you go rescue her, why don'tcha?"

Carson had him, and Evan knew it.

"Your job, Carson, not mine. Guess the only thing for you to do is find some extra ways to go fuck yourself."

"They teach you to talk like that in them bars and saloons you frequent?"

"Nope," Evan replied. "I learned that all by myself. Special kind of language I studied up on just for you."

Carson set the bottle down on the veranda rail. "You stay here and drink the whole thing," he said. "Maybe you'll find some sense way down near the bottom."

Evan smiled. "Oh, I doubt it, big brother. Been looking there a long time, and all I found is more reasons to go on drinking."

310

Carson took his glass with him. Took his anger and his resentment, too. Evan could feel it behind him in the house, like the sound of someone breathing, like the certainty that something was right behind him and it did not wish him well.

Several people saw Carson Riggs leave the offices of Warren Garfield the following morning.

It was a little after ten, and Carson—according to reports—"looked like he'd swallowed thunder and had the indigestion to match."

Voices had been raised. That much was known. Specifics and details were unknown, but common sense said it had to involve the last will and testament of William Ford Riggs, deceased. Something had happened, something about which Carson Riggs had been both angry and confused, and when he returned to the farm, he took Evan aside and asked him point-blank if he was planning on staying back and running the farm.

"You know I ain't gonna do that," Evan said, "but that don't mean we can't get a farm manager in, pay him a good wage, keep the place going for Ma. I've spoken to her, and she feels that would be best. I think that's what Pa would have wanted—"

"Hell, Evan. Seems to me you're the last person in the world to have any kind of opinion about what Pa would have wanted."

"What did Garfield say?"

"What did he say? What do you think he said? Place is fifty-fifty. You and me, little brother. We gotta make some decisions."

"What's the hurry?"

"The hurry?" Carson frowned. There was something in his face that Evan had seen only a couple of times before. Carson was angling for a fight, and a real one at that. "You gonna stand in my road, Evan? Is that what you're gonna do?"

"Don't see there's a road for me to stand in," Evan replied. "Where the hell you think you're headin' anyhow?"

"Future lasts only so long as it's there," Carson said.

"The hell does that even mean?"

"Means you're gonna come to see Garfield and we're gonna sign some papers and we're gonna start talking to them oil people and make enough money to take care of Ma and ourselves for the rest of our lives. They want drilling rights here, and I am set on givin' 'em just exactly what they want."

"Is that so?"

"Sure is, and I don't wanna hear a goddamned word of resistance

311

about this, Evan. Matter of days you can head off back to Austin or wherever the hell you wanna go, and you will go richer than you could ever imagine."

"And if I don't got no interest in bein' richer than I could ever imagine?"

Carson frowned. He tilted his head to one side as if trying to see his younger brother from some new angle. Then he started laughing. "What in God's name are you talkin' about, boy? You don't wanna fill your pockets with gold and head out of here like a king?"

"I have no such interest, Carson. Right now I am interested in two things and two things only. Firstly, I wanna see Ma settled down. She's grievin', Carson, and she's gonna be grievin' for a good while yet. Let her deal with this, okay? Let her deal with this before we start throwin' even more confusion and craziness into her life. There's time, man. This business can wait a couple of months. Hell, if there's oil here, it ain't goin' nowhere. Been here a million years; will still be here five years from now."

"Five years? What—"

Evan raised his hand. "Listen for a minute, Carson. You got yourself fixed up as sheriff, and you are so busy bein' big boss with the hot sauce that you ain't hearin' anythin' but your own goddamned voice. Well, let me have a chance here. Like I said, there's only two things I am interested in. Helpin' Ma deal with everything she's gotta deal with, and that means we change nothing, do nothing, let everything settle for a while. Second thing, and this is something I plan on doing right now, and that's go see your wife up in Ector, give her my condolences about her pa, see she's all right, have a talk with them doctor people and find out what they plan on doin', when she'll be out, an' all that. She's pregnant, Carson. You're gonna be a daddy. You need to be dealin' with that."

Carson said nothing. His eyes were cruel slits out of which he glared at his younger brother. "You are *not* to go and see Rebecca," Carson said. His voice was emphatic.

"Sorry?"

"I told you. You heard me. You are *not* to go and see my wife."

Evan laughed. "Carson, you may be the sheriff of this here pokehole, but when it comes to telling me what I can and can't do, you can go to hell."

Carson stepped forward, his fists clenched.

Evan frowned. "What is this? You gonna arrest me? You gonna fight me? What the hell is going on with you?"

"Don't go up there," Carson said. "I'm tellin' you now, and I ain't sayin' it again, Evan. Don't go up there."

"Well, fuck you, Carson. More times you tell me, the more determined I am to be contrary. I'm gonna go up there right now and visit with her, and there ain't nothin' you can do about it."

Another step forward, Carson and Evan now no more than three feet from each other, the tension palpable, the sense of threat and bottled violence both potent and real.

"I told you twice, Evan. There ain't gonna be a third time."

"What the fuck—"

Carson grabbed Evan's wrist. Evan wrenched his hand free and pushed his brother away. Carson lost his footing, stumbled backward, his right thigh colliding with the small table. Carson grabbed at it instinctively, but the table fell sideways with a crash. He ended up on his ass, looking up at his younger brother. It was the final ignominy.

"You have become such an asshole, Carson," Evan said, and before Carson had a chance to say a word, Evan had stormed back into the house and slammed the door behind him.

Carson heard the engine of their father's pickup gunning into life, selfsame pickup he'd been driving when he met on the road with Ralph Wyatt. Carson got to his feet and ran after his brother, caught a final glimpse of the truck as it passed the end of the driveway and reached the road. Evan was headed for Ector County Hospital and Rebecca Riggs, oblivious to the fact that just as his dalliance with her after the party had resulted in a life, so his reunion with her now would result in, not one, but two unnecessary deaths.

If God was at work, then he was a fiercely retributive God. Seemed that this was the way of things, and there was nothing that could be done to avert it.

FORTY-EIGHT

By the time Henry Quinn came to in the emergency room at the County Hospital, it was all over Calvary that Sheriff Carson Riggs had gone crazy, was holed up in Roy Sperling's house, that Sheriff's Department people from both Sonora and Ozona were on the way, if not already there.

Clarence Ames showed up, took one look at Henry's busted-up face, at the shocked and wan expression with which Evie returned his wordless gaze, and he took off again.

Doctors came and went. Someone told Evie that Henry needed X-rays, that his cheekbone might be broken, that there were signs of busted ribs, other things. There was some mention of internal bleeding, but no one seemed intent on doing anything to determine this one way or the other.

"What the fuck is happening?" Henry asked Evie. He lay on a gurney. She stood beside him, held his hand.

"Sheriff Riggs took off," she said. "Apparently, he went over to Roy Sperling's place. I don't know what he's doing there. I don't understand any of this . . . I really don't . . ."

For a moment it seemed as though she was set to cry, but she gathered herself together, her jawline resolute even as she finger-tipped tears from the corners of her eyes.

Henry started to get up.

"What the hell are you doing?" she asked.

"Getting up," Henry said. "I ain't lyin' here waitin' for him to come back and beat the shit out of me some more."

"He's not going to come back," Evie said. "He's over at Roy's place—"

"Roy Sperling is one of the people who knows what's really going on here," Henry asked. "What if he went over there to kill him?"

Henry was on his feet, wincing and holding his side. Evie knew she wasn't going to convince him to do anything other than exactly what he wanted to do. He'd proven his stubbornness plenty already.

She turned back toward the hallway as she heard a familiar voice.

Her father was running down the corridor, head going left to right as he sought her out.

"Dad!" she hollered, and he came rushing, threw his arms around her.

"Jesus Christ Almighty," he said. He took one look at Henry and visibly paled. "I heard Alvin Lang shot himself."

"He did . . . Shot himself right in front of us," Evie replied.

"And Riggs did this to you?"

Henry nodded, his eyes narrowing as the pain in his face reminded him of how hard Riggs had beaten him.

"And he's where now?" Chandler asked.

"We heard he was over at Roy Sperling's," Evie said. "Henry thinks that Roy knows what's really going on here and that Riggs might kill him."

"This is unbelievable," Chandler said. "This is just utterly beyond—"

A confusion of voices erupted from the far end of the hallway. Both Glenn and Evie turned. There were uniforms coming, three or four of them, and Glenn recognized the Ozona sheriff, Ross Hendricks, and a couple of his deputies, Al Hines and Jim Newell.

Hendricks saw Glenn Chandler, made a beeline for him.

"So, what the fuck is going on here, Glenn?" he said. He looked at Henry. "This the guy you told me about?"

Glenn Chandler nodded. "Henry Quinn, this is Ross Hendricks, Sheriff of Ozona."

Henry grimaced, trying to smile. "Excuse me if I don't get all excited about meetin' another sheriff," he said.

"So, what in God's name has been going on here, boy?" Hendricks asked.

"Sheriff Riggs beat the hell out of him is what's been goin' on," Evie said. "Lang shot himself, Riggs showed up, beat the hell out of Henry, and then took off. Last word was that he was over at Roy Sperling's house, doin' whatever the hell crazy shit he's set his mind to doin'."

"I crossed paths with Bob Arnold coming down from Sonora with a couple of his boys," Hendricks said. "Said he was headed over there. Don't know what the hell you done started, boy," he said to Henry, "but you got two sheriffs and a half dozen deputies chasing Carson Riggs down. And Lang done killed himself. Lord Almighty—"

"He shot himself right in front of my kid," Chandler said.

"Had my way, he woulda shot hisself a good long while back. Him and his father and his father before him. Assholes, the lot of them."

"You have any idea what Riggs is into?" Chandler asked.

"Don't know and don't want to know," Hendricks said. "Lesson learned from hard-won experience . . . If it don't concern me, I don't get concerned."

"I want to get out there," Henry said, and once again moved toward the corridor.

Both Hendricks and Chandler stepped up.

"Best stay right where you are," Hendricks said. "You look like the sky fell on you. You don't know what the hell you done broke or busted, son. Don't make it worse."

Henry smiled grimly. "What's the worst he can do?"

"He can kill you," Evie said. "Seems to me he's lost his mind already. Lord knows what he's capable of."

"Son, seriously—" Hendricks started, but Henry interrupted him with, "Look, I been on this from the start. I gotta see this through one way or the other."

"Seems like a foolish thing to be doin'," Hendricks said. "But hey, I can't stop you. You ain't done nothin' I can arrest you for."

Henry moved, grabbed Evie's arm, and she held him up. Chandler stepped in, took Henry under the shoulder, and Henry sort of moved awkwardly until he could lean against the wall.

"I'll be okay," he said. "I'm just a bit unsteady. Ribs hurt, face hurts, but I can walk."

Hendricks motioned for one of his deputies. "Jim, go get the boy some painkillers. Anything. Half a dozen of something that won't knock him out."

The deputy complied, then met Hendricks, Chandler, Evie, and Henry outside as Henry was maneuvering himself into the back of Sheriff Hendricks's car. Evie got into the back from the other side, Chandler fetching his own car and pulling up behind them.

Hendricks wound down the window and took a bottle of painkillers from Deputy Newell. He gave them to Evie, and she took a couple out for Henry. He crunched them dry, wincing at the taste.

"You and Al follow us," Hendricks said. "Get Al to call ahead. Speak to Bob Arnold and find out what in God's name is going on over there, will you?"

"Will do, Sheriff."

The convoy rolled away, Hendricks up front, Chandler behind him, the two squads behind Chandler. It was no more than a half dozen miles out to Sperling's place, but before they'd even made it halfway Al Hines patched through on the radio to say that Bob Arnold and one of his deputies, Maurice Whyte, were out in Roy Sperling's front yard, and Carson Riggs was hollering at them from an upstairs window. Said he was gonna shoot Roy Sperling if someone didn't get John Lang down there.

"John Lang?" Henry asked.

"Alvin's pa," Hendricks said. "Big shot in Texas Corrections, far as I recall. Hell, the whole family are a bunch of liars and thieves. Don't give a damn what anyone says, Lieutenant Governor Chester Lang is about as straight as a sleeping rattler. If Carson Riggs is neck-deep with them, then there's gonna be something awry going on, for sure."

Evie leaned forward, her face between the front backrests. "Alvin said something about shame." She looked back at Henry, holding on to his side as the car jolted and bounced on the uneven road. "You remember what he said?"

"Something about the past," Henry replied. "Said it all comes back. Something about shame, and that only real shame was that he wouldn't see Riggs's face when it all fell apart. Something like that. I don't remember exactly. I just remember the fucking gun he was waving at us..." Henry grimaced again, reached for the bottle of painkillers in Evie's hand.

They hit the end of the street where Sperling's house was. Sonora Sheriff's Department cars were parked at angles in front of the house. Bystanders and onlookers huddled on the facing sidewalk.

"Goddamned circus already," Hendricks said. "Haven't these people got lives to be gettin' on with?"

He drew to a halt thirty yards away. Chandler and the two deputies drew up behind him, and for a while it seemed as though no one was going to move.

Then Hendricks opened the driver's side door and got out. Everyone followed suit, Chandler coming forward to help Henry up out of the back of the vehicle.

"Right," Hendricks said, "let's go see how deep a hole Carson Riggs has dug for himself and who else is gonna fall in."

FORTY-NINE

Evan Riggs's voice was like some sort of air-raid warning, careening back and forth between the walls, echoing down the corridors as he charged through Ector County Hospital looking for her.

"Rebecaaaa! Rebeccaaa!"

People got out of the way, wondered if this was one of the crazies from upstairs gotten loose. The receptionist tried to stop him, but he pushed past her and took off on his own. She called the police, and hospital administration sent for three or four orderlies from the fourth floor with orders to detain the man before he did any real damage or disturbed too many people.

Evan was cornered on the second floor by a man called Richard Deacon. Ex-US Navy, came out of the war with a half dozen medals, insomnia, blinding headaches. He was not averse to a fight.

"I just want to see Rebecca Riggs," Evan said.

"You gotta calm down, sir," Deacon said.

"I am calm. I just want to see my sister-in-law."

"You don't seem too calm to me, sir. You gotta stop shoutin', okay? You gotta stop runnin' up and down these corridors. You are upsettin' people, and that upsets me."

Evan was breathing heavily, sweat running down the inside of his shirt. He felt light-headed.

"You know her? You know someone called Rebecca Riggs?" Evan asked.

There were other orderlies now, tough-looking, didn't look like they'd have a problem getting him down on the ground and dragging him out of there.

"The pregnant girl?" Deacon asked. "The sheriff guy's wife? She's your sister-in-law?"

"Yes, that's her," Evan gasped. He felt as if he was going to puke right there. He leaned back against the wall, right there in the corner of the stairwell, and then he slid to the ground.

Deacon turned and waved back the small gathering of orderlies. It was okay. He could deal with this.

The crowd dissipated. The place started to resume its own order. The hum and murmur of routine traffic and voices.

"So, what's the deal here, man?" Deacon asked. "What you doin' here?"

"I came to see my sister-in-law," Evan said. "I don't even understand why she's here."

"Her husband . . . your brother, right?"

Evan nodded. "Yes, Carson. Sheriff Riggs. He's my brother."

"Well, she's only been here a couple of weeks. Came in here all wound up and distressed. Don't know details, you know? I just make sure these folk don't do themselves any injury. Some of them are pretty wild."

"Can I see her?" Evan asked, getting to his feet, holding on to the banister and pulling himself up.

"What's your name?"

"Evan. Evan Riggs."

"It ain't visiting hours, Evan," Deacon said. "You're gonna have to cool off someplace and then come back when it's visitin' hours. This is a hospital. There are rules and regulations. You can't just have anyone and everyone wanderin' in and out of here like it's—"

"I really need to see her," Evan said. He looked at the name tag sewn across the pocket of Deacon's scrubs.

"Richard, right? Richard Deacon."

Deacon nodded.

"Well, Richard, I gotta see her. Somethin' wrong is happening here. She shouldn't be here, you know? There's nothing wrong with her. She doesn't belong in any psychiatric place—"

Deacon smiled sardonically. "I hear that every day, Evan, both from the visitors and the people they come to visit. It ain't nothin' to do with me. If they're here, then they've been put here by family, and usually there's a doctor behind that and a lawyer, too. Folks don't wind up in here because someone takes a dislike to them. There's a process, you know?"

"I need to see her, Richard . . . I really do."

"I understand you, Evan, but I gotta abide by the rules and regulations myself. Visitin' time is visitin' time, and there ain't nothin' I can do to change that."

Evan stood up straight. "I don't want to cause any more trouble—"

Deacon smiled. "Believe me, you ain't gonna cause me any trouble, Evan."

"I reckon I can have a pretty good go."

"You're tellin' me what I think you're tellin' me?"

"I am."

"I can put you down real fast, my friend. Done it before. Will do it many times again, I'm sure."

"You served?"

Deacon nodded. "I did. US Navy."

"I did infantry," Evan said. "Learned a few things. We get into this, then neither one of us is walking away undamaged."

Deacon laughed. "I like you, man. You got a bad fuckin' attitude, but I like you."

"I like you, too, Richard, but if you don't let me see Rebecca, then I am gonna give it my best shot and they're gonna be stitchin' up your face."

"What happened here? You get up this mornin' and decide to be the worst asshole you could be?"

Evan shook his head. "No, sir. I got up this morning and found out that my brother is the worst asshole he could be, and he's put his wife here for some reason I do not understand. She is pregnant, and now I am getting scared. I need to see her, Richard, and I need to see her now, and we're either gonna agree on that or we're both gonna wind up in triage."

"That's really the way it's gonna be?"

"It is."

Deacon looked Evan up and down, shook his head resignedly. "Third floor," he said. "But I'm comin' with you."

Rebecca looked at Evan as if they were dreaming different dreams. Her eyes seemed washed-out, almost devoid of life.

She lay in a bed in a room on the third floor of Ector County Hospital Psychiatric Facility, and when Evan appeared in the doorway, there was little enough recognition for him to even be aware that she knew who he was.

"Jesus Christ, what the hell . . . ?" he started, and Richard Deacon walked with him to the side of the bed and watched him as he sat down and took Rebecca's hand.

He could so easily see that she was pregnant, and the fact that she was evidently drugged into some sort of mindless stupor concerned him, not only for her own well-being, but for the well-being of the child.

"What have they done to her?" Evan asked.

Deacon shrugged resignedly. "I don't know. I'm no doctor. Like I said, I'm just here to make sure the really crazy ones don't kill the less-crazy ones."

"Does she have a doctor?"

"Sure she does."

Rebecca smiled weakly. "Evan," she whispered.

"Rebecca," he replied. "Jesus, I am sorry . . . What happened here? What the hell is going on?"

"Get me out of here, Evan," she said, and the way her gaze drifted toward the window made Evan feel as if she were halfway toward being a ghost.

"I am gonna get you out of here," he said, and with that he turned and looked for someone to speak to, someone in charge, someone who could make a decision and let Evan take her home.

"Hey, hey, hey," Deacon said. "She's not goin' anywhere, man. You can't just take her out of here, and she sure as hell can't discharge herself."

"She's coming with me, Richard. Now either you help me, or we're gonna get into even more trouble."

"Wait a minute now—" Deacon started, interrupted then by the sound of commotion and voices at the far end of the corridor.

"Ah, hell," Deacon said, and walked to the door. He looked out and down the hallway, shook his head, turned back to Evan.

"We're both in the crap now, my friend," he said, and before the last word left his lips, a group of orderlies, doctors, and nurses appeared in the doorway. Following them was Carson, and he looked at Evan as if he had now brought all the anger and hatred the world had to offer along for the ride.

"Get the hell away from her," Carson said. His voice was hard and bitter. "Get the hell away from my wife right now."

One of the doctors put his hand on Evan's shoulder. "Sir, you need to get up off the bed. You need to step away from the patient—"

Evan shoved the man aside.

Deacon stepped up.

The doctor turned on him. "Get back, Deacon. You are on notice. You let this man up here."

Another orderly tried to grab Evan, but Evan pushed him back into the doctor and the two of them lost their balance and fell against the wall.

Carson charged through the group and grabbed his brother. Before Evan had a chance to wrestle himself out of Carson's grip, Carson had cuffed one hand and pulled Evan down to his knees.

Carson was half a head taller, in better shape, and Evan was at a disadvantage. Before Evan knew what was happening, his hands were behind him, cuffed hard and fast, and Carson was standing over him.

Rebecca fought to sit upright. She possessed no strength, it seemed, and she just collapsed back to the mattress and started to cry.

"Carson . . . I'm so sorry . . . I never meant—"

Carson turned and glared at his wife. "Enough," he said. "Not another word, Rebecca."

The doctor was on his feet. "I need you all to leave," he said. "I need this room cleared. This is outrageous. I cannot have this kind of commotion and noise—"

"We're leaving," Carson said. He pulled Evan to his feet and turned him toward the door.

"Evan!" Rebecca called after him. "Tell him how sorry I am . . . Tell him we never meant to hurt him . . ."

Carson turned on her once more. "Silence!" he shouted. "That is enough from you!"

"Evan!" she called again.

Evan looked back over his shoulder at her.

"I need you here . . . I need you to be with me, Evan. I want you to see our baby . . ."

The world stopped.

There was silence, as if throughout the entire building.

The doctor looked at Carson Riggs, his face now red and livid, his eyes wide with hatred. Carson pushed Evan aside and rushed to the side of the bed.

Rebecca barely had time to raise her hand in self-defense before Carson rained punches down on her like a whirlwind.

It was Deacon who dragged Carson Riggs back, but by that time it seemed that the place was bedlam once more.

Rebecca was screaming for Evan, Evan screaming at his brother, Carson hollering abuse at his wife, how she was a bitch, a good-for-nothing tramp, a whore.

Orderlies were tasked with getting everyone but the staff out of the room and out of the building, and they did so. It was a running battle through and out of the front doors, and before either of them really understood what had happened, Carson and Evan Riggs were standing face-to-face on the driveway of the hospital,

Evan still cuffed, Carson holding a gun in his hand, the expression on his face as if he possessed every intention of using it.

"You are going back to Austin," Carson said, his voice measured and certain.

"You can go fuck yourself, Carson. What the hell are you doing? What the fuck—"

Carson raised the gun and pointed it directly at Evan's face. "You, my little brother, are going back to Austin. I am even going to take you there. You will not come back here again. You will not see Rebecca again. You will never speak to me, and you will never speak to Ma."

"You can go fuck yourself, Carson . . . You are fucking crazy. You can't make me go. You can't fucking make me do anything . . ."

Carson swung the gun sideways. It connected with Evan's right cheek and sent him to the ground.

Carson stood over him, brandishing the sidearm, every word from his lips like a bullet.

"You fucked her. You fucked her the night before she agreed to marry me. You are not my brother. You are not my blood. You betrayed me. You betrayed Ma and Pa. You are nothing to me."

Carson stepped back and let fly with a harsh kick to Evan's ribs. Evan howled in pain, turned onto his side, and pulled his knees up to his chest.

Carson got down on his haunches beside his younger brother and pushed the barrel of the gun beneath Evan's chin.

"I should shoot you right now. To me, you are dead already anyway. You're going back to Austin. I am taking you, and you're going back now. You will never come back. That is the way it is going to be."

Evan tried to push back against his older brother, but Carson just jabbed the gun hard into Evan's face. His cheek now cut, the blood ran down the side of his nose and Evan could taste it on his lips.

"Not another fucking word, Evan," Carson said.

"You cannot—" Evan started, but Carson shook his head, raised the gun, and brought it down on the side of Evan's head with such force that the lights went out completely. No one intervened when they saw Calvary's sheriff dragging an unconscious man to the black-and-white parked just a few yards away. He was the law, after all, and when it came to the law it was wise not to get involved.

*

323

Evan Riggs was arrested in Austin at approximately eleven that night. He was found slumped in a doorway by a beat patrol. Not only was his face bruised and swollen, but his clothes were ripped, stained with blood, and he was rank with stale liquor.

Seventeenth Precinct house took him, threw him in the tank, and called a doctor. Despite the stench of liquor, it appeared that he had not been drinking. He was dazed and confused, said something about his brother, that there was a girl in trouble, but little of that made sense. They held him, the doctor recommending he get a psych eval before they let him out.

In the morning they let him go. Seemed whoever might have been interested in determining the mental state of Evan Riggs was no longer interested. To the duty sergeant, he was just another of the many dozens of drunks who dragged their sorry stink in and out of the precinct house on a routine basis.

Evan Riggs walked a block and a half and found a bar. He was drunk before noon. By three he was haunting regular spots, arguing with folk he had no business arguing with, deep in a well of despair and self-loathing. It was a place he'd been before, knew it well, though this time there was more than enough reason for him to be there. He understood that Rebecca was pregnant. He also understood that he was the father of this soon-to-be child, and yet she was not only married to his brother but now locked up in the psych ward at Ector County Hospital. Carson was right. He had betrayed his brother, his folks, his own integrity, and he was an asshole of the first order. He drank more. Seemed the only solution.

By five, Evan Riggs was through and out the other side of the depression. He was angry, bitter, the shame and ignominy he felt for what he'd done somehow turning back upon itself. Carson deserved everything that had happened to him. Carson never really loved Rebecca; he just wanted her as some kind of trophy. Carson didn't know what it meant to feel what Evan felt. Carson was the bad guy here, not because of what he'd done, but because of what he'd failed to do.

Evan would take her away. He would go back to Ector, get her the hell out of there, and the two of them would somehow disappear. Rebecca would have the child, and Evan . . . Evan would change everything. He could be a good man, a good father, and Carson could go to hell, for all he cared.

Evan showed up at the Excelsior Hotel, little more than a flop-house on the west side of Austin, at around six that evening. It was a regular haunt for those late nights when he couldn't make it back to where he was staying, or had no place to stay. They knew him there, not only a regular face but a regular tab that they let run to thirty or forty bucks before turning away. That evening they took him in. He was drunk, but Evan was always drunk. No change there.

Evan Riggs lay on a cot in a first-floor room. While the ceiling swam in circles above his head, he put his life back together, if not in reality, at least in his imagination. Tomorrow he would go back to Calvary. He would straighten it all out. He would make everything good. He could do that. He really could do that.

It was with a sense of positive optimism that Evan responded to a knock at the door. He was feeling a little better. It was still early. He could clean himself up, go out, have just another drink or two. Tomorrow was the demarcation point between the past and the future. Tomorrow the bottle would be part of his history.

The man in the hallway was a stranger to Evan Riggs.

"Mr. Evan Riggs?" the man said.

Evan nodded. "Yeah . . . who are you?"

The man held out a sheaf of papers. Evan instinctively took them.

"You've been served, buddy," the man said.

"Served? What the hell?"

The man took a step backward. "Go within three hundred yards of Rebecca Riggs, speak to her, call her, attempt to gain entry to the hospital, and you will be in violation of that injunction," the man said. "Okay?"

The man started to turn.

"Hey," Evan said.

He turned to face Evan.

Evan threw the papers at the man.

The man was implacable, had seen it all before. "Buddy, you've been served. That's just the way it is."

Evan took another step forward, pushed the man's shoulder.

"Okay, now you're crossing another line, my friend. I am an officer of the court. Touch me, and you're in deeper shit than you could even imagine."

"Take your goddamned papers!" Evan snapped, the anger surging inside him. How dare this stranger tell him that he could not see Rebecca. How dare he ferry a message from Carson and think

325

that this would carry some weight. What the hell did he think was happening here?

"Seriously, you need to think about what you're doing, buddy boy," the man said. "Back the hell away. You raise your voice or your fists to me, I will have you arrested right here and now; then you will be dealing with an assault charge as well as whatever other bullshit you've caused for yourself."

"How dare you come in here—"

"Hey," the man said, raising his hands. "This is not me, mister. This is due process. You can't tell me anything I ain't heard a thousand times before. You are just one more sorry asshole who fucked up his life, and I am not the target here... You deal with whatever you gotta deal with, and you keep me the hell out of it."

Evan was incensed. He took another step forward, his fists raised. "You take those papers back to my fucking brother and you tell him—"

"Okay, that's it," the man said. "I'm outta here. Next stop for you is the drunk tank—"

Evan swung, connected hard. That fist came like a runaway train and caught the man on the jaw.

The man went down hard, and Evan was over him, fists flying, a drunken rage powering every muscle, every vein, every nerve, every sinew.

Evan could see nothing but Carson's face in that final moment outside Ector Hospital, the way he looked down at him, the condescending sneer, the knowledge that Carson would do everything he could to keep Evan away from Rebecca, from his own child.

Evan Riggs was no flyweight. Lessons learned at Fort Benning were not forgotten. The process server didn't have a chance. He may well have been a fair-minded and decent man, a good father to two small boys, a faithful husband, a hard worker who believed that doing the right thing was always the easiest way out of any trouble you might experience in life, but he was no fighter. He served papers to recalcitrant husbands, loan defaulters, errant wives, folks who missed payments on mortgages and cars, and on weekends he liked little more than a barbecue and a couple of beers in the backyard, his pretty wife in a cotton print dress bringing hot dogs and corn for him and the boys.

His name was Forrest Wetherby, and the papers he'd delivered had come from Warren Garfield at the request of Carson Riggs. How Wetherby had found Evan Riggs was part experience, part dogged persistence, part sheer luck, but those papers were the very last he would serve.

Evan Riggs couldn't have hit him more than a half dozen times, but they were decisive blows, driven by a fierce and uncontrolled rage. The throat, the chest, the solar plexus, finally some blows to the head that put Wetherby back against the wall. The final strike caught him full in the face, and it was the thunderous impact the back of his skull made against the wall that precipitated the fatal hemorrhage.

Forrest Wetherby's legs gave way like those of a newborn heifer. He was dead before he hit the worn-out linoleum hallway on the first floor of that Austin, Texas flophouse.

The hotel people found Wetherby right where he'd fallen, blood running from his ear due to the sustained trauma to which he'd been subjected.

Evan they found sprawled across the mattress in his room, drenched in sweat, his clothes spattered, his knuckles raw.

Every other room was empty. No one had entered or exited the building following Wetherby's arrival.

Evan didn't even realize what had happened until he woke in a cell three hours later with a murder charge on the books. He'd already been booked for drunk and disorderly the day before, said he didn't remember a thing. Coincidentally, he went back to the seventeenth, and they held him there for arraignment. A public defender was assigned, and he came down on Monday the twenty-second. By that time, Evan Riggs had lost whatever semblance of self-possession he had formerly maintained.

Evan Riggs was done for. He knew it. He reconciled himself to fate, and had it not been for the intervention of Governor Shivers, he would certainly have gone to the chair. Forever after, folks would listen to *The Whiskey Poet* and hear a man confessing, even though those songs were written long before Evan Riggs crossed paths with Forrest Wetherby. Maybe a man could confess in advance, seek forgiveness for something he was yet to do. Maybe some people just knew that bad things were on the way, things they would do and things that would be done to them, and they were getting ready for it ahead of time. As had been noted so many times before, people were always of a mind to think what they wanted, and there was often no relationship between that and the truth.

*

327

Rebecca Riggs gave birth to a daughter in the second week of November, 1949.

It was Grace Riggs who got word to her younger son that he was now the father of a beautiful girl called Sarah.

Carson had expressly forbidden Grace to contact Evan and did not learn that his mother had gone behind his back until after Christmas. By that time he'd already found her a place at Ector County Hospital, her committal papers countersigned and processed by Roy Sperling and Warren Garfield. The last will and testament that William Riggs had authorized before his death—the very document that William had delivered into Garfield's hands after learning what Carson, Garfield, and Sperling had done to Rebecca—was conveniently lost. An earlier will was processed, a will that left the house to Grace, also financial provision for the remainder of her life, the land then divided into equal parts between Carson and Evan. Evan was already in Reeves, would be there for life, and thus by law he had no defensible position. Carson Riggs called in a longtime favor from Alvin Lang's father, John. John Lang, not only the eldest son of Congressman Chester Lang but a significant authority in the Texas Department of Corrections, had words with the Redbird County DA. The DA made a call to Warren Garfield. Warren Garfield was unreserved in his willingness to cooperate, and any right Evan Riggs might have had to contest Carson's decisions about the land were summarily waived.

The Riggs farm was broken up into lots. Before Grace Riggs was even admitted to Ector County, Carson had signed away every one of those lots to the Naval Petroleum Reserves Department. A good number of people became a good deal richer with a single signature. Proceeds from that sale found their way into the pockets of both Chester Lang and his son, John. Warren Garfield and Roy Sperling were taken care of generously. George Eakins, Clarence Ames, and Harold Mills, all three of them members of the Calvary Residents' Charter, were impressed upon sufficiently to overrule a petition to revoke the drilling rights granted by Carson Riggs.

Carson Riggs ran for sheriff again, once more uncontested and unchallenged. Where questions might have been asked about the veracity and fairness of that election, those questions were answered with contributions to church renovation funds, civic projects, licenses issued by the Redbird County Sheriff's Department for roadworks to be undertaken, construction permits granted, building certificates authorized. A great deal of money found its way into a great many hands. Those payments served to tuck in corners and tidy away any unsightly threads. All was well that ended well.

Sarah Riggs was taken from her mother when she was four days old. Between that day and the day Rebecca died in June of 1951, mother and daughter did not see each other again.

That was Carson Riggs's wish. He was sheriff of Calvary, had been for five years, and it looked like he was going to be sheriff for as long as such a position was available. He knew people, he had money enough, and all that had happened with Evan was a matter of history. People knew not to speak of it, and so they did not.

That history would remain right where it was until one Tuesday in May of 1972, when Warren Garfield's heart stopped in the middle of a telephone conversation. Perhaps it was the burden of guilt that finally killed him, not only for what had happened with William Riggs's last will and testament, but the committal of Grace, of Rebecca, and his collusion with Roy Sperling and Carson Riggs in a matter that went back many years earlier to a time when America was calling on its loyal sons to fight the good fight in the European theater of war. No matter what Carson might once have said about the Second World War never reaching the United States, it had done so, and those who did not volunteer were ever aware that conscription might remove any power of choice.

With the death of Warren Garfield, a closed chapter was opened. Despite that Garfield had conspired to overturn Williams Riggs's final wishes as to the division of land and wealth, Garfield's final wishes were honored, one of them being the dispatch of a letter to Evan Riggs at Reeves County Farm. Ironically, it was Roy Sperling who insisted Garfield's wishes were abided by, perhaps to mitigate the burden of guilt Sperling himself had carried for as long as memory served.

That letter arrived just a little while before Evan's cellmate was due for release, and it was to this cellmate that this letter was then entrusted.

"This is for my daughter," Evan Riggs told Henry Quinn. "Her name is Sarah. That's all I know. I need you to find her and give her this letter. Start in Calvary. My brother is the sheriff there. He will know where she is."

Calvary was where it all started, and Calvary was where it would end.

FIFTY

Roy Sperling possessed no uncertainty. He knew his nose was broken, his left wrist, too. He was a doctor, after all. He had fulfilled that position in Calvary for as long as anyone could remember.

He sat in a chair in his own kitchen. Blood had coursed down his chin and soaked the front of his shirt. He looked much the same as Henry when Henry had been admitted to triage.

"We're done for," he told Carson Riggs. It was not the first time he'd said such a thing. The second time had prompted the swift right hook that broke his nose.

"Shut the hell up," Riggs had told him. "John Lang is gonna come down here and fix things up."

"You really believe that, Carson? He's a functionary in the Department of Corrections. What the hell—"

"Shut the hell up. This is gonna get fixed."

"That kid has screwed you, Carson. Evan sent that kid down here and he has screwed you. Screwed both of us. Only reason Warren isn't getting screwed is he had the good fortune to fucking die before the shit hit the fan."

Carson Riggs, face like a hammer, stood with his back against the sink and looked at Sperling.

"I am not going down," Riggs said. "And if I do go down, you and the rest of them go with me."

"Ha! You are an arrogant asshole, Carson. Always have been, always will be. You are dealing with the lieutenant governor of Texas, you dumb son of a bitch. You think he's gonna let some small-town sheriff from the middle of nowhere fuck his life up? He may very well have hailed from here, but he is a big shot now, Carson. Politically, that man is even more powerful than the governor. What happened was nearly thirty years ago. His sons are long grown-up. The war is over. Jesus, you are living in a world entirely of your own creation."

Carson Riggs raised the gun in his hand and pointed it at Sperling's face.

Sperling looked back at him, his expression less of surprise and more that of someone anticipating the predictable.

"You're gonna shoot me? Is that what we've come to, Carson? Alvin Lang is dead, or did you forget that already? His father isn't coming down here, no matter what the fuck you say or do—"

"He is coming down here. Chester Lang, too... They're gonna come down here and sort this out."

Sperling started laughing, and blood bubbled from his nose. "You are just downright crazy, Carson Riggs. You and that lunatic fucking brother of yours. Jesus, why the hell me and Warren ever got involved with you, I do not know."

"Because you were greedy and you wanted the money, that's why... Same reason as everyone."

"Ironic though, wasn't it...? You and your dumbass brother. He beats some poor schmuck to death and spends the rest of his life in jail. And Charlie Brennan may very well have been a fucking useless sheriff, but he didn't deserve what you did to him. You beat Charlie to death in just the same fucking way... beat the poor son of a bitch's brains out because he wanted a bigger cut and you wanted his fucking job. Well, you got the bigger cut and you got his job. You also got a dead wife, a crazy mother, and a brother in Reeves. And what the hell has happened now, huh? Some poor naive kid who doesn't know his ass from his elbow comes wandering in here with a letter, and your whole fucking world falls apart. Hell, you don't even know what's in that letter, do you? I bet that's been driving you fucking crazy..."

"Shut the fuck up, Roy! Just shut the fuck up," Riggs snapped. "You don't know a goddamned thing about this—"

"Is that so?"

Riggs's expression changed for just a split second. He sneered at Sperling. "You don't know a goddamned thing about what's in that letter."

"You think? You don't think my oldest and dearest friend, Warren Garfield, didn't tell me that he was gonna screw you sideways over a barrel if anything ever happened to him? He always knew you were crazy as a shithouse rat, Carson. He guessed that one day you might even try to kill him. Well, he died anyway. His heart gave out... And you know what I did? You wanna know what I did? I followed his last wishes exactly, and one of those wishes was sending a letter and a very interesting document out to your brother in Reeves—"

Riggs lunged forward and grabbed Sperling around the throat

with his left hand. He held the gun close to Sperling's face. Sperling looked back at him implacably, a response that seemed to anger Riggs even more.

"Fucking shoot me. I am done, Carson. I am gonna die right here and now, or I am going to jail for the rest of my life. Hell, I might even get to room with your brother—"

Riggs let go of Sperling's neck. He swept the gun sideways and brought it back to connect with Sperling's cheekbone. Sperling both heard and felt it crack. He nearly passed out as the lance of excruciating pain almost took his head off his shoulders, but within moments he was looking back at Riggs with that same determined and defiant glare.

"That will your daddy wrote when you put your wife in Ector . . . That's what Warren sent to your brother, Carson. He sent him the last will and testament of your father, the one you overruled, the one you thought would never come to light. That was Warren's dying wish . . . that the truth of what you did came out. You fucking killed Charlie Brennan. You beat the poor, greedy, stupid, dumbass son of a bitch to death, and I falsified the death certificate. You got what you wanted. You got the land, you got the oil rights, you got all the money, and you've paid your way into the Sheriff's Office for the last thirty years. Well, fuck you, Carson. It ends here and now. That kid is gonna find Evan's daughter, and he is gonna give her that letter, and she is gonna find out who you are and who her daddy is and how you robbed her of her inheritance. Because that's what your father did, Carson . . . He left everything to Evan's daughter. You betrayed him, you betrayed your ma, your brother . . . You betrayed everyone far more than Evan ever betrayed you. Your daddy knew that, and he took everything away from you. He wanted you to have nothing after what you did to Rebecca and that baby. You killed Charlie. You saw your own wife dead after what they did to her up at Ector, and you might as well sign your own mother's death certificate, because she is gonna die up there soon enough—"

"Shut the hell up, Roy! You shut the goddamned hell up right now. There ain't no will—"

"There is. I seen it, Carson. I seen it with my own eyes. I was the one who got it in the mail after Warren died, and I knew exactly what I was doing. And I am fucking glad, Carson . . . I am fucking glad. I made a lot of money from what we did back then, but you have held court and controlled this town and told us what to do ever since, and it ends here—"

Riggs grabbed Sperling by the throat again, squeezed it hard, a cruel and fierce madness in his eyes as he looked down at the bleeding man on the chair in front of him.

"Kill me, Carson... and then if I were you, I'd kill yourself. Them Langs... man, they are not gonna let you bring down their family. They have way too much power and way too much money. Hey, I bet you they even got it rigged that you killed Alvin. Shee-it, I bet you that's the way it's gonna turn out in the papers. Would they want a suicide on their hands? No siree, Bob. Suicide makes it looks like the Lang family has got something to hide. Deputy sheriff of Calvary shoots himself for being complicit in what? Hell, I don't believe they want that kind of scandal slurring their upright and prestigious family name. But Calvary sheriff goes crazy, shoots his deputy, shoots the town doctor, and then shoots himself... Well, man, it's the South. These things happen. Three weeks and no one will even remember that you knew the Langs."

"You were in this as much as me, Roy," Riggs snarled. "You were right in there with Warren and me. We did what we did for the Langs. We arranged everything, covered everyone's tracks—"

"Sure we did, Carson... and you got Alvin's daddy on your side, and he called the Redbird DA, and Warren destroyed the last will... or so he said, and you got the farm and the oil rights and more money than you knew what to do with. But it was never about the money, was it, Carson? It was about the authority and the power and being able to do just what the hell you liked. Christ, man, you've spent your whole life getting revenge on people for things you made them do!" Sperling started to laugh, but the pain shot through his face and he grimaced. "We cooked up those medical records and affidavits, my friend. We did what we did. We hid both of Chester Lang's sons behind a veil of lies so they wouldn't have to go to war. We did it for Chester Lang and for anyone else who had the money. Go take a look in the cemetery. Memorial down there for all our brave boys who died in the First War, but is there anything for the Second? Hell, no. Fucking ironic that the only one with any balls when it came to the war was your dumbass brother. Second irony is that the most powerful and influential families in West Texas are still the most powerful and influential families in West Texas. They had the money to pay us, and we did what they asked us. You think they're gonna let some greedy small-time sheriff expose their cowardice? You think they want the world to know that they paid to keep their kids out of the army? You think they are gonna admit what they did and say sorry and be all ashamed? Hell, you are even fucking crazier than I took you for—"

Riggs hit Sperling again. "You shut the fuck up—" he started, but his words were interrupted by the voice of Ozona sheriff Ross Hendricks. That voice came loud and clear through a bullhorn, and the message was unequivocal.

"Sheriff Riggs! You hear me in there, Sheriff Riggs? This is Hendricks out of Ozona. We got some kind of trouble here, and we've come down to try to sort it out. Now, whatever the hell has happened, we can straighten it out, but I am told that you and Doc Roy Sperling are in there and there's some kind of problem. Well, I am a reasonable man, just like you, and we can straighten it all out. You come on out here and we'll get to talking, and you might be surprised how easily we can fix whatever the hell is going on."

Sperling tried to laugh again. "Jesus Christ in a chariot, they don't have the faintest goddamned idea of what you did, do they, Carson?"

"You did the same, Roy . . . You did the fucking same, and you are going down, too . . ."

"Difference is, Carson, that I know I'm done for and I don't care. I've had enough. Shoot me, or let them shoot me. Put me in Reeves and throw away the key. I'll just tie a bedsheet around my neck and hang myself. It's over, Carson. Warren bailed out. I'm an old man. I don't think of anything nowadays but what we did to your wife, how they drugged her and stuck things in her brain and whatever . . . all to make it look like she was crazy so she would never have a hope of taking that land and that oil off of you. I just have to close my eyes for a second and I can see her screaming her head off in the back of that hospital car as they drove her away. "

From out in the street, Hendricks was hollering through the bullhorn. "Sheriff Riggs . . . Carson . . . you gotta come out of there and talk to me. I don't wanna have to come in there, my friend."

"Lang will come," Riggs said, his tone desperate, as if he was now struggling to believe what he was saying. "John Lang will come to find out what happened to his son . . . and if he doesn't come, then Chester will send someone, and this will all get straightened out."

"They're gonna find the girl, Carson. They're gonna find Sarah. Hell, she lives no more than twenty miles from here. Terrible shadow that must have been. Keep her close or send her far away. How that must have tormented you. Well, it wouldn't have mattered, because that dumbass kid from Reeves is gonna deliver that letter. This whole house of shadows will come crashing down around you . . . and you won't even hear it. Only person they're gonna send, even if they do send someone, is gonna be here for one reason and one reason only. To make sure you never say a goddamned word about the Langs and what we did back in forty-four. John Lang, Robert Lang, the Webster boys, the Deardens, the Wesleys, all of them fit and well, all of them more than eligible for armed service, and we hid them all. While honest German people were hiding Jews from the Nazis, you were hiding the sons of the rich and powerful so they didn't have to go to war. You really think the lieutenant governor of Texas wants America and the world to know what we did?"

Riggs looked at Sperling like he was facing his own executioner.

"Carson Riggs!" Hendricks's voice bellowed through the bullhorn. "Come on out now, or we're comin' in!"

"It's all over, Carson," Sperling said, and then Carson Riggs raised the gun once more and shot him in the chest.

Even from the kitchen, Carson Riggs heard the response to that single gunshot. It sounded like an army was advancing from the street.

He looked at Sperling. He looked at the gun in his hand. He had just murdered the doctor. That, if nothing else, would see him in Reeves for the rest of his life.

And it was that thought—the thought of seeing Evan every day—that turned the tide of his thoughts.

He looked once more at Sperling, and then he turned toward the door.

Sheriff Carson Riggs went out there, gun raised, pulling the trigger even before he'd exited the house, and the sound that welcomed him was something Vernon Harvey—he of Snowflake, Arizona, he of the pocket watch that Evan himself carried to a different war—would have recognized. It was a cannonade, an assault, and Carson fell forward from the veranda and never got up.

Ross Hendricks came through into the kitchen.

Doc Sperling stirred.

Hendricks hesitated for just a second, and then he was hollering for a medic, a doctor, an ambulance.

"Sto-o-op," Sperling slurred. He tried to raise his hand, tried to motion for Hendricks to come close.

Hendricks went to the man's side.

"Too l-late," Sperling gasped. "He-Henry Qu—"

"Henry Quinn," Hendricks said. "He's here. He's outside."

335

Sperling seemed to smile then. "G-get h-him h-here. Get h-him h-here. Need to tell hi-him . . . tell him wh-where th-the girl i-is . . ."

Hendricks sent for Henry Quinn. Henry came at a run. Evie, too, the two of them kneeling beside Doc Sperling to hear the last halting syllables that left the man's lips before his eyes rolled white. He died right there in his own kitchen, and with him went the truth of how Carson Riggs had held sway over him and Warren Garfield for nearly thirty years.

The Langs would never have come to Calvary. In truth, Carson Riggs had known that all along. In the end it was face his Maker or face his brother, and he had chosen the former.

Somehow that had seemed the easier option after all the wrongs that had been done.

FIFTY-ONE

She did not look how Henry had expected her to look. There was so little of Evan in her. Perhaps she simply took after the mother she'd never known.

It was early on the morning of Thursday, July twentieth, and behind a small house off the highway between Sanderson and Langley, just a stone's throw from the Pecos River, a woman of twenty-two called Sarah Forrester hung washing on a line. Nearby there was a basket, within it a baby, and she sang to the baby, and the song was something simple and sweet, and Sarah's voice was soothing, and the baby gurgled and cooed as if joining in with the song.

Henry stood there at the edge of the road, Evie beside him, the letter from Evan in his hand, and he looked at Evie and the question was in his eyes, same question he'd been asking himself ever since Roy Sperling had told him where Sarah now lived and the name she had married into. Sarah Forrester. Twenty-two years old, alive and well and now a mother, living with her husband in a small house off the highway between Sanderson and Langley.

It was that complex, and then—all of a sudden—it was that simple.

Henry looked down at the letter in his hand, a letter secreted beneath the lining of his guitar case ever since he'd arrived in Calvary, and he wondered how this had all happened. It was the twentieth of July. He had arrived in Calvary on the thirteenth. One week. Seven days. Three men were dead. He felt like he had known Evie his whole life. He felt as if he had never been anywhere but here, never done anything but chase the ghost that was Evan Riggs's daughter.

And now here she was.

He could see her.

And she did not look at all as he had imagined.

"Go," Evie urged, and Henry left the side of the road and walked across the dried and rutted track to the fence that bordered the backyard.

337

Evie hung back a step or two.

This was Henry's job now, and most of him knew he needed to do it alone, despite what he thought or felt.

"Mrs. Forrester," he called out.

The young woman stopped singing. The baby stopped singing, too.

"Yes," she replied.

"I am Henry Quinn," Henry said. "You don't know me. I have been looking for you. I came to deliver a message."

"A message?" Sarah asked. "About what?"

Henry held up the creased and grubby envelope. "I don't know," he said. "I don't know what the message is."

Sarah Forrester smiled and shook her head, puzzled, wondering what this was all about.

"Who is this message from?"

Henry held out the letter. "I think you need to read this and find out for yourself."

The young woman came forward and took the envelope from Henry's hand.

She studied him closely for a second, glanced at Evie, a fleeting frown across her brow like the shadow of a cloud across a field.

Had Evan been there to see her, he would have recognized that expression. She looked like her mother. So much like her mother. Snake hunting. The rats' nest. The bundle of clothes on the veranda. The way she looked as they hid in the barn and waited for Gabe Ellsworth. The expression on her face when he glanced back at her on the night of the party, the guilt of what they had done somehow extinguished by the passion of having done it.

Sarah Forrester read the letter.

She looked at the enclosed document; she looked at Henry, at Evie, back at Henry once more.

She read her father's letter one more time, and then she started to cry.

FIFTY-TWO

Roy Sperling was buried in Calvary on Friday, July twenty-eighth. Alvin Lang was already gone, his family plot somewhere near Fredericksburg. Clarence Ames, George Eakins, the Honeycutts, even Ralph Chandler went out there for the service. They'd known Alvin, many of them since he was a child, and they wanted to pay their respects.

"It's done now," was the only comment her father made when Evie asked him why he wanted to attend. "When they're dead, they gotta deal with a far higher power, I reckon. Who are we to judge?"

The Lang family did not order an independent inquiry into the suicide of Calvary's deputy sheriff. Seemed they wanted the whole thing laid to rest and forgotten along with Alvin. Likewise, the killing of Roy Sperling seemed to be now the only motivation for Carson Riggs's actions. Why had he killed Sperling? What was it that took place between those two men in that kitchen that resulted in Carson killing the town doctor and then walking headlong into a hail of gunfire, the only outcome of which would be his own death? Folks like Clarence Ames and George Eakins perhaps knew, but they kept their mouths shut and looked no one in the eye. There were theories, of course, but theories would always remain theories without the evidence to back them up. And no one was looking for evidence. Seemed no one was interested in finding it.

For the people of Calvary, the Sperling funeral was somehow significant, perhaps even cathartic. All that was left of the Riggs family was a crazy old woman in Odessa and a killer in Reeves. Aside from the girl. Rebecca's girl. She showed up alongside Henry Quinn and Evie Chandler the day before Roy Sperling was buried. They told her what they knew of her parents, her grandparents, of the events that pulled her family apart so violently. They took her out to the old Riggs place, now nothing more than a footprint of the original farmhouse and tracts of land, all of it marked and bordered and punctuated with sinkholes where drills had punched deep into the ground in search of oil pockets and reservoirs. Whatever fortune came from that land was either gone, or buried so deep in legal paperwork that it would probably never surface. Carson Riggs had been spending that money for more than twenty years, and when the lawyers and the tax collectors and the court officers were done with it, it would very likely turn out that he owed the state.

Whatever the details, Sarah Forrester wanted none of it.

"This is not my life," she told Henry Quinn and Evie Chandler, and then she asked if Henry would be so kind as to drive her home. Her husband had the baby, and he needed to get to work.

"What about your father?" Evie asked her.

Sarah looked away once more toward the horizon, across land that had seen the tracks of unknown predecessors, people whose names had only come to mean something within the last few days, people for whom she perhaps should have felt something, but somehow felt nothing at all. These people, like the land before her, were as distant and unfamiliar as the far side of the world.

Sarah turned to look at Evie. "What about him?"

Henry thought to speak, to say something, anything in Evan's defense, and yet there were no words to find. A drunk, a traitor, false-hearted and irresponsible; an absentee father, a man who deserted his family and friends for the promise of some other life never attained; a killer. Henry had known him for three years. In truth, Henry hadn't known him at all. The message had been delivered; he had kept his word. Upon reflection, it would seem that getting that letter into the hands of Evan's daughter was less about keeping a promise to Evan, even less about Sarah, and more about Henry Quinn proving to himself that he was not the kind of man that he'd perhaps believed himself to be. For all their apparent similarities, he and Evan Riggs were altogether different.

And so, the day before Roy Sperling was buried, Henry Quinn and Evie Chandler drove Sarah Forrester back to the house off the highway between Sanderson and Langley, just a stone's throw from the Pecos River, and her husband was there to greet her, standing inside the doorway with the baby in his arms.

Sarah got out of the car, and she looked back at Henry. "I don't really have anything for him, you know? I mean, even if I met him, I wouldn't know what to say."

"I understand," Henry replied, thinking in that moment of what he would do were he suddenly presented with Jack Alford, a father he himself had never known, a father who—more than likely—knew nothing of him.

"Do you want me to go and see him?" Sarah asked. "In Reeves?"

Henry shook his head. "I think it would kill him," he said. "I think he would realize what he had missed all these years, and it would break his heart."

"But you? You came all this way, and there's been all this trouble?"

"The trouble wasn't mine, Sarah, and it wasn't yours, either. The trouble was here long before us. I walked into this with my eyes closed, just like you." Henry looked away for a moment, his expression pensive and uncertain. "Now I am wondering whether I shouldn't have promised your father that I would find you."

"I am glad you found me," Sarah replied. "Of course, I knew I was adopted. I never had a problem with that. My adoptive parents never hid that. They didn't know who my real parents were, and after a while it didn't seem to matter." She smiled to herself, as if now understanding some small mystery. "When you don't know who your parents are, there will always be things about yourself that you can't explain... things that come from some unknown place, you know? I know his name now. I know who he was and what he did. That's enough."

"But the money that should have been yours?" Evie asked. "You were supposed to inherit that farm, all that land..."

"You can't miss something you never had," Sarah said. "Do I want to fight battles with lawyers and the courts and all that? No, I don't, Miss Chandler. I want to raise my daughter and be the best wife and mother I can be, and that's all I need right now."

"Sweetheart?" Sarah's husband called from the doorway of the house.

Sarah turned and waved and then looked back at Henry and Evie.

"I have to go," she said. "I would say thank you, but I think this was more for my father than for me."

She started toward the house.

"If I see him," Henry said, "is there anything you want me to tell him?"

Sarah shook her head and then hesitated. "Yes," she said. "Tell him that I will find a copy of his record and listen to it."

"I can send you a copy—" Henry started.

"It's okay, Mr. Quinn," Sarah said, and smiled so artlessly that there was nothing else to be said.

Henry watched Sarah Forrester disappear into the shadowed hallway, knowing then that the sound of Evan Riggs's voice would never reach her ears.

The following day, the funeral done, there was a small gathering at the saloon where Henry had first met Roy Sperling, George Eakins, Harold Mills, and Clarence Ames. Ralph Chandler came, too, and Henry and Evie sat with them, and they all looked at one another as if each expected an explanation they knew would never arrive.

"You heading out now?" Clarence asked Evie.

"I am," she said. "Henry an' me are gonna go on up to San Angelo and see Henry's ma."

"And then?"

Evie looked at Henry and shrugged.

"Take it as it comes," Henry said.

"You gonna make a record?" George Eakins asked.

"Maybe," Henry said. "We'll see what happens."

"I seen the girl," Harold Mills said. "Evan's daughter. Yesterday."

"We took her out and showed her the old Riggs place," Evie said.

"Hell, if she don't look just like her ma," Mills added. "And she just let it all go . . . everything to do with her family here."

"What family?" Clarence Ames asked. "Only family she got left is a crazy woman and a homicidal country singer."

For some reason Henry started laughing. The laughter traveled the table, but it died within a few seconds. It was symbolic, if nothing else, of the surreal nature of what they were discussing.

"Hell of a thing," Evie's father said, and that seemed to be the punctuation mark that ended the conversation.

Outside, Evie shared words with her father, trying to refuse the money he was offering her. Clarence Ames approached Henry Quinn. Henry stepped away from the back of the pickup and walked with him a few yards.

"I knew there was bad history here," Clarence said. "I knew there was Lang trouble. I knew Roy was in something up to his neck. I had some ideas, but they were only ever ideas, and now that he's dead, I don't want to know. I even wondered if Carson had Evan fixed up and thrown in jail. Ain't nothin' those folks couldn'a done had they wanted. Anyways, it's all bad water under burned bridges now, eh?"

"It is, yes," Henry said. "Leave it where it is. No one wants to dig up the dead."

"You gonna go see Evan, tell him you got the letter delivered?"

"I am, yes," Henry said. "A week or two. I'll go tell him what happened."

"You think it's gonna break his heart... that his girl don't wanna see him?"

Henry looked away toward the horizon. "I don't know, Clarence. Maybe it was never about fixing anything for himself. Maybe it wasn't about her either..."

"It was just about revenge, right? Getting Carson back any which way he could for what he done to Rebecca."

"Maybe. Only Evan knows."

"Crazy goddamned brothers, the pair of them."

"We're all crazy, Clarence," Henry said. "It's just that we all think that our own kind of crazy is the good kind, right?"

Clarence Ames reached out and gripped Henry's shoulder. "You do good, okay, son? Take care of that girl. She's a sweetheart."

"I will do just that, Mr. Ames."

"Can't say I am pleased we ever met, Henry Quinn. Done lost another good friend because of what you brought here, but Carson Riggs is gone, and I think that's gonna be good for Calvary."

"I hope so."

"Travel well, boy," Clarence said. He started to walk away, and then he paused. "You know... When I seen you the first time, there was something about you that reminded me of Evan. Ask me what, I couldn't tell you. Same with Evie, how she had something of the Wyatt girl in her. Seemed ironic, I guess. That record Evan made. *The Whiskey Poet.* Song on there called "Mockingbird." You know it, right?"

"I do, yes."

"A mockingbird mimics the song of all other birds, you know? Beautiful though it may be, it pays by sacrificing its own individual voice."

"You still think I'm anything like Evan?" Henry asked.

"No, son, I don't," Clarence said. "I don't reckon you're anything like him at all," and with that he turned and walked back to the saloon.

They drove away then, the sun high and bold, the sky clear, the highway just running the straightest of lines toward an unknown horizon.

Evie took off her shoes and socks, put her bare feet up against the dash. She rolled a cigarette and lit it, passed it to Henry, then rolled one for herself.

"I never did hear you sing," she said. "Never did heard you play no guitar, neither."

"Time enough now."

"How bad are you?"

"The worst," Henry said.

"Like a pet store burnin' down, right?"

"Worse than that."

"And there lies our fortune?"

"Sure does."

"Oh hell."

Evie started to laugh.

Henry tried to laugh with her, but his face just hurt too much.